Praise for M

"It is part action-adventure novel, part off-road motorcycling memoir, part philosophical meditation about the nature of danger and courage, about love, both lost and found, about friendship and trust, about aging and death, about the pure pleasure of revenge. This is a spooky, beautiful dream of a novel."

—Chuck Kinder, author of *Honeymooners: A Cautionary Tale* and *Last Mountain Dancer: Hard-Earned Lessons in Love, Loss, and Honky-Tonk Outlaw Life*

"Once 'on the road,' Maynard's characters make us want to follow them as far North as their endurance will take us."

—Gary Fincke, author of *The Proper Words for Sin* and *A Room of Rain*

"It is a rollicking contemporary picaresque—a tale of friendship and adventure and a personal quest for meaning. If *Zen and the Art of Motorcycle Maintenance* had been written by Edward Abbey, it would be Lee Maynard's *Magnetic North*."

— Doug Van Gundy, author of *A Life Above Water*

"A buddy quest on motorcycles in Maynard's tough-as-nails voice."

—*Kirkus Reviews*

# MAGNETIC NORTH

# MAGNETIC NORTH

## LEE MAYNARD

VANDALIA PRESS

MORGANTOWN 2015

© 2015 Vandalia Press / an imprint of West Virginia University Press

All rights reserved

Printed in the United States of America


22 21 20 19 18 17 16 15 1 2 3 4 5 6 7 8 9


ISBN:

Paper 978-1-940425-48-1

Epub 978-1-940425-49-8

Pdf 978-1-940425-50-4


Library of Congress Cataloging-in-Publication Data


Maynard, Lee, 1936-

  Magnetic North / Lee Maynard.

    pages;          cm

  ISBN 978-1-940425-48-1 (pbk.) -- ISBN (invalid) 978-1-940425-49-8 (epub) --
ISBN (invalid) 978-1-940425-50-4 (pdf)

  I. Title.

  PS3563.A96384M34 2015

  813'.54--dc23

                              2015001847


Cover design by Michel Vrana

To G. L. and Kelli Scarborough
ultimate and ever friends
&
finders of souls
who have always helped me keep track of mine

sometimes, it's what's in the rearview mirror . . .

# CONTENTS

# INTRODUCTION

All of life is an introduction
to something else

Sometimes, it is simply an ending to the memories

1.

# WILD HORSE CANYON, SOUTHERN NEW MEXICO

April

NOTHING FELT RIGHT.

My mind had taken a solid, heavy form and weighed inside my body. It was in darkness and would not move, and I could not see tomorrow.

A late evening breeze ghosted through the giant cottonwoods that rose from the flat canyon floor and spread over the tiny world I lived in. The air had a smell I had come to associate with the desert, a smell I imagined fine crystal would smell like, if crystal had a smell. The air brushed the sides of my old adobe house, washed through the open windows, eased through the shade of the front porch, and softly cooled my face. The porch did not belong on an adobe house, but I wanted one and so built it there.

I sat quietly on the porch and watched a giant bull snake move with silky grace from beneath the worn plank steps and on across the bare earth in front of the house. He was in no hurry.

I knew that snake. He lived under a shed out beside the house. I called him Hillbilly. Yeah, I'd named him. I didn't hate snakes, but I didn't particularly like them. They were symbols of things I needed to bury. But I loved that fucking snake. Funny thing was, one of these days I'd rip off his head and then eat him. Even funnier—I think he knew it, too.

The big .45 semi-automatic was digging into my hip, so I eased it out of its holster and laid it on the porch railing—it never crossed my mind to shoot the snake. I tilted the cane-bottomed rocking chair back, put my boots up on one of the railings, lifted the battered, stained Stetson off my head, and let the breeze take sweat from the long graying hair that hung far down between my shoulders.

Another rocking chair sat close enough to mine that I could touch it. It was painted in bright colors, and the cane bottom had been replaced to make it more comfortable. A straw hat hung from the top of one of the spindles, the hatband nothing but a faded pink ribbon tied with a bow, the ends of the ribbon fluttering in the soft air. A heavy layer of desert dusted the chair—it had not moved, or been sat in, for months. I thought I would give the chair to one of the Apache women. But not yet.

The two chairs were alone on the porch. As was I.

Less than twenty yards to the east a narrow stream slowly wound its way through giant cottonwoods that sheltered the house. The stream was one of my favorite things. It sprang from a jumble of rocks on the north end of my land, pushed up into the sunlight by some unknown artesian force. There was just enough water to make a stream, and it ran far too gently to make any noise, and I could sit beside it and still be covered by the near silence of the gentle rustle of cottonwood leaves. But then, cottonwood leaves always rustled. The only real friend I ever had, Slade, said that the passing of a fair-sized snake would cause cottonwood leaves to rustle.

Rancho. It was only fifty acres, part of it edging up into the canyon behind my house, the rest of it stretching south and rolling out as though flattened by the hand of a nature that had tired and simply stopped building things. Behind me, pines of various types reached up from the canyon, growing taller as the land rose. When the air moved gently down out of the slope, I could smell the pines in my sleep.

In front of me, brittle tumbleweeds collected against the far southern fence. I left them there. I would rather see tumbleweeds than wire.

Rancho. Arturo said to be proper I should call it a ranchito. Sometimes that old Apache was a pain in the ass. He always seemed to be around—at the village miles to the southwest, at the rancho, everywhere. He was old beyond old and wise beyond the ken of men. And he was always trying to teach me things that we both knew I might never grasp. But I loved him anyway.

Nothing felt right.

The sun had slipped behind the low ridge far enough that only the tops of the cottonwoods glowed like precious metal on the edge of melting. A high, thin cloud layer stretched across the western horizon, and the falling sun was reaching into it with layers of fine, dark gold, heated to a gentle red, like the color of thin blood. I pulled my feet off the railing and leaned forward in the chair and felt the muscles in my back resist the movement. When I reached out to pick up the small Mason jar from the porch railing, my arm and shoulder felt awkward and stiff. As I reached for the jar I saw a tiny scuttling movement by my boot. A scorpion, working his way across the porch. I watched him as he disappeared under one of the rockers of my chair and then I rolled forward, hearing the tiny crunching sound as the rocker flattened him into eternity. I had a history with the little bastards. I once wrote that scorpions were born pissed off and stayed that way through their miserable lives. They were the only nonhuman critters that I actually hated.

Humans were another story. I had a lot hate left over for some humans. Hate is like love—there is a beginning to it, but there is no end. Not for me.

I stood up and reholstered the .45. I spent a moment or two adjusting the fit and hang of the big gun. It didn't need adjusting. I just liked to touch it. I didn't know which felt better in my hand, the Mason jar or the .45.

I left the scorpion where he was.

I clumped down the steps from the porch, feeling my knees grind and my legs tremble, then shuffled slowly around the porch to the old, wooden, tin-roofed shed that stood between the house and the stream. Everything on the rancho, except the porch, had been built before I owned it, and I was never sure what held the shed together. It might have been ancient hand-forged nails. Might have been bailing wire. Might have been spit. The wind, rain, and sun still worked the wood and had turned the sides into a silky softness that seemed alien to wood but so very personal to the touch. Feminine. Somehow, the old warped planks stayed in place, tiny shafts of sunlight spearing through the cracks and into the darkness of the shed when the doors were closed, as they were now.

I stood in front of the tilted old building, put the Mason jar on the ground, and pulled open the big plank doors that made up almost all the building's south end. A hasp and lock hung there, useless. The lock probably worked, but I couldn't remember the last time I'd locked the shed, and I had no idea where the key was.

The smells from the old building belonged there. I could smell ancient leather and the faint aroma of horse shit from when it had probably been a tack shed. Motor oil. The tiniest hint of perfume. Perfume.

I stepped back and out of habit checked the ground in front of the shed, but I knew Hillbilly was not at home. Probably still out to dinner.

On the left side of the shed a dented, almost trashed-out Kawasaki motorcycle leaned heavily on its side stand. An old boot sole under the stand to kept it from slowly sinking into the dirt floor. It was a KLR 650, a so-called dual-sport bike; on-road, off-road; big and bony; pure ugly. I hadn't ridden the bike in a couple of years. Every now and then one of the Apache kids would haul it out and chase cows with it, but they said it didn't run right. Whatever the hell that meant. What it meant, Arturo said, was that some of the Apache kids could outrun the bike.

The other side of the shed was a different story. Sitting on its center stand was a twenty-four-year-old BMW K75, gleaming in its custom paint, the engine completely rebuilt, every piece of the bike polished and ready, its new, black, cushy seat puffed up and waiting for the even softer ass of the woman. Who was not here.

I wished Slade were here. I would say, "Everything has its time . . ." and Slade would fall on the ground laughing, wanting to know who the hell I was and what the hell had I done with a guy named Morgan.

In the far back of the shed the remains of my life hung on cracked wooden pegs and rusted hooks—out-of-date mountaineering equipment, white-water river gear, western riding tack, worn packs, and now-useless survival crap. Junk like that. But no guns. The .45 was the only gun left. I seldom remembered the stuff was there, seeing it only when I went to the shed for one of the motorcycles. Even worse, rodents probably chewed on it and it would certainly kill me if I used it.

I knew that would happen when I hung it there.

All I could do was stare at the K-bike.

Soon, now.

I stepped back and closed the doors.

The light was weakening. And maybe so was I. The black flight-ghost of a raven landed in one of the cottonwoods and made some sort of guttural noise that sounded vaguely like an insult. Might as well be a buzzard, I thought. "But not yet, you bastard," I muttered in the general direction of the raven. "I'm not ready. I'll let you know when."

I had always liked birds, loved them, but ravens weren't birds. They were messengers. Most of us never learned how to hear what they were saying. Because we wouldn't like what they have to say.

I picked up the jar. I hadn't eaten anything since early morning, and the bourbon was beginning to work my bloodstream.

I walked over and stood beside the crystal running water. Where the stream moved past the house I had long ago hollowed out a small pond and piled some rocks at the downstream edge. The pond was big enough for two people to lie down in.

It was time for my bath. I stripped off my boots, jeans, and shirt, and left everything in a pile by the water. I left my hat on and left the .45 where I could reach it. Old habits don't die quickly.

Baths in streams are what we were born to do.

I carried the Mason jar carefully into the center of the pond and sat down. The water was only deep enough to cover my belly so I eased back against the bank until the water flowed gently under my chin. I drank the last of the bourbon, set the jar on the bank, and tilted my hat down across my eyes.

And I breathed.

And still, nothing felt right.

When I thought the water had done its work I got out of the pond, pulled on my boots, and strapped on the .45, then walked naked downstream beyond the cottonwoods. A dirt road was down there, somewhere right outside my fence, but it was the color of desert, and I could not tell where it ended and the desert began. Sometimes the colors of the desert blended into a constant spread of dry liquid that seemed to hang at the edge of the sky, waiting for mere humans to make a mistake as they walked toward it.

I walked down and across the road and stood leaning on a sagging wire fence that the Apaches had built to keep their longhorns from wandering too far away. I looked across the desert floor and into the far purple distance at the mountains that rose against a darkening sky. I looked down that way every evening.

My eyes strained against the distance, looking for a shape, a movement, a sign that there was something looking back at me that would tell me that I was still alive. But there was nothing but the rapidly falling Earth that promised a soft and folding night.

*  *  *  *  *

Two months ago, Arturo had sat in the painted rocking chair. At least I think it was two months ago. Sometimes it seemed that Arturo was always there. He was the only one who could sit there without violent consequences. I sat in the other chair, both of us holding small Mason jars. The bourbon bottle sat on the porch between us.

We sat silently for long minutes. I had learned long ago that it was not necessary to fill in long silences, or any silences, with Arturo.

Then, I said, "I think I'm done, Grandfather. Nothing feels right. Seems like there's nothing left for me to do except be pissed off and tear shit up."

Arturo stared into his Mason jar. He could sit for a very long time without speaking. Then, "You need to see the buffalo," he said, almost under his breath.

Oh, shit, I thought, here we go again.

I waited.

"When you see a buffalo that no one else sees, it means that a part of your life is still undone. And you must finish it."

A buffalo no one else sees. I had heard some wacky Indian shit from the old man, but this was the absolute wackiest. I couldn't stop myself from grinning.

"So, let me get this straight," I said. "If I see this buffalo, how will I know what it is I'm supposed to do?"

The old man poured himself some more bourbon. "You

white guys, you want all the answers handed to you. Sometimes you have to figure things out for yourself."

Another one of his fucking "lessons." But something bothered me—I had learned long ago that when Arturo said something that sounded like pure bullshit, it usually wasn't.

"All right," I said, "I'll look for this weird buffalo. And then I'll go do . . . whatever it is I'm supposed to do. And then what? Do I go looking for another buffalo?"

The old man looked directly at me and grinned. "Think about it, Morgan. How do you know when you've seen the last buffalo?"

I didn't say another word.

\* \* \* \* \*

Standing there, looking at the darkening sky, I didn't see the buffalo or anything else.

I stared into the distance, a man nearing old and feeling older, wearing nothing but boots and a battered Stetson, my hand resting on a gun as big as a lunch box and my dick just a hair's breadth from barbed wire. I'd forgotten to bring the Mason jar, but it was empty, anyway, as it should be.

Behind me, a silence thick enough to see washed down out of the canyon as though the ranch knew it was empty of all life, except me. My rancho. My hacienda. My home. Fifty acres, a tiny mud house, a shed with two old motorcycles in it, a little bitty creek. Some old cottonwoods that always dropped at least one branch on my truck. I'd tried to hide the truck behind the house where there were no trees, but the trees always knew where it was, and in the middle of the night I would hear a small branch bounce off the roof of the cab, and in the morning I would find another small dent. Ten yards from the nearest tree.

My home, the only home I'd ever owned, a place with practically no furniture but with every wall covered with bookcases I had built, stuffed with books.

A place I'd wanted to stay in until I died.

But things change. Or maybe they don't. Maybe I never really wanted that.

Inside the house, on a small, crude, wooden table that I'd built, were piles of yellow note pads, pencils of all lengths lying on them, or on the floor. Sometimes it would take me an hour to find the notepad I had been working on; putting the right notepad back in the right place had never been important to me. I could always get notepads—I bought them by the dozen—and I could always get pencils—I bought them by the hundreds.

I no longer wrote on a computer. Fuck computers. People killed you with computers.

I looked up beyond the house and trees into the dark and narrowing canyon. Somewhere up there—neither the Apaches nor I cared much where—the land became Apache ground. The Apaches, heading up canyon, came and went through my property as they wished, quietly, without hesitation. We had an arrangement. After all, it had been their land to begin with, back in the day. The far day.

Up where the Apache ground took over, the canyon walls climbed sharply toward the sky, the east wall scarred by a so-called road etched into the rock and hard-gristle dirt, nothing more than a track that disappeared at the first opportunity. The Apaches had built it to get their horses and hand-built carts up there to haul out the deer and elk they killed. Good for hauling out white men, too, they said. Sometimes they smiled when they said that. Sometimes they didn't. I liked it better when they smiled.

I was going to leave something up in that canyon, far up into the high ground. The Apaches knew—Arturo had told them—but they didn't care. It would be a good story. A crazy white man story. They liked crazy white man stories.

I had stuffed the cell phone into one of the bookcases and it took me a while to find it. I had never wanted the damn thing but there was no landline into my house. In fact, no lines of any kind led to the house—no electric line, no gas, no water main. I loved it. On the roof Slade had installed a small solar panel that could not be seen from the ground, which powered the computer and charged the cell phone. But there were no electric lights. I had two kerosene lamps, one of them bright enough to read by. When I needed heat, the kiva fireplace in the living room kept the front of the house warm. I cooked on the little two-burner wood stove that sat in the kitchen to the side of a narrow table, the heat from the little stove combining with the fireplace to make a space that was never cold.

I carried the phone outside. Sometimes it worked, sometimes it didn't. Six months ago I'd wanted it to work, and work well, always. But that time was gone and would not return.

Tonight I wanted it to work. I punched the only number stored in the phone.

In the state north of mine, in a living room that I knew well, a room with the windows open and country music drifting on the air, in a room with copies of my books strewn on random tables, the phone rang.

Modene answered. Modene. Slade's woman. A woman like no other woman. A woman who knew me better than Slade, a woman on whom bullshit, especially my bullshit, would never, ever, work. A man needs that in his life.

"Morgan," she said softly. Her voice never seemed to change. Even when she spoke softly her voice was full of light and lilt and strength, a voice that could be felt, as well as heard.

"Modene," I said. And then I waited. But she said nothing. "I . . . nothing feels—" I was mumbling.

I heard a small click and thought she had put the phone down. I waited. And then I realized Modene had hung up.

I stood there in the dim last light of day, naked, wearing a hat and a gun, and feeling old and foolish. I wanted more bourbon.

The goddamn flimsy phone rang, a tiny sound that came with the phone, a sound I hated but had never bothered to change.

I punched the button.

"It's been five months," Slade said. His voice had an echo quality that meant he was on speakerphone, Modene listening. "I've never seen you like this, pardner. Not over a woman, especially one who kicked you to the curb like dog shit—*by a fucking e-mail!*"

"It wasn't just the e-mail, Slade, it was what she stole from me . . ."

"What the fuck?!" Slade shouted into the phone. I thought he was done, but I should have known better.

"Hell, Morgan," Slade finally said, "there's nothing on that damn ranch worth stealing."

He waited for me to react. I didn't.

"So what the hell did she steal that could drive you into the place you're in?"

Words came to me that I never planned on saying, words I'd only say to Slade.

"She stole . . . tomorrow, Slade. Tomorrow. She was my last chance, and she stole it."

Slade didn't hesitate. "Jesus, pardner," he said, "don't you think it's about time you took your head out of your ass and started realizing just how hollow she is? Arturo called her a Smoke Woman, someone who bends in the slightest breeze. And those friends of hers were all the breeze she needed."

Arturo? "Have you been talking to Arturo?"

Slade didn't answer.

"Morgan." It was Modene. "Don't do anything—"

I hung up.

# 2

# WILD HORSE CANYON,
# CENTRAL NEW MEXICO

April,
days later

SOMETIMES DAYS WOULD GO by when I didn't talk with Slade or
Modene. This was one of those times.

I was lost on my fifty acres.

I hadn't written a word since the Smoke Woman left. Lancey.

Tomorrow existed only as a flat panel of anger, left over from
some ancient storm that grew in my mind and grew larger with
each rising of the sun.

I stood in the living room looking at the computer, one of
those new, state-of-the-art demons. The box, the monitor, the
printer all made a pile in the middle of a small table that I had
bought in a thrift store. The damn thing was powered up, waiting. My publisher wanted something I could use to send my
stuff in by e-mail. That's why Slade hooked it up to one of those
satellite systems.

And so it sat there, waiting for me to do something. Anything. The only thing I did was check the e-mail every day, but

there was nothing. Lancey had sent me the last e-mail I would ever get from her.

The computer waited for me to do something. So I did. Somewhere behind my eyes a connection seemed to burn out, and in the brilliant darkness I wrapped my arms around everything that seemed to say "computer." I ripped the entire mess off the table and dropped it on the floor, power cords dangling, plastic cracking, and some other tiny agony noises I did not recognize, as though the thing were alive.

The little table suddenly looked better, maybe a place where I could sit and have coffee. On the wall above the table, hanging from a piece of dry cottonwood root, was a Seneca wampum belt that had belonged to Kateri. I had been married, once upon a time. My wife was mostly Native American. Kateri was not her name, but it was what I called her.

I should never have put the computer near the belt. Bad juju. I knew the belt would live a better life, now that the computer was gone.

I pushed the wheelbarrow up to the fence. It was loaded with all the computer junk, rolled into one gigantic ball, an ungodly lump held tightly together by duct tape so old it was frayed at the edges. An even older lariat lay coiled on top. I picked up the lariat.

Some of the longhorns ambled in my direction, thinking maybe there was something to eat in the wheelbarrow. I opened up the loop in the rope and tossed it easily over the horns of the big steer nearest me. He was pissed off at being roped, and he tossed his head and, pulling hard, tried to tear the rope through my hands. I took a quick dally around a fence post, hoping the steer would not tear down the whole goddamn fence. I would have a hard time explaining that to the Apaches.

I tipped the wheelbarrow over and dumped the huge lump on the ground, took the end of the rope and threaded it through the ball of computer crap, tied it off, then picked up the whole mess and threw it over the fence.

It was the second time I had dumped a bag full of mind-aching shit south of my property.

I whipped the dally loose from the fence post. The steer stood there, eyes wide, looking at me with naked hatred, shaking his head slightly, his breath coming in hard bursts, confused at what was going on. He didn't move.

This wasn't going like I thought it should.

I pulled the .45 and fired a shot over his head.

And then things changed. The steer wheeled and roared away through the rough desert, the bundle of computer stuff bouncing behind him, little pieces of it flying off into the brush. Dust rose behind the steer in a low adobe-colored cloud, as though the steer were plowing a furrow in the desert. Which it was. I already had the gun out, so, what the hell, I fired another round over the steer, and then another, and kept firing until the gun's slide locked back, my ears ringing loudly enough to peel brain matter from the inside of my skull.

And that was the last I saw of the steer.

Or the computer.

It was a bright night under a big moon. I was standing out next to the creek. The air did not move. But the silence did, flowing down out of the canyon in a presence so thick that I could feel it pressing against my face.

Slade was on the phone. "You haven't answered my e-mails. You okay? Sick?"

"Nah, I'm okay. Don't have a computer anymore." I thought for a moment. "It went . . . away."

There was silence And then Slade said, "Are you out there, next to the creek?"

I didn't answer.

"I know what you are doing, goddammit. You're standing out there in the moonlight, naked, half full of bourbon, wearing a gun, feeling sorry for yourself. Just like you've been doing for weeks, now—the same damn thing you did when Sylvia left."

If ever a man was lucky enough to have one really good friend, it would be Slade.

"And the computer didn't 'go away,' did it? You trashed it."

He stopped talking, and I knew enough to say nothing.

"So what's the problem?" Slade wanted to know. "What's different about tonight?"

"I've been looking. Hard. I look every day. But he's not there."

I was talking about the buffalo.

I could hear Slade breathing into the phone, his breath steady, solid. "Goddammit, Morgan, I love Arturo as much as you do, but you've got to stop listening to that old man—no, you've got to stop *believing* that old man." He paused, waiting for me to argue. I didn't.

"Morgan, I want you to hear this clearly . . . *there is no fucking buffalo!*"

"Yeah, I know, but . . . goddammit, Slade, I'm not ready yet. It isn't right for a man to just lie down and die when he isn't used up. You have to be used up, and then you die. That's the way it works. I'm not ready to go to ground yet."

"You were ready to go to ground when the woman was there."

I didn't say a fucking thing.

"We can't go back in the business," Slade said. "That's all behind us, now. We're too old. Too slow."

"Well, then, let's do something easy. We aren't dead yet!"

Slade was quiet. I knew what he was thinking. And then he said it.

"You don't want to get away from the ranch. You want to get away from her. And you want to get away from the fact that you haven't written a damn word in . . . what? . . . months?"

I ignored his crack about my not writing. I waited for him to say something, but sometimes Slade could outwait me. "Goddammit, Slade, a little adventure sure wouldn't hurt anything."

"You know, Morgan, the problem with your 'adventures' is that they always turn out to be 'misadventures.' Every fucking time."

"Hey, Slade, isn't that always the fun part? And besides, we're getting to be senior citizens. Maybe even the misadventures will be easier."

"With you? Easier? Fucking *never*!" I thought I could hear his smile.

"That time in Papua wasn't bad, was it?"

"Which Papua?" he said. "There's a bunch of 'em."

We sat for a while, each of us silently holding our phones.

"Morgan?"

"Yeah, Slade."

"You holding my .45?"

Shit. "Depends on what you mean by 'holding,' I guess." I pulled out the pistol. "Got my hand on it. Hammer's cocked. Safety's off. Grip safety's pressed." I held the pistol up in moonlight. It was velvet black, checkered walnut handles. I remembered Slade tossing it to me like a chunk of scrap metal wrapped in a piece of smelly canvas, all those years ago.

"Morgan, put the gun away."

Fucking Slade, always giving me orders. I put the gun away.

"Morgan, you know if we go on another one of your 'trips,' it's not going to change anything. It's over, Morgan. Just like it was over with the other women." He paused, but I said nothing. "Didn't you learn anything from Arturo? You can't keep doing this, *old man*."

Old man. Slade wasn't being cute. I was an old man. "Hey, wait a minute! I thought you said I wasn't supposed to believe all that crap that Arturo puts out!"

Slade laughed. "Well, maybe not word for word. You have to be selective." He laughed again.

We were both silent. Thinking.

"Bike trip," I said. "Long one. Let the fucking machines do all the work."

I knew he was thinking about it, but I also knew he'd already made up his mind. "Okay," Slade said, "I'm in."

And then his voice changed. "And Morgan," Slade said softly, "if you're still moping around the next time I see you, I'm going to take back my .45 and beat you to death with it."

"Okay, I'll—"

But Slade had hung up.

I stumbled inside in the dark, the .45 banging against my leg. The old house smelled of piñon smoke and bacon and desert perfume. And somewhere in my brain another small piece of electrical meat shorted out and burned apart. I didn't even smell it, but I knew it was burned beyond repair.

And I had not seen the buffalo.

3.

# WHITE SANDS NATIONAL MONUMENT

Southern New Mexico

May

THE DUNES WERE NOT white. They were a void in the conscious-ness, an absence of substance and color that began as wonder and ended as pain.

Slade and I sat at the bottom of a dune on insulated pads, not moving, our legs folded in front of us, wide-brimmed hats drooping down to our dark sunglasses. Somewhere above us, somewhere we dared not look, the sun hung in a thin sky and poured molten light down on dunes so glistening hard that I thought I could hear the strike of the light on the rounded curves of the dunes' tops.

The heat rolled across the dunes and washed against our shirts, cooking the cloth to our skins. Our only movement was the quiet roll of our breathing, and even that caused sweat to run into our eyes and down across faces coated with a dust as pure and fine and white as the breath of angels.

And so we sat, two clumps of breathing darkness baking quietly in a world so intensely crystal it had no boundaries that could be seen by ordinary eyes. This was our second day.

At some unknown hour the sun quit the fight and retreated toward the far edge of Earth, the hard light finally fading. We took off our sunglasses, sipped water, and did not speak. Now and then one of us would stretch his legs out in front and shake the tiny cramps from strangled muscles.

And then the moon came out.

It was a different kind of light, thicker, moving slowly, a golden cream flowing down the sides of dunes that now looked like the curves of a woman's body, gentle, rhythmic, bending into a place in the mind where they would stay, always.

Lancey liked it when the light got that way. Sometimes she would strip to her waist and dribble handfuls of the warm sand over her breasts.

I rose slowly, unfolding one part of my body at a time, until I stood in the moonlight, a body ready for slow flight. I turned and started moving along the side of the dune, climbing the ghost-like powdery side, moving up a step and then sliding back but keeping at it until I was at the top.

I'd not climbed to the top to commune with nature in some hippie version of sanity, because, deep down, I knew I was not sane. If you *know* you are not sane, can you really be *insane?* I thought so.

I was there for something else. I was there to try to stay alive. I stood quietly, not staring in any particular direction of the outside world. I was staring into my mind.

I was there to see the buffalo.

The tops of the dunes looked like ghost waves rolling away and into the far reaches of time and space, into a place in the world that few of us have ever seen—but where Slade and I had lived.

I stared, but I saw nothing.

Getting down from the top of the dune was easy. I stepped over the side and leaned forward. The dune gave way beneath me and I slid down its face in a gentle glide, floating almost weightless.

I stopped only few feet from Slade. He was lying back on his pad, his hat over his eyes. I thought he was asleep. Wrong again.

He started mumbling from beneath his hat. "You've been moaning for a couple of years about riding a motorcycle to Alaska to the Arctic Circle. You have any idea why you haven't done that?" He had driven down from Colorado Springs just to make sure I had not done anything truly crazy. Or more stupid than usual.

"Hell, yes! It's *cold* in Alaska! I hate the goddamn cold!" I shut my mouth and thought for a minute. "Well," I said, dragging the words out of my mouth, "at least it's not going south through all that stinking jungle and dodging mean brown guys who want to learn to play the drums on my teeth." I picked up a handful of warm sand and dribbled in onto Slade's chest.

He ignored the sand. "That part's over. Don't think we can do that again. It's just you and me now. Besides, I don't think anybody really cares, one way or another. Maybe they never did." He paused. "Unless, of course, you fuck something up, like you usually do—then *somebody* will care a lot." He laughed.

I reached behind me and pulled the .45 out of the back of my pants and held it up in front of my face. I could smell the gun. I thought it glowed, thought it was actually alive.

"They left us, Slade."

Slade crossed his arms on his knees and dropped his head on them. "Oh, Jesus, Morgan, are you still hanging onto that?"

"Yeah, and I'm keeping it. They left us. They threw us out like trash. They never meant for us to get out alive," I said through gritted teeth. I was gripping the .45 so hard that it shook with the beat of my heart.

"Let me ask you something," I mumbled. "When we're gone, do you think anybody will ever know we were here?"

"Give me the .45," Slade said.

"Why?"

"Because I'm going to beat you to death with it."

Shit. I had been whining, and Slade hated whining. And I hated it when he called me on it.

And then I thought about Modene. "Modene," I said. "If we ride bikes to Alaska, we might be gone for . . . hell, I don't know. A month? Longer? You do realize Modene will kill you?"

He didn't even have to think about it. "Modene's the center point. She understands me. But you, on the other hand, she might actually kill."

I thought he was joking. But I wasn't sure.

"Besides, there's more than one kind of death, pardner. You taught me that."

Once, years ago, it had been Slade and Modene and me and Kateri. Once.

And then, decades later, there was Lancey.

For a while.

* * * * *

Lancey had her old yellow battered pickup parked in front of the house, the bed full of pots and flowers and garden tools. She had been very careful—none of the tools were mine. She could have taken everything if she'd wanted. I would have given it all to her. On the surface, there wasn't much to give.

She slid into the driver's seat and closed the door, then turned to look at me. She looked surprised to see me. She thought I was up canyon with the Apaches. I had been, but something had brought me back to the house. And now I knew what it was. She was going to leave without seeing me. Without saying a word. Without remorse. Just like Arturo said.

She turned those enormous, piercing amber-colored eyes on me, eyes that matched her hair. And then, as I was staring into them, her eyes seem to change color, changing to something I had never seen before.

She didn't speak. And she drove away.

To go into town. To the Snake.

And to send an e-mail.


An "intervention," the e-mail said. Her friends, "The Girls," had pulled her into a cabin and convinced her that she was going nowhere, that I was going nowhere, that it was time to change from being nowhere . . .

The Girls, the goddamn girls, her only friends, women with no lives, aging, homely, clueless, lonely women, going to cheap bars, drinking cheap whiskey until some cheap guy started buying them more cheap whiskey, and they got a cheap buzz going and then went to a cheap motel and had a cheap fuck.

I had once described them to Slade. "Jesus," Slade had said, "I want to meet these women!"

"Nah, you don't, pardner. In a very few short years the only way these broads will get laid is to pay some drunk to fuck 'em. And he'd better be pretty damn drunk."

I hated The Girls. I would always hate them.

But the thing that saddened me most was how fucking dumb she and The Girls must have thought I was.

And I was.

She didn't take the painted rocking chair.

* * * * *

It was still dark. I dozed, not fully asleep, but not fully awake, my arm across my eyes. I thought I could smell the sand. How could that be? How can you smell sand? Maybe even sand has an aroma if you heat it up enough.

"The river," I mumbled.

"What?" Slade asked. "Hold it, Morgan." He sat up and shook my shoulder, his voice firm. "You can *not* take Lancey to the river."

I was wide awake, now. Slade's voice could do that to me. "Not Lancey. She's just a self-absorbed pawn. Really easy to influence." I hesitated. "The Girls. All of them."

I was holding the .45 again.

"You already did it, didn't you?" His voice was soft with resignation.

"Yeah. I did."

"A'anka and Red Hawk, they let you do it?"

"Yeah."

He was silent for long moments. The moon had disappeared behind the dunes, and the darkness seemed to underline

Slade's silence. Then he muttered, just above my hearing, "The girls will never know why all the shit is coming down on them."

We had another of our silences. Then he said, "A long bike ride."

I'd been breathing shallowly, waiting. "Yeah. North. Arctic Circle. Maybe we'll find something up there . . ."

"Yeah. When you're involved, we always manage to find something." He turned to look me squarely in the eyes. "Do me a favor, Morgan," he said, "nobody is chasing us. For God's sake, let's keep it that way. You know what I'm saying, pardner—don't go and shit in your own backyard. I've gotten to like moving around in this country without looking over my shoulder."

He said it lightly, but I knew he wasn't kidding.

I managed to upright my body and picked up the thick foam pad I had been lying on.

Slade unfolded his lanky body. As usual, he was ready to go, no fumbling around.

"You got the wire cutters?" I asked him.

The strange tool appeared magically in his hand.

The Colt was still in my hand. I held it up over my head.

"I guess we're both ready," he said.

"Do you know, Morgan, really know, how fucking old we are?"

Even Slade could ask a stupid question.

We started mushing off through the sand, our feet making large dimples that would be gone with the first breeze. And then I realized that Slade had dribbled sand into every opening in my clothing.

4.

# THE KLR

THE KLR LEANED ON its side stand in the middle of the cluttered shed. It was absurdly tall, bony, the gas tank bulging in all directions, its collective parts seeming to belong to other bikes, on loan to this one for some unknown reason. The thing looked like an ancient stork ready for flight, not knowing that its flight days were long gone. It was dead but had not fallen over yet.

Somewhere along the way Lancey had balanced an empty flowerpot in the middle of the cracked seat. One of her bras still dangled from the left handlebar. Lancey said the KLR was better for hanging clothing than for riding.

A guy had owed me some money. He offered the KLR instead. I took it. It was a '91 with only four thousand miles on it. A '91! With only four thousand miles! That should have told me something. But who the hell could resist?

It was the worst deal I ever made.

I'm not sure why I didn't like KLRs. I knew these bikes and had ridden them in strange places. Parts would fall off, the seat would come loose and fly off into the bush, and the bikes would keep running. I thought they were too damn big to be real dirt bikes and too damn clattery to run wide open on the road.

But it was the bike I had, and it was sitting there, mine. For better or worse.

I could have, of course, chosen to ride the K75. It was in perfect condition and probably would have made the ride easily, even though it was not a dirt bike. But the K75 had a different future.

And, besides, the KLR was a bike Slade loved.

We were going to ride to Alaska, explore some back roads along the way, ride the Cassiar Highway, find some mud, get a little dirty. Slade was fond of pointing out that he had been, and still was, a pilot, one of the best, and that he rode KLRs. And therefore his taste in machines was impeccable.

I had been a pilot—not much of one, it seemed, although Slade had tried his best to teach me. And as for motorcycles, well, I rode whatever the hell was stuck out there in the shed. It didn't matter. Apparently, I had no taste at all.

The KLR in my shed was a piece of crap. And I had less than three months to get it ready. Yeah, three months. We were going to ride to Alaska in September.

That bright morning I flung the flowerpot out into the desert. I pulled the bra from the handlebar and carefully hung it on a small nail on the wall above the bike. Sometimes I punish myself in odd ways.

I rolled the bike into the sun. I was wearing the .45, of course, and if the bastard bike didn't start I was going to shoot it and walk away.

It started right up. Crap. I was stuck with it.

I rode it around the cottonwoods and down the narrow dirt road, then circled around the house and went part of the way toward the narrows, where the canyon started to close in and then rise in earnest. The bike seemed sluggish, the engine changing rpms without any input from me.

I had very little time to get the damn bike up to speed. I knew what Slade would do. He would go down to a Kawasaki dealer, buy a new bike off the showroom floor, fill it with gas, and be ready to go.

Shit.

I backed the bike inside and started in on it, doing what I could do. In a very short time I realized that the problems of the bike, whatever they were, were beyond my limited mechanical abilities. So I took the bike to Juanito, Arturo's grandson, who lived about ten miles away and was one of the best mechanics I've ever known. Juanito used to race dirt bikes. He never had the money to buy a bike, so he gathered up old parts and built his own. In the process, he learned how to make an engine scream, even when it had lost its voice.

Once Juanito got his hands on it, I didn't see the bike again for ten days.

But he left some stuff for me to do, and, finally, the bike was back in my shed.

But there was a problem. The shed wasn't really that big, and every time I turned around I bumped into the BMW.

I needed room.

It was time to get it over with.

It was not yet breaking daylight. I rolled out of my bed and hauled on the riding gear that was piled in the middle of the floor, silently, not wanting to break the black mood that piled up in my chest.

I walked slowly out to the shed and opened the doors.

And there were the bikes, one a bony piece of shit, that I thought might actually take me to Alaska, and the other, shining like a blood-red star, even in the darkness. The 1990 BMW K75. Before I found it, it had spent most of its life in a storage barn, fading, hardening, its fluids turning to mush that neither ran nor dripped, its tattered tires flaking from the rims. And in all that time, it had been ridden less than nine thousand miles.

I had approached it like a work of art and had taken almost a year to revive it both as a motorcycle and as a thing of beauty, to put it back together, to make it work like BMW had intended it to work. To make it right. A year of firing custom paint and chasing parts and finding things that couldn't be found. But I had found them.

Lancey had never driven a bike before she met me, never felt the abject freedom that only came from a bike, a machine that only you controlled, a machine that could go anywhere, if you were good enough.

A bike, driving her own bike, was on her list of things that the men in her life had kept her from doing. I was not one of those men. I would not hold her back from anything. I would teach her how to really drive a motorcycle.

But Lancey never gave me the time.

I opened my jacket and took out a carefully folded piece of paper, a title to the BMW. In Lancey's name. I had signed the bike away to a woman who made my fingers ache and shoved pain through the very cords inside my spine and powered undiminished into my brain. The bike was hers, and she didn't even know it. And if you don't know the *why* of what I was going to do that morning, well, then, stop thinking about it. You won't get the point. Not ever.

I slipped the folded paper into the little storage well at the back, behind the seat.

I put on a small daypack, hauled my ass across the bike, started the engine, and rode away in the dark.

Was I just angry? Or was it more than that? If I could reason with myself, if I could ask myself if I was mad—crazy—was I then truly crazy? Oh, hell yes.

I wasn't wearing a helmet. I wanted to feel the black air move past my face.

I started up into the narrow canyon. As the trail rose the jagged rock walls closed in more tightly, and the light thrown by the headlight made the rocks dance, some of them reaching for the bike but never quite making it. The dirt road quickly changed to nothing more than a trail, more for dirt bikes than anything else. The K75 wasn't a dirt bike, but it would be one on this dark morning. I geared down. So far, I'd managed to keep the bike upright in the rock and hardpack, but more difficult stuff was coming up. I powered on. Rocks and gravel and pieces of cholla rattled under the engine and bounced off the hard luggage that clamped to the back side of the bike. The bike was going to take a beating. I didn't care.

I hit a long stretch of fine earth, sand-like, stuff that made me crazy on a bike. I shifted all the way into low to keep control. I shouldn't have done that, should have kept the speed up to stay on top of the sand, but, hell, there was hardly enough room to keep up what little speed I had. So I left the bike in low gear—too much power, too little speed.

The track became worse. It didn't matter. I was already in a fine, high, rage, as some guy once wrote. Rage. I had come to love the word. It was so . . . *right*. Rage so pure and buried so deep that it almost seemed a normal condition. I thought—I was afraid—that I was coming to look forward to it each morning, or in the middle of the night when I woke up reaching for the .45 and wishing there was some reason to fire. I was like that almost all the time, now, trying to act normal in front of people I did not know—or did know—while the universe was burning. Where does such a rage come from, and where does it go?

So I left the bike in low gear and twisted the throttle, the rear wheel throwing sand and small rocks behind in a hard, striking spray, the engine screaming, me screaming, the bike wallowing and jumping in the soft dirt, the rear wheel wanting to be the front wheel, the front wheel trying to survive. Waiting for the engine to blow. But, nah, this was a BMW. The engine was not going to blow.

I rode on, the bike and I making obscene noises that crashed against the canyon walls and slid down the rock like old tar in the heat of the desert. I wanted to feel the same pain as the bike, power stored in a beating heart, charging at nothing in front of me but another piece of useless space, wondering why the hell the road didn't stop and get it over with.

And so it did—the road stopped.

It was as good a place as any to stop, there on the top of the sharp canyon wall among tall black trees that had a right to be there and I did not, where I could look far back and see the sharp outline of the southern mountains, the sun still so far around the planet that it lit absolutely nothing in the world where I rode, except the crest of those far mountains. I had been on the tops of every one of them, all of them. Back in the day.

The light kept coming, gray and cold, a light that brought no joy. The odometer said I was more than eight miles from my house, but I wasn't ready to stop. I wrestled the bike toward what looked like a wider spot in the track. I wound the engine and took off, and the speed built.

I never got anywhere. About twenty yards farther the bike hit a rock and veered sharply to the right. I tried to get the wheel back in line, but I had never been very good at that stuff, especially on a road bike, and the K75 kept going off to the right, and I knew I was at the end of wherever it was that I thought I was going. The front wheel jammed into some low brush and stopped instantly. I went over the handlebars and hit something that felt like a tree that sprang forward and then slammed me back across the bike. I ended up face down on the ground.

The bike's engine died.

I didn't move.

The light was up hard now, flowing among high desert brush so thick that the bike was still upright, jammed into the hard, spiny limbs. I was lying right beside it, my face in the dirt. I could smell the dirt, smell those years of slow regression of dying things melting back into the soil. Some of the dirt was sticky and I was bleeding somewhere on my face or head. I went through an internal inventory, checking that I was still breathing, that I could still think, that my arms and legs moved, that there were no major blood leaks. I was stunned but not really hurt.

If I stayed where I was the damn bike might fall over on me, but I was still in some state of semi-consciousness and couldn't make myself move. I slowly twisted my head. There was enough light for me to see that the bike's custom paint job had been damaged maybe beyond repair, but that only made me smile.

The smile went away quickly enough.

A snake lay about a foot in front of my face, an enormous rattler. My mind was supposed to be in a time and place where I didn't give a fuck about anything, big or small, harmless or terrifying, but a rattler that big overrode all my senses. He was looking directly at me but seemed stiff from the early morning cold, only his ugly little tongue flicking now and then, smelling me.

A rattler. An animal that could kill me. Or an animal that I could kill.

A snake—I knew who the Snake was that killed Lancey and me. Or just me. Lancey had been willing. I tried not to think of Lancey being willing, with someone else. But the image wouldn't leave my mind.

I could see every tiny scale, each seeming to throw a slightly different muted color from the back of the snake. And the longer I looked the more I hated that goddamn snake. That Snake. The Snake who now had Lancey.

I had the gun, but that was too easy, too detached, too remote. I hated that Snake, and I wanted him to know the depth of that hate, wanted him to know that there was a hate he had never imagined.

I stared at the snake, easing my arm forward. I'd seen a couple of Native guys do this to a torpid snake, but I'd never tried it. Maybe I'd win. Maybe the snake would win. And then the bike fell over. It fell away from me, exposing its belly, the guts of the bike, the center of its power.

The snake watched the movement. I snapped my arm out and grabbed the slimy bastard right behind the head. That woke him up. He went berserk, wrapping himself around my arm and thrashing as hard as he could. Jesus Christ! He was bigger than I thought and getting up to my knees and holding the snake out in front of me took me a while. I looked in his tiny eyes and squeezed his throat until his tongue came out and stayed out and then I squeezed harder until I could feel hard things inside his throat. I held him above my head and watched his coils thrash on my arm and listened to his rattles and all I could think of was that I wanted him to scream. But he did not.

The underbelly of the bike was there beside me. I held the snake out in front of me and fell toward the motor, jamming the snake's head again and again into the flat, hot metal of the K75's engine, finally feeling the coils loosen on my arm. As the snake began to dangle from my hands I whipped it again and again into the side of the engine until the snake stopped moving, hanging limply in my hand. It died, little parts of snake still burning on the metal. It stank as the life leaked out of it, just like a human.

I held the snake in one hand, reached back to my belt with my other hand, unclipped my knife and flicked open the heavy blade. I trapped the rattles under a knee and stretched the snake into its full length. The snake could not scream, but I could. I screamed out into the empty canyon below me, screamed into the mountains still ahead, screamed into the bloody face of the snake and I slit him open like a tube of rotten meat. I longed for a bigger Snake that I could crush.

I flung the pieces of this one into the canyon.

There was more light, now. I surveyed the bike's damage.

Not bad. Not really good but not bad, not nearly bad enough. I tossed the daypack onto the trail beside me. I had work to do.

I took a last look at the bike. I didn't buy the bike for Lancey, not originally. But now it was hers, the title neatly tucked under the seat. She would never know that. But I would.

I found a dead tree limb as big as my arm and I dragged it to the front of the bike. I raised the heavy club with a strength that I had thought was long gone, and in my mind I could see Snake there, under the glass of the instruments. I could see everything I hated at that very moment. I crashed the club down between the handlebars, glass cracking, tiny parts flying, small indicator lights popping.

Everything in my world was in pain.

I always had an idea of where I wanted to go on a bike when I bought one. I never rode a bike to a grocery store, or on any other mundane mission. To me, bikes were for something else. An adventure. A goal. Some reaffirmation of the stuff of life. That was why I rode. Unless, of course, I was simply running from someone.

But this bike was different. When I first saw it—faded, dusty, tires flat, battery gone, seat cracked—I knew there was a bike soul still in there, so I had to have it. I didn't know where I would go on it. I just wanted the bike, *that* bike.

And then Lancey came storming into my life and suddenly everything I'd thought about for the last several years changed. I discovered I had life left, and I had to rethink every minute of it. I was not alone anymore.

And then it was all clear. I knew where the bike was to go— to Lancey. I would restore this bike for her. I would put her on the back of it and ride the most incredible roads we could find.

We would stop by streams and sleep under stars and eat in tiny cafés and talk about the wonder of it all. And I would write while Lancey dozed and stretched the curves and mysteries of her body and made me feel alive again.

That was my plan, my secret. I had bought all her riding gear and now had it folded carefully in the hard saddlebags—helmet, armored jacket, sunglasses, boots, gloves, a scarf. Only the best of everything.

And I would teach her how to ride. And then I would give her the bike. God, how I would love that.

I got the limb under the front wheel and levered it out into the dirt track, then did the same with the rear, the bike scraping over rocks, dirt packing into every possible space. The gas tank was nearly full and I had to work hard at lifting and twisting the big stick, grinding it against the bike and feeling it bite into the metal and the soft dirt of the trail. In a few minutes I had the bike at the edge of the canyon wall, on the lip of the flat cliff face, the front wheel spinning slightly, hanging over hundreds of feet of space, and I was sweating enough to feel the gentle movement of the high, sweet canyon air. After three or four more levered shoves with the big stick the bike seemed to teeter on the edge of the canyon. I screamed again. I could not help myself.

And then the bike was gone.

It tipped into the canyon with only the slightest sound from the gravel that followed it over. But then there was sound to marvel at—the bike hitting rocks and bounding, crunching, parts flying off, the screams of metal ripping scars into hard surfaces . . . the screams sounding almost human. Some screams coming from me. I loved that part, the screaming.

The sounds stopped. I eased out on the rock ledge and looked down at the dead bike, about fifty yards below me, jammed between two huge boulders, upright, clamped terminally in place, not even touching the ground, in a field of rocks so jagged and tightly packed that jackrabbits would have had a hard time getting across it—no grass, no brush, none of the little spiny trees that cling to life in the damnedest places. Just ancient rock. I thought the gas tank was ruptured, thought I could see a dark stain spreading across one of the boulders. It didn't matter. If it wasn't already ruptured, I would take care of that.

A thick cloud pack had started to form over the canyon, but, even in the heavy early light, I had a good view of the wreck. I pulled the .45 from beneath my riding jacket and lined up the sights on the gas tank and held the sight picture until my hands began to shake. I didn't see the bike in front of the gun. I saw the Snake.

I hadn't realized that I had been carefully bringing the trigger back until the shot caught me by surprise, and the big gun let loose and let the world know what a .45 sounded like. I hardly heard it. I was screaming at the time.

The bullet went straight through the gas tank. It was a relatively long shot but I was a relatively good shooter. I fired more rounds, pulled another magazine from my pack, fired more rounds, not really aiming, just pulling the trigger. Somewhere in there, a bullet hit something that sparked.

A fireball shot up fifty feet. The bike became a sun flare in dull morning light.

I watched the fire until it bubbled and bent the hard saddlebags, the fire eating them from the trashed bike like dessert after a good, hot meal. I knew the helmet, the gloves, and all the other items meant for Lancey were gone. The seat was gone and the bike's title would be a wafer-thin ash that would disappear in some random movement of hot air. The paint bubbled, and tiny things exploded, and the tires seemed to melt, the rubber sending up black smoke. The wheels slightly glowed, dramatic in the heavy light. I had never watched a motorcycle burn before, but I watched this one.

I slammed a fresh magazine in the .45 and started back down the trail. I was moving very, very slowly, limping from some bang to my leg that I hadn't known was there.

The cloud pack thickened and blackened, and it started to rain, and in minutes I was a slowly moving bent figure bumping through water that seemed intent on covering Earth, hobbling down a steep canyon that men had hobbled down for centuries. The bike was gone. My sanity was gone. But Lancey was still in my mind. I wondered how long she would live there.

I kept walking, the rain dripping from the big gun dangling from my hand. Something else on the way back should need killing.

I sure as hell hoped so.

5.

# TEST RIDE

from Wild Horse Canyon
Southern New Mexico
Late June

My ranch was in Mescalero County, in the bottom of a small, wide, shallow canyon about five miles from the nearest house, about twelve miles from town. Where I could be left alone, if I wanted to be left alone. Where there was no traffic, no siren noise, no gunshots . . . well, except for mine. Where no lights burned at night and only jackrabbits and coyotes were traffic hazards. And they were safe, because there was no traffic.

Wild Horse Canyon. There hadn't been a wild horse in the canyon in a hundred years, but that's what the Apaches called it. It was their canyon. And I loved the name, anyway.

I left the canyon before daylight and screamed north on the KLR, sticking to the two-lane roads and trying to make the bike do something it should not—I had no idea what I meant by that; I'd let the bike figure it out. I met up with Slade in Southern Colorado. Salida. We were both loaded with the gear—far too much gear—that we thought we'd take to Alaska. The KLR was running well, and I was impressed once again with the power of the single-cylinder engine and with Juanito's abilities. Slade, not a man to mess with older equipment ("Why should I buy into somebody else's problems?") was riding his new KLR. Just like I knew he'd be. Fucking show-off.

We wanted to ride on dirt with all that gear on our bikes, wanted to feel the wheels on something other than blacktop. We rode south out of Salida, started up Poncha Pass, and then turned west, powering up a narrow dirt road, heading high into the mountains toward Marshall Pass. I was riding behind Slade, watching him handle the bike. I knew he had been doing some riding, getting ready, but I was still surprised at his ease on the bike. Slade had flown in Vietnam, had taken planes into places where planes didn't belong. He was one of those guys who can bring skills back into his consciousness, skills he may have had and used in another life, but which never seem to leave his mind, his muscles, and his nervous system. He could have been off bikes for decades, and it wouldn't matter.

I stayed on the throttle up the mountain as long as I could, keeping the engine under strain, but a sharp switchback caused me to ease up on the gas. The engine died instantly.

Slade was somewhere up ahead and didn't know I had a problem. And I didn't know what the problem was. I tried everything I knew, but the bike would not start. And so I sat.

Within ten minutes, Slade was back. He pulled up beside me and gunned his engine, just slightly, just enough show that his engine was running . . . and mine was not.

He tried everything *he* knew, but the bike would not start. And so we sat, trying to figure a next move.

We abandoned the test ride.

I turned my bike around and started coasting off the mountain. Twenty minutes later we broke out on the highway, me still coasting on a silent bike.

We sat on the side of the road and didn't speak. I hated unreliable equipment, and I was thinking of running the damn KLR off the highway and into a shallow canyon. Riding with Slade back to Salida. Renting a car. Just driving away. Before I went, maybe I would put a couple of rounds into the fucking KLR's gas tank, watch the bastard burst into flames—that's the way it happened in the movies, any vehicle in trouble always burst into flames.

That's the way it happened with the BMW.

This was shit. I wanted to kill something. Something was seriously wrong with me. I started fumbling in my gear, angrily shoving stuff aside.

"You're looking for the .45. Christ, can't you even keep track of a fucking pistol?"

I whirled on him, waiting.

"You actually going to shoot the bike? That temper of yours going to take over again?"

I sat, my teeth grinding, feeling foolish.

"Morgan, you're not exactly broke—you could buy any bike you want. Why don't you just do that, and get it over with."

That would be the sensible, sane thing to do, I thought. So why would I do that?

"You had another bike," Slade said quietly. "Damn fine bike. You could be riding it, right now . . . or I could." He paused.

"A bike is just a bike."

"Not to you, it isn't. Not the BMW. That bike was a symbol. And you're damn good at killing symbols." He thought for a moment. "And sometimes killing the real thing."

He shut up, waiting for my reaction. Any reaction.

He got nothing.

* * * * *

It wasn't very long after Slade and I had been to White Sands. I lay on my bed in the ranch house, staring up at a dark ceiling I couldn't even see and wondering which night Slade would call.

This was the night. The fucking phone rang at a little past three in the morning. Its noise and its little light were like techno-bombs in the peace of Wild Horse Canyon. I didn't even bother looking at the phone; I knew the call would be from Slade. And he knew I would not be asleep.

The phone was in the center of the old wooden table near the bed. I got up and stared at the arrogant little light. A few more rings, and it quit. And then I picked up the half-empty bottle of Knob Creek and rammed the bottom of it down on the phone as hard as I could. A satisfying crunch sounded, and all the tiny little twinkling lights on the phone went out, and it died without a gasp. The way death really worked. Yeah, the movies again, always wrong. There usually is no noise—most things die quietly, die without a gasp, without a scream.

Like humans. Most of us die in silence.

I swept the ruins of the cell phone off the table and onto the floor. Killing the cell phone had made a small crack in the whiskey bottle, enough to let a drop of bourbon begin to form on the outside. I set the bottle carefully where the phone had been and watched the whiskey droplets soak into the cracks and gouges of the ancient table. After a while, the table should smell good, I thought, really good.

There was another phone around, somewhere. Another damn cell phone. I had intended to cancel the thing a long time ago but just never got around to it. I found it behind some books. I called Slade's number.

Modene answered.

She didn't even say hello. "You wearing the Colt?" she asked.

"Yeeeep," I said softly into the darkness of the room. I drew the word out, knowing it would piss her off.

"You going to do yourself?"

"What? *Hell no!*" I knew she was prodding me, but I couldn't help myself; I reacted exactly as she knew I would. "She'd have to be one helluva lot more woman than she is before I'd pull the trigger over her!"

I could hear her breathing. Modene was one of the few women I had even known who tell you what she thought, just be breathing. "Really?" she said quietly. "Are you listening to yourself?" And then she hung up.

Slade called back. I told him about the Beemer.

He was quiet for a long time. Then, "What a waste," he whispered, "what a waste."

Neither of us knew where to go from there. Finally, Slade said, "Well, at least you didn't kill the real Snake, that would have been—"

I put the phone in the center of the table and picked up the whiskey bottle. Slade was still talking when the bottle killed the second phone.

*　*　*　*　*

I hit the starter button. The mentally retarded bike started instantly, as though nothing had ever been wrong.

But the test ride was over, goddammit, over! And my bike had failed the test. Slade turned north, toward Colorado Springs.

I turned south. I managed to ride the damn thing all the way to Wild Horse Canyon without it dying on me. Not once.

Back to Juanito.

This became the order of things: long test ride, engine dies, get it started, back to Juanito. For most of the summer.

I once even rode back to Salida—and the engine died. Still, Slade and I got in a couple of complete test rides, enough to reduce our gear load, make things more compact, more essential, enough time in the saddle to get our blood going.

The jumping-off date was fast approaching, and the bike finally seemed to keep running, although neither Juanito nor I could figure out why. To hell with it. I was riding to Alaska, one way or another. If I had to abandon the damn thing along the way and buy something else, that's what I would do.

This ride was not about bikes. It was about something else.

I was figuring it out. I was getting closer.

6.

# THE RIDE

Day 1
Monday, August 26
6:45 a.m.
from Wild Horse Canyon
Southern New Mexico

THE PACKED AND STRAPPED KLR 650 seemed heavy, but it rolled easily out of the old shed and into the early silvery light of a New Mexico morning. I stood by the bike and let one thought run through my head. By the time day was in full hot light, I would be on the way to the Arctic Circle. I was in New Mexico, and I was going to ride to Alaska. Lots of good riders had done it. But I had not.

I rode slowly down the dirt track to the slightly larger dirt track that pretended to be a road and slipped through the sagging fence that marked the southern edge of my rancho. I turned west, rolling to the far southwest corner of the property. I stopped the bike and shut down the engine. I got off, took off my helmet, and stood there in the silence, breathing early morning air that smelled like piñons and ancient earth. I looked back at my so-called ranch. The house was closed up. The doors of the shed were pushed closed, the rusty padlock hanging useless in the hasp. I had pulled my old pickup around to the far side of the house—a little farther away from the goddamn cottonwood trees, disconnected the battery, and tied a heavy tarp over the cab. That was more protection than the truck had ever had. I left the key lying on the dash.

I could barely see the tightly capped full bottle of bourbon on the railing of the porch tucked into the shade next to one of the posts, a small, empty Mason jar next to it. I had left them there for Juanito, or Arturo, or for anybody who wandered by. It was a rule—no bourbon on bike trips. Maybe some other stuff, but not bourbon. Slade had made me set the rule. Damn him, anyway.

Juanito would come by now and then and check on my place. If it were still standing, then everything was all right. If it wasn't standing, Juanito wouldn't try to get in touch with me. After all, if the place was not standing, what the hell could I do about it from Alaska? Or anyplace else?

My eyes drifted to the very corner of my land, where the fence stopped going west and turned north at a right angle. Inside the corner, almost hidden now, deep within the pile of dry, brittle, brown tumbleweeds, lay shards of crockery, broken glass, and faded, tattered pieces of what was once a sheet. In the dim light I could see the dull glint of something metal—a fork, maybe, or table knife. In the dirt at the edge of the pile, some ivory-colored flakes, maybe left from bones. The wind, rain, and various small animals had almost completely removed the aging trash, the detritus of a picnic. Or rather, a Thanksgiving dinner. I knew the trash well. It had been there for more than seven years. I had made a pledge to myself never to touch it.

I don't know how long I stood there, staring. Must've been a long time. I mounted the bike and rode slowly away, so slowly that I had to work at balancing it. Something inside me wanted to make this goodbye last. Something inside me knew more than I did.

As I lost sight of the ranch I carefully opened the throttle, a little at a time, until, eventually, I was screaming in high gear along the dry dirt road and leaving a plume of dust rolling like a thin brown cloud high in the air behind me. My face shield was up and the sweet air packed inside my helmet and brushed whisper-like past my face. But the sweetness was already pumping into heat, coming up boiling hard, and by mid-afternoon there'd be no way I'd be able to keep from roasting inside my jacket. I should've been thankful for the heat while I had the chance. In the days to come I'd beg for heat.

I rode the bike hard, feeling its movements, its guts. The machine felt awkward, heavy with road gear and spare bike parts. The odd, heavy 650cc single-cylinder engine thumped. I'd heard this sound many times before, but now it sounded different. It seemed to be a new sound, a sound that was saying that everything felt right. But I wasn't sure about that—feeling right. This was the jumping-off point, the leaving, those few minutes when you know you are going away. And when you can change your mind. I didn't change my mind. I flipped my face shield down and powered on.

And almost ran down Arturo, standing squarely in the middle of the dirt road.

I stood on the rear brake, trying to keep the ass of the bike from catching the front. The awkward bike slid to the left in a soft half-circle that brought it to a stop a foot from Arturo, dust, dirt, and small stones flying in a screen that almost hid the old man. The engine died.

I ripped my helmet off and threw it into the tall grass at the side of the road, furious at the old Apache for holding me up, ready to take him on, yell at him. Anything . . . he had ruined my leaving. Now, instead of the rancho, I would remember almost killing Arturo. But then I took a good look at his face. He was crying.

"Arturo?" I said.

"You are a hard man, Morgan. Angry." It was that voice again, the voice that he used when the words were more than words. When the words were wisdom. "I hope the inside of your mind and body find peace." Arturo turned and looked out across the desert, as though looking at his own kingdom "It's been good to have you here, Morgan." And he walked away.

Good to have me here? I thought. Goddammit, I was just going on a long ride.

Just going on a ride.

Just going.

There was nothing I could say. As Arturo walked across the desert I realized I'd never known where he lived, had never been to his house, did not even know if he owned a phone. And when I was with Juanito, working on the bike, Juanito never mentioned him. It was Arturo who said he had a grandson named Juanito; Juanito never told me he had a grandfather named Arturo.

I straightened out the KRL and pointed it along the road. By that time Arturo was out of sight. I looked for him. In the direction he'd taken, there was nothing large enough to hide him and yet he was gone. Silence came over the land and I couldn't even feel the air stirring. I found my helmet, looking around almost furtively as I got back on the bike, as though I were doing something that shouldn't be done. The engine started instantly and I rode away. I did not look back.

At the intersection of two narrow blacktop roads I turned right and headed north, knowing that I was riding the early miles of another long ride, always a feeling of excitement in me, a feeling that I was going somewhere, anywhere, and that not many—maybe no one—knew where I would be or why I would be there. No better feeling exists in the minds of riders like me.

And then I passed the other road that turned to the west. West, to the town where Lancey now lived. Some of the Apaches had said she had moved in with the Snake, but that is all they would say, and that is all I really knew. It had been so easy for Lancey to kill me, never really giving me a reason, never talking with me, just crushing my chest and disappearing.

But I knew the Snake was there, in that town. It really wasn't his fault, not entirely. Maybe he was just the bag of shit The Girls picked out for Lancey, convincing her that she would be far better off without me. It didn't matter. One of these days I knew I'd make *him* pay for what Lancey had done. The Snake— I knew his name, and where he lived, and where his office was, and what he looked like. But I'd never say his name aloud. Another promise I'd made to myself. I would hate his ass forever.

I decided to open up the KLR, give it a chance to do whatever the hell it was going to do, right now, while I could still just drive it off the road and leave it in a bullet-riddled pile.

It came to me that I was angry. Imagine that.

The KLR was building speed, running smoothly, the power of the thumper engine advertising what it could do, the bike, me, and all the gear ripping north in a mad rush to go, just go, the needle climbing above seventy, and then eighty, leaving the ranch and the town behind me . . .

And then I realized I was slowing down. The bike was losing speed in a very subtle slipping of everything that made speed. But it was not the bike, it was me. I was slowly letting the throttle slip, backing off the fuel until the bike crawled along the road, lugging down, barely fast enough to stay upright.

A dirt lane to my right led across the rolling plain, and I turned onto it. In the distance tiny dots of pronghorns fed on a ridge. They were too far away to be concerned about me.

The area around the lane had been used to load cattle, the ground torn and pulped, low ditches and high bumps. I rode the KLR in large circles, working the wheels and the load, working the engine, wanting to ride faster but going more slowly.

What the hell was wrong with me?

The bike faced back out toward the highway. I dropped into a lower gear and moved slowly back toward the blacktop. And then I turned left and rode south, over the road I had just ridden, riding back to the turnoff to the town, Lancey's town. And Snake's.

I turned onto that road.

There was no doubt about it. It was his office. Hell, maybe he owned the whole building. It was a low-slung two-story fake adobe that looked like a thousand other fake adobes in New Mexico. A polished brass plaque hung beside the door, his name the only thing on it, no title, no alphabet of initials. It was an announcement—you were supposed to know what he did inside that ugly building without being told. If you did not know, then you were standing in front of the wrong building.

The next thing I knew I was standing beside the bike,

pushing the .45 farther down into the left pannier where it rode in a plastic bag. I thought about sticking it inside my belt, but if I ended up in cuffs I didn't want to be carrying the gun. My helmet was dangling from a mirror—Slade hated it when I did that. I took off my riding jacket and draped it over the bars beside the helmet, then pulled on my thin leather riding gloves and tightened them on my hands.

And I just stood there.

Now was the time to change my mind, be adult, be what Slade and Modene wanted me to be, put my gear back on and ride away. It was over. Let it be, stop thinking about it. It was a game, and I lost. She was a Smoke Woman, a gorgeous piece of useless crap that had crawled into my mind and dug in like a parasite. I wouldn't take her back if she were lying naked in the middle of the road cupping her tits in her hands.

Now was the time to change my mind, be an adult.

Fuck that.


I pushed open the heavy door and slid to my left two or three steps and waited, my hands at my waist. The room was huge, heavy carpeting, overstuffed leather furniture supposed to look expensive but was probably cheap crap.

The only person in the room was a woman, maybe in her early fifties, Latina, attractive, every hair in place, her clothing expensive and tailored. She stood at the edge of an enormous desk gingerly holding a garish coffee cup in front of her, like some sort of offering. Steam crawled over the edge of the cup. The woman stared at me and didn't move.

Obviously, I was scaring the hell out of her just by standing there. I held up my hand, palm out. Peace. I mean you no harm. She still didn't move, gripping the huge cup.

Just beyond her was an ornate door that went into another office. The Snake's office—had to be. My lucky day.

*"Teresa, where's my goddamn coffee?"*

The voice was loud and demanding, and it clawed its way out of the other office like some sort of putrid life form. I thought I could *feel* the voice. He didn't use the Spanish pronunciation of the woman's name.

The woman dropped her head slightly, her eyes down, embarrassed that a stranger, even a stranger she might fear, was there to hear him.

I stepped softly in front of her, pointed at the coffee cup and raised my eyebrows in a question of . . . is this his coffee? Teresa nodded so slightly I waited a moment to make sure she'd moved.

I put my hands on the coffee cup, with hers. "Con permiso, señora," I said very softly. And I took the cup from her hands.

In two quick steps I was at Snake's office door, shoved it open, and stepped inside.

He was standing in front of his desk, an open file in his hands. When he heard me come into the room he turned his head and opened his mouth.

*"Teresa, where the hell . . . !"* and I hit him straight in his open mouth with the cup of hot coffee. The cup shattered and blood flew from his mouth. Scalding coffee covered his face and soaked the front of his snow-white shirt and his dark gray suit coat. He flopped over backward and bounced off the front of his desk—another oversized piece of ugly junk. He came up

on his feet almost at once—I didn't expect that—trying to blink coffee from his eyes. His mouth was curved in a mad snarl and I could see some jagged teeth. His face seemed out of shape, crooked, and I realized the cup had broken his nose. He put his hands up in what he thought was some sort of martial arts thing. I kicked him in the balls.

His body snapped forward, folding like a closing pocket-knife. He went down hard, landing on his hands and knees in front of the desk. Retching started from somewhere down in his guts and he puked and convulsed, spraying vomit across the cheap carpet. Before he could move again I stepped to the side and kicked him in the ribs, and the ribs made that beautiful cracking sound of splintering. He flopped over on his side and didn't move.

I wondered if he would choke on his own puke.

I didn't care.

I stood there for a few seconds, looking at him. He lay in his own vomit, his eyes partially closed, his breath coming in soft, tiny gasps that almost weren't there. He slowly slid his arm out across the carpet as though looking for something to grasp, his hand flexing, long fingers, manicured nails . . . a hand that had been on Lancey. I grabbed the hand and jerked him upright, wadded his filthy suit coat into my hands, lifted hard, and threw him on top of his own desk. There wasn't much on the desk— a small brass lamp was bent double, some wooden trays flew off and smacked into a nearby chair. The best part was, he had one more little vomit reaction and dumped it in the middle of a leather desk pad.

I slid around the side of the desk, opened one of the heavy drawers, shoved his Lancey-hand down on the edge of it and kicked it shut with everything I could put into it, which was considerable. If I had done it right, I had broken at least some of his fingers.

He didn't make a sound.

Damn, I thought, it was now definitely too late to be an adult.

I pulled the bastard off the back of his desk. He landed in a pile in front of his leather office chair and curled into a fetal position. I squatted down in front of him. He was bleeding badly from the mouth, nose, and some other places. Puke covered his clothing. He lifted his arm slightly and tried to look at his damaged hand but his eyes would not work and the hand just hung there. Blood and spit dribbled out of the corner of his mouth, snot out of his nose, his eyes swelling rapidly. He mumbled, "doctor." I hooked him across his broken nose with an elbow.

I glanced through the open office door. Teresa stood frozen in the exact spot where I had left her. There was no expression on her face, no anger, no fear.

I tried to pick a place on his shirt that wasn't covered with blood, snot, or puke, and I grabbed him. Oddly, I remember thinking I'd never had my hands on a shirt that expensive. I leaned in close. He said something I had trouble understanding because of his swollen tongue and fractured teeth. "You hurt me," he mumbled, in a little-boy incredulous tone. He held his broken, swollen hand up in front of his face, squinting at it, trying to get his eyes to work.

"Hell, Snake, I was just getting warmed up. I should take you outside, strip you naked, and show you how it's really done."

His eyes got as big as the swollen tissue would allow, and he shook his head, no.

I pulled him closer. "Listen carefully, Snake. "One of these days I'm going to come back. You'll never know when. You'll just walk into your bathroom to take a shit, drop your pants, and sit down—and I'm going to be there. And before you can move I'll stuff you in the toilet with your own crap. But by that time, you won't smell a thing."

My face was practically pushing against his broken nose.

He didn't move. His shirt was getting slippery so I let him drop. I stood up. "I don't know if she'll stay with you, Snake. But she's a Smoke Woman. So probably not."

I could see that I wasn't getting through to him.

It was time to go. He was already curled up so it wasn't difficult to stuff him into the foot well of the desk. I shoved him completely out of sight. Strange thoughts come shooting out of my mind at strange times, always have, and one hit me at that moment—I wondered whether Lancey had ever hidden in that foot well and given the Snake a blow job while he yelled at Teresa for more coffee. I guess I was never going to find out.

Back in the outer office, Teresa hadn't moved. I picked up the phone from her desk and held it out to her. She looked at the phone and then at me. She shook her head, *no.* I tossed the phone on the desk.

"Lo siento, señora, about that mess in there."

"Ni modo, señor. It will be the problem of another. I think I do not work here anymore."

"May I have cinco minute—before you call?" I asked softly.

Teresa smiled up at me. "Make it veinte," she said. "I have to clean out my desk."

7.

# DAY 1— THE SAME DAY

Monday, August 26

IT WAS DIFFICULT TO hear my brain over the sound of the engine and the rush of air past my helmet. Normally, I wore earplugs when I rode, reveling in the near silence of the bike's piercing passage through space and distance, but I hadn't taken the time to put them in when I left Snake's office.

So I tried hard to hear my brain. I'd learned long ago my brain and my body sometimes worked separately, each telling me something different. How the hell does that work? Who is the "me" that my brain and body are speaking to? Is it some spiritual intellect that exists in the ether of my being? I've never really figured it out. All I know is—it's there, and it listens.

My brain was being rational, logical. There was no way that Snake was going to let this pass. I'd become an outlaw in my own backyard—the very thing Slade had warned me about. Sooner or later there would be a price to pay. That's what my brain said. That's what my brain felt.

But there was another part of me. I searched through my body, searched for pain, searched for anguish, searched for guilt, searched for anything that would make emotional sense of what I had done. And what I would do again, when the blackness came upon me. I found only one thing, one feeling, one surge up through my spine, leaping into my lungs and heart.

Good. I felt good. I felt better than good.

The narrow streets of Santa Fe had once carried burro carts and men with long, hammered knives stuck carelessly through sash belts, within easy reach.

I wasn't worried about riding through those narrow streets. I wanted to play motorcycle-tourist for a few minutes before heading farther north. I was in no particular hurry. I thought it would take Snake a few hours to be able to make sense to any cops who were interviewing him.

It had not rained for weeks, and the drought became more hard-baked and brittle as I passed through Española and rode up the dried, cracked valley of the Rio Grande. I could glance into the canyon and see the bottom of the river, some of the rocks barely damp. I knew a professional river runner in the area, a guy named Toran, one of the most skilled outdoorsmen I ever knew, and one of the toughest. I knew it had been a bad year for guys who made their living on moving water, and I wondered how Toran was doing. But I knew him—natural obstacles, even disasters, were part of his life, and it was a part he loved to live in, and survive.

Once, I had taken Lancey to meet Toran, a mistake that I could not undo.

The earth was still brittle when I reached the high country of Taos. I thought about stopping in Taos for a while, but I was not really there, not in my mind, not in Taos or any other place. And besides, by now, maybe someone was looking for me. I was sure that Snake had found his balls and gotten his smirking mouth working by this time.

So I drifted further into my riding mode, when being on the bike was the thing, the life. The *life*. When being on the bike meant no one could find me, could not reach me. Pure freedom. I was screaming out of the little town, twisting the throttle through the small, gentle canyons to the north, pushing the bike hard toward the high plains, the jagged peaks of the Sangre de Cristos seeming to press against my right shoulder, holding back the horizon.

In the middle of nowhere, not yet to the Colorado border, I saw a kid, far up ahead, walking on the side of the road. As I came up behind him he stopped, turned, and watched me go by. We were at least five miles from nowhere and I wondered where he had come from, where he was going. Somewhere back there toward a far ridge there must be a small farm, a cabin, a dirt-poor home kept by a dirt-poor family that had produced a kid who was walking on a road five miles from nowhere. Heading nowhere.

I knew that kid. I'd been him.

He was still standing there, his arms hanging straight down at his sides, when I lost sight of him in my mirrors.

And then I was in Colorado.

My stomach was in a knot. The bike was acting up again. On the shakedown rides I had looked for everything about the bike that might jump up and bite my ass somewhere in the wilds of the Yukon. The main problem was that, for no discernable reason, the fuel to the engine would simply stop flowing—like when the engine quit back there on our first test ride. It seemed always on the edge of dying—at least in my mind.

But I was there, north of Taos, jumping off into the ride of a lifetime—and the goddamn bike was not cooperating. I had tried to explain the problem to Juanito, over and over again. Finally, he would get tired of hearing me talk and would wave me away so he could concentrate.

Finally, Juanito found a tiny leak somewhere in the fuel petcock. The KLR's fuel delivery system was vacuum operated; when enough air seeped through the pinprick, the vacuum didn't work, and the engine died. At least, that was all Juanito could find. He installed a new petcock, gravity fed. Yet, each morning when I tried to start the bike it coughed and spit, puked, gagged, and hacked—the most cold-blooded damn bike I'd ever owned. When I finally got it started it would hardly run until I really warmed it up, and then it would run like a banshee. But when I stopped for gas and then tried to restart the bike, I still had to use full choke to force the engine to life.

I've never liked starting out on any sort of adventure, expedition, trip of any sort, with anything less than perfect gear—or as close to perfect as I could get. With this bike, I wasn't even close. And now I was intending to ride to Alaska, to the Arctic Circle. I began to understand that my ego-desire to ride an old KLR that had been sitting in my shed was, simply, a fucking mistake.

Screw the bike. I rode on anyway.

It was late, and clouds had covered the tops of the mountains. A hard wind came down the Grand Canyon of the Arkansas, bending everything in front of it. My body ached from the first full day's ride, and my mind ached from the anticipation of seeing flashing red lights in the mirrors, or the bike's engine quitting, a sort of constant alert that took a lot of energy without my even knowing where it went. I gave up for the day. I rode into the woods near Cotopaxi, hid myself in the trees, and rolled up inside a large, lightweight poncho. I didn't bother with the tent. Or food.

I was still wearing my waterproof riding gear, stuff I'd worn for so many rides it seemed to be grafted to my hide. It wasn't the first time I'd slept in it.

# DAY 2

Tuesday, August 27
from Cotopaxi, Colorado

IT WAS ODD. THE rain pattering softly on the poncho was awakening me, and yet the same sound was telling me to stay where I was, don't move, close my eyes, breathe gently. I was safe, dry. I could stay there under the trees until the world became warmer, and the water stopped trying to find its way inside the poncho.

The feeling was natural. My ancestors, and I mean *ancestors*, must have felt that, done that, for thousands of years when the weather was chilly and wet. They stayed in the cave, or inside the skin lodge, or turned the boat upside down and slept under it. They weren't stupid—other, drier, warmer days would come. I knew very well those feelings were still inside me.

But I wasn't in a cave or a skin lodge. I was wrapped in a high-tech mountaineering poncho in the rain, and I had places to go. And the only way to go there was to get up and get on the bike.

The world smelled like only a forest can smell in the rain. It was still falling all the way to the far mountains when I left the woods and rode down through the foothills. Rain, in a time of drought. By the time I reached Ute Station and the Arkansas River the clouds sat tightly on the peaks and pressed me into the narrow canyon.

I knew what was coming—more rain—and there was no place to hide and no reason to hide there. I was on a bike, trapped by the weather. It was one of the most familiar feelings I've ever had.

I stopped at the lone gas station at Ute Station—the lone anything; Ute Station *was* a gas station, a couple of pumps outside a tiny store. The place seemed empty, huddled in the rain. I pulled up to a pump and shut down the engine, the hot metal making tiny clicking noises in the dim light. I topped off the tank, trying not to let the water ooze into its innards.

I pushed the bike off to the side of the pumps and bumbled my way inside the little store, the heavy riding gear hanging on me like leaden Spanish moss.

A skinny guy stood behind the counter. He was sitting on a stool, looking at something on a computer, his damp hair hanging down over one side of his face. He didn't look up, didn't speak. But the coffee machine was working. I poured some of the stuff into a large cup and took a strange-looking sandwich out of the cooler—a sandwich that must've been made when Teddy Roosevelt was still mucking about in the West. Through the filtered light that came through the mist on the store's windows I saw the wavering image of a pickup truck glide slowly in beside the pumps. I stood sipping my coffee. Nobody came into the store, and nobody was pumping gas. I leaned to my right, to the far edge of the window where I could tilt my head toward the glass and see the KLR.

There was a guy sitting on my motorcycle.

*Sitting on my motorcycle! Without asking me!*

I remembered an old buddy, Chaser, saying that a guy who would just climb on your motorcycle was the same as a guy who would walk into your house and climb on your wife. Except worse.

I took off my bulky riding coat and went outside into the light rain.

He was a tall guy, young, stringy, wearing a sweat-stained western hat, a faded denim jacket with holes in the elbows, and ragged jeans. He sat on the bike in the rain as though it were a bright Sunday afternoon just before the picnic. He had the bike balanced up off the side stand and was squeezing the clutch lever, twisting the throttle, tapping the brake. . . . If I'd left the key in the bike, he'd have started the engine.

Another guy sat in the truck on the passenger side. He was looking straight ahead and made no move to get out.

I walked up and stood beside the bike, just out of reach of the bastard sitting my saddle. He didn't bother looking at me, just kept toying with the bike's controls and tugging at straps, running his hands over the panniers.

"This is one ugly fucking motorcycle," he said casually, still not looking at me.

I waited a moment. Then I asked, "You done?"

He grinned. "Don't know, just yet. I'll let you know when the time comes, old man."

The .45 was still inside the left pannier, still wrapped in plastic. I began to think that was not a good idea. If the guy stuck his hand in there, I'd be in deep shit. I'd have to take him off the motorcycle before he found the gun. I took a quick look around for something to give me an edge. A shovel leaned against the side of the store.

"You're done," I growled. I was surprised at the sound of my voice, surprised at what was coming up through my chest, surprised at the realization that I was energized.

Surprised that I was happy.

He leaned the bike back onto the side stand but made no move to get off. He turned his head slowly toward me, rain streaming off his hat. His eyes were wide, pupils like black marbles, his lips twisted into a sneer, his teeth stained black, one tooth chipped. A tweaker. He took his right hand slowly off the handlebar and eased back the edge of his jacket—to show me the butt of a pistol sticking up from inside his belt. "You're way too old to fuck with me, grampa. I'll git off the bike when the right and proper mood strikes me . . ."

But I already had the shovel.

The surprised look on his face was worth the price of admission. He probably thought I was going to swing at his head and his arms shot up. He was wrong. I swung the shovel in a short arc and cracked the edge of the blade into his knee. He screamed and reached over to grab at his leg, the bike moving slightly. And then I brought the shovel up into his face. His hat flew off into the rain, and he hung there on the edge of the saddle for a moment, blood gushing from his nose and a cut somewhere on his forehead. Then he toppled off the bike, lying in a jumbled heap, rain washing the blood from his face. The bike slowly fell over on top of his legs.

But I knew it wasn't over. I charged around the bike, grabbed the pistol out of the guy's pants, and threw it as hard as I could up and over the roof of the store. And then there was the truck—if the other guy was going to join in, I had to head him off before he got organized. I ran to the passenger door and whipped it open. The guy was the same type as the other one, tall, stringy—they could have been brothers. He stared at me, and at the shovel, eyes wide, hands in the air as though I had a gun.

"I ain't a part'a this, mister. I tole that dumbass not to mess with no guy's motorsickle . . ."

I reached in, grabbed him by his old leather jacket, and pulled him out of the truck. He hit the ground like a puppet without strings and did not move. I thought maybe the guy was stoked out of his mind on some sort of high-powered shit. I didn't care.

I bent over him, ran my hands quickly under his jacket, around his belt. "If you move, you fucking tweaker, I'm going to use this shovel to kill you, and then use it to bury you." He didn't move a cell in his body.

I checked the guy lying under my bike and then ran back inside the store—the clerk was nowhere to be seen—and grabbed my gear. Outside, I thought about grabbing the .45, but neither guy had moved. Instead, I leaned into the truck, yanked the keys, and flung them over the top of the little store. I liked throwing things over the store. The Arkansas River was back there, but I couldn't tell if the gun or the keys had made it that far.

Lifting the bike was not easy, but I was pumped from the action, and it came up off the guy without much trouble. It started instantly. I dropped it into low and almost let it leap forward. But I held the clutch in and looked back at the two guys, still lying there, one of them unconscious, mostly, and one of them scared shitless. I was looking for other dangers. There were none, unless the clerk in the store had called the cops. If he had, I didn't want to be there when they showed up.

In less than two seconds I was headed east, my coat flapping in the rain. Not a problem. I would stop and button up when I thought I was safe.

I thought about the guy I had hit. Young, high on some sort of shit. I guessed he may have seen me through the store's window, saw the color of my hair, thought he would amuse himself. He probably would have kicked my ass. But I had the shovel. I didn't think of it as a shovel. I thought of it as a club.

Whacking a young stud with a club.

I was going to have to quit doing that.

\* \* \* \* \*

If I didn't ride with Slade, I rode alone. A few years ago I felt the years stuffing into my heart. In the shed, I had an old bike that I was trying to bring back to life. I decided to take it for a test ride. I climbed on and lit out, as Slade would have said.

I ended up in South Dakota . . .

An ancient, solitary bull stood on a small ridge and looked down on the group below. Females and their young stood with immature males, young bulls that watched the old bull as he stood against the horizon. One of the young bulls, larger than the others, stood between the group and the old bull on the near ridge. Watching. Supremely confident.

The old bull was massive, standing more than six feet tall at the shoulder. He was almost twelve feet long and probably weighed nearly two thousand pounds. His head, neck, and forelegs were covered with dark, shaggy hair, and his horns, which he never sheds and which grow throughout his life, had begun to chip and lose the luster of his youth.

I sat quietly, leaning back against a stump, my feet propped on a dead limb lying in front of me. The limb, as big around as my arm, looked polished, as though the buffalo had rubbed it hard out of sheer boredom. Or out of rage. I was less than fifty yards from the old bull, my bike and my riding gear hidden in a dry wash at least a quarter mile behind me. I held my binoculars on him, steady, my elbows propped on my knees. I could see the breath streaming in heavy bursts through his wet nostrils and the insects buzzing in tight little circles around his eyes, the eyes staring at nothing. Certainly not staring at me. He couldn't have cared less that I was there. Clumps of earth hung in the hair of his massive neck and I thought I could see blood oozing from a slash in his side and an old scab at the base of one of his horns, a cracked horn. With the tip broken off. Wide awake, he was standing there, dreaming of something. Something lost. I put the binoculars down and simply watched the bull, waiting for something that would never come.

I could see his age, that he'd lost his speed and stamina. He could neither chase the young bulls from his group nor fight them when they came. He knew that, now.

And so it had happened.

To both of us.

A young male now controlled the group. The old bull had been driven out and wouldn't be allowed back. His time had come, and gone, and there would be no other times for him. The young bull stood out from the small herd, now and then glancing my way, but not really caring that I was there.

The old bull had done what he was supposed to do—he survived, and he made his contribution to the survival of his kind. And now it was over.

He turned and eased down the far side of the ridge and out of sight of the group, and I could see that he stumbled slightly, not caring, now that the others could not see him. He walked unsteadily out of sight.

I waited, thinking maybe he would top the next rise, but he never did.

I slid backward, out of sight of the herd, and slowly walked back to my bike. I felt as though I'd been to a funeral and was now trying to sneak away in the falling light, sneak away before the not-quite-dead knew what was happening. I didn't want to witness that.

I dropped over a low rise and down into the wash and looked at the bike. It seemed oddly out of place, not a part of any world that was happening within my reach. It was an old Yamaha, the paint faded, the seat cracked. But it ran. It had brought me all the way up here and now would have to take me home.

I put on my gear, swung my leg over the saddle, stood the bike up, and booted the side stand up.

I touched the key.

A shadow fell across the bike. And me. I did not want to turn my head but I had to, I had to see, even though I knew what was there.

It was the bull.

He stood on the edge of the wash, the low light throwing his shadow completely across the bike. He seemed tilted, as though he were struggling to stand upright. Other than that, he didn't move. He seemed not to be breathing, but I knew he was, knew he would breathe until something took the breath from him and took him from the wilderness of the living.

We did nothing but look at each other.

Somewhere, a part of my mind opened and took him in, an image, a being, a living thing that wasn't supposed to be there, but which I knew would be there for the rest of my days.

I got off the bike and took off my helmet. I could hear him breathing, then. I met his eyes. He knew. He knew that whatever had driven him was gone, spent out from his being.

And he knew it was happening to me.

He turned and walked down the edge of the wash to the rim of a small valley. He simply stopped there. He did not look back. He knew, when he turned, that I'd be gone. He awaited death with a patience developed over centuries, a style and a fate that had been handed down to him.

And to me.

But there was a difference between us.

I would not wait.

Something slowly formed behind my mind, something that I wouldn't even try to resist. Something totally insane. I wished Slade were there. He would keep me sane.

I hung the helmet on a handlebar.

I left all my other gear on—the armored jacket, the gloves— and I walked back to the top of the ridge. The tiny herd was still down there, grazing, content. The big young bull still stood guard, not too far down the ridge.

This was crazy. I was going to die. Fuck it. Only Slade would understand. And Modene.

I picked up the dead tree limb. It was bigger than I had

thought, but I could handle it. I hefted it casually on my shoulder and walked very slowly down the ridge. Toward the bull.

He never moved. He watched me come, but he never moved. These were only half-wild buffalo, living on a park, used to seeing tourists stop their cars, take pictures, hold their children up to the "see the big animals."

I walked right up to him.

The tree limb seemed to come up off my shoulder without my thinking about it. It rose above me as something flowed through my body that must have been energy but was more than energy. It was a force that I had never felt, never knew was there, a force from all the years behind me, a force, I knew, I would never feel again. Because I was going to die there.

The bull never moved.

The force brought the limb down between his horns, the wood cracking, splintering, twisting, the sound of it firing across the others in the small herd. I don't remember any of them moving. I staggered a short step backwards and then realized my old bones and my aging body were empty. There was no force, no muscle, no will . . . nothing.

I sank to my knees, closed my eyes, and waited for his charge. I was ready. It was a good day.

He went to his knees in front of me. And stayed there.

I tried to see into his eyes but they had left him, searching in his universe for the reason for it all, not knowing that there was no reason. Except that he was young and I was not and I hated him for that.

The ground was soft and wet and my knees sunk in and so did his and we stared at each other in some sort of wonder at something that had happened that perhaps had not happened before in the history of men and buffalo.

I guessed I would not die that day.

I got up and hobbled away stiffly.

\* \* \* \* \*

And I had one other thought—the .45 was not going to live inside a damn pannier where I couldn't reach it. From now on, it would live inside my belt.

Rain. I didn't particularly like riding in the rain, but the land needed the water. I thought I could hear the earth sucking the water into itself, pulling the wet so hard that it seemed like an hour before there was enough water to puddle on the side of the road. I hoped the rain made it all the way to the rancho.

But riding that particular piece of highway was not as simple as it looked. The road was narrow and twisty. If I rode at fifty, trucks stayed on my rear wheel. One mistake and I would be road kill. If I rode at seventy, I could feel the bike skim slightly in the turns, as though losing its grip on reality. I tried to hang in the middle, but there was no middle.

Mist and mud coated my face shield and I had to turn my head constantly from side to side. Water drove under my helmet and oozed inside the back of my collar, slipping down my spine like a cold snake. A truck threw mud so hard that it hit my chest and spattered up inside my face shield. I had to stop, take off the helmet, and clean it while rain soaked into my hair and swept down inside my jacket. It was late August, and I was cold. How could that be? I hated being cold.

I was less than two days into a thirty-day ride, and already I was questioning why I was doing it. Halfway from Ute Station to Colorado Springs the old, old question came again . . .

What the hell am I doing here?

It was the question that had come to me, over and over, throughout my life, every time I had waded into shit I hadn't planned on. But then I thought about Slade, and his philosophy about riding in weather. ("Hell, it's just weather!") And I was on my way to join up with him. I must have been out of my mind. Of course I was.

I rode into Colorado Springs in the rain, parked the bike at the side of the house in the rain, walked up the steps in the rain.

Slade stood there on the tiny porch, all 6'3" of him. "Isn't this great?" he said.

In the rain.

# 9

# DAY 3

Wednesday, August 28
from Colorado Springs, Colorado

MODENE WAS THERE, COMPACT and blonde, beautiful, with a smile that would stop traffic and a mind that constantly throws out ideas that stop your thinking. Looking at her, all I could think of was Slade saying, "center point."

But they weren't married. How could Slade not be married to Modene?

I looked at the small house, the narrow driveway to the little garage, a garage too small for cars but perfect for a motorcycle. Once, when we'd been sitting at the edge of the jungle, listening to the night noises and talking softly about home, I'd asked Slade who owned the house, him, or Modene. Slade stared off into the darkness. He was silent for a while, thinking.

Thinking? He didn't know who owned the house?

That was a part of Slade. Some things that were important to him and some things that were not. If the things were not important—to him—most of the time they simply didn't exist in his mind. Things like owning a house.

"I'm not sure who owns it," he mumbled. "Never really gave it much thought." He listened to some sort of noise from the jungle. "Guess I never paid much attention. I signed a bunch of papers once, stuff that Modene had, but I'm not really sure what they were. Modene had them, so I signed them." We sat in silence for long moments. And then Slade said softly, "One thing I do know—Modene and me? We own each other."

Modene made breakfast. We sat at a small table in the kitchen. Modene watched Slade out of the corners of her eyes, as though trying to see as much of him as she could while he was still there.

"Modene," I said, almost under my breath, "there may be somebody calling here. Maybe somebody dropping by. Maybe trying to find me. Might even be, uh, some sort of cop. Everybody who knows me knows about you and Slade, so they might call . . ."

Modene and Slade stopped eating. Modene looked at me. Slade did not.

"Oh, God, Morgan," Modene said, "what did you do?"

I sat there, my chin on my chest, my mind flashing back to the Snake. I waited for the shame to overtake me, but all I felt was hot energy that still boiled in my gut.

Oddly, the tweaker at Ute Creek never crossed my mind.

"It might be better if I don't tell you," I said, my voice seeming to come out of somebody else.

Modene stared at me, wide eyed. The edges of a small smile were on Slade's lips, but he didn't look at me.

Modene looked at Slade. "Do you know what you're getting into, if you get on that bike and ride out with him?"

Slade waited, thinking. "Getting into? I haven't known that since I broke him out of that cage in the river," he said quietly.

Modene rested her elbows on the table and put her head in her hands. We sat in silence.

"Morgan, do you remember what Kirk Judd used to say?"

Kirk was a buddy out of the past, a poet from the mountains, one of those guys who express a hundred thoughts in a dozen words.

I remembered his words clearly: "If you can see the edge, you're not on it," I mumbled.

"Morgan," she said, "you can't see the edge, can you?"

There was a minute of silence, like a silence for the dead.

Modene leaned toward me and put her hand on mine. "Morgan," she said, "you know I love you. But you are truly, truly, truly . . . fucked up."

And then she laughed, and Slade laughed, and all I could do was grin in the face of truth.

We finished breakfast, feeling good. I loved feeling good.

And then it was time to go.

Slade rolled his bike out of the tiny garage and parked it next to mine, the bike, like mine, heavy with gear. But, heavy or not, it was the gear we thought we needed. Later, I would notice that each time we unpacked and then repacked, the load seemed to become smaller, more concise. Maybe we tossed some gear away, but I don't think so. We just got better at doing what we were supposed to do.

I could smell rain in the air, and I thought our first day of riding was going to be a mild sort of hell.

Slade was walking toward the house, his helmet under his arm. Going to say goodbye to Modene, I thought.

Before he got to the back door, I heard an engine fire up. Modene's car pulled away from the front of the house and disappeared down a side street. Slade stopped and stared after her, not moving, not seeming to breathe.

He walked back to his bike and threw his leg over the saddle. Before he put on his helmet he said, "Girl hates goodbyes." And then he started the engine and rode away.

We left Colorado Springs under heavy cloud cover, the sun streaking through breaks in the overcast just enough to keep us happy. But it didn't really matter. I had joined up with Slade again and we were actually, really, for damn sure, on our way to Alaska.

We headed northwest, out of the Springs and over the nearest high ridge and then down into a valley that I had not ridden through before, and that's when it all began to feel real to me. Almost.

I didn't realize it then, but those points of departure, those places where "it would feel real to me," would come almost every other day. Each time we passed some real or imagined landmark, some mystical turning point in our journey—Yellowstone, Whitefish, the Canadian border, the Alaskan border, the Yukon River—each time, without fail, I would think, "now, it feels real." Almost.

But, no, it never actually felt "fully real," never felt as though what I were doing was a true and exciting thing, never felt as though I were actually in some place and time that the days and mileage and maps and the weather said were *there*, and that *I was in it*. It was all just a little . . . "unreal." Sometimes I felt as though the bike were not touching the highway, or the dirt, or the mud, or the gravel, or whatever it was supposed to be touching at the time. The bike was just floating, with me on the saddle, having nothing really to do with where the bike was going. I was along for the ride, a piece of dunnage, strapped to a machine that had a mind of its own, a goal of its own.

How did it get to be that way? How did the bike work all that out without my participation? But it had. Any minute now, I would awaken, and the ride would be over. A dream.

It never felt real. Not quite. Somewhere out there, up there, beyond there, was the Arctic Circle. If we made it, maybe, then, it might seem real. Maybe.

Slade rode ahead, his tall frame settled into his bike like he was born to it. I watched him lean into the curves, thankful that I had a friend like Slade. I thought of other guys I knew, guys who were sometimes fun and sometimes not, guys I could only sometimes trust—and if you can't trust someone all the time, then you can't trust him at all.

You can be a male and not be a man. Slade was a man.

We were totally self-contained. Each of us had a tent, a sleeping bag, a ground pad, cooking gear, and all the other stuff that makes loading and balancing the bike difficult, but sure as hell makes life easier if you need the equipment. We were prepared to stop anywhere, camp anywhere, sleep anywhere. Other than food and gasoline, we were dependent on nothing and no one. But that wasn't all the gear we carried: we carried bike parts, maintenance supplies, tools, oil, chain lube, spare tubes.

And me? I had a handful of notebooks stuck in the bottom of one of the panniers on the back, those weird, old-fashioned composition books with the wide lines and hard black-and-white covers, the sorry-looking things that kids used to use in school. Back in the day. Six or eight of them, all blank as a new-born baby's ass.

We were prepared for anything short of absolute disaster. And if disaster came, well, it would just have to be part of the trip, part of the fun, part of what we were looking for.

And I also carried what I always carry—the Colt. The incident at Ute Station showed me that the Colt was useless if I couldn't get to it. Now, the Colt rode inside my belt.

Slade never carried a piece.

"Why should I?" he would grunt. "You've always got one—belongs to me, in fact. When you're around, I don't need one, and when I need one . . ."

I knew what was coming next.

" . . . you always seem to be around."

"You sayin', it's when I'm around, that's when shit happens?"

"Just sayin'."

We got almost an hour out of town before it started raining. How can we ride in the rain and ride through absolute drought at the same time? But that's what we did. We rode in the rain through country so dry the raindrops rose dust from the land.

We were on the roof of the world. Rabbit Ears Pass lifted us into a time and place that made our ears ring. And when we dropped off the pass I knew, for real, that we would be on our way again. Dropping over the pass would be like sailing out of sight of land. We would be really committed to the ride, crossing over onto the Western Slope, and any rain that fell on us would end up in the Pacific. What's more, the Arctic Circle was now only four thousand miles in front of us. No problem.

The rain had stopped, and the sky was littered with clouds.

Bolts of crystalline light shot through the holes in the cover and tried to find the bikes—a sort of celestial shooting gallery.

I caught myself thinking about Modene, vibrant and sufficient, getting on with her life, keeping everything together while Slade and I hiked high ridges in the far mountains, rode over hard desert, and flew airplanes over impenetrable jungle, chasing some mystical balance in our lives. Maybe trying to make a difference. But I'm not sure we ever did.

And now here Slade and I were, chasing another mystical balance. At least Slade was. Me? I was just . . . chasing. I remembered something Modene had said to me at breakfast: "You aren't just on a bike ride, Morgan. You're trying to get away from the fact that you lost something, and you don't like to lose *anything*. It pisses you off beyond belief. You get so angry . . ." And then she stopped talking and all of us sat in silence for a while.

Now, I wondered if Slade was thinking about her. But I didn't ask.

We pulled off the road and parked the bikes on a sharp outcropping, high among the clouds. I dug my favorite sunglasses out of my luggage and walked west, then stepped through the trees and edged out onto the lip of a rock face. Mountains dropped away, flying toward the horizon, falling away until they were blue, then purple, then fading to gray as they disappeared over the edge of Earth.

There are times on rides when the bike, any bike, stops, knowing there is something that needs seeing, wants the touch of eyes, demands the grace of emotion that, I think, only long-riders may have. This was one of those places.

The earth simply fell away. I was standing on the edge of the world, looking west at a landmass that stretched beyond imagination. The colors blended, one into the other, until there was only one softly intense color of unknown name that painted the earth and faded into the sky.

I sat on the edge of the rock ledge and dangled my legs over. Between my feet, hundreds of feet below, sat the tops of trees. And I knew the question would come again.

What the hell am I doing here?

This time, the answer didn't matter. I was here, and I was happy.

Slade pushed through the brush and sat beside me on the rock ledge, staring off into the west.

"Those are the sunglasses Curry gave you." It wasn't a question.

"Yeah. You know they are." I thought of big John Curry, sitting beside some slow, green, sun-dappled river, making love to his guitar.

"Those are the coolest glasses I've ever seen," Slade said. High praise, since Slade thought there were no sunglass styles other than aviator.

"That they are," I said, very pleased with my cool self.

"Then why are you wearing them?"

"What . . . ?"

"Big John is fighting a losing battle." Slade was grinning. "He's *never* going to make you cool."

I thought about shoving Slade's ass off the rock ledge, but he had already walked away.

By the time I got back to the bike, it was raining.

# 10

# DAY 4

Thursday, August 29
from Steamboat Springs, Colorado

SLADE GOT UP SINGING, and I knew I was in trouble.

He loved to sing, and he sang for only two reasons—he was happy, or shit was about to hit . . . us. With Slade, that was sometimes the same thing. So I never knew, until it happened, why he was singing. I think that morning he sang because he was happy—his voice sounded like rotten apples falling on a tin roof, always a good sign. If I could ever get him in one place long enough, I'd buy him voice lessons.

Last night had been the first real night on the road. We had spent the night in a motel in Steamboat Springs, unloading all our gear and carting it inside, trying to get it dry. We'd parked the bikes out of sight at the end of the parking lot, and in the morning when I went to check them a misty rain was still falling, and I could smell the high mountain scent of moisture that, somehow, is different from rain in the desert. So much for dry gear.

But there was something else in the air: I could smell wood

smoke, a thin pervasive aroma that came in over the moisture and hung in the air. Piles of damp, smoke-soaked fire gear had been dropped almost haphazardly down the hallway of the motel, on the floor and hanging from doorknobs, any place exhausted firefighters could drop their equipment when they came out of the woods, before they fell into bed.

Slade and I were probably the only guys in the motel who were not wildfire fighters.

God bless 'em, bless 'em all, was all I could think of.

\* \* \* \* \*

Once, I fought a fire in West Virginia.

There were four of us in my group, in the late evening and then into the dark, working frantically on the side of a steep ridge, hacking and raking the dirt and loam of the forest into a raw line that was supposed to stop the flames. But the flames paid no heed. When it came to the line, it merely leaped across as though we'd never been there. And then there was fire in front of us and fire behind us and fire in the tops of trees that lit our world with an unbearable intensity. We broke, charging down the ridge, running through a roaring wave so thick that I knew what the end of time would sound like, carrying our heavy fire rakes and trying to breathe through rags we'd tied around our faces. The air that came through the rags burned our throats and our lungs, and we knew we could breathe fire into our bellies or not breathe at all. Tears ran from our eyes in steady streaks of reflection cutting through blackened faces.

We made it out the bottom. We started hacking another line, but there was a sense of time running out, of something that was not going to work out, no matter what we did. The fight was worth the fighting, but it was a loss from the start.

And then I realized I was alone, left behind, the others lost from sight in the smoke and heat. It didn't matter. The fire was high above us, now. We had lost.

I heard a radio crackling somewhere in the smoke below me, and I followed the sound. The others were already there. We were being pulled out of the fight. The fire burned for days, but I never got back there.

And I never fought another fire.

\* \* \* \* \*

The rain stopped within minutes. Maybe our gear would stay dry. Maybe the firefighters could go home.

Slade and I drank coffee in a small café near the motel, then strapped stuff to the bikes. We were almost ready to go when I looked up and saw, about a half block from us, a cop car cruising slowly in our direction. Normally, I paid no attention to cop cars, or cops, figuring they had no idea who I was, what I looked like, or where I was going. But this time I wasn't so sure. Slade wasn't paying any attention to the cruiser, just kept on packing his bike.

I pulled on my helmet and stood at the back of the bike, my body shielding the license plate. The copy went by slowly, staring at the bikes, and at us. As he rolled past us Slade looked up, noticed what was going on, and then glanced at me, standing there with my helmet on.

In less than a minute we both were packed and on our bikes, engines running. I started rolling slowly forward when I saw

Slade hold up his hand. He dropped it to his side, where only I could see it, and pointed up the street. The cop car was turning around in the middle of the next block. Slade made sure I was looking at him and then he jerked his head to the side, toward the back of the motel's parking lot. He wheeled his KLR slowly, not in any particular hurry, and started toward the rear of the lot. I followed, the tension running down my back like fresh cement.

The back of the lot was blocked by a heavy cable strung between short concrete posts. Toward the right end of the cable a load of small gravel had been dumped, making a pile maybe three feet high. The gravel covered a section of the cable. Slade rode a 360, looking at the cable and the gravel. Then I heard his engine revving, and he went straight for the gravel pile, stood up on the pegs, leaned back and drove the KLR straight into the rock pile. In two seconds he was over the top and down the other side, kicking the bike to the left and heading down the alley.

All I had to do was do what he did. Sometimes following Slade wasn't easy, but this time it was.

He didn't go to the end of the block. He saw another parking lot to his right, one that had no fence, and he rode into it and onto the next street over. He did this two more times. I followed. He finally pulled to the corner of two narrow dirt streets, stopped, raised his face shield and sat there, scanning everything he could see. So did I.

"West," Slade said. "And if that cop wants us—and finds us—we go cross-country. And we stay cross-country until he has us, or we've lost him."

"Roger that," I mumbled.

We rode slowly away, attracting no particular attention from anyone.

Five miles out of town the rain came again and stayed, a hard, driving, steady opening of the heavens. I was surprised at how well the bikes handled the wet surface. There was a growing sense of confidence in the machines that maybe I once had about KLRs but had long since forgotten. So we cracked the throttles open and bore through it, heading for Maybelle. There, we shot instantly into spare and desolate country, unlike any Colorado that I knew of.

There was no sign of the cop car.

The road went west but we wanted to go north so Slade turned onto a raw dirt track—a raw *mud* track—that dropped off into a flat and disappeared into a canyon cut so narrow that it would have been difficult to get the bike past a truck, if a truck had been crazy enough to venture into that place.

I saw Slade's taillight grow quickly smaller through the rain, and I knew he was into it now, driving his bike hard into the muck and gravel and standing water and rain so dense that his taillight simply disappeared. And then we disappeared—into an even smaller part of the canyon with walls so steep the canyon itself appeared, what we could see of it, to have been dug by machines, flat, steep walls that closed in against the sides of the bikes. We were doing forty miles per hour over mud and gravel and through running water, bits of stone flying out from the sides of the tires and pinging against boulders at the side of the track, mud sticking to everything that moved. If a truck had come from the other direction, we'd have been very wet roadkill.

The rain kept coming. Our riding gear tried, and failed, to keep us dry. In this rain, even a whale wasn't waterproof.

It couldn't get any worse than this. But, in the end, much farther north, it did.

We broke out of the canyon, saw flat riding ahead, and kept our speed, mud flying from the bikes like motorboats on a calm lake. Slade's rear tire was throwing a rooster tail of mud fifteen feet in the air and I had to drop farther back to avoid the downfall.

And I realized that I might possibly be in love with the KLR. I wasn't sure, but I thought maybe I was getting there—if the engine kept running. I'd felt the movement of it on the bits and pieces of dirt that we had ridden so far, but nothing like this. This was a major piece of off-road crap that tested every bit of remembered skill that I could summon. The road through the sharp, confining canyon was as big a problem as I ever wanted to encounter on a bike. The temptation was to slow down and walk the bike along, to keep my feet out to the sides, to try to protect myself in any way I could. But Chaser, the best dirt rider I ever knew, had once told me that there were very few problems on a bike that couldn't be solved by more gas—something Slade also believed in. And so I gave the bike more gas, gradually catching sight of Slade, who'd already figured the whole thing out.

We blew out of the north end of the canyon like we were squirted out of a tube, the hard ridges behind us giving way instantly to a brown plain that ran knee-deep in water and mud. But farther to the north, a tiny sliver of sunlight showed, and that was enough to calm my breathing.

At the top of a low rise where most of the water had run off onto the plain, Slade plowed his bike off the road and let the mud bring him to a stop. I followed, pulling up beside him.

We turned off the engines and sat there looking at each other, the rain still drizzling on our helmets, a thick coating of mud on everything that we thought was ours. I couldn't see Slade's face; I didn't know how he could see to drive the bike through all the muck on his face shield. We were wet, cold, tired, hungry, almost too stiff to pull our legs off the bikes. But we did. We had to. I needed to piss so bad that my bladder was painful. Everything was so wet I thought I could just piss inside my pants and no one would know. Well, maybe Slade would know. He always seemed to know when I was so fucked up that I was about to piss my pants.

We stood beside the bikes, listening to the rain drum lightly on our helmets. Slade was taller; other than that, no one could tell us apart, two men wearing bulky, mud-covered gear standing by mud-covered bikes in the middle of mud-covered nowhere. Somehow, water had pooled in the bottom folds of Slade's jacket, and, when he stood up, had burst inward and sloshed down inside his pants, soaking him from the crotch to his knees. He couldn't have cared less. We stood in the rain, looking at each other. Then our hands came up and we both raised our face shields. We were both laughing, and then screaming.

I grabbed him and hugged him. And then I hugged the KLR. I resolved to love that ugly bike. And I did, right up until later when the fucking engine finally went crazy.

It couldn't get any worse than this, I thought.

It couldn't get any better than this, I thought.

I was wrong on both counts.

Somewhere in there we crossed into Wyoming, and I finally stopped checking my rearview mirrors every thirty seconds.

By five o'clock we'd skirted Rock Springs, found hot soup and berry pie at a roadside stop called Cruel Jack's, made a side trip to Fontenelle, and then were deep into the Green River Basin. In the tiny town of Marbleton, almost touching the equally tiny town of Big Piney, we found a two-bay car wash that looked closed, but wasn't, standing vacantly at the edge of a slab of broken concrete. We wheeled in, parking both our bikes in the center of one of the washing bays.

Before we turned on the water, I put my hand on Slade's arm. "How'd you know the cop might've been looking for me?"

Slade gave me a half smile and shook his head. "I knew he wasn't interested in me, and then I remembered who I was riding with."

"Back there, in New Mexico, I . . ." I never got to finish. Slade held up his hands, palms toward me.

"Wait," he said. "I'm not ready yet." He paused. "Fuck, Morgan, I may never be ready!" And then he laughed.

We turned on the high-pressure hose and sprayed the bikes, our gear—everything, including us. Fully clothed and laughing like idiots, we took turns spraying each other until, once again, we could tell the color of our riding gear. And then we stood outside, dripping wet, and watched the sun go down, feeling the gradual creep of the cold into the mountain country.

I'd never had a better bath.

And baths are important.

* * * * *

The house was ordinary, looked pretty much like any house you might find in deepest Appalachia. Front porch, back porch, a jumble of small rooms on the inside, cold water from a pump, wood-burning stove. No bathroom, but the outhouse wasn't too far away—outhouses were built just out of smelling range, which, in the heat of an Appalachian summer, wasn't easy to do.

Bath time. The fire in the stove was built up, and a large metal washtub was banged down onto the center of the cook-top and filled with water, bucket by bucket, from the pump. Bath time had to be planned ahead—it took a long time to heat the water.

Another larger tub was kept on the far end of the back porch. To take a bath, we carried the heated water, again bucket by bucket, from the stove to the tub on the back porch. You didn't try to sit down in the tub. You just poured the water, a little at a time, over your body, soaped up, scrubbed, and poured more water to rinse. It took a long time, carrying the water, standing there naked in a washtub, trying to get rid of all the soap. I kept a Mason jar on a windowsill where I could reach it from the tub. I used the jar to dip water from the tub and pour it over my head. Years later there would be other uses for Mason jars.

When you were finished, you tilted the tub over and let the soapy water run off the back porch and out into the yard. Wasn't much of a yard. Seems as though soapy water didn't make good fertilizer.

In the winter, the process was exactly the same. But colder.

I came to hate baths.

And then one day I thought about the creek, down and across the cornfield, its light green water flowing quietly, less than a hundred yards from our house. One hot afternoon, I took a bar of hard soap and went to the creek. I sat in the warm, gently moving water, soaped up, and took a bath. I lay back and felt the rays of sunlight filtering through the overhanging willows, watched the dragonflies maneuver in their graceful trajectories, coming from somewhere, going somewhere.

Bathing in a creek. Primal. Incredible.

I probably killed every fish within fifty yards, but I never thought about that at the time. I never took another bath in the washtub, not even in the winter.

11.

# DAY 5

THE TETONS WERE SUDDENLY there, another unreality in the many on this trip of pure and instant unrealities. Nothing could look like that, like those mountains. Nothing could impress like that. The size of the human mind simply was not sufficient to comprehend.

But I had not yet seen the Yukon.

Riding north, I could look far to the east at the outline of the Wind River Range, wondering if maybe we should have ridden over there. And then I turned my head back . . . and the Tetons jumped out of the west, a magnificent wall of challenge, a natural show of force.

We stopped, took pictures. And we knew, to the north, was Yellowstone.

We rode under heavy cloud and in a growing cold that didn't belong here, not yet, maybe not for another month or so, but here it was. Yellowstone reveled in the cold. The unearthly—or maybe earthly—heat that roiled beneath its surface provided a contrast that we had seen in no other place. While you were watching the heat punch through the surface—enough heat to boil you alive—you could freeze to death.

We eased into Yellowstone like trespassers, riding tenderly, lest we disturb some natural balance that would release punishment on us and our pathetic loads of gear. But Yellowstone is not some weekend place, some little park where you can see the whole thing in an afternoon. We rode across the park boundary and still had more than fifty miles to go before we really got inside.

And then we were.

We were going to stay a couple of nights. We rode past the main visitors' area and on to a campground to the north. We pitched our tents in the chill of the afternoon, hills rising around us. Before we'd properly set up camp, the temperature dropped to thirty-four degrees, another sure sign that we were riding late and fast and that any thoughts of riding in the dry and the heat were dim memories of another time, another trip, another place.

It was late.

It was cold.

And we were old.

"What the hell are we doing here?" Slade mumbled the question out of the top of his heavy, armored, cold-weather riding jacket, the collar pulled all the way to his nose, a fuzzy-fleece cap pulled down to the tops of his eyes, his gloved hands shoved under his armpits.

We huddled on a hard bench looking at a hole in the ground. The air was full of icy mist that seemed to hang like a curtain in front of our faces, not really raining, but keeping our bodies on the edge of shivering in the late Wyoming light, the light, itself, nothing more than a shield against any thought of warmth.

"It was your idea, as I remember," I muttered, knowing that it hadn't been his idea, and knowing that I'd piss him off. I'd pulled my own collar up, my own heavy, fleece hat pulled down hard. All you could see of our faces were our squinting eyes, our hunching shoulders, trying to keep the liquid ice from making thin lines down inside our insulated shirts. Trying to watch the hole in the ground.

Tourists scuttled by, their arms wrapped around their chests, heads down, feet shuffling across blades of grass that seemed to make crinkling noises as they passed. They looked at us with a look combined of wonder and pity. Mostly pity. They were on their way to the lodge or to their rooms where they could bring heat to themselves, where hot drinks and warm fires would bring them back to normal lives, to comfort. Tourists not caring about the hole in the ground.

But Slade and I wouldn't be going to a lodge. Once we'd seen the hole in the ground do its thing, we'd be thumping our butts down on the hard, cold seats of our motorcycles and riding north, back to the campground where our tents stood, ice crystals forming on the flaps, sleeping bags spread inside on ground that, I thought, had never, ever, been warm.

We'd light our tiny stoves and make thin soup and sip it from clumsy insulated mugs and try to finish before a skin of ice formed across the tops. The temperature was still dropping—our cold-bound fingers wouldn't uncurl properly when we tried to set the mugs down. I knew that. And I hated it.

But, for now, we sat on the hard bench.

"Nope, the idea was yours, way back there, somewhere. While we were at Mesa Verde, maybe? Or Yucatán? Twenty years ago, maybe? It was your idea—all I did was say, 'you're an idiot.'" Slade's voice was so muffled I hardly heard him.

"I have some really fucked-up ideas, now and then. You ever notice that?"

"Like I said . . ." he muttered. "On the other hand, I think that's what makes you so interesting. Fucking crazy, but interesting."

But, still, I thought about the question: what the hell were we doing here? And I knew it was *my* question, and always would be.

Right there, right now, I guess we were there because we cared about the hole in the ground. It was something to do. We'd ridden hundreds of miles to see it, and damned if we were going to leave until the son of a bitch blew—Old Faithful, in Yellowstone. And so we waited in the falling light.

And we waited.

"Fuck it," I mumbled—seems as though I were always mumbling something to Slade. "I'm going to get some coffee. You?"

"Nope," he said, "I'm going to wait right here until this bastard bitch blows. If it blows and I miss it, I'm going to pour cement down the damn hole."

The gigantic log building with the gift shop and café was packed with human bodies and the rising invisible steam that comes from cold bodies in a very warm place. I shuffled toward the counter where people were buying coffee, and I had to stand in line. I was in a national park, established to preserve wilderness . . . standing in a line.

A man and woman were standing behind me, arguing quietly. I tried not to listen, but the argument started sliding toward loud. And then I heard the woman say, in one of those stage whispers designed to be overheard, "Get your hands off me!"

My boot heel squeaked on the floor as I whirled around. Maybe I was interested in protecting the woman, or maybe I thought that a guy in a public place who'd grab a woman with any sort of physical intent might decide to grab me. He was holding the woman's arm with both hands, his face red, his mouth twisted in a sneer. She was trying to pry his fingers off.

They both looked at me.

I could hear the voice in my head. Hit him now, it said, before he can adjust.

\* \* \* \* \*

Everybody has to be someplace, and Santa Barbara was as good a place as any. Or so I thought.

It was downtime. I had nothing to do and no place to do it in. I tried to make these times happen, now and then. I'd pick a place where I'd never been, where no one knew me, and no one knew I was even there. A place that, I thought, might offer some change from the rest of my life.

But usually I fucked it up someway.

This time, it was Santa Barbara.

The room I rented near the beach was good enough; it was on the second floor, had a bed and a shower, a door that would lock, and a window that was large enough to crawl out of, if I had to. I paid for a week.

The guns were in a black bag that looked enough like my other gear bags to pass casual inspection as luggage. I took the bag out of the pickup, lugged it up to the room, and hid it above a utility trapdoor in the bathroom. As a hiding place, it was such a cliché that it might actually work. I figured anyone breaking into the room would not be looking for guns, so I left a few dollars in cash lying on the nightstand. If some clown broke in, maybe he'd just take the money and run.

The restaurants in Santa Barbara were good. It was nice not to sit with rain dripping down through the bush and have to dig maggots out of my food. Of course, you could never get all the maggots out, but some of them were pretty tasty.

I ate in the restaurants, walked the beach, looked at the art displayed in stands on the beach walk, went into a couple of bars . . . bad idea. The bars were loaded with people roughly my age, but with whom I had absolutely nothing in common. The women seemed vacuous, and the men delighted in hitting on vacuous women. That was okay, as far as it went. After all, that's why those people were in the bars.

But there had to be something else.

Maybe. Maybe not. In two days I was bored out of my skull.

The soft air from the channel came up State Street and swept gently into the foothills behind the city, leaving the taste and feel of the ocean resting on the night of Santa Barbara. I stood outside a restaurant, not wanting to go back to the room. I wasn't really dressed to go anywhere that mattered; I was wearing worn sneakers, tan chinos, and a heavy denim shirt that hung outside my pants, covering the .45 holstered inside the back of my belt. Other than the .45, I thought I looked like a wannabe college boy. Maybe a graduate student.

The theatre marquee hung out over the sidewalk about a block away. I didn't pay attention to what movie was playing, but it didn't matter. It would keep me out of the bars.

There was a line outside the theater. I hadn't stood in a line since . . . well, I couldn't really remember the last time. It was almost a new experience for me, standing there, within breathing distance of people I didn't know. Not actually touching, of course. In America, the only actual touching of strangers I'd seen was on subways, where men could stand groin-to-groin with women they had never seen before and would never see again.

I glanced around, out of habit. There were not many people on the street, mostly just the line I was standing in. In front of me a young couple held hands but did not talk. Behind me an attractive woman, dressed as though she had just come from the office, stood reading a book from the light of the marquee, her face a mask of wonder, perhaps fear. I could see the title— *Fatal Light*. Reading a book in a movie line. I was impressed. Must've been a helluva book.

Up the street behind me a homeless guy leaned against some sort of tall, bushy plant, the sort of thing cities plant in square holes in sidewalks and dogs piss on until the plant dies. He was tall and rangy, wearing a tattered military field jacket, his hands jammed into his pockets, dirty high-top sneakers with no laces. He was at the edge of the light from the marquee, but I could still see that he was staring at each person in the line, checking, then his gaze moving on. When he got to me, our eyes locked. I kept my face in neutral, nodded once, and then turned away from him. But I took my hands out of my pockets.

The line began to move. People reached into pockets and purses for ticket money—and that must have been what the homeless guy was waiting for. I could hear him working the line behind me, bluntly asking for money. No finesse, no story, just a harsh demand for cash.

Intimidation. And anger. I knew about those.

I didn't like the tactic, but the guy had balls. I was trying to decide whether to give him a couple of bucks, when I heard him approach the woman directly behind me.

"How about some money, bitch?"

Bitch? Like I said, intimidation.

I was turning toward the guy when the woman said, "Let go of me!" And then she twisted away from him, stepped out of line, and was standing directly at my side, putting me between her and the street guy, her hand reaching out and touching my shoulder, as if to make sure I stayed between them, or perhaps implying that we were together. She was looking past me at the street guy, ready to do whatever necessary to keep me in the middle as a barrier. Smart chick.

And then the guy grabbed me by the right shoulder and pulled hard. His grip was damn strong and he kept pulling, thinking maybe that I'd try to jerk away from him. Instead, I let him pull me into him, bringing my right arm up vertically in case there was a punch coming. There wasn't—just a surprised look on his face that I could be moved so easily. Hit him now, I thought, before he has time to adjust. The surprised look was still there when I whipped my elbow around and caught him flush in the middle of his face. Bone and flesh gave way before his head snapped back, and he lost his grip on me, staggering backward, his hands coming up to cover his face. Blood oozed out between his fingers.

The theater line disintegrated, people disappearing into the growing night like snowflakes fluttering in darkness. I found myself standing there with only three or four people who seemed paralyzed by what was happening.

And the street guy lying on the sidewalk.

And a cop.

The woman with the book was gone.

The others in line were jittery, eyes big, tense, wanting to leave, wanting to run from the scene with a cop standing right there, looking at them.

Christ on a bicycle, where the hell did the cop come from? And then I glanced across the street and saw his cruiser parked in a traffic lane, the door standing open, another cop leaning against the rear fender. Pretty damn relaxed procedure, I thought.

"Everybody just stay put," the cop said. He didn't sound unfriendly, just serious. "What happened here?"

For a moment, no one spoke. Certainly not me. And then a short, stubby guy who had been in the back of line said, "I didn't see anything, officer. I was waiting back here when something happened up front. Couldn't see anything." He wouldn't look at me. Lying little bastard.

No one else said a fucking word.

The homeless guy sat up, still holding his hands over his face. But I could see his eyes and I didn't like what I saw.

The cop looked at the guy. "Stay where you are, sir. There's an ambulance on the way." The guy stayed on the sidewalk, never taking his eyes off me.

"Okay," the cop said, turning squarely toward me, "it's your turn."

So I told him my story, in detail.

"Is that what happened?" the cop said, turning to the others.

No one said a word. Except the street guy.

"Mutherfucker hit me when I wasn't even looking," he said from between his fingers. "I wuz just walkin' down the street, not doin' nuthin.'"

The cop turned back to me. "That's not what you told me."

"No, it isn't," I said. "And no matter how many times you make me tell it, my story will not change."

"You been down this road before, seems like."

"I don't know anything about a road, officer. I'm just a guy standing in line to see a movie."

"Let me see your ID, sir."

"Of course," I said. I reached carefully into my front pocket—I never carried ID, or anything, in my back pockets—and pulled out a thin wallet. I took out a driver's license and handed it to the cop. He looked at it carefully.

"Mr. LaRue," he said. "Mr. Alfred LaRue. Prescott, Arizona." He paused. He seemed to be thinking. "Mr. LaRue, I'm going to send this other gentleman," he said, nodding at the street guy, "for medical treatment. But he has some pretty serious injuries, so I'd like you to come with us to the station to make a statement."

I didn't say anything. He didn't ask me to go to the station, he told me. And he kept my license.

I wasn't really worried about the license. Alfred "Lash" LaRue was a cowboy actor from the forties and fifties, an actor who could use a bullwhip like an artist used a paintbrush. I loved watching the guy in old films, loved using his name on bogus drivers' licenses. Often wondered whether Lash would mind.

It wasn't the license I was worried about. In most ways, it was a real license, and it would take a little time for them to find out that I wasn't Alfred LaRue. What I was worried about was the .45 in the back of my pants. This was fucking New Age California, antigun to the center of its being. If the cops found the .45, I'd be a visitor in Santa Barbara for a very long time.

The ambulance pulled up as the cop was taking the names of the other people still standing, motionless, on the sidewalk. The medics loaded up the street guy . . . and I thought from the looks on their faces that this was not the guy's first trip with them. But they said nothing.

"Mr. LaRue, if you will come with me, we'll get this over with, and then we'll bring you back to your car," the cop said.

If I had a car, I'd never see it again, once I walked into that police station.

We walked across the street to the cruiser. It was parked facing downhill, the passenger side away from us. We walked around the car and the cop opened the back door. Behind us, the neon signs in the cluttered window of a bar bounced unreal colors off the black and white of the car. I couldn't see a single face in the window. Perhaps there wasn't room for a face. Perhaps the people inside didn't give a shit about a minor street scene.

I put my hand on the open door and ducked my head, then rose quickly, staring across the street. "Well, that was quick," I said sharply. "He's back already?"

"What?" the cop said, taking his hand off the door and stepping quickly to the side, looking hard across the street. When he saw nothing, he turned back to me. I was gone.

It probably took him a second or so to figure out where I went—straight into the bar.

I burst through the door. "There's cops outside!" I yelled. "They're coming to roust this place! Body searches!" And I charged through the crowd toward what I hoped would be a back door.

For a moment I thought I'd blown it. People seemed rooted in place. And then the room erupted in a mixture of laughter, anger, and thrashing movement. Some of the patrons just sat there, lifting their glasses. Others checked their pockets and purses. Most were standing, milling, making it almost impossible to move. But at least two guys made mad dashes toward the back. I followed, bowling over a drunk in the process, straight to, and out of, a back door.

The cops would certainly start canvassing the hotels for Mr. Alfred LaRue, especially since Mr. LaRue had avoided being detained. I needed to stay invisible. I walked the side streets back to the little hotel on the beach and managed to sneak up to my room without being seen by anyone. I gathered my stuff, including the bag inside the utility trapdoor, made my way back to the pickup, and drove slowly out of town. I was headed north, but I didn't like that. It was shorter out of California if I went east. And so I did.

* * * * *

The guy's face was very, very red. But when he looked at me, he didn't like what he saw. He let go of the woman and stomped out of the café.

I said nothing to her, just turned around to get my coffee.

And the hole in the ground finally blew—in its own damn good time, an anticlimactic event that we'd look back on and wonder why we bothered, wonder why we cared that it was important to see Old Faithful.

But we knew why. Because *we* had not seen Old Faithful, and men should see things they've never seen, no matter how gigantic or how insignificant. It's the way of us. Some of us. It was the way of Slade and me.

No one made us be there. We chose to be there, there, in the grinding cold and dark. It was only early September, but we were in a land where summer turned to winter in a dozen beats of a buffalo's heart, and where old men would shiver in their sleeping bags, feeling their bones crack, knowing what tomorrow would bring.

Yeah, we'd ridden hundreds of miles to be there, and we still had a few thousand miles to go, due north, thousands of miles only to stand on a mythical, invisible line on Earth where many men had already stood. And no one cared.

But we cared. *We* had not stood there.

We had no idea that this night would be one of the easy times, one of the ordinary times. We'd seen Old Faithful, and it wouldn't be one of the most gripping or amazing or scenic or startling or exciting things that would come before us on this trip. Not even close. In fact, it was nothing.

I felt Slade move on the bench beside me, trying to get smaller inside his riding gear. Getting smaller was hard for him. He still had the rangy build of the gangly Texas ranch boy that he had been and, in many ways, still was. But now he was like me. We were old, and we were doing things meant for younger men. The difference was, Slade was still handsome— but I certainly would never tell him that. I felt him move, and I thought for one brief flicker of time that I might lean forward and look at him and say, "Let's get the hell out of here. Let's ride south."

But I didn't say that. If I rode south, I'd be riding alone. Slade wouldn't be with me. He'd be headed for the Arctic Circle.

The temperature kept dropping. We'd left our bikes a half-mile away and walked to the observation area to look at Old Faithful. Old Faithful had taken its own good time, but finally it was over. We walked back to the bikes and grabbed just about every other piece of clothing we had, putting on everything. Didn't matter—it was still cold.

It was my turn to ask it: "What the hell are we doing here?" I mumbled out of the depths of my heavy coat.

Slade, of course, didn't answer.

By the time we got back to camp I was hammered by the wet and the cold. And I was depressed—worried about the bike. Since its stellar performance in the canyon back in Colorado, it had performed well. But it had been coughing and jerking most of today, the engine changing rpms with no throttle adjustment. Same old problem.

We still had thousands of miles to go, and the thought of actually making the distance, actually doing it, was all that calmed my mind. I looked at the bike, sitting there in the dark, mocking me.

"Fuck you," I said. "I love you—I think—but I can sell you in the next city, buy something else, and you can go to the fucking scrap yard."

Jesus, I was talking to the bike as though it were a person. I was losing my mind in the cold.

I sat at a picnic table in the dark and fished a blank journal out of my luggage. My journal, my everlasting, always-fucking-there journal, my millstone, my dead weight. Once, I'd stood on the edge of a canyon and thrown every journal I had out into the dim emptiness of space above red rock and brown river. I watched them disappear. I never wanted to write in a journal again.

And I hadn't—at least not since Lancey left.

Not the journal. Not tonight. Tonight was not a night to begin.

And then I realized I was not depressed about the bike. My mind washed with darkness, and I could see, I could *feel*, Lancey there in my head, see her sitting in the pickup, see her sitting naked in the pool beside the house. I could feel the rage simmering somewhere in my bowels, and feel my hands on Snake, and hear the coffee mug cracking against his teeth. I gripped the journal until I had folded it in half, the hard edges leaving tiny hash marks on my hands.

Slade didn't know it, but I'd some pills to take at times like this. Got them from a doctor in Mexico. I never told Slade or Modene. They might think that only crazy people took pills because they were crazy. Problem was, the pills sometimes trashed my mind, building weird images that flashed behind my seeing, hallucinations that sometimes intrigued me, sometimes terrified me, but always, always, turned the demons loose. Made some people look like other people, people I either wanted to see or never wanted to see again. And I never knew when it would happen. Truth is, I'm not always sure it was the pills that caused the hallucinations. Modene asked me about the hallucinations once, not knowing about the pills, but I didn't answer. And she never brought it up again.

No, I wouldn't write in the fucking journal tonight and maybe not ever again. I stuffed the journal back out of sight, swallowed a couple of the pills, fished a Chuck Kinder novel out of my luggage, and managed to get inside my little tent and struggle into the sleeping bag. I lay there reading by the beam of a tiny light strapped to my head, amazed at the lilt and flow of Kinder's words, the realness of the prose, thinking that Kinder and I had more in common than he would ever know.

Slade was moving around outside. Then I heard him squatting down beside the wall of my tent.

"How come you're not writing?"

"Not tonight. Don't feel like it. Can't write for thinking about the fucking bike," I lied. "Makes me feel like catching a bus south—going home."

Going home. I never thought I'd say that to Slade. But then I realized that "home" was no longer within my reach, if it ever had been. I'd fouled my own nest. But there must be some place out there I could go, any damn place but here. Someplace warm.

Slade was silent for a while, but I knew that he hadn't moved. "All that stuff you wrote in the past, all those things—you just going to quit and leave all that hanging out there?" He paused. I could hear him breathing. "Seems like kind of a waste."

We hung there, silently, me inside my sleeping bag, Slade outside the zippered door of my tent.

"The words won't come," I mumbled.

I heard him move away from the tent, could hear his boots on the frozen ground. I thought maybe I'd pissed him off.

A heavy zipper was pulled, and Slade rummaged around in some bike luggage and came back to my tent. He opened the flap and stuck his hand inside. He was holding one of the blank notebooks and a pencil. He dropped them on my chest.

"Let 'er rip," he said. "If there aren't some words in there tomorrow morning, I want the .45 back." And he walked away. Singing.

A few minutes later, he mumbled something in his tent, but I couldn't understand what he said, and I didn't ask. And then I didn't hear him anymore.

I put down the Kinder book and picked up the pencil. Writing. Back in the day, I had started to write to see if I could do it, and the writing became a habit, and then an addiction, and I realized that I'd been heading for the addiction from the time I began to understand language. The addiction became hardwired; I couldn't stop.

The pencil began to move, and the words began to come. I stayed with it most of the night. After all, this was Day 5; I had a lot of catching up to do.

And besides, I did *not* want to give the .45 back to Slade.

The hallucination that night was only a small one. But weird.

12.

# DAY 6

IT WAS TWENTY-TWO DEGREES last night. I slept cold. I woke cold. I breathed the cold into my body in liquid form, the heavy air filling my chest, the sort of cold that can only happen in the stillness of a morning that promises nothing. There was no movement in the world outside the tent. Even the dying leaves hung motionless from the stark, hard limbs of trees.

I didn't want to get out of the sleeping bag, but I could see the tent walls beginning to lighten and I knew Slade was probably already dressed and gone, walking in the early light. Scouting. Old habits . . .

I dragged my ass out of the bag and into my clothes.

When I crawled outside there was cloud cover as far as I could see, moving quickly, rolling in from the west and smothering the steam boiling up out of the Yellowstone Valley.

We wanted to see the steam vents, the pools, the blistering cracks in the earth. It was what we came for.

By the time Slade came back, and we were ready to ride,

the temperature had risen ten degrees. I wondered if the cold would bother Slade. I wondered if anything bothered Slade, at least to the point where he would complain. I'd never heard Slade complain. About anything.

We started south, riding back toward the main part of the park, looking at everything that could be looked at, soaking the images into our minds. Two elk sauntered across a wide field to the west. A bald eagle sat in a tree above a small stream, watching, watching. Twice, buffalo wandered along the road, and I stopped both times, looking hard at each animal. Making sure.

Slade would wait patiently—he knew what I was doing.

Within an hour, the sun was with us. We rode on, joying in the light and warmth.

We rolled into a small parking area beside a steam vent and stood looking at the curl of moisture that rose endlessly into the sky. A car pulled in. A guy and his wife got out and stood beside us. The guy eyed the bikes. I knew he wanted to say something, and I knew what it was.

Finally, he turned toward me.

"You know," he said sadly, "I had a friend who was killed on one of those."

I should not have done it, but I simply couldn't resist.

"Really?" I tried to effect an amazed expression. "He was killed *on* the bike? What killed him?"

The guy looked perplexed, as though he was speaking to an idiot. (Maybe he was.) He grabbed his wife by the arm and started to walk away.

"Say, mister," I called after him, "if he died *on* the bike, how far did he go before he fell over?"

Slade was sitting on his bike, his head resting down on the handlebars.

By noon, dark clouds were pressing in over the treetops, hiding whatever was behind them. We slipped into West Thumb and walked by the steaming pools, the mist rising hard and fast from the ground. The earth was raining upside down, and we walked as though in trances, our legs moving through the rising water, our eyes and minds so caught by what was on the ground that we didn't notice the actual rain, the rain from the sky, the rain that began to hit our faces until we had to put on our helmets and try to keep the water from running down the backs of our necks.

It didn't work. We didn't care.

We walked slowly back to the bikes and pulled on more gear as the water began to fall in huge, hard drops, making noise on our helmets like tiny mallets drumming some universal beat that only the rain gods would understand. And dance to.

We rode east along a lake, trying to ride out from beneath the storm but only managing to ride constantly under it. Through the rain the look of the forest seemed to change. The trees became thinner and darker and stood against the gray light like blackened stalagmites on the floor of a cave with only the sky as a roof. What light there was drifted through the stands of brittle timber with little to hold it back. I swung into a pull-off and raised my face shield. And looked into a dead forest.

It was an old fire, maybe a year, maybe more, and I was looking at it through cold rain. But in my mind I could feel the still, hot air coming up from the surface in heavy waves, wrapping around the bike and pouring into my clothes. The sensation of heat was as strong as if the fire were still alive, and I was still inside it. And suddenly I was back in West Virginia, running for my life.

Even sitting on my bike in a chilling rain I knew what the forest earth felt like, what that air tasted like, knew how the sunlight was kept from my face. I knew what it was like to walk a dead earth in heavy boots and shuffle through steaming loam and ash and the bones of trees flung onto the ground as though something gigantic and angry had been there. I knew what it was like to kick the ash and see it hang in the air like maniacal snow, some of it white, some of it black, some gray, all of it clinging. It was desperate ash, the last vestige of life once lived, now dead in the heat of the earth.

And the veins of trees spilled smoke.

We stared into an unbreathing forest until the black and gray painting of the woods left by the fire was burned into our minds.

About an hour later we pulled into a small marina at the edge of a lake and took shelter under an overhang, a sort of porch. We stood there, leaning against the wall, staring into rain, each of us thinking of some other time, some other place.

A woman and her family came out of a gift shop, the three kids eating ice cream cones. The biggest kid looked at his cone, wrinkled his face, and tossed the cone out into the rain. The woman stopped, not because of the kid throwing ice cream, but because of us, as though confounded by the sight of huge men, dripping water, our bikes standing like exhausted horses in a storm.

"At your age, you should know better," she said.

Out of the corner of my eye I saw Slade drop his head and put his palm to his forehead.

"Ah, but that's the problem, ma'am," I said. "At my age, I know different, but I don't know better." She stared at me. The husband was looking off into the distance. "Kind of like that kid there," I said brightly, "throwing that ice cream on the ground. Does he know better?"

She gathered one of her kids—a boy—into her arms and walked quickly to the other end of the porch. The husband followed her. Neither of them looked at us again.

Slade still had his hand to his head. "Can I look, now?" he said through his fingers.

"Yeah. Just another dull day in the rain."

Briefly, the rain stopped, and we got back on the road—and ten minutes later *hail* was pounding a blinding tattoo on anything in its way. The mushy stones pinged off the gas tanks and thunked against our helmets, splattered off our fenders, and stung our hands, even through our gloves. It covered the road and shattered against guardrails, piled up in the curves, and coated the landscape like pearls on the beach of an infinite ocean. We slowed, trying to feel the kiss of the tires against the road, waiting for that first greasy slip of rubber on ice.

It never came.

Ten miles later the hail stopped.

Slade eased off the road into a pull-off. I rode up beside him. We raised our face shields. Slade was grinning from ear to ear.

I thought, yeah, we're going north.

And so we did.

13.

# DAY 7

Sunday, September 1
from Yellowstone

FROST COVERED THE TENTS and the bike covers.

My bike cover was nothing more than the bottom of an old tent that I'd cut loose and pounded grommets into around the edge so I could fasten it down with tiny bungee cords. Perfect cover for a KLR. Looked the part.

Just for fun, I loosened the bungees and gingerly lifted the cover, stiff and still formed to the bike, into the air. I wanted a picture of this. Oh, yes. I would brag about this.

And then a huge black bird flew into it. The bird smacked into the center of the cover, dragged the thing from my hands and everything landed on the ground in a crumpled mess. I leaped onto the cover and covered the bird-lump with my hands, trying not to hurt the bird.

The bird did not move. Shit, I thought, it broke its damn neck.

I felt around under the cover, thinking maybe that, some-how, I could save the bird.

And then Slade stomped on the bird. Just walked over and stomped on it, one hard smash of his heavy motorcycle boot, and there was nothing now but a flat mass, inert, still under the cover. I could imagine the blood, guts, sodden feathers, and bird shit on my bike cover.

I stood up slowly and faced Slade. I don't think, even after all these years, that we'd ever had a real argument, an *angry* argument, a fight, where our faces turned red and the veins stood out in our necks. Some disagreements, yes, but the type of disagreements that were more fun than not. But not a fight.

We were going to have one now.

He was taller; I was wider. It would be a good fucking fight, even though I knew Slade would probably beat the crap out of me. But we would fight, oh yes, because the bastard had maybe killed the bird.

And birds were very, very special.

* * * * *

It was supposed to be a training exercise. We were supposed to run around in the jungle, and they were supposed to try to find us. They said it had to be as real as they could make it. They were really going to look for us, and if they caught us they would make us wish they hadn't. They said everybody had to do it. It was training.

Fuck that.

What could they do to us? We weren't even in their ragged outfit. We were contractors, along for the ride to make a few bucks. I didn't even know the others, and I was too damn young to know that what I didn't know could, in fact, get me killed.

So there I was, before full light, strolling through the dense growth, waiting for the "enemy" to find me. I thought, if they did, I would go back to camp and sleep until they caught the rest of our bunch.

The guy dropped on me out of a tree. He just let go and came straight down on my head and shoulders, and I crumpled like a gum wrapper. I rolled over on the ground, dazed, vaguely aware that there were more than one of them. A boot came down on my rib cage and all the air shot out of my body. Before I could do anything else they ripped the rifle strap from around my neck and dragged away my pistol belt and ammo pouches. I was disarmed, all my gear taken away, even my hat, my hands lashed behind my back and a hood yanked down over my head. The hood smelled like someone had pissed in it, a long time ago.

I was done up like some sort of trophy. And they did it all without saying a word. Bastards. This was a training exercise! But I had to admit—these guys were good.

Whoever it was—I never actually saw them—cut my hands loose and shoved me through some sort of wooden grating. I fell into water that was deep enough to make me want to scramble to my feet, which is what I did. I ripped off the hood.

I was in a cage anchored in the edge of a clear, rippling river. A total cage—walls, floor, ceiling. And I was alone.

About a foot of water ran through the bottom of the cage. I could stand up, barely. I could sit, if I wanted to sit in water. If I lay down, I was lying in water deep enough to drown me. If there were a heavy rain and the water came up, I'd probably drown, anyway.

The cage was made of some sort of heavy jungle vines, as

thick as my wrist, wired together so tightly that the wires cut deeply into their sides. The wires were heavy and stiff, the ends cut at an angle and pounded into the wood, too strong for my fingers to work loose.

For the first day I looked for a tool—they had even taken my belt buckle—running my hands down through the bars at the bottom of the cage and into the mud of the river bottom trying to find a rock, a stick, anything that I could use to loosen the wires. There was nothing.

In a fury I grabbed the heavy vines, shook them, levered my legs up, and pushed against one side while the rest of me pushed against the other.

I never made a dent in anything.

I had no food. No one came to check on me. I could not get dry and yet I could not get out of the sun. If this were a training exercise, I didn't want to experience the real thing. By the second day I was beginning to withdraw, to pull inside myself. I had to concentrate to keep from talking to myself, to keep from yelling, to keep from crying.

The bird came on the third day, some sort of jungle bird, the size of a small chicken. I thought all jungle birds were supposed to be flashy, lots of colored feathers. This one was not. I was kneeling in the river, throwing water on my head and drinking as much as I could hold, trying to fend off the hunger pangs, when I heard him land on top of the cage. Him—I thought of the bird as a him. He sat there and looked down at me, wondering, I suppose, if it were worth the trouble of trying to get down into the cage where he could take a bite out of my wet ass.

And I wondered if I could get my hands on him. Raw bird meat or not, he was food.

And then he was gone.

He came back the next day, before dark, sitting in the same place on the top of the cage, looking down at me. I eased up toward him, gathering my legs under me, trying to figure the best angle to make a grab for him.

And then he started to talk to me.

He made small, low gurgling sounds deep in his throat, and he made them while looking directly at me. I could see his throat move, and I could see his eyes, and I knew he was talking to me, and I knew I was not smart enough to know what he was saying. But I listened.

I remembered back in the mountains, where I grew up, remembered, as a little kid, how I always thought the birds brought the dawn. As the dawn lit up the tops of the sprawling hardwood trees the birds would sing and move with the light, as though they were pulling the brightness with them as they went. And they sang when they did it, happy in the work they had been doing since there were birds.

And now this big bird kept talking to me until the dark came full, a darkness so thick I had to touch the heavy vines of the cage to make sure they were still there. And then his voice fell silent, and I knew he was gone.

He came back the next day.

I began to talk back to him, sometimes trying to copy the sounds he made, sometimes thinking, maybe, I was teaching him my own words. Now and then a small plane would fly over the canopy of the jungle, but it never came close enough for me to see it, no way to signal it. So there was only me and the bird.

We talked for three days.

And that's when I finally admitted to myself that no one was coming back for me. Whatever had happened out there, back there, somewhere, anywhere—whatever had happened I was not a part of it anymore. My part was over, really over.

I sat in the far corner of the cage, in the deeper end of the water, facing the trees and the dense growth. I stared at nothing. The bird sat on top of the cage, still talking, but I didn't care.

One of the mottled green shapes at the edge of the woods moved slightly, and that prickly sensation ran down my back. I sat motionless, hardly breathing, waiting.

The shape rose up. It was a man, tall, slender, fully dressed in jungle camo, packs and straps and bulges hanging from his body, his face painted in a grotesque mask, a boonie hat jammed on his head. Even his hands were painted, but that didn't hide the ropes and cables under his skin as both his hands gripped an automatic weapon, some sort of short carbine. He was either one of theirs, or one of ours. From the look and shape and dress of him—and the fact that he wasn't pointing the gun at me—I thought he might be one of ours.

He walked slowly up to the cage.

The bird didn't move.

I stood up, waiting for him to speak. He didn't say a fucking thing.

"I guess the training exercise is over," I mumbled.

He stood there, looking into the cage, glancing up at the bird. He wore aviator sunglasses. I thought I recognized him, even through the face paint. He didn't smile.

"You're the pilot," I said. "What? They sent a fucking pilot out here to get me out of the river?"

The guy twisted his mouth, as though he had just eaten something that tasted like shit. "Nah," he said, from deep in his throat. "Unfriendlies overran the camp and rounded up everybody they could catch. They knew there was a guy still down here at the river. They sent one of their guys to get you. He had a very big knife. This one, in fact." He reached behind him and pulled out a sleek machete. "I don't have any idea what he had in mind." But the way he said it, I knew. And he knew.

"So what happened to him?"

"I followed him. He didn't make it."

For a few moments, neither of us spoke.

"So it's over," I said. "They just walked off and left us."

"Didn't walk. Ran. Burned the camp and ran."

"But the motherfuckers left us. They left us!"

He looked at me as though I were some sort of unruly child, upset at something trivial. And then he sighed and said, "You want out of there, or what?"

"Hell, yes, I want out of here. But you're probably going to have to hack out a piece of this fucking cage. I think they built it with airplane cable."

He stepped closer and looked at the wire, then turned and put most of his gear up on the dry part of the riverbank, carefully balancing the gun on top of the pile. He reached to the back of his belt, ripped open a long narrow pouch, and pulled out a pair of heavy wire cutters. The things were long, with a snout like a miniature bolt cutter, yet somehow almost delicate. They looked like they could cut through a redwood.

"Best tool ever invented," he mumbled.

He started toward the cage, then stopped, turning his head, listening, looking back at the jungle behind him.

I knew enough not to move or speak. We stayed motionless for a long minute.

Still looking at the thick, tangled growth behind him, he slowly shoved the big wire cutters into his belt and picked another bundle out of his gear, stepped down to the cage, and handed it to me. His eyes never left the jungle.

He'd handed me a piece of brown, oily cloth wrapped around something that was heavy for its size. I unrolled the thing, careful not to let whatever it was fall into the water.

It was a pistol, a .45 model 1911, a gun I loved, mine taken by one of the "trainers." It was cocked and locked. I checked the magazine and the chamber—the pistol was loaded to the max.

The pilot had gone back to his pile of gear but was still tuned to something in the jungle. Finally, he pulled out the wire cutters and turned toward me.

I whipped up the .45, double-handed, pointed it toward his face, and fired.

At the last moment he saw what I was going to do, but it was too late. The gun blast drove him backwards over his gear, so violently that his feet left the ground and for a millisecond he hung horizontally in the air, his hands flying up and covering his face, the wire cutters tumbling as though he was juggling them. And then he hit the ground flat on his back. I didn't hear him hit the ground, of course—the blast from the .45 still banging inside my skull.

He lay still, then slowly raised his head and looked at me. I stood stone-still, my arms extended in his general direction, the .45 still pointing at where he had been standing.

I flicked the muzzle of the gun up, pointing beyond him. The pilot rolled slowly onto his side and looked behind him at the jungle. At the base of an enormous tree a man sat on the ground, his legs folded under him at odd angles, his arms bent at his sides. He was wearing some sort of out-of-date uniform, originally dark green, now faded and tattered. In the center of his forehead was a large, dark hole, a tiny trickle of blood running down to his nose and then across his cheek. His eyes were open wide, giving his face a dead surprised look. In his right hand was some sort of Uzi-type weapon. Above him, where he'd been standing, a dark red splotch glistened on the trunk of the tree, a streak of the red running down the bark to the back of the man's head where he sat on the ground. Along the streak I thought I could see brain matter and bits of bone. While we looked at him, he toppled forward, his face hitting the ground. The back of his head was gone.

The pilot eased himself up from the ground and walked slowly to the dead man. He carefully took the stubby gun out of the guy's hand, dropped the magazine, threw back some sort of bolt. A live round flipped out of the chamber. And then the pilot threw the gun and the magazine into the middle of the river.

The pilot stepped to the edge of the water, squatted, and scooped up water in his hands, sluicing it over his face and hair and running his fingers in and out of his ears—seriously messing with his camo paint, I thought. He took his time. Finally, he got up, still blinking his eyes and probing his ears with his fingers. I thought his face was stinging—his ears ringing loud enough to drown out church bells.

He rummaged around in the tall grass behind his gear until he found the big wire cutters. He walked back to the cage and stood there, looking at me, the way that fat housewives look at the monkeys in the zoo.

"Jesus Christ," he mumbled, "you have to be that fucking guy they call Morgan." He paused. "Shit, I'm not sure I should let you out of the cage. World might be a better place if I didn't."

I couldn't tell if he were kidding. I was standing there with a .45, and all he had was a pair of wire cutters, and yet he stood there like he was thinking it over. Jesus Christ, who was this guy?

And then he grinned and stepped up to the cage and started in on the wires and bits of cables with the huge cutters. In less than ten minutes I was standing on the riverbank.

The pilot said nothing more, just picked up his gear and started into the jungle. I struggled after him, trying to make my legs work properly.

I stopped and looked back at the cage. The bird was gone. Immediately, I felt a sense of loss, some deep, molten mass that seemed to roll inside me, far too heavy to be about a mere bird. But maybe it was, because the bird had left me, and I thought he was all that had kept me sane.

"You got anything to eat?" I said over my shoulder.

He reached into his pocket and pulled out a small bag of something and tossed it in my direction. I grabbed it out of the air and ripped it open. Beef jerky. Damn! Just like home! When I looked up to thank him, the pilot had disappeared into the jungle. It took me an hour to find him.

We lay at the edge of the rough airstrip and looked at a short row of crude huts on the other side. From what was left of the charred roof smoke drifted lazily upward into the hot, still air. In a flat area scraped at the end of the huts two small aircraft were burning. The flames were the only movement. I could smell the smoke, smell the oil that made dark patches in the packed earth of the airstrip, smell the rotted food that I knew had been thrown into the edge of the jungle. And there was another smell, one that will never leave your consciousness—I could smell decomposing bodies.

The camp was deserted.

The pilot was holding the carbine in one hand, his other holding a pair of small binoculars to his face, scanning the camp. I still gripped the .45.

"Why did they burn 'em?" I wondered, nodding at the planes.

"They couldn't find me. No one else could fly them and they couldn't leave them operational."

"So, our bunch, they just left us. We're expendable. Do you think they even knew our fucking names?"

The pilot said nothing, just slowly stood up and started adjusting his gear.

"We'll have to walk out of here," I mumbled.

"Yep," he said, "that we will."

"I remember their names," I growled, "and sooner or later . . ." I was gritting my teeth.

"Get over it," he said. "That much anger is one helluva big load." And he walked away.

I sat for a moment, staring at the burning planes, then took a deep breath, trying to release some of the "big load" into the jungle. It didn't work.

"Hey," I said, scrambling after him, "when we get wherever the hell it is we're going, will you teach me how to fly?"

He stopped and looked at me. "I hear tell you can shoot." There was a tiny smile at the corners of his mouth.

"Some."

"I can fly some. We could trade."

"Deal," I said.

And he tossed me a belt with the machete and a bunch of ammo pouches hanging from it. And the holster for the .45.

I stood looking at the gear in my hands, my mind wandering back to the river. "How come you threw away the Uzi?"

"Wasn't an Uzi," he growled. "One of those knockoffs they gave their guys. Piece of shit. Thing gets off a short initial burst, maybe two, then jams. You might make one kill, and then you're dead. They gave me one to put in the plane. I threw it out the window over unfriendly territory."

"Does this mean I get to keep the .45?" I asked quietly.

He just looked me for a moment, me still holding the gun. "Tell you what," he said, "you keep it until I ask for it back. When that day comes, you hand it over, no questions asked. I might give it back to you. Might not."

"That sounds like we're going to hang around together for a while. How do you figure that?"

"Karma. I must have fucked up big time a couple of lives ago. You're my long-term punishment."

Bastard. I just looked at him. He wasn't smiling. And then he started walking away again.

"Hey," I called after him, "so the gun's a loaner. Okay with me!" I gripped the gun. It felt like mine. It really did.

I started off after him. "You got any more of that beef jerky?"

He stopped and looked back at me. He had an odd expression on his face, something like a Cheshire cat.

"Wasn't beef," he said. "Was paca."

"Paca? What the hell is paca?"

"Think rat," he said, walking away. "Big rat."

Fucking guy. Turns out, his name was Slade. Took me two more days to find that out.

\* \* \* \* \*

I didn't know what to say.

Birds were special. And ever since the bird landed on my cage in the river and talked to me, birds were *really* special.

Now, Slade had killed the bird, just stomped on it like it was a cigarette butt.

There was nothing to say. I was just going to hit him and hope for the best.

Slade didn't move, just stood there with that stupid grin on his face. I hated that grin . . .

Grin?

Now he was trying to keep from laughing.

He was wearing only one glove.

It began to dawn on me. I backed slowly off the bike cover and carefully lifted the corner until light peeked underneath, and I could see Slade's other heavy, black, insulated glove under there, where he had thrown the damn thing, hard and whirling, a "bird," to break up the frost on my bike cover.

Slade walked away, singing. Jesus Mother, I wish to hell he would not sing.

*"Okay, you bastard, tonight you buy the beer! And I'm having a shot of Old Crow!"*

Oh, fuck, I thought, that didn't come out right.

It took us a while to get the bikes warmed up, mine in particular. We stood by them, engines idling—quietly, we thought— until I noticed a guy in another campsite glaring at me through the mist. Ah, well . . .

We left camp, driving west out of Yellowstone, Slade leading.

We were riding gently, easily, in no real hurry to leave the park, watching the sides of the roads and the far valleys for elk and buffalo. The road climbed, clinging to a steep hillside to our right, the left side dropping just as steeply into the grass of a heavy valley, its floor dipping and rising in easy cadence, ending at a dark stand of timber far to the side. The miles slid by in a soft dance of near distance, and then we rounded a gentle curve, and I could see cars stopped up ahead in our lane, other cars stopped in the oncoming lane, cars stopped everywhere. Slade's brake light came on. He slowed, then stopped. I eased up beside him. We raised our face shields. Three or four car lengths in front of us the back of an enormous buffalo rose above the roofs of the cars, the animal too big to be anything but a bull. And he was hopelessly penned in by the cars and the steep bank to the right.

A bull. An old bull.

We put down our side stands, stepped off the bikes, and started forward, carrying our helmets, moving quickly.

The buffalo turned his great body and looked at me, directly at me, something in his eyes that was less than recognition but more than cold indifference. Clots of mud and patches that looked like blood matted his hair. At the base of one of his horns a piece of his scalp had been ripped from his skull and dark scab glistened with new bleeding. The tip of the horn was broken off. Mucus ran from his nose and a string of spittle hung from the side of his mouth and then dropped as he swayed slightly on his feet. He swayed, not from being unsteady, but in preparation for flinging himself into some fight that only he knew existed.

I knew him. Maybe I'd always known him.

He swung away and tried to move away from us, his huge head swinging from side to side. In front of him, wide-eyed kids were pressed against the glass of every car window, the tiny flashes from their cameras constantly going off in a silent display of neuron-like explosions, muted giggles coming from behind the glass.

The bull swung around and looked at the line of cars blocking the other lane, bumper to bumper, doors locked, windows rolled up, more faces flashing their puny little cameras in the early light. The bull rolled his giant head to look at the sheer bank that rose to the right, too wet and too steep for him to climb, mud and gravel dribbling down onto the road. The cars in front of him were still not moving, the other lane a metal chain of cars sitting bumper to bumper. The car behind him in our lane was a BMW sedan, expensive, shiny, and it was edging slowly forward. The bull was trapped.

And then the stupid son of a bitch driving the Beemer blew the horn.

The bull jumped and whirled, facing the car, his huge eyes trying to find the noise, the danger.

We could hear the idiot horn-blower laughing. His window must have been down. Didn't the asshole know that the buffalo could totally, *totally*, destroy his Beemer?

Slade looked at me. I knew that look.

Here we go.

I was insanely happy.

Slade moved quickly forward until he was standing in front of the Beemer, looking at the bull. I slid back past the driver's door.

"Hey, old man!" Slade yelled at the bull, at the same time slamming his hand repeatedly on the hood of the BMW. He yelled again, "Hey, old—" and the bull charged. Slade disappeared instantly along the side of the Beemer. The bull did not. His great head centered on the front of the car, driving the metal back toward the engine. A horn was hooked into the tiny grill and the bull lifted, the horn ripping open the front of the car like opening a can, the hood of the Beemer popping loose, a mangled flag of expensive metal.

Horn Blower was raging, struggling to get his seat belt unfastened, his body thrashing, arms jerking. A woman sat beside him in the other seat, looking embarrassed, her head down, one hand on her forehead. I caught a glimpse of red hair and a hand without a wedding ring.

Slade slid between two of the unmoving cars, the kids inside frightened now, knowing in a little-kid way that something bad was about to happen. Slade yelled at the drivers to try to make room, get off on the berm, become invisible—*anything*.

Horn Blower finally untangled himself and slammed the driver's door open, his beefy legs shooting out like pile drivers, arms flailing as though he thought the car were holding him back.

Maybe it should have.

I wound up and hit him in the side of the head with my helmet. When he went down, he went down silently.

The bull spun and tried to climb the muddy bank, only to slide, spinning, back onto the road, his hooves making soft thunking noises on the blacktop.

Slade rapped on more car windows, trying to stir the drivers into some sort of motion, any motion, Slade didn't give a damn—move just a little, backward or forward. *Do something.* He just wanted enough of a gap to let the bull slip through.

The bull turned fully now, fixing me and Horn Blower with a look of timeless hate that must've gone back to the beginning of men and buffalo.

I didn't want to be there, where the bull could reach me, but I thought if I ran and left Horn Blower there, the bull might stomp him into molecules.

Not a bad thought, actually.

Slade had managed to get a gap opened in the line of cars, but I didn't know if the bull would see it. Instead of running away, I screamed at the old bull.

He turned to face me, seeing me as another danger, his head down. I thought he would charge. I could see his enormous eyes, deep with the weight of death. I'd thought the bull was frightened—the cars, the flash cameras, the people, the horn, the engines. I was wrong. I could see in his eyes only a rage and a hopelessness, a deep knowing that, no matter what, there would, one day, be no place for him. Not here. Not anywhere.

And then Horn Blower made a mistake. He got up, staggered forward, and came face to face with the buffalo.

The buffalo made only the smallest of movements: the big head lowered, twisted, raised, and Horn Blower left the ground. He landed in the middle of the crumpled hood of his own BMW and lay very, very still.

The fight was over and the bull knew it. He saw the opening in the line of cars, the valley floor stretching to the near mountains, sunlight sparkling on wet grass. He blundered through, a ton of living flesh, an animal-tank pressing forward. He was gone.

Even in his heavy riding clothes, Slade was faster than a snake sliding on shit. He jumped to the side of the BMW, hauled the guy off the hood, wrapped his arms around him, and gently lowered him to the pavement, carefully arranging his arms across his chest. He looked good that way, I thought, sort of looked dead, except that he was making soft little mewling sounds.

A guy in a Smokey hat came running down between the lines of cars. He had a radio in his hand and I could hear him say something about needing a bus—an ambulance. He skidded to halt and looked at the guy on the ground. Then he looked at us, the guy's eyebrows raised in the universal question . . . "What?"

"Officer," a soft voice said, "my boyfriend was trying to get the buffalo off the highway. The buffalo seemed to take exception. These gentlemen," the redhead turned to face Slade, "were coming to my rescue when the buffalo ran off."

She'd said "these gentlemen," but she only looked at Slade. Fuck. What did I expect?

The giant idiot on the ground said nothing, still making his pitiful little sounds. His eyes were closed.

The ranger looked at us and smiled. "I see you met Viejo," he said, flicking his head toward the disappearing bull. "Thanks for helping."

"No problem, ranger," Slade said, "my buddy and I were just about to—"

"Viejo?" I stepped slightly toward the ranger. "He's been around here for a long time?"

"As long as I've been here," the ranger said, looking closely at me.

"Has he ever been anywhere else? I mean, did you guys ever truck him in from somewhere?"

"Viejo? Oh, hell no." The ranger stared out across the valley. "He's been here as long as anybody can remember. Might wander off, now and again. Always shows up, sooner or later. He belongs here. Only here."

I thought I heard a catch in the guy's voice, but I wasn't sure.

Slade put his hand lightly on my arm, but he was looking at the ranger. "Anyway, sir, we were just passing through. Okay if we just keep going?"

"Please do," the ranger said. He was smiling.

The redhead reached out and touched Slade's arm, then took his hand.

"I just want to thank you again," she said. They stood that way for a moment, and then Slade turned and went back to his bike.

She never looked at me.

And we mounted up and rode out of that place.

A half-mile up the highway, away from the ranger, we pulled off, took off our helmets, and looked back at the vast meadow where the old bull had headed. Slade pulled off his glove. He had a piece of paper in his palm. I knew what it was—I didn't even have to ask; it was the redhead's name and phone number. How the hell does he do that? Me? I have to work my ass off for a woman to speak to me. Slade? Hell, the redhead was probably writing the note while Slade was hauling her boyfriend off the hood of his own car.

Slade hunted around in his riding coat until he found his Little Black Book—he actually had a Little Black Book. He folded the note from the redhead and slipped it into the pages.

\* \* \* \* \*

We should be too old for this shit.

But maybe not.

We could see a tiny black dot in the distance, far across the meadow. I couldn't tell if it were Viejo. The dot seemed to be grazing. I was glad.

"By the way," I said, "what made you so sure the bull would charge the car?"

Slade grinned. "Wasn't sure. Just wanted to get the guy out of the car, see if you could handle it." He paused. "Good thing you had the helmet. You might have been too old to go at him empty-handed."

The bastard grinned.

We stood quietly.

"We're both slowing down," Slade said. He nodded toward the old buffalo in the distance.

I watched the dark dot far across the meadow.

We started to pull on our helmets. I looked at Slade. "Did you notice that the ranger never asked our names, never looked at the bikes, never took any information?"

Slade thought for a moment. "Never question good luck," was all he said.

# 14

# DAY 7—THE SAME COLD DAY

Sunday, September 1

from Yellowstone

IT WAS THE HARDEST day's ride yet. There was no rain, but the wind blew, and never with us. We were headed north, and the wind came sharply and steadily out of the west, shoving the bikes hard toward the shoulder of the road. We rode with the wind whistling under our helmets and tearing through our clothing, rode fighting the strain and constant tension.

High cloud cover muted the light, and the wind carried a dense infusion of everything it could scour from the earth. I could smell the dust from the flat earth to the west of the mountains and feel the bits of hard things pinging into my helmet and snapping against my jacket. The riding wasn't exactly fun, but at least we were riding.

By the time we got a few miles to the south of Twin Bridges I was ready to look for any kind of shelter from the wind. The tiny town was there in front of us, smiling, I thought. And then the wind stopped. Just like that.

The main street of the town was totally empty, no cars, no motorcycles, no people. We pulled into the only gas station—at least the only station we could see: two pumps and a little wood-fronted convenience store.

Although I thought we didn't need gas, I was glad to stop, and I knew we would. It was hard to get Slade past a gas station. Slade was now and forever a pilot—it showed up in almost everything he did, like stopping for gas.

"The only time you have too much gas," he would say, "is when you're on fire."

We pumped our gas, moved the bikes next to the store, and went inside for a cup of coffee.

There was a single traffic light in Twin Bridges—you could see the entire length of the little town—and when we went inside there wasn't a car or bike in sight. We got our coffee and sat at a tiny table by the window, staring out into the empty street. It was Sunday in Twin Bridges, and people were quietly doing whatever they did here on a Sunday. And whatever they were doing, you couldn't see them doing it. Every time I was in a town like this one I would think . . . what would it be like to live here? To start new? To get up in the morning, make my coffee, get out my pad and pencil and write until I didn't feel like writing any more? What would that be like? What would . . . peace . . . be like? Could I live here? I always asked myself those questions, but I never yet tried to find the answers in one of those little towns. I think I was afraid. But there were little towns still to come.

As we drank our coffee a biker on a huge Harley rode up to the gas pumps, and then another, and then the place filled with bikers, engines turning in that deep, wonderful *basso profundo* that Harleys make, that I thought was their contribution to the music of riding.

We went outside to see dozens of huge bikes, bikes parked at the gas pumps, on the town's only sidewalk, lined up in rows by the side of the street, stacked up in the driveway. One guy rode a Harley up the front steps of a closed store across the street and parked the bike on the porch. No one seemed to care.

The bikes were mostly Harleys, a few Triumphs, a couple of Victory heavies, all ridden by a bunch of great, colorful people out for a long weekend ride.

And then I realized that tomorrow was Labor Day.

We spent some time talking to the riders, getting tips on the best routes up through the state, just enjoying the company of others who liked to ride. Some of them looked at our bikes, grinning and shaking their heads.

"Those things are almost motorcycles," one guy said, grinning at me.

Another guy: "Ain't there some pieces missin'?"

A woman driving a custom-built trike pulled into the gas pumps. She dismounted, looking at us like we were aliens. And I guess we were, wearing the gear we were wearing, riding bikes that, next to the Harleys, looked like underfed steel dragons, gear strapped to every part of them. She was tall, red-haired (yeah, another one), and built like a lean wrestler, one of those people who knew what she could do, fearing nothing, holding her place with the good ol' boys on their Harleys.

She wanted to know where we were headed, and I told her. I was watching her closely, and she got a sort of wistful look on her face, then turned and stared at the horizon.

I had learned to watch for that look. When we gassed up the KLRs or stopped at a café, when we sat at the side of the road and someone stopped to talk, when we were pitching tents for the night and another biker was nearby, that look, that wistful look, would come over their faces when they realized that we weren't out for an afternoon's ride. When they realized they might never see us again but that we would be doing something, really doing *something*, and when I saw that look on their faces it made me realize that Slade and I had spent a good part of our lives *doing something*. Even if it was wrong. And sometimes it was—very wrong. Those were the good times.

But sometimes it was right.

The redhead's trike was big, shiny, and built for comfort, the front wheel extending like a probe of the road. The seat was plush with padding and fit snugly in front of the rear wheels, chrome glistened, and no dust spotted the mirrors. Slade walked over to the pump and took the hose down. The redhead opened the tank behind her seat and Slade pumped the gas. Through the whole process they looked at each other, neither saying a word.

Me? I was no longer in the redhead's world, or even on the planet.

Slade put the hose back, and the redhead capped the tank, reached into her jacket for her wallet.

Slade held up his hand, palm out. "On me," he said.

The redhead looked at him. "Next time it can be on me," she said softly. "Literally."

But the redhead didn't try to prolong things. She simply climbed back onto the trike, started it up, and revved the engine. She reached for the shift lever that stuck up almost a foot high between her legs. She put her fingers on it lightly, looking at Slade. The shifter was a huge, rubber penis.

Slade stepped up beside the bike and looked at the shifter. He grinned at her. "Not quite big enough," he said, and I could hear the chuckle in his voice.

From somewhere inside her jacket the redhead pulled out a card and handed it to Slade. All I could think of was, what the fuck, another card? Another phone number? That's two in one goddamn day!

Slade took the card, and the woman grabbed the shifter. When she grabbed it, she looked at Slade and me, grinned, holding the shift firmly, lovingly. And then she drove away from the pumps, her fingers still wrapped around the shaft. She never looked back.

We rode north for two hundred miles. The wind came again and never stopped. We had been on the road seven days and there had not been one calm, cloudless, still, dry, warm day. But this wind was nothing compared to what was waiting for us. Of course, we didn't know that at the time. If we had known, maybe we would have . . .

Would have . . . what? Ridden off in another direction? Turned south? Bullshit!

We stopped just short of Missoula, Montana.

Slade found a dry flat at the edge of a wash. The flat was thick with short evergreen growth, and the ground was a mat of old needles, soft from age. Ten yards away a small stream rumbled over rocks and green spikes sticking up out of the water. Slade reached down and grabbed a handful of mud, raising it, letting it ooze between his fingers and drop back into the water. I knew he wanted to ask me something, wanted to fill in a gap that had been bothering him, but he did not. He washed the mud from his hands and came back to the campsite. We pitched our tents, and I broke out the Irish Mist and the cigars.

Slade and I have a small tradition. I carry thin, fine cigars and Irish Mist, both sealed in unbreakable plastic bottles. On every ride we had ever been on, over all the years, I always brought the Mist, the cigars, and small metal sipping cups. Neither Slade nor I are really smokers. And Slade wasn't much of a drinker, but I tried to make up for his shortcomings in that department. On cold, dark evenings, before slipping into frigid sleeping bags, we'd sit on the ground, huddled in our riding gear, sip the Mist, fire up the cigars, hold the smoke inside us, and wait for that buzz that was the absolute best, better than weed, better than straight alcohol. The mellow tobacco and the silky slide of Irish Mist down our throats kept us in touch with things from worlds that we'd somehow slipped away from. Or had never known.

This evening, we weren't even going to bother eating.

Slade peeled off his heavy coat and started taking things out of the pockets. He always took inventory at night, checking to see that everything he wanted, everything that he might need, was still in his pockets. He laid the Little Black Book on a rock and held it there with his folding knife. And then he took his cigar and went off to take a piss.

I looked at the tiny book. I found another rock, a flat one, put it in the center of our camp, and put a small pile of needles and tiny leaves on it. And I put the Little Black Book on top of the pile.

When Slade came back, I was holding a burning country match in my fingers, a few inches from the book. Slade just sat down and didn't move until the match began to burn my fingers. I blew it out.

He smiled, took a sip of Mist, pulled out another match, lit it, and held it until the flame was at his fingers. He put out the flame.

"Think I'll see if I can call Modene," he said, getting up and pulling his phone out of one of the tiny pockets inside his coat. He wandered off.

When I crawled into my tent and into my sleeping bag, he was still gone.

And the Little Black Book was still there on the tiny stack of tinder.

# 15

# DAY 8

Monday, September 2
Labor Day
from Missoula, Montana

WIND SHOOK THE TENT all night. I'd pegged the tent down like I was tying down a steer—taut lines holding the frame, had every zipper closed tightly—and yet the tent vibrated like the cover on a cheap bass drum. When I woke up, I wanted to lie there until the wind stopped. But I didn't.

The thought of coffee brought me out into the open. I thought I was up early, but Slade was already gone from his tent, out taking another one of his walks.

We were going to go into Missoula for breakfast, but I wanted coffee. Now. I dug into my saddlebags and found my tiny stove and the coffee that I always had in there, right next to the Irish Mist. I fired up the stove and was able to drink two cups before Slade got back.

I had never been in Missoula.

I loved the place.

There was bright sunshine from the moment we broke

camp, and we rode into the town in a state of euphoria, moving through air warming us like kisses. And the light from a clear sky stayed with us all day. I was almost uncomfortable with it; a week on the road, and this was the first clear, warm day. How the hell was I going to handle it?

The human body and the human mind can get used to a horrible pantheon of conditions. Almost get comfortable with them. Once, I had trudged step by agonizing step on a long traverse five hundred feet above tree line, low cloud cover hiding anything beyond fifty feet, sleet nailing the side of my face no matter how many times I tried to cover it. It had been that way for three days. And then I topped a ridge and suddenly broke into the open, the clouds hard behind me, the sleet gone, liquid sunshine warming me. I stopped, staring at the golden lay of the mountains in front of me, below me. The challenge was gone. I was almost disappointed.

Now and then, in a café or gas station, almost anywhere on the road, we'd walk past a newspaper box, never looking at the paper showing through the glass. If there were TV in a café we moved away from it, not wanting to hear what was happening in the outside world. We wanted to be isolated, alone. Once, in a restaurant, we walked through a bar with a large-screen TV showing an NFL game—beer drinkers, smokers, people cheering for the teams, TV blaring crowd noises, and the repetitious patter of announcers. At home, we might have stopped and watched, maybe had a beer with the folks in the bar. But here, on this trip, it was grating. We hustled through the bar and out into sunshine, breathing it in while we could.

I'd read somewhere that Missoula was a place where writers lived, a bunch of them. Or had lived. Real writers. Kinder had once lived there, and guys like Burke and Crumley and Welch, guys who could write sentences that made your eyes water from the beauty of the words, who could contract your chest from the intensity of what they were saying.

I don't think we got off the bikes in Missoula. I was content to leave it to those guys who knew what they were doing.

I really had no idea where we were going from Missoula, what route we would take. But Slade's attention to travel detail and map reading was amazing. He brought his piloting skills to the motorcycle. As long as I could keep his taillight in sight, I knew I'd end up where I wanted to be. Or someplace better.

Polson was one of those "better" places. We eased into town in still-brilliant sunshine, saw the small orchards in backyards, knew that the fruit from the trees might already be in baskets sitting on kitchen counters, waiting to be canned for Thanksgiving and Christmas dinners. I was sure of that.

We watched the sails on Flathead Lake, small boats handled by skilled men and women, content to be on an enormous lake that most people to the far south had never even heard of.

Polson. I realized that there were people there who might actually be real. Polson, another town where I asked myself the questions again, where I thought I'd switch off the engine and see if there were a room to rent—for the rest of my life. It was where I wanted to be. Polson.

What the hell was going on here? I kept falling in love with these little dinky towns. What was I looking for? Why didn't I just stop here? Not go any farther. To hell with Alaska! How could it get any better than this?

I didn't want to leave.

But, of course, we did.

There was some sort of pull from Alaska that I didn't understand, or even try to.

We ended up in Whitefish.

It was the shortest day's run we had made.

# 16

# DAY 9

Tuesday, September 3
from Whitefish, Montana

I'D HEARD OF WHITEFISH all my life. Why, I'd ask myself, would anyone voluntarily live in Whitefish, Montana?

And now I knew the answer. Whitefish, quite simply, was America's hidden hometown.

Another little town. I won't even tell you how many times the old questions came flooding behind my mind.

The kid didn't help.

We cruised down a narrow residential street and saw a dirt lane that led to . . . who the hell knows where it went to, it just went, and so did we. I peeled slowly off the street and followed the land down a gentle slope and then onto a well-beaten path that stopped at a small stream. There, at the end of the path, by the stream, was the kid.

He was squatting by the water, playing in the cold mud. We stopped the bikes and got off, just to watch him. We had nowhere in particular to go.

He paid no attention to us. He was building something out

of the mud at the edge of the water. I couldn't be sure but he seemed to be building . . . mud dolls.

I eased up beside him—he still had not turned around—and marveled at his concentration on the dolls. And then I realized he was an Indian. I slowly stood up and backed away. From somewhere inside I could feel another world pushing up, a world of my own making, wavering visions of things not here. I struggled to keep the visions down.

Slade had never taken his eyes from me. "The kid's just playing, Morgan. It doesn't mean anything."

"It does to me, Slade."

Slade slid out of his saddle and stood in front of me. "I know you've already done it. And I've been thinking about asking you about it. But what I know or don't know doesn't really matter. What *you* think is what matters—and it's way too late now to be sorry. There's nothing you can do to call it off."

"That the trouble, my brother. I'm not sorry, and I don't want to call it off. I want to go back to the river and do it again."

"You're a hard man, Morgan.

"Funny, that's what Red Hawk said."

\* \* \* \* \*

The two old Indian men stood in piercing sunlight at the edge of the hard-dirt plaza, almost shoulder to shoulder, looking at me. I'd known them for thirty years.

They could've been brothers, but I knew they were not. They were short, stocky, their skins a soft nut brown that Anglo women paid to achieve in tanning parlors. Their wrists were thick and their hands knotted from hard labor in the fields down by the river. Both were barefoot. They wore thin, faded jeans, threadbare flannel shirts. Each wore a wide cotton headband. A'anka's headband was red, or it had been at one time. Red Hawk's was blue. That was the only outward difference between them.

Sweat ran down all our faces.

And then, softly: "Morgan. You have not been here for a long time. We thought the Apaches had cut off your balls and fed them to the hawks." A trace of a smile was on his lips.

"No, Grandfather A'anka. The Apaches have no need of my manhood," I said. "But I have need of your power."

"You stay away for years, and then you come back to the river," A'anka said. He looked at Red Hawk. "He comes because of woman trouble. That's your department." And he walked away.

I thought maybe I was done. Couldn't tell with those two. Depended on what signs they had seen that day, or whether they thought I was being respectful. Or disrespectful.

A'anka was walking away across the bright plaza, the tiny adobe houses standing like oversize brown bricks, their small windows looking out on a world they neither wanted nor truly understood. Red Hawk let A'anka walk out of sight around the old adobe church before he turned back to me. But I spoke first. "How did he know it was woman trouble?"

"Morgan, we have known you for a very long time. We sent you cornmeal when you were in the jungle. And, still, you do not really understand."

I stood there, my head raised, looking into the blue of the world. "Something happened," I said. "I'm a fool. I need to fight back."

"You always feel the need to fight back," Red Hawk said,

"even when it's your fault." He turned and started padding across the plaza. "Especially when it's your fault," he said over his shoulder. "That's why you are such a hard man."

I followed at a respectful distance, down a narrow path to the river. We sat on the downed trunk of an ancient cottonwood. "Tell me," he said.

And I did. I left nothing out, including how foolish I was. Red Hawk knew white men were foolish—especially me.

"Explain to me, Morgan. You said you were happy when the woman was with you." He took a deep breath. "How did you know?"

I looked at him. "How did I know . . . ?"

"I do not know if you have ever put your hands around happiness, Morgan. Life. It is usually not a matter of happiness. Life is something else.

"No one can describe happiness, not even you, Morgan, with all your writing magic. So how do we know what it is, this 'happiness'?" He sat staring across the water.

"It's a smoke, Grandfather. That's all I can see that it is. A smoke." I looked at the old man, waiting. But he said nothing.

"Grandfather, I learned long ago that happiness is not something to be described, to be had and held, to claim, to store beside the warm robe in my home. It's only something to try to live through because there is an end to it, and we have to get to the end, thinking we will find the truth of it. There, at the end. Thinking that it is something to strive for. But we are wrong. We don't know where the end is, and we never quite make it. And just when we think we have it, it is over."

The old man got slowly to his feet, grinning. "You are making up words that sound like Indian words. You always did that," he said softly, smiling, not looking at me.

And then he got serious. "We live through tragedy, not happiness," he said. "We can deal with tragedy. We can recover. We can only worship happiness. And we seldom recover."

I'd never thought of it that way.

"Yes, happiness is a pursuit of smoke," Red Hawk said, "and you never know, even when you catch it, what it is. How do you know when you have caught smoke? What signs tell you? What drum song plays in your mind? And then, at the end of it, where does the smoke go?"

I stood up, facing him. I knew there was something else.

"And sometimes the smoke catches you," he said. "Especially if the smoke is a woman."

I had no fucking idea what Red Hawk was trying to tell me.

We were silent for long moments. And then Red Hawk looked at me. "What does Arturo say about the woman?"

I was surprised by the question. I didn't know Red Hawk had even heard of Arturo.

One day, while Arturo was riding his pony, and the young men were running up the canyon chasing cows, Arturo had stopped by my porch.

"Do you see her, Morgan?" He didn't use Lancey's name.

Arturo did not mean "could" I see her. He meant "do" I see her. See her *really*.

"I think so," I mumbled. "But maybe not."

Arturo leaned down from his pony, as though he might fall off. "That is the trouble, Morgan. I do 'see' her. And I don't want to be on the same land with her." He waited for a moment, but he was pretty sure I wasn't going to say anything.

I sat silently until Arturo rode away.

I told Red Hawk what Arturo had said.

"You should have listened, Morgan. Those Apaches are right about some things." And he walked away.

I sat alone in the sun on a broken lawn chair at the edge of the plaza. I didn't know whether to leave or to wait. Maybe I should've gotten back into my old truck and driven away from that place, that place that I loved.

"Let me understand," he said. A'anka was standing behind me—I hadn't heard him come there. His voice was that soft, mellow Indian voice that seemed soothing, even in times when there was nothing but anger in the world.

"Red Hawk and I have talked. If we do not help you, you will try to find some other way. And that way will be more evil than this."

He was still standing back there, motionless. But I wouldn't turn and look at him. I was angry, and he did not like anger.

"Let me understand," he said again. "There are these women, The Girls, you call them. How many women?"

"Four, I think. That's all the names I have, anyway. There may be more, but the four are the ones who . . ." My voice broke slightly and I stopped.

Red Hawk fell into a silence that was deeper than sleep, but he never closed his eyes.

I waited.

"You asked us to tell the river to take the spirits, the will, the power of the women."

It was not a question.

"Yes, Grandfather."

The old man waited.

"I want them to be as miserable as I am, Grandfather. Forever."

"It is your right, Morgan, as one of us." He paused. "What hardened you, Morgan?"

"I do not know, Grandfather. Maybe it was because I did not fit . . . anywhere. Maybe it was because of women with eyes that changed color."

A'anka got up and walked away.


It was not yet full light, and the mist rose from the river in soft streams that curled through the cottonwood limbs and disappeared into air of the world in a quiet statement of life.

A'anka and Red Hawk stood ankle deep in the mud at the edge of the brown water. Both were naked.

I stood upstream, looking at them, waiting to be told what to do. I dared not begin until told. I was naked. All our clothes were thrown up on the high weeds, away from the water and the mud.

"The mud you stand in is mud that our ancestors treasured," A'anka said. "They put it around the bits of planted corn and patched their houses with it. They spread it on burns from wind-blown fires, and they made their masks of it. It is powerful mud."

I said nothing.

"Go ahead," Red Hawk said. "Build the women."

I kneeled, and at the very edge of the water I began to shape mud into four small mounds, each less than a foot high. The mounds were wider at the bottom, came in at the waists, had crude arms, and smaller clumps of mud for heads. I pulled some grass from the riverbank and used it for hair. With my finger, in the front of each doll I made a groove from where the navel should be down to where their legs should be joined at the tops, and then farther down, all the way to the mud at the bottom. Around each waist I tied a thin piece of green vine that was growing near the water. When I'd finished, I'd built four short, crude, ugly dolls. I had made women of mud.

And when I was done, I built one more, quickly, a little apart from the rest.

Red Hawk and A'anka hadn't moved.

"Do you have the leaves?" Red Hawk asked.

"Yes, Grandfather. They're in my shirt pocket."

A'anka carefully took the leaves from my shirt. He looked at each of them. "These are the names?" He was looking at the writing on the leaves.

"Yes, Grandfather. I wrote them with blood from my hand, as you instructed."

He handed the leaves to me. "Plant them," he said softly.

I pushed each leaf by its sharp stem into the top of the legs, where they joined—I pushed the names into the cunts of the dolls.

"There is no leaf in the last one," Red Hawk said. "Is that the woman of unhappiness?" Red Hawk asked.

"No, Grandfather. It's an extra. An extra, in case there is a woman who has escaped my notice, a woman of no name."

The two old men silently looked at each other, and then walked away, their naked brown bodies shining softly in the sun.

I stood by the water, looking at the dolls. The old men had been gone for hours. The sun was almost gone. Other than that, nothing had changed.

I had to wait until the sun rose the next day. I had to stay naked beside the river. I couldn't eat. And I knew I shouldn't piss. By sunrise, if the water had risen and taken the dolls, the magic was in place. If the water didn't rise, I could either walk away and leave the dolls, and the women, in peace, or I could wash the dolls into the river. In another way.

I sat down at the edge of the trees.

There was no moon.

By first light I was bleary from not sleeping, shivering from cold. I got my creaky legs under me and staggered to the dolls. The river hadn't taken them. They stood silently, shoulder to shoulder, staring out across the river, secure, their cunt-leaves solidly in place.

The Girls. I hated them. I wouldn't walk away.

I stood directly behind the first one, my bladder bursting. And then I pissed on the doll, and then pissed on each of the other dolls. I pissed until I could piss no more.

The dolls stood there, their forms eroded from the hot stream. They no longer looked like dolls. They looked like lumps of piss-stained mud that the falling of the next rain would wash away.

No sign of the dolls would ever be seen again.

I started to walk away toward the plaza, no longer concerned about my nakedness. I thought I heard something. I stopped and listened, but I couldn't quite make the sound come clear. I lay face down on the mud at the edge of the river and turned my head, putting the side of my face into the mud. I could hear faint screaming, female voices, voices in agony. The Girls. The Mud Girls, on their way to the Gulf of Mexico. I could stop them now, if I wanted to. I knew how, and I knew Red Hawk was watching me from somewhere back in the trees, waiting to see if I stopped them. But I did not. I wanted my pain to be their pain. And it was.

And then, from somewhere, high on the bank, far back into the cottonwood trees, beyond where the grasses once more gave way to the brown things of the world, I heard the words from a voice that was not A'anka or Red Hawk. It was a voice out of time and pain, and it said, clearly: "May the ancient flow of the river forever rot the knotted spirits of The Girls."

And I covered my head, and I cried.

The old pickup was where I left it. I put on my clothes and was ready to slide behind the wheel, and then A'anka and Red Hawk were suddenly standing by the door.

"Be careful, Morgan," Red Hawk said. "Listen to Slade. He is your true brother."

"He's my white brother," I said.

"If we shed our skins, we are all the same," Red Hawk said.

"Even a snake?"

"No," Red Hawk said softly. "That is true. When a snake sheds his skin, he is still wearing the skin of a snake. He is a snake all the time, I am thinking."

The old men touched me lightly on my shoulders.

"You are lost in anger," A'anka muttered. "But you are not really angry at that woman back there. Deep inside, she is nothing to you." He lowered his head, not looking at me. "You are angry at the sky."

I was not sure I heard him. "At the sky?" I said.

He still hadn't raised his head. "The sky is larger than Earth," he said softly. "Your anger is larger than Earth, so you must be angry at the sky."

And they walked away.

\* \* \* \* \*

The kid was gone.

We sat on the bikes, watching the water.

"When I called Modene the other night," Slade said, "she said that some sheriff from down your way called the house, looking for you."

I said nothing.

"Modene told him the truth—she said that you had been there, but she never saw you leave. Which, technically, was true. She drove off before we left." He paused. "Modene said he didn't even ask if she knew where you were going. Odd, don't you think?"

I said nothing.

"Looks like you're a wanted man," he said, grinning.

"I'm glad somebody wants me," I muttered.

Slade laughed. "Don't get too used to feeling sorry for yourself," he said. "Doesn't fit your personality. If you had a personality, that is."

He laughed again.

Bastard.

17.

# DAY 9—THE SAME DAY

Tuesday, September 3

from Whitefish, Montana

A COUPLE OF HOURS north of Whitefish, we entered Canada.

We rode into country that was real.

We rode into a country we had imagined, where the road instantly became a thin black path into some sort of adventure that spiked in our minds.

We rode across the border without ceremony, knowing that the actual port of entry was a few miles away, a few miles into a new being, a new way of riding. And, again, the thought hit me: we were in *Canada*, and for the first time, Slade and I were really on the road, really going to ride north until something, or somebody, stopped us.

We had actually left home.

Again.

We rode through heavy mist, tall, green-black trees on each side of the narrow road seeming to hold the mist in a gentle pledge of sunlight somewhere farther on. Just from breathing the air, I thought most of the world's crystal must be in Canada and had escaped into the wind around us.

Within a mile or so we came to the official Canadian point of entry. It stood against the side of the narrow road, a neatly painted, slender, tiny, official-looking building that seemed to be alone in the Southern Canadian wilderness. There were no cars, no activity around the building, nothing to show that there was official business to be conducted there. Slade and I rode up to the building, stopped outside a window that opened onto the road, and killed our engines. We took off our helmets and dug out our passports. The window slid open. A uniformed border agent leaned out. He looked at us, nothing showing on his face.

"And where might you gentlemen be going on this fine, foggy morning?"

"Alaska," Slade said.

The agent looked surprised. He said nothing for a long moment, letting his eyes wander over us, our bikes, the gear strapped neatly into place. Noticing the color of our hair.

"And where might you be from?" he finally asked.

"Colorado," Slade said.

"New Mexico," I said. And then a lump formed in my throat. I was holding a passport and had told a border guard where I was from. Shit. If they were looking for me at the border, this was it. The next thing I'd see would be a gun.

But the agent's expression didn't change. He didn't even look directly at me. The lump in my throat grew smaller.

"Do either of you gentlemen know what time of year it is?" he asked.

Slade and I looked at each other and grinned. It was the

same question, the same look, we'd been getting since we left Colorado Springs.

"Yeah," I said, "it's September, and we're riding north, and everybody else is riding south."

"And you planned on doing this, when there's a Canadian winter somewhere up there," he flicked his head up the highway, "waiting to hammer you right out of your saddles?" He paused for a moment. "Why?"

Slade and I looked at each other. "Maybe it's because we're riding north . . ." Slade said.

" . . . and everybody else is riding south," I said.

The agent said nothing for a long moment. Then, "There aren't many of you left." He shook his head slightly. "You gentlemen have a nice ride—or whatever ride you're trying to find." And he closed the window.

Slade and I sat for a moment, staring at the passports the agent never asked to see. We thought of some other borders we'd crossed in our travels together, borders with men no older than high schoolers standing over us with fingers on the triggers of automatic weapons, waiting for something, *anything*, to happen that would allow them to pull those triggers, to relieve the boredom of watching foreigners come and go across their borders.

But not in Canada.

The agent was wise beyond his job.

Instantly, I loved Canada.


We rode away from the tiny building and immediately ran out of civilization. Houses became rare; there was no roadside advertising, no junk, no litter. The road and the country were as clean, crisp and beautiful as any I'd ever seen. Here, only a few miles from the United States, was a land as fresh and inviting as a newborn day under a light mist that you knew would burn off to show forested mountains that would stop your heart.

Canada. I made a promise to myself. I would never tell *anybody* about Canada. I didn't want any more Americans to come up here and fuck it up.

About fifty miles later Slade pulled to the side of the road. I pulled in beside him, our engines still running. We raised our face shields.

"Back there," Slade said, "when the border guy said there weren't many of us left, I don't think he was talking about tourists."

"No. He wasn't. He was talking about us."

For once, we didn't seem to want to immediately get back on the road, just sitting there, feeling the vibration of the engines coming up through the seats.

Then Slade said, "This is Canada." His voice was serious.

"Right. So it is."

Silence again. Then, "Pistols are illegal in Canada, any place, anywhere," he said.

I thought for a moment. "Hmmm, so they are." I paused. "I'll keep that in mind."

Slade just kept looking at me, his face a blank. And then a tiny smile curled his lips. "Never made any difference to you anywhere, did it." It wasn't a question.

"Nope."

We popped our shields down.

And then Slade popped his shield up again. "Where the hell did you put it? I mean, what if the guy back at the border had wanted to take a look at our gear?"

"I wasn't a bit worried," I said. I leaned over and shoved my hand under the top of one of his soft saddlebags and pulled out the .45. "I hid it in your luggage, of course," I said, stuffing the gun into one of my panniers.

I gunned my engine and was a half-mile up the road before Slade could get his face shield down.

We stopped at Wasa for lunch, at Marie's Café. A single car was parked out front, a beater with faded paint and a cracked windshield. It was loaded for the road, clothing and boxes stuffed to the ceiling, other boxes tied on top with what looked to be clothesline. A fellow traveler, I thought. Jut getting the hell out of Wasa.

Marie wasn't there. Marie wasn't anywhere. Didn't own the café, anymore. Didn't even live in Wasa, anymore. Marie was smart. All that Wasa was, *was* the café. And now the café was owned by Jade—that's what it said on the little sign tacked to the outside of the door.

Slade and I walked in—there was no one in the place. Every table was empty, no one behind the counter. There were no napkin dispensers or salt and pepper shakers on the tables. In fact, there was nothing of any kind on the tables. We ambled to the center of the room and sat down. No problem; there was plenty of room.

We sat and waited for . . . somebody? Anybody?

Jade?

Except, it was Lancey. Or so I thought.

The slender woman walked out of the back room, the same determined walk, the same stride, the same worn jeans, rodeo belt buckle, amber-colored hair pulled severely back in a pony tail, paint on her hands, a rag hanging out of her pocket. But her eyes were amber again.

Something popped in my brain. Pain shot through my body, my eyes clouded over, I couldn't see. The woman wasn't Lancey—I *knew* that, knew that Lancey couldn't be here. I'd taken a couple of the magic pills this morning and my iron-covered, pill-loaded brain was fucking with me. My eyesight wavered—like looking through old glass, my throat closed, and I began to make growling sounds from somewhere in my chest. "Lancey" was all I could say. And I said it again.

"Lancey . . ."

I rose out of my chair and backed up across the café, then put my hands out behind me, feeling for the door to the restaurant. Something started boiling behind my eyes—pure unadulterated anger.

"Who the fuck are you?" I growled, bringing my hands up, leaning forward, my body rigid.

Slade jumped up and stepped quickly in front of me, grabbing my shoulders, shaking me.

"Morgan! Morgan! Wake up!"

I woke up. The rigidity flew out of my body as quickly as it had arrived. I was vaguely aware that Slade was between me and the woman, trying to watch her and keep an eye on me at the same time.

The woman stood frozen at the edge of our table, her face a mask of bewilderment, a lone woman watching a man obviously in the throes of some sort of mental train wreck.

I looked around like a drunk man, not really knowing where I was or what it was that was going on in my mind. The door-frame was against my back and I twisted around it, through the door, shambling across the small porch, lurching down the steps, and then out in front of our bikes, where, for some unknown reason, I sank onto the gravel.

There was something wrong with me. I had known it for some time, even before Lancey left. Something burned under the skin of my aching body that lay there, smoldering, waiting for an excuse, any excuse, to burn its way to the surface. I lay in the gravel, staring up at the sky. I never wanted to rise again.

Slade was on me instantly. He squatted down and looked into my eyes.

The woman—Jade, not Lancey—was on the porch, watching intently. And then she disappeared. In a moment she was back with a glass pitcher of water, ice cold. Slade poured half over my head and held the rest ready. If I tried anything weird, I knew he'd simply hit me with the half-full pitcher, glass or not. I stayed as still as I could.

It was over in a few heartbeats. The woman squatted beside me and used the tail of her shirt to wipe away the water, gently, patting it more than rubbing it. When the shirt was wet, she used her hand, rubbing my forehead gently, a caress I had not felt in. . . . I could not remember the last caress.

She leaned closer and took by face in her hands. "Listen to me," she said. "Are you listening?"

Slade backed away, eased up the steps, and went back into the café.

All I could do was look at her and nod repeatedly.

"I'm not . . . Lancey. I'm Jade. I don't know any Lancey, probably will *never* know any Lancey." She waited for some sort of reaction from me, but got none. "But let me tell you something, biker boy, I really wish I were. To have somebody show that much feeling . . . and I wouldn't care what the feeling was."

"It might be hate." It was all I could say, but I wanted her to know the truth. I squeezed my eyes shut. I felt like a goddamn fool.

And then she pulled my head against her breasts. There was nothing sexual about it. It was an offer of comfort.

I accepted.

And so we sat, me and this woman who was not Lancey but who could have been her twin. This Jade. And we hugged tightly as the sun moved past noon and the air cooled slightly, two grown people, total strangers, sitting on the gravel of parking lot in front of two ugly, trip-laden motorcycles, arms wrapped around each other.

Slade, God love him, never came back outside.


Jade. She was Jade. She was the owner, cook, waitress, cashier, and dishwasher—and comforter of a lost old man who maybe in his whole life had only been with one other woman as fine and true as Jade of Wasa. Jade, hidden in the forests of Canada, Jade who belonged in the arms of a man who would make her the only living being he could possibly care about. Jade, with a smile that you could read a menu by. Jade, the owner of a café in Wasa, a town that wasn't even a town, miles from anything, in the middle of Canadian wilderness so imposing that I didn't know if I would be able to ride out of there with a whole soul. Part of my soul, I knew, would have to stay there. Maybe with Jade.

We went inside and sat at a table with Slade. We just sat there and talked. No reason to hurry—the café was closed.

Actually, I was glad the place was closed—no other customers. I wouldn't have wanted to be seen sitting on my ass, crying, in the middle of a parking lot on a sparkling day, in Wasa, British Columbia.

So we talked. We told her we were going to Banff, and then farther north. Going to Alaska. Maybe to the Circle. Most people would not have believed us, at least not right away. But based on what she had already seen, I don't think there was anything we could have said that would have surprised her.

No, Jade was not Lancey. She was far, far beyond Lancey. And Lancey would never know.

But I would, and so would Slade.

Every so often, Jade would reach over and touch me, ever so lightly.

Slade and I stalled as long as we could, trying to string out the conversation, wanting more time with Jade. But, finally, we had to leave. Either that, or toss a coin to see who married Jade. And I would shoot that fucking coin right out of the air.

We walked out on the tiny front porch and Jade walked out with us. We stood there in that small, awkward silence before leaving someone we liked, knowing we would never see them— her—again.

We struggled into our gear and stood by our bikes. On the porch, Jade pulled the door shut and locked it from the outside, dropped the key into a flowerpot. She took off her apron and hung it on the doorknob, then came down the steps and walked up to us. And she hugged us both.

Tears were running down her face.

And then she stepped into the loaded old car and drove slowly away. South.

She went away. She got into that fucking overloaded beater and went away.

Slade and I stood there for at least half an eternity, watching Jade's car carve slowly around a turn in the far distance and disappear. The woman was gone from Wasa, and gone from our lives.

We looked back at the now-deserted café, Jade's apron hanging from the doorknob, looking at a building that would seem empty for the rest of our lives.

As I hauled my leg across my saddle I noticed a tiny sign nailed to one of the posts on the porch. It said, "This café for sale. Inquire inside." It was a very old sign. And we knew there was no one inside.

The apron hung motionless from the doorknob. I got off the bike and walked slowly back up on the porch, took the apron, folded it carefully, and tucked it into a pocket inside my riding coat.

Slade said nothing.

We hadn't started the bikes. I raised my face shield and looked at Slade. He raised his shield.

"What happened to me in there," I said, nodding at the café, "if it ever happens again, I want you to take the .45 and shoot me."

"With pleasure," he said. I think he chuckled, but I wasn't sure. "And it will happen, if you don't stop taking that shit."

The pills! How the hell did he know about the pills? Fuck.

We rolled the bikes side by side to the edge of the parking lot.

There was a car coming, from the south. With boxes tied to the top.

Jade.

She pulled into the lot, got out of the car, walked straight up to the bikes, and stood between them. She put her hand on my handlebars, but she looked at Slade. "Banff is a good place to lay over. Let people catch up."

"Yeah," Slade said. "I've heard tell."

"Don't desert him. He'll be there."

"I don't desert people. Especially him."

Slade and Jade were speaking some sort of code that I didn't understand. And I was trying hard.

"I'll see you around, then. Sometime," she said, looking at Slade, but still holding onto my handlebars.

Slade rolled slowly out onto the blacktop, pointed north, and rode away. He didn't gun the engine.

Jade finally turned and looked at me. "You can ride it around back and leave it under the shed. I'll open the door back there." She walked up on the porch, fished the key out of the flowerpot, and opened the door.

I hadn't moved.

She turned toward me. "What's my name?" she said, almost in a whisper.

"Jade . . ." was all I could manage to choke out.

She stood there, looking at me. "Well," she said, "are you coming?"

When I finally rode out of Wasa I didn't know why I was riding out of Wasa. Or any other place.

I left the café, and so did Jade, but we drove in different directions.

Maybe Jade was looking for the same thing we were. But then, what the hell were we looking for, anyway? Maybe, for me, it was right there in Wasa, another tiny spot of humanity smack in the middle of nowhere. Maybe a spot where I could come to feel at home. I could have just unstrapped the bike . . .

Or I could've followed Jade.

It was the same old shit going through my mind like it always did. I shoved it back into that mental compartment labeled "do not open" and left it there, with all the other shit.

I wondered whether I would find what I was looking for. I wondered whether I'd really know it if I found it.

Whatever it was I was looking for, it wasn't Radium Hot Springs.

Radium Hot Springs—that's what the sign said. I did not go there. There were some hot springs somewhere in the neighborhood, but I didn't stop. I love the hell out of hot springs but I really wasn't too enthusiastic about getting into hot water labeled "Radium."

But the ride out of Radium Hot Springs . . .

There comes a time in every rider's life when he finds the ride that might be indescribable. Every time I had found that ride, tried to really tell others what it was like, how it felt—I found a new ride that surpassed it. And the road from Radium Hot Springs to Banff and on to Jasper did just that—surpassed everything I'd ever ridden through. It wasn't that I was riding through the deepest gorge, or over the highest mountains, or through the thickest forest, or any of that stuff. It was that *every* view was off the scale, every curve a doorway into some other paradise. Each piece of everything I saw had been tweaked by nature in some small way that made it, well, not special, because that word simply is too plain to even begin to describe what I saw. The road to Jasper was dream-like. For a biker, it made no sense to go any farther. I could simply have ridden that road again and again until the bike just gave it up and fell apart.

My hands rose from the grips and I could feel the saddle

drop away from my body. I couldn't hear the engine. There was a sensation of moving and yet not moving, the bike seeming to ride itself, me carried along above it, doing nothing but looking, seeing, feeling the warm, comforting air sliding through my clothing. No cars came. No trucks. The road was mine, and mine only. Tall, silent, green trees melted past the edge of my eyes. The road was black, but for once the black was welcoming, a black invitation to something even more comfortable, even more to be driven toward. I was not touching the bike. The bike was not touching the road. The road was not touching Earth. It was the only time I'd ever ridden in a true dream state.

I could never compare that ride with anything. There were no other mountains that came close, no other mountain passes that I'd ridden over that were as vivid in my mind, nothing that developed the sensory overload that I experienced on the road to Banff.

I wish I had better words. I don't. I never will.

Would the ride have been half so mystic if I hadn't known Jade?

For once, I didn't try to figure it out.


I rode into Banff, the Aspen of Canada, where I caught up with Slade. It was simple. All I had to do was look for a KLR parked in front of some motel.

Banff. Streets without a cigarette butt. Stores that looked like sets from a Disney movie. What the hell was this place doing here in the middle of Canadian wilderness? But I could ask the same question about Aspen. And I knew the answer to both questions.

I just wanted to get the hell out of there.

And I wondered where Jade was.

18.

# DAY 10

Wednesday, September 4
from Banff, Alberta

Twenty-six degrees.

Another day of foul weather. Heavy clouds hid the tips of the mountains that cupped Banff like a child holds a precious toy. Rain drizzled lightly. We stood by the bikes, amazed that we could see our breath, wondering whether the bike covers would ever really get dry—they hadn't been dry since we left Colorado Springs.

Actually, I don't know why we bothered with the bike covers. Nothing but an avalanche would harm the KLRs—and I thought the avalanche might regret the encounter.

Today, we would cross Bow Pass, a major crossing in a major bunch of mountains on our way north to Jasper, and I wondered about ice on the road.

We were strapping gear on the bikes.

"Damn," I muttered.

"What's up?" Slade asked, his breath coming in a cloud.

"Lousy weather. Again."

Slade looked at me, smiling slightly. "We're nearly two thousand miles from home. We're riding motorcycles. Are we *not* going to ride because it's cold and wet?"

Damn, I hated it when he did that.

In my life, there have only been two or three guys I cared anything about riding with. Slade was one of them. He was, and is, the Number One of them.

But back in the older, scarier days, there had been Chaser . . .

\* \* \* \* \*

Nobody told Chaser that he shouldn't ride a motorcycle when the weather was bad.

When the rain began to slam across the highway and bikers dived into friendly gas stations or huddled under overpasses, Chaser kept riding. The others would catch up if and when they sucked up their courage and got their asses out into the wet. But Chaser would be long gone. Chaser was out there to ride.

He always called it "heavy weather." It didn't matter what sort of weather it really was, didn't matter that the wind was pounding his bike to a dead stop in the center of a wild and blackened road, didn't matter that the rain was piling water deeper across the pavement than his bike could run through, didn't matter that it was cold enough to freeze his leathers to the saddle, didn't matter that gale-driven dust was drilling into his chest like shot-gunned sandpaper—it just didn't matter. It was still just "heavy weather." And he still just rode. It took me a long time to figure out why he did that.

I learned part of it one night when we were on a high ridge

just off the Blue Ridge Parkway, wrapped in sleeping bags at the edge of a small clearing, working on a fresh bottle of Wild Turkey. The bikes were under the trees, mine covered with a nylon tarp, Chaser's covered with a quilt. ("Hell, I sleep under a quilt. What's wrong with a bike being under a quilt?") We were watching the sun go down, waiting to get sleepy, and looking into the valley far below at the tiny, twisting highway that we would ride tomorrow.

"That road down there," he said. "You ever notice that most roads are black? And that roads always run away from you? That black line running down there, it's always running away. It's important to know that, to know that roads run away."

Whiskey talk, I thought. Dumb hillbilly.

"Kid," he grumbled, speaking slowly and softly, as though to a child, "you just don't understand yet. But you will. See, I don't really live to ride, and I sure as hell don't ride to live. That's Harley PR bullshit. It's more than that. Riding is just one way to do it. There have been other ways, and there will be other ways still, long after all the motorcycles have been melted down to make deodorant cans. Some of us will always find a way to be, and being is what this is all about. And being is more than just riding. Hell, it's more than just living!"

At the time, I though he was full of crap—I was riding motorcycles long before I met Chaser, and I thought I knew something about riding. And living. And being, whatever the hell he meant by that. But, now, thinking back, I think Chaser knew a lot more than he ever tried to teach me. Some things, he just let me learn on my own, over the years.

To Chaser, riding was an expression. It was Chaser's way of sculpting, of painting, of making music, of creating some sort of art that only he understood.

And so I rode with Chaser, even in heavy weather.

His motorcycle was an ancient Harley, with a seat large enough for Chaser and any two women he happened to pick up along the way. The bike was heavy and powerful, strong enough to carry anything, and Chaser had bolted just about every attachment to it that he could hammer together in the barn out back of his house. He chose his bolt-on attachments, and the gear they carried, to fit his mood. He had a bow rack, and a gun rack, and a bunch of pipes and nylon straps that unfolded to make a chair. And sometimes a beach umbrella, carried head-down in a heavy tube behind the seat. I've seen him in the crystal light of a bright summer day, parked on a hill overlooking the river, the bike in the shade, the chair unfolded and padded with his leather jacket, the beach umbrella spread and shading him as he sat, book in his lap, reading and watching the river flow. When the weather wasn't heavy, he said, a man could also enjoy himself.

But it was the heavy weather riding we really shared. Once, near Myrtle Beach in South Carolina, we were caught in a hard blow—a small hurricane the locals said, nothing to be worried about. But it blew hard enough to move the Harley on its side stand, and that was the first time I ever saw Chaser look intently for cover—no bullshit about it, just find a hole to hide in. We ended up riding down off the highway, dropping over an embankment, and gunning the engines as the heavy bikes wallowed in the soft coastal Carolina soil, heading for the black mouth of a huge yawning culvert under the highway. In a culvert. In a storm. We were out of our fucking minds. And we stayed there for twenty-four hours, waiting for the water that never came.

And the late fall day in Greenbrier County, West Virginia, when Chaser decided he wanted lobster. Two days later we were parked on the waterfront at Freedom, Maine. Chaser couldn't find anywhere to buy lobsters. And then the coast of Maine seemed to forget that it was only late fall, not winter, and snow fell and collected on the leaves that still clung to some of the trees, and we lost the craving for seafood as our clothes soaked through and then took on that clinging, numbing cold that brought our hearts down below idling speed and kept them there. We tried to get away from the coast, but riding motorcycles in the snow was never one of my strong points, and we holed up again—this time in an abandoned garage. At least we thought the garage was abandoned. But when the lady who owned the garage saw us ride inside, she called the sheriff, whose four-wheel-drive vehicle had no trouble at all with the snow. He even brought a trailer so that we could load our bikes. So that he could haul both of us straight to the local jail. Where he put us up for the night in a warm cell with dry clothing, thick blankets and hot food. But no lobster. He even put a tarp over the bikes. Good man.

Never did get any lobster.

When I was younger I wanted every day to be perfect, full of sunshine from front to back, warm, calm, and windless. But that's not the way it is with riding. I learned that if I rode long enough and far enough and hard enough, if I rode when no one else was riding, if I rode in the black and in the light, and if I rode to take the full measure of the horizon from side to side in a single day, then, like Chaser, I would be a rider. And, like Chaser, I would make my own painting, play my own music.

But I always seemed to play my music alone.

Over the years, there weren't more than four riders I cared about being with for any length of time. I rode mostly alone, heard the music alone, covered the distance alone, beat down the road alone. There was a time when I climbed alone, afraid that my aching body and diminished skills would combine to harm anyone who went with me into the mountains. A time when I got broken alone, clubbed on the back of the head in a bar just outside of La Paz. I even loved alone, never seeming to be in the right place at the right time for the women I wanted to be in love with.

Over the years, it became a pattern.

And then one day I started to write, and I realized that I was writing alone, the stories all in a tight box that measured no more than the distance I could see down the road in front of me, the width of the highway I was on. I worried about writing like that, worried that there was not enough scope, enough magnitude.

And then I realized that, as a writer, I was only grinding out the detail on the path in front of me.

In other words, I was being.

Chaser would understand.

I lost Chaser somewhere in the years. He just disappeared. I rode back to his place in the mountains one time, but the gate was locked and the house had that forlorn look that houses take on without human beings in them. Chaser was gone.

I kept putting on the miles, wearing out my life on two unstable wheels cutting into tiny two-lane black roads in places with no names. Scribbling on the wrinkled pages of rain-soaked notebooks. Even after finding Slade.

But it was more than riding. More, even, than riding with Chaser. And it was more than the motorcycle. It was the searching-after that got to me, the constant moving about. It was the journey. The destination didn't seem to matter. It was the riding in heavy weather, yes, but it was also the riding when everything was perfect, when the bike flew on its own course, when nothing I did seemed to have any effect on my destiny, and I knew that whatever the day brought, that I had had no hand in any of it. It was the riding when the riding was totally incidental to what was really going on, when the riding just brought me there, and if I hadn't been riding, then I would have found some other way to find the bits and pieces of my life.

It wasn't just the motorcycle.

It wasn't just the riding.

It was the idea of the thing.

It was the looking and the finding out.

It was the black line running.

\* \* \* \* \*

We shook the icy water off the bike covers and cranked the engines. My bike had lulled me into some idea that it might just be curing itself from whatever mysterious ailment that afflicted it. But this morning it slid back into its old behavior. I used full choke to start it but had to keep the choke on long past normal. The engine seemed to rev on its own, and then fall back down, and then rev again, me standing there with my hand on a throttle that was not moving. But, finally, it seemed to settle down.

We started out of town—and the engine died. By now, Slade was used to the totally crazy actions of my bike. I waved him on past me, gave him a thumbs-up, and settled back to wait for the fucking engine to make up its mind.

I didn't know whether to love this bike or hate it. The engine would simply quit—and then start again. Like now. I rode the hell out of there, chasing Slade, listening to the engine like I had never listened to it before, wondering if I should duct tape the damn throttle wide open, hang on, and see how far I could go.

To love it or to hate it. Maybe that was a theme in my life. Love or hate, no middle ground. Because that's how I felt about Lancey.

The RVs and the camping trailers were slow. We were fast. We climbed steadily up the south side of Bow Pass, finally parking at an overlook. We took pictures, stretched, ate some trail food. We stood looking back the way we had come, down and off the pass and into the rapidly narrowing distance, tracing the road that we had ridden, watching as it disappeared into a thick mist that was chasing us up into the mountain range. As the mist flowed up the mountains like an incoming tide, the road below us disappeared into the wet gray. Standing there, it was as though I were looking into a deep mountain pass from before the advent of any mechanical thing that made men the soft and callow things that stare back at us from mirrors. There was nothing below me but steep canyon wilderness that formed a fold in the earth that could hold and hide a man until his time was finished. I could have stood there, maybe . . . until *my* time was finished.

Slade appeared beside me, looking.

"We were born a hundred years too late," I mumbled.

He said nothing, just looked into the distance. And then he breathed deeply. "Well, pardner, I think I might have been born at the right time. 'Course, I've spent a great deal of my time trying to drag your sorry ass into this century. I sort of consider it my obligation to society. And it's not easy—we have computers I could hide in the crack of my ass and you're still writing with a pencil and a pad of paper."

We stood silently, grinning, and then I heard tiny sounds, like grains of sand dropping softly on canvas. But it wasn't sand; it was snow, the hard little flakes hitting the shoulders of our riding jackets and bouncing down inside our collars.

I knew Slade was waiting for me to bitch about the snow, about the cold, but I didn't open my mouth. I mean, how could I say that I was born too late, and then bitch about a little weather?

And right then and there I knew what this ride was all about. It wasn't about the weather. I knew the weather would play a major role in everything we did on this ride, but the ride wasn't *about* the weather. This ride was about *us*, about Slade and me, about two aging, scarred humans who were still looking for something.

Maybe that really was all that Slade and I had been doing over all those years. Just looking for something.

That was okay with me.

That is, after all, what humans should do.

For the rest of the day we watched snow appear on the tops of the mountains as we rode through country that was too astounding to register properly in our minds. We rode in pristine beauty and loneliness. There were no billboards, no roadside tourist stops, no litter, no overflowing trash barrels, no utility poles lined up like wooden soldiers guarding the roadside. There was only the narrow black road running away, and away, and away.

The farther we rode, the farther the snow crept down from the tops of the peaks. Days later, we'd make a game of trying to measure the snow creep, trying to see how much farther down the mountains—how much closer to the road—the snow had come during the night.

We could see the Athabasca Glacier from the highway, and we slowed for a closer look, then wheeled the bikes off the road and down into a heavily graveled area where we parked. Slade had been on a couple of glaciers before, but I had not. Glaciers were, after all, cold, and I had carefully avoided them. What I knew about them was only what I had read. I did not know what to expect.

And I certainly did not expect the damn thing to have a personality.

The glacier was a huge, dark, foreboding mass that stretched away to the far ridges, the dark, dense ice brooding in the weak sun, as though waiting for some sort of creeping death, the quiet desperation written across its steeply tilting face. I could not figure it out. Was this glacier really different? It was, after all, nothing more than a thunderous collection of ancient ice.

A trail led from the gravel up a rise and toward the ice that glowered in the pale light. It was still spitting snow, and I was stiff from the freezing ride from Banff, glad to be able to walk for a while. Slade and I wore our riding clothes and crept along the gravel, approaching the glacier as though it might resent our presence.

There was a small wooden sign at the right side of the trail. It said, "1944." I wondered what had happened there in 1944 that merited a sign, a sign with no other information. And then we passed more signs—1955, 1972—and the reason for the signs became obvious; they marked the limits of the glacier in those earlier years. In ten minutes, we stood on the glacier itself and looked back over the decades to where the ice had been.

This glacier was dying. And it knew it.

From what I had read, I knew that seventy-five percent of the earth's fresh water was tied up in glaciers . . . and they were melting.

Where the hell would the water go?

We climbed steadily, on the ice now, working our way above the tracks of the few tourists who had been there since the last snow. An hour later we stopped and stood silently on the old ice, the fresh covering of snow already melting and making tiny grooves in the glacier, like age wrinkles. I tried not to dwell on the similarity.

We looked at the bikes down below, tiny rounded specks in the distance, parked where once the glacier had reached and covered, where no sane person would have walked, where now our bikes and a few cars desecrated the space of one of the world's largest natural things.

And then the personality, the emotion of the glacier was even clearer to me. The glacier was dying, but it was also very, very angry.

And so was I.

And we were both angry about the same thing.

Slade and I went back to the bikes and rode away from that place. I don't remember our speaking a single word while there, as though we were attending the wake of a famous person, didn't belong there, and had nothing to say that would make a difference.

Hours back on the road.

Maybe we really didn't have this figured out. Birds and tourists were moving steadily south as fast as they could go. Slade and I were moving steadily north. When tourists talked with us as we stopped beside the road, you could tell they thought we were crazy.

It never failed to intrigue us, the number of people who came up and talked to us. They showed amazement ("You're riding to *where?*"), concern ("Don't you know what time of year it is?"), fear ("Aren't those things dangerous? I mean, I know a guy who wrecked one . . .") Inevitably, they gave us warnings. ("Don't . . .")

And we probably were. Crazy. That was the fun part.

It was raining when we quit for the day. We parked the bikes parallel to each other with some space in between, then suspended a light mountaineering tarp over the space. We sat under the tarp and smoked cigars and let Irish Mist trickle down our throats.

Every day was hard.

Every day was a joy.

And everything was okay.

19.

# DAY 11

Thursday, September 5

from Jasper, Alberta

WE'D BEEN ON THE road for more than two thousand miles.

We rode out of Jasper under heavy clouds, riding due west. We thought the cloud cover would keep the temperature in warmer ranges, but we were wrong. This was Canada. The cold was with us when we got on the bikes, and before we were out of town it had ground its way up our arms and into our chests, and within fifty miles the cold had our heads and ribs shaking and our bladders bursting. When we had to piss we never bothered looking for a gas station or a café—in Canada, those things didn't line the roadsides. We just stopped wherever we wanted and walked into the heavy brush at the edge of the woods. There would always be woods and heavy brush.

We stopped at the same time, turned off the engines, and staggered into the trees, our legs stiff from the cold. If I could have pissed without taking off my gloves, I would have. But, somehow, that seemed like a bad idea. I tugged off the thick gloves and fumbled with my clothing, fingers slow and clumsy, arms not wanting anything to do with what was going on. I unzipped my armored riding coat, the heavy material stiff and unyielding. I unzipped my liner. My kidney belt covered the buckle and the top of the zipper on my insulated overpants, so I had to rip it off. I just dropped the damn thing on the ground. The buckle on the overpants was one of those fail-safe things, designed to stay put, once buckled. I could not get the thing open and thought I was going to piss in my pants. Finally, I got the buckle opened, only to encounter the snap at the top of the overpants' fly, and then the fly's hook-and-loop closure.

"*Fuck!*"

I got the snap and closure open, unzipped the fly, and then had to push down the sewn-in wind panel that covered the fly even when it's open. I pushed my overpants down to get at the hard-weave pants I wear to ride in, unzipped the pants, and reached inside, and fumbled with the fly of my heavy long johns. I finally got through those and then had to get inside the *thinner* pair of long johns that I wore next to my skin . . .

"*Goddammit!*"

"What's up?" Slade asked through the brush.

"*My goddamn dick is not long enough to pull out through all these goddamn layers! I think I'm gonna piss in my pants!*"

I could hear Slade laughing through the woods.

I don't think Slade ever had that trouble.

I didn't piss in my pants. Pure luck.

We didn't watch television, didn't hear the radio, didn't read newspapers, didn't go to movies. We had to think about it, sometimes, when we were curious as to what day it was. I could always look in my journal, but knowing what day it was did not seem to matter.

And somewhere in there, somewhere in those long, languid stretches of Canadian two-lane and dirt track, I once again reconciled with the machine, came to feel as though it were a part of me. When we stopped and got off, no matter the reason, all I wanted to do was get back on, even when I thought the damn thing was not running properly. But at least it hadn't quit on me. Not totally.

When we started this trip, the riding was something we did between stops for food, to piss, to sleep. It was how we filled in between the places where we stood still. But then, things changed. The riding, the wind, the road, the cold, the machine . . . they were all. Everything else was simply an interruption. If I was not moving, if the motorcycle was not moving, if the trees by the side of the road were not slipping by outside my face shield in steady, flowing progression, then I was uncomfortable. The tiny towns, smoke-filled cafés, cold camps, hot meals—no longer meant anything. They passed in a blur. We rode, ate, slept, and rode again. It was hard for us to stop to take pictures, or to stop at all, for any reason. Riding had become almost automatic. When we pulled into a roadside stop, we seemed to be almost in a hurry to mount up, ride off, keep going.

Gradually I realized that when we stopped for the night it seemed to be only preparation for the next day's ride.

I felt at ease only on the road.

And somewhere, there was a life in the riding.


The wind and the rain and the cold wore us down. We climbed stiffly off the bikes and staggered around wearing our heavy riding suits under which we had put on every supposedly warm thing we had. Yeah, yeah, I know, we could have equipped ourselves with electric vests, electric gloves, even electric jock straps. But we did not; that didn't even enter our minds. Especially my mind—there wasn't room for anything else in there. We didn't want electric, we wanted basic, elemental, hard rock. And that's what we got, and more.

All day we looked at the mountains, the valleys, lakes, rivers, at the clouds packing against the peaks. We were on some sort of overload, our minds not capable of seeing another mile of landscape too grand and too awesome to be believed. It all ran together and almost seemed to lose its importance.

Only the riding had meaning.

We stood and stared at Mt. Robson, the massif leaning against the sky. There was a time when it would have pulled me, just looking at it, knowing it was waiting, knowing it was there to be climbed. But no more. Robson and its kin could still call to me, but I had no desire to answer. Either that, or I didn't hear them. Perhaps I didn't want to hear them.

But it wasn't always that way. Life was not always on a motorcycle. Once, there were the mountains . . .

\* \* \* \* \*

My body always complained. Although I was driven into the mountains by some heat source that could only be dampened by climbing, my body never joyously attacked the trail or the mountain or charged my brain with intoxication at the thought of twelve hours of nonstop labor. For me, the pain came early and stayed, every time I started into the mountains.

Thirty minutes on the trail in the mountains, always the first thirty minutes, were the toughest. If I got past those, the other minutes began to dull and close until they ran into each other in an endless procession of meaningless time.

Thirty minutes, and never a downward step; each step a little higher, on and up, again and again, higher, staggering and straining. No level ground.

Maybe I'll never know why I did it.

Maybe the knowing is not important.

But one thing I do know—the days were not wasted. No day in the mountains is wasted, even if you do nothing. Because it's impossible to do nothing in the mountains.

The trail. Strangely, this may be the real heart of an expedition, the ultimate test of will, ultimate pushing of limits. In the mountains, there are many of those short, shocking, fearsome, adventuresome moments, moments that take away your breath, crush your chest, tighten your throat. But the trail, the boredom, the grind. Nothing so spectacular, so startling, just facing the undecorated truths of life, of learning that it can be done, of making something out of nothing, of just getting there.

Climbing the mountain was the reward. Getting to the mountain, that was the price you paid.

The best trails get a jump on the sun, running out of camp and into a fresh world long before first light comes splashing through the passes. It's a time to walk quietly, stepping into a world of which you are still a part. I always left camp in the dark and quietly.

Soon, on the trail, my body hummed and steamed, the parka shell came off, my collar opened, hat stuffed into a pocket. The sun flicked beams between rocks and trees, then climbed above me and began to cook my nose and the top of my head. I hiked for hours, grinding out the elevation, trampling out the distance. I was a free human in the free mountains with no place and every place to go.

The trail went on, and I went with it. I was part of the rock and the light, of the green trees and the blue and white sky, of the water and the earth, of the snow and the air, the heat and thump of booted feet, the sweat and the pull of shoulder straps.

And the weight on my back was not a burden. And I was not a stranger to Earth. The pain which came early and stayed was no longer an enemy. It was merely there, a reminder of the price and the reward, a constant notice of a lesser time when the body rebelled, but the mind pushed on.

And I forgot about it. And I was alive.

But we get older. We try different things to see if we are still alive. The challenges change, the body changes. I no longer dreamed of climbing Nanda Devi. Now, the mountains were all inside my mind.

\* \* \* \* \*

We started off slowly enough, that day, but as the ride got under our skin we rode faster, the bikes cutting the highway. And then, there by the side of the road, a black bear simply stood looking at us. We slowed slightly, but did not stop. Thus far, we had seen white-tailed deer, mule deer, elk, moose, buffalo, bald eagles, fox . . . and now this bear, staring as we went by. It did not move. We moved, sliding quickly by, its image a snapshot in our minds. But the picture on the top of my mind was not a bear. It was a buffalo, a thousand miles away.

We kept riding. We looked at more mountains, more rivers—the most beautiful rivers I had ever seen. So many rivers, so many river-names, that eventually, the river-namers had just given up: we crossed a bridge with a sign that simply said, "River."

Prince George, British Columbia. And the goddamn bike was making odd noises. I didn't know if it would last the trip. If it was going to quit, now would have been the time. I could have bought another bike in Prince George.

Too bone-cracking cold to camp. We got a room.

# 20

# DAY 12

Friday, September 6
from Prince George, British Columbia

WE STUMBLED OUT OF the room and into the northern light of
Prince George like bears out of hibernation, blinking, stiff, frozen, and absurdly hungry.

We ate stacks of pancakes dripping with butter and honey;
hash brown potatoes fried crispy on the bottom, eggs nestled
into their hot centers; and bacon layered over everything. We
drank orange juice and hot coffee. We ate as though we had not
eaten before, ever.

The temperature was twenty-eight degrees, and the bike covers were still frozen with ice and hard frost.

If the bike gave me trouble this morning, I was done with it.
But the damn thing started easily, even in the cold, and I didn't
hear the strange noises I'd heard yesterday.

By the time we left Prince George we were riding in brilliant
sunshine, hoping for one of those truly incredible days of being
on the road.

Bullshit.

Within thirty minutes we were in fog so thick that water condensed and ran down our face shields, inside and out, like rain from a tin roof.

As near as I could tell, our visibility was about twenty yards. We coasted down to a slow roll, trying to see the pavement that was as gray and wet as the frigid air that enclosed us, everything blending to form some sort of alien environment that seemed thick enough to hold the bikes upright, even if they weren't moving. This was crazy. If a truck came along, we would neither hear it nor see it. We would be unconscious.

We kept riding. We had to. We were nowhere, and that was always a bad place to be.

Every time I thought we'd ridden in the coldest conditions yet, the next day proved me wrong. And the ride out of Prince George was the coldest riding of all the days. The frigid temperature and the wet air—water hanging in the atmosphere like a shroud—stiffened our hands around the grips.

And then providence eased up on us . . . a little. A tiny roadside café. Slade was leading and he didn't see the thing until he was right in front of it. He wheeled hard to the left and for a moment I thought he was dodging something on the road. I wheeled over after him and then there we were, in the café's parking lot. There was only one car already there. One car—not a good sign.

We covered the bike seats in a vain attempt to keep the mist from condensing on them, and then clumped into the café as the Frankenstein monster must have walked. But the monster, as I recall, never drank coffee.

Amazingly, even though there was only one car outside, there were five or six locals sitting at the tiny tables.

We sat there for nearly an hour, too damn cold to be polite, saying nothing to the locals. I think Slade did nod his head, but my neck would not work so I simply sat like I had a log (instead of a stick) up my ass. We sipped our coffee and waited for the fog to lift, waited for our bones to thaw, waited for the world to change. It didn't.

The locals sneaked looks at us, slowly shaking their heads, feeling sorry for two Yanks dumb enough to be heading north, on motorcycles. They knew why we were in the café, what we were waiting for, and you could see smiles play now and then across their faces.

And there it was again, that wonderment that was always with me, that fleeting mental exercise that would put me at a table with the locals, being one of them, drinking coffee, and looking across the room at two dumbasses frozen nearly solid with nothing in front of them but more of the same. I wondered what I'd do, as a local, when I finished my coffee and walked out of the café. Would I go home? Did I have a job? After all, what was I doing in a café in the middle of nowhere, in the middle of the morning, on a workday?

When I left the café, was there a woman waiting for me?

For a brief moment, I thought about Lancey, wondering where she was and what she was doing. And who she was doing it with. And Snake, who apparently had called the cops. I wondered if he locked the door when he sat on the toilet.

I looked at Slade. He sat silently, motionless, his eyes and his mind not in the room. I thought maybe he was thinking about Modene, wondering, maybe, why the hell he was here, farther north than men on motorcycles were supposed to be at this time of year, wondering why he was not with Modene, drinking tequila, a fire dancing in the fireplace. But I did not ask.

The locals knew the fog wouldn't lift, and it never did. So we rode on. That was why we were there.

An hour later we rode out of the fog into sunshine.

We stopped for lunch in Burns Lake; had some really decent food. But that was not unusual. Almost every place we stopped had good food.

We ate, drank some more coffee, and went outside, carrying our helmets. When we went into a café we always tried to leave the bikes where we could see them through the window, but this time that hadn't happened. So we hadn't noticed as a small clump of young guys, probably high schoolers, gathered around the bikes. We wanted to talk to them but the moment we appeared in the doorway of the café they melted away, moving down the street in a practiced dance of not-too-fast, but definitely not-too-slow.

I realized it was a school day. Other young people walked and sat in clumps along the town's main street—maybe the town's only street, probably on lunch break. I leaned against my bike and watched them, wondering if young guys were pretty much the same, no matter where you found them.

Four young guys, Indians, sat on a long wooden bench on the sidewalk near our bikes. Across the street some white girls lounged against the front of a small restaurant and sat on the trunk of an old sedan parked at the curb. White boys were scattered along the street, watching the girls. Watching the Indians. The girls called across the street to the Indians, laughing and making comments behind their hands. It seemed good-natured, but I wasn't sure. The Indians looked at the girls, but they never moved, never spoke, never smiled. One of the girls walked out into the middle of the street and stood, feet apart, hands on hips in a classic suggestive pose out of some bad movie. She said something to the Indians, something low in her throat that I couldn't hear.

One of the Indians stood up.

The girl quickly retreated to the far curb. At the same time, one of the white boys stood up and hitched up his pants, took a couple of steps toward the street. I've always wondered how such a simple gesture as hitching up your pants could be threatening, but it was. Just depended on when and where, I thought.

I could see the tension in some of the other whites. Another white boy stepped forward. One step. The rest were waiting.

The Indian stayed on his feet, but did not move.

The first white boy took another step.

And then Slade ghosted up behind the bench. He made a small, slow show of putting his helmet on the ground, and then he just stood there.

The boys across the street thought it over. And then they simply left, sauntering away down the sidewalk.

The girls piled into the old sedan and drove away, smoke trailing from the exhaust pipe.

The Indian, still on his feet, turned and looked at Slade.

"We could handle it," he said quietly.

"There was never any doubt," Slade said, picking up his helmet and walking toward the bikes.

We got on the bikes and started to put on our helmets.

"Thanks, anyway," I heard the Indian say, just loud enough for us to hear.

Slade put his helmet on, looked at the Indian, and nodded. And punched the starter button.

When Slade and I rode out of town, the boys still sat, staring across the street. I wondered, for a First Nations boy in high school, how wide that fucking street was.

I thought about Kateri. She would have known the width of that street. I thought of her every day. The memories had long since stopped being painful. Now, they were like a warm blanket that sustained me.

I needed sustaining. Riding out of town I knew how close we'd come to something bad. Slade and I used to sit beside some stream in the deep woods, watching the water, talking about how close we were to the cave. Not a real cave. A metaphoric cave—the cave we all lived in at one time, a cave where we watched for others coming into our territory, within reach of our cave. The others may have looked like us, maybe not. No matter; we were scared of them, and probably hated them because we were scared, all before any of us had spoken a word, made a sign, reached for a weapon. That shit was still in most of us, immediately under the skin, where it could burst out into the emotional atmosphere at even the slightest provocation.

We were still protecting our cave.

Some of us still lived there.


The lake appeared through a long gap in the trees off the left side of the road. I paid no particular attention to it. It was long, narrow, and I couldn't see where it began and where it ended, the sun, for once, glistening from the dark water. I was trailing Slade by a few hundred yards, and when I glanced ahead I realized that he had wheeled left across the road and had stopped in a patch of grass, facing the lake. He got off his bike and stood looking at the water. I parked beside him.

We stood there, our helmets off, a tiny breeze cooling our faces. I had no idea what we were doing there, but I knew Slade would explain it, sooner or later. Or maybe not.

I heard the sputtering engine of a plane, the sound coming from far down the lake, the plane out of sight behind a thick stand of trees. Slade pointed in the direction of the sound.

"A float plane," he said. "Heard him coming in. His engine was not running right. Saw his floats—looked old, used hard." Slade glanced at me. "It's an old plane. Don't know what's holding it together."

I said nothing.

We stood there, listening to the pilot fiddle with the throttle, the engine fighting his every move. And then we heard the unmistakable sound of an airplane engine being revved for takeoff. But this engine was still sputtering.

The plane came roaring into sight. As we watched, the pilot got the aircraft up onto plane on the water, and his speed increased. And then the engine stopped sputtering, winding under full power, dragging the plane from the water and throwing it into the air. In a few seconds he was gone, far down the lake and skimming the tops of trees.

Slade glanced at me, then looked down the lake where the plane had disappeared. "Could have used some baling wire," he muttered.

Strange, I thought, how small things can trigger big memories. Slade stood silently, staring. I knew where he was.

\* \* \* \* \*

We saw the old airplane land on the pitted dirt strip. It was a piece of junk, a clumsy high-winger, seemingly held together with duct tape and spit. The wings looked as though they did not belong to the fat fuselage, and the prop made an odd sucking noise as it wound down. But that pieced-together thing had been in the air. The pilot and two other guys got out. They didn't even tie the plane down, just walked away to a battered pickup truck and a rusty van that were parked across the strip. They got in the truck and drove away, didn't look at the van.

We needed that plane.

We lost a man in Baja.

Well, we didn't exactly lose him. We knew exactly where he was—Rico's body was rolled up in canvas, lying in the brilliant sunshine, rapidly heating up.

I looked back at the old airplane that maybe once upon a time had been some sort of Piper. The wing struts probably were held on with baling wire. Nonetheless, I thought the plane might make it back into the air. So did the Cuban.

For once, we had not been doing anything illegal. Just four Norte Americanos, wearing shorts, boat shoes, sunglasses, and floppy hats—for once, trying to look and be exactly what we were, tourists, fishing off a little dirt-ball town on the west shore of the Sea of Cortez, our boats far out into the miles-wide channel across to Carmen Island, the water as smooth as the surface of a mirror, Slade and I in a tiny sailing vessel, big enough to hold us and a fish or two. And some beer. Rico and the Cuban were in sea kayaks, paddling maybe fifty yards away, at peace, soaking into the solitude, fishing lines dangling behind their boats.

And then the other boat came. It was some sort of powerboat, large, the throb of its engines rolling across the water. The boat had sneaked around the south end of Carmen Island and was loafing its way toward us, in no particular hurry. A couple of men stood on the front deck, relaxed, leaning against the railings.

It was obvious the boat was coming toward us. Slade and I took in our little sail and went dead in the water. The kayaks were about fifty yards away. The big boat seemed to ignore them, heading straight toward Slade and me. I could hear the engines being cut and the boat slid silently closer, its hull painted a mixture of dull white and mottled blue.

Slade and I put down our fishing gear.

The men on the bow did not move and neither did we. And nobody smiled.

A door on the side of the cabin opened and another guy stepped through and moved up between the guys at the railing. He looked over at the kayaks, and then back at Slade and me.

"Where is it?" he asked, his voice just loud enough in the silence of Baja for us to hear the stone in his words, no trace of an accent.

Slade and I looked at each other. "Where is what?" I said, trying to sound mystified. And I was. I had no idea what the guy wanted.

"I will ask again, politely," the guy said, a slight smile on his face, "and then I will stop being polite." The smile went away.

Slade and I glanced at each other. Whatever it was that the guy wanted, we sure as hell didn't have it. But I was certain the guy on the boat would not believe that.

"We have nothing that would interest you," Slade said, his voice soft and level.

In a smooth motion, one of the other men reached behind him and brought out a short-barreled rifle, an enormous magazine sticking out of the bottom. He didn't point the gun at us—he pointed it at the kayaks.

"You gringos come here and you interfere with our business. You bring your own merchandise and you hide it on our islands." He flicked his head in the direction of Carmen. "Naturally, we take offense."

Yeah, I could see that.

"Now, one last time, please tell me where it is."

We were in some serious trouble, but there was absolutely nothing we could do. We did not have what the guy wanted—believe me, we would have given it to him—and we had no means of escape. Rico and the Cuban had guns, but they would be useless against the men on the boat. Slade and I stood up and put our hands over our heads. If they were going to shoot us, we made great targets.

The guy with the gun twisted toward the kayaks, brought the gun up, and fired a short burst at the Cuban. He was good. If he'd meant to hit the Cuban, the Cuban would be dead. Instead, the bullets tore off about a foot of the bow of the boat. The Cuban flipped over sideways and dumped himself into the water. The Cuban was very good in the water and I knew he would try to stay out of sight. But I also knew that if the big boat wanted to find him, it could.

I could see Rico shaking his fists, arms waving. I knew he was screaming at the shooter.

And then he made a mistake. He dug down inside the cockpit

of his boat, pulling gear out. The butt of a rifle stuck up into the sunlight, both of Rico's hands on it.

Goddamn dumbass kid.

The guy on the boat calmly swung on Rico, lined up, and opened up, the gun chattering a deadly cadence. Rico's arms flew up, and he slammed backwards out of his boat. The rifle flipped up into the air, then disappeared into the Sea of Cortez. I thought one of Rico's legs had tangled in the gear that he had been thrashing through, but I couldn't be sure.

The guy kept shooting.

Then the universe went silent and still. Nobody spoke or moved, not us, not them. Slade and I still stood in our little boat, our hands still up. I had never felt more impotent, more useless, in my entire life.

The door of the big boat's cabin slammed open and another guy stuck his head out. "Vámanos!" he screamed. Without waiting for the men to get off the deck, the boat's engines came alive like hard thunder, the stern dug into the water, the bow rose, and in a very short time the boat was skimming away to the north on a hard straight line.

We didn't know what scared them off, and we didn't care. We had oars on our little boat and we got the thing moving toward Rico.

We never got there.

From around the south end of the island—exactly where the other boat had come from—another boat appeared, a gray metal, clunky, military-looking speed boat, a .30 caliber machine gun mounted on the front. They were pushing the boat hard, not quite making a plane, still enough metal in the water to throw a heavy bow wave, slamming past the kayaks close enough to reach out and touch them. Or turn them over. It didn't matter. There wasn't much left of the kayaks, anyway.

I couldn't see the Cuban, or Rico.

The gunboat swung toward us.

Federales.

And then the bastards fired over our heads just for fun, making Slade and me duck and finally fling ourselves into the water. When I came up I saw the Cuban swimming for the island. We swam after him. The Federales kept firing, concentrating on our little sailboat. The three of us managed to get ashore but our bullet-riddled boat was trash, floating on the gentle waves like a broken toy.

And that's when we saw Rico's boat.

What was left of Rico's kayak was floating upside-down, the bottom of the hull barely breaking the surface, most of the cowling around the boat's cockpit sawn off by the stream of bullets, bits of fiberglass blown away like confetti in a breeze.

Rico's body dangling in the wreckage. Rico had taken heavy hits in the head and chest.

Rico, the kid from Kansas City who wanted to be a part of an adventure, a part of anything, whose family—whose priest—said to stay away from us; we weren't real. "Please, Rico, don't take a job like that." But Rico went with us. To Rico, we were real.

The Cuban wrapped Rico's body in the tattered sail from our boat. He would not let us help.

The fishing trip was over. I don't know how many times over the years we did something for fun, and got fucked for doing it. And it had happened again.

I could hear Slade arguing with the Federales. I could see his hands curled into fists. I stood up.

And then Slade came back to us, trailed by the Federales, six of them, all carrying automatic weapons.

The Federale in charge, El Capitán, was fat. I always wondered about that—why was the guy in charge always fat?—and he did not smile.

"He says the shooting was in defense of Mexican sovereignty. Says they saw a drug transaction taking place, and an American pulling a weapon from his boat. They knew they could not catch the other boat, but they could catch us."

"Motherfucker," the Cuban muttered, looking directly at the capitán. The capitán pretended not to understand. Maybe he didn't.

I could tell from the way Slade was talking that he thought the capitán knew the whole thing was total bullshit.

"There's more," Slade said. "He's going to hold us all overnight in the local jail, then take us to La Paz for questioning, give us the opportunity to 'clear ourselves.'"

I started for the fat captain. Slade grabbed my arm. "No," was all that he said. The capitán looked surprised that I would even move.

They loaded us into the patrol boat and headed west across the channel. They left what remained of our gear on the island.

On the way over, Slade whispered to me, "If we go to La Paz, we're going to be in Mexico for a very, very long time." And that's all he needed to say.

We put ashore at a ramshackle wooden pier just north of the tiny village where we originally had bought our supplies for our fun fishing trip. Our van was gone. We staggered ashore, the Cuban carrying Rico. We moved away from the beach, up the slope, seeing a few lonely shacks on a nearby flat and what appeared to be a dirt landing strip. There were no planes on the strip, only an old pickup and a rusted-out, ancient van.

The capitán looked at Rico, then gestured to Slade. They stepped aside, the capitán talking and gesturing. The other Federales stood in loose formation around us, their fingers on the triggers of their guns.

This could not be good.

Slade came back to the Cuban and me. "Once again, there's more," Slade said, his mouth twisted in a sardonic smile. "Down here, the capitán says, we have only a short time to bury a body. Mexican law. Health reasons. To keep the people safe. We have to bury Rico within the next few hours, or we all go to the local jail, even what's left of Rico."

The capitán was smiling. "Ahora!" he said.

"Let me get this straight," I said to Slade in English, "first we go to jail here, in some fucking little village, and then when—and if—we get out of there, we go to La Paz, where we probably will be held for fucking ever!"

Slade just looked at me. I knew that look.

The Cuban slowly stood up. The Federales had never searched us and I knew he had a gun in a plastic bag strapped under his shirt. Slade reached over and put his hand on the Cuban's arm. He said nothing, just put his hand on the Cuban's arm. The Cuban stood motionless.

The capitán caught the movement. He nodded and his men casually spread farther out on both sides of us.

"But I am a reasonable man," he said in Spanish, still not smiling. "In the town, there is a man who does funerals, an empresario. What do you call him? Yes, an undertaker. I know him quite well. He is my cousin." He paused again. Got no reaction from us. "If you take your friend to my cousin, the . . . undertaker . . . he will prepare him properly and will see that you get an extra day, perhaps two, to make the correct arrangements."

The fat bastard paused again. Nobody moved. Slade still had his hand on the Cuban's arm.

"And he is a fair man. His costs are very reasonable."

I could feel the Cuban tensing up, could see Slade's fingers tightening on the Cuban's arm.

"We will all leave now. We will go to my cousin's, the empresario. And, of course, we wish to be of help, so I will have one of my men lend you his autobus. That is it, over there." He nodded toward the ancient van parked at the edge of the runway. "And, of course, he will stay close with you, just to show you the way, and to be of any other service. It is not far. It will take only a few minutes. And, of course, you have no other place to go, and nothing to go there in . . ." he chuckled at his little joke "so I am sure I will see you at my cousin's."

The bastard nodded at his men, and they strolled back to the dock and their boat. The last two guys did not get in, just stood there while the boat pulled away. They turned and looked at us, their automatic rifles dangling from their hands. One of the men pointed toward the old van. "Aya, ahora," he said.

And that's when we saw the plane come in and land on the dirt strip. It was like a gift.

I took a step toward the Federales. "Do you speak English?" I asked.

They said nothing.

We all spoke Spanish, but that wasn't the point. I wanted to know if we could speak openly in front of him, in English.

Turns out, it didn't matter.

The Cuban walked within a couple of paces of the Federales. Their hands tightened on the rifle straps, but they didn't unsling the weapons. Thank God for bad training.

The Cuban had a big smile on his face and his hands held casually behind him. In one of his hands he held his pistol, still wrapped in plastic. He stepped in front of the biggest man.

"You smell like a pig. That's probably the smell your sister has. You got it from her, when you dropped her off at the whorehouse last night. Just before you fucked your grandmother on the steps of the church." The Cuban held his big smile.

The big Federale looked at each of us. We all smiled. And then he smiled and said, "Sí." The fucker did not speak English. If he did, that crazy Cuban would have gotten us all killed. The other man didn't move.

The ending was not very dramatic.

The Cuban simply slammed an elbow into the side of the Federale's neck and the guy went down instantly. At the same time, he whipped the pistol around and pointed it at the other guy's face. The pistol was still in the plastic, but the Cuban's finger was clearly on the trigger. The Federale let his weapon slide to the ground.

We took their weapons and extra ammo, tied them up with their own belts and straps, and left them stashed behind some rocks.

The Cuban said to them, very quietly, "If I see a head come up above the rocks, I will shoot the top of it off."

We grabbed Rico and walked, as casually as we could, toward the plane.

It was time to take Rico home.

The plane looked like something from a scrapyard covered with wing-like awnings to keep the junkyard dogs out of the sun. One wing strut was, in fact, held on with the help of baling wire, but we didn't give a damn. We put Rico in the back, Slade tossed his wire cutters to the Cuban, and then we stood at the side of the plane with one of the Federale guns. The Cuban got underneath the plane's control panel with his knife and Slade's wire cutters. In about three minutes the prop was turning. The Cuban got in the back with Rico, Slade took the controls, and I sat in the copilot's seat with the guns.

Slade messed with the controls. The engine sputtered and spit, but Slade kept doing his thing, and we rolled out onto the end of the runway. It's tempting to say that Federales came running after us, firing at the plane—just like in the movies—but that didn't happen. There was absolutely no one anywhere near the strip. Slade opened the throttle, the fucking engine fighting him all the way, Slade talking to the engine, threatening it, I think. And we left the ground. The weird old plane did everything but roll over to try to dump us out on Baja, but it was being flown by Slade. It would do what it was told.

Slade curled the plane out over the Sea of Cortez, all of us looking down at where we'd just been and probably would never be again.

When we landed on the mainland I thought we'd be shot on sight. But some civilian guys came running out to help us, actually help us. I was afraid they'd recognize the plane, but, if the did, they gave no sign. We told them that we had come from a tiny town to the south, that we needed our plane gassed up. In the meantime, we said, we were going to walk into town and find a café.

They pushed the plane in front of a ramshackle hangar and went about their business with the gas. And the Cuban stole a van. No big deal—he just stole a van. We loaded Rico and the guns, and we drove away, away from the Federales, away from the patched-together plane.

Rico was not expendable.

Rico was not forgettable.

We took Rico home.

# 21

# DAY 13

Saturday, September 7
from Smithers, British Columbia

WE CAME INTO SMITHERS in the early evening, the air crisp and clean, the town almost silent.

I had been cold all day, and I desperately needed yet another layer under my riding coat. Slade and I walked around until we found a sort-of clothing store. Maybe sort of like an American GI-surplus store. Maybe not. There was only one person in the store—the woman behind the counter. I tried to get her talking. I was always interested in the locals, how long they'd lived there, why they lived there, what was next in their lives.

Bullshit. I was always interested in women.

But the woman said little, just stared at us in our heavy riding gear, a look on her face that I came to recognize. Maybe I'm being dramatic, but the look said, "Wherever you are going, I want to go, as long as it's away from here." I'd see this look again, and then again.

I saw the look every time I looked in the mirror.

The store was not into high-tech stuff. The warmest thing

they had was wool, so I bought the heaviest shirt I could find, thick, high collar, weighed a ton. It would have to do.

We rode out of Smithers in crystal sunshine, the air so warm that I was sweating inside all of my clothes, riding with my jacket open, the warm, sweet air filling my sleeves like balloons. I stopped and took off the shirt I'd bought the night before and stuffed it in my luggage.

Within thirty minutes the sun was gone, and we were in the rain again.

We swept into an easy turn, then straightened out for a mile or so, the speed creeping up, the rain blowing across our face shields. Then, for a moment, we popped out into the clear. No rain. The heavy mists capped the trees, and the highway was a narrow black line boring through a gray tube of thin light, focusing our attention on the misty world in front of us.

And then the bear cub appeared out of the thicket on the right side of the road and stopped dead center, not more than fifty yards ahead of me. I got off the throttle and let the bike run down. The cub, startled, looked back the way it had come, unsure of what to do next. I thought I knew what was back there, and I was right—the mother bear shot out of the thicket on the right and hit the cub on a dead run, knocking it like a huge, soft eight ball farther across the road and into the brush on the left side. Without slowing, the mother bear turned back, slammed into the brush, and reappeared almost at once, pushing another cub in front of her. The mother and the second cub jammed into the heavy growth on the left side of the road and all three bears disappeared instantly.

We eased the bikes forward, slowly gearing down, ready to bolt away from the mother bear. I had read once that black bears can run at thirty-five miles per hour, and I wasn't about to get caught in a gear that couldn't get me up past forty and get me up there damn fast. But the mother bear was not about to come back out on the road. As we went past, we could see the two cubs up in a tree not more than five yards off the side of the pavement, the tree so skinny that the weight of the cubs was bending it toward the road. The mother crouched at the bottom, her back hunched, ready to take on all comers.

Not us. We gassed the bikes and got the hell out of there.


At Kitwanga we were supposed to turn north onto the Cassiar Highway. And we did, for about fifty yards. The rain was coming down in a heavy mist, not exactly drops, not exactly fog, the mist so thick I thought it was more like the foam in whitewater than actual rain, so cold it seemed to be sticking to my face shield.

The intersection at Kitwanga was as desolate as any place I had seen on that ride. At the side of the road, dark gravel ran with water like the bottom of a streambed. Three or four old, leaning, wooden buildings hunkered blackly at the edge of even blacker trees that seemed to be frozen in place, the trees held upright by a sheer force of nature, surviving against all odds.

But one of the old buildings was a café.

Slade and I have always operated pretty much on the same wavelength, but, still, it sometimes surprised me. I wheeled off to the right toward the café, only to find Slade right beside me. We'd come off the road at exactly the same time. We parked the bikes, not attempting to cover the saddles. It was too late for that.

There were no cars in the parking lot, and yet there were a half-dozen men in the café, lounging deep into their chairs, sipping from hot cups, and, of course, looking at us.

The scene always repeated itself: a tiny café; no cars, and yet men inside, looking at us as though we were crazy. Where the hell did they come from? How do men in Canada, and, we would learn later, in Alaska, materialize inside cafés not large enough to hold a decent brawl? We never figured it out.

Sugar has never been a big thing for me. I seldom eat dessert, and I can't remember the last time I bought a candy bar. But when we got our coffee and sat down, Slade noticed a pan of brownies on the counter. The brownies had already been cut for serving, and they were the size of bricks.

Sometimes I wonder about the things I remember, or don't remember. I have to concentrate to remember the details of how I broke a particular bone—but I knew I would remember the taste of those brownies for the rest of my life.

Later, Slade and I agreed, those were miracle brownies. They had saved our lives.

Back on the road, the rain had quit fooling around. No more heavy mist, no more rain-like substance. Now, it was pissing down in a torrent.

But we were on the Cassiar. *The Cassiar.* Slade and I had been looking for this place. The highway ran due north, and for the first time I felt as though I were actually heading for Alaska. Yeah, I know, I'd had this feeling before, but, damn, here it was again. We were heading *due north*.

The rain severely limited our vision, and the highway seemed to grow narrower as the thick, low ridges on both sides closed in to press the bikes against the road. It wouldn't be long, I knew, before we would hit the mud. No short run through a small canyon, like back in Colorado, but real mud, miles and miles of it.

And we did.

The Hazelton Mountains, and then the Coast Mountains, pushed in from the west and squeezed the Cassiar into a lush valley heavy with mist and cold. The trees were still green, but every now and then some tiny patches of gold showed on the branches, and the scent of snow was in the air.

Hours later we rounded a gentle turn, rolled down an easy slope, and came to the Belle Lodge, a Tyrolean-type hotel and cluster of cabins in the middle of the wilderness. It was like finding daylight at the end of a frigid tunnel. It was early, but we couldn't resist. We turned into the driveway, and looped around in front of the lodge, and shut down the engines. We'd had enough rain for the day.

It looked as though we might have the place mostly to ourselves. There was only one car and a box truck—some sort of delivery truck—parked there. The truck had a damaged British Columbia license plate, as though the driver had continually backed into something and didn't give a damn about the plate. But the thing that caught my eye was a very bad painting of a wolf's head on its door, the wolf snarling out through a coating of mud.

Here, at Belle Lodge, we found civilization—a warm cabin, a restaurant, hot food.

We removed our wet clothes, took hot showers, put on anything that was dry, and went to the restaurant in the main lodge. There was only one other customer, a thirty-something guy, thick through the shoulders and heavy through the body, who sat at a table in the far corner, his huge arms surrounding his plate as though guarding his food. He was bald, his head shining. A gnarled mustache rose and fell as he chewed. He did not look up.

We had hot, thick vegetable soup, freshly baked bread, and pot roast, as comforting a meal as I'd ever eaten.

We were in bed before it was even full dark.

# 22

# DAY 14

Sunday, September 8
on the Cassiar Highway, British Columbia

THE CASSIAR HIGHWAY.

I had to get ready for the rest of it. I went outside and checked the bikes. My bike cover seemed to sag oddly, and when I touched it, it cracked, or more like . . . crinkled. It made tiny ice sounds as the material tried to shed its layer of thick frost. Heavy cloud cover kept the light muted and gray, and I could feel moisture in the air that was too heavy for mist and too light for rain. I stared at the sky for about a minute, then went back inside, my ass beginning to freeze.

Slade was already packing. We gathered our gear and loaded the bikes. My bike started easily, for once, and we rode the short distance to the parking area in front of the restaurant. Again, the only other customer in the place was the big guy, at the same table, his arms again circling his plate, guarding his food. He did not look up.

We hurried through breakfast, eager to get back on the road, although we knew it was going to be a cold, wet, muddy day. But it was what we had come for.

The big guy at the other table left just before we did, and through the window I could see him getting into the box truck.

Slade and I went outside and started our bikes, leaving them to warm up on their side stands. As we were pulling on our riding gear the box truck started to back up, swinging in a wide arc as the driver turned the front of the truck toward the highway. But the truck kept turning, the heavy rear bumper heading directly for my bike. If it kept coming, it would pin the bike between the truck and some heavy timbers that bordered the parking area and bend the damn thing like a wet pretzel. For a few seconds I thought the driver would see our bikes and stop, but then I realized he did not. Or that he did not care. And by then it was too late to grab the bike and shove it the hell out of the way.

"*Hey!*" I screamed. "*Stop, goddammit!*"

The truck kept coming.

I jumped to the driver's side of the truck as Slade jumped to the other side. Both of us pounded on the side of the truck and yelling. The truck stopped.

The truck door opened and the big guy got out. He walked to the back and looked at his bumper, which was actually touching my bike's rear wheel. And then he stared at me.

"Don't ever touch my fucking truck again," the guy growled, his voice coming from somewhere dark.

I could feel the old blackness rolling up through my chest, could feel my body tense. I shifted my feet slightly, thinking that I could get a shot at his throat before he could react—and then, out of the corner of my eye, I saw Slade lift his hand. Think about it, he was saying.

I thought about it. This guy wasn't the Snake. He was just an asshole whose old man didn't use a condom.

While I was thinking about it, the guy turned and walked back to the cab, got in, and slowly pulled away onto the muddy road. Very slowly. Telling us he was in no particular hurry to get away from us.

Slade and I stood there, watching the truck drive out of sight into the rain that was now misting down into the valley. It took less than half a minute to disappear.

My hands were clenched at my sides, my body shaking, my teeth grinding. The trees across the road marched through the mist, tall spiky solders moving in unison. I squeezed my eyes shut, knowing that my mind was falling into some anger-driven vision. But even with my eyes shut, I still saw the trees, could still see the truck.

Slade's hands were on my shoulders and he was shaking me gently. "C'mon," he said, and he turned back toward the restaurant.

"What?"

"I haven't had enough coffee," he said, grinning. I knew he wanted to snap the vision, bring me back to a lonely highway in the rain. I also knew he just didn't want me to get on the bike and chase the truck. Sometimes Slade could be a real pain in the ass.

We stood by the bikes, realizing that we were underdressed. While we were back inside the restaurant, the temperature seemed to have hit bottom, the stuff falling out of the sky unsure whether it was supposed to be light snow or thick mist. I rummaged through my gear and dragged out everything that I thought could provide warmth, including my new shirt. I put it all on, every shirt, every liner, *everything*. I stood at the side of the bike, wondering how the hell I would raise my leg high enough to lift it over the saddle. I had so many clothes on that my arms would not hang straight down at my sides; they hung outward at an angle, like Charlie Brown dressed for the snow.

We left the lodge in the rain. At least it wasn't snowing . . . yet. The Coastal Mountains seemed to crowd the highway even more, the road rising with the hills and pushing the bikes up into the mist. Clouds sat on the ridge tops and seeped into the canyons, heavy with moisture, the rain drizzling constantly. We could see only the lower slopes and the tops of trees that seemed to hang on the near horizon. The temperature was trying to make up its mind. If it stayed like it was, we'd ride in the rain. If it became colder, we'd ride in the snow.

It did. And we did.

And then the realization hit me. It was all so very clear . . .

*The Cassiar was no fucking highway!* Highway? That was just some PR story the Canadians threw out there. Two narrow unpaved lanes ran swirling through a choked, wet valley, pressed hard to the west by the Cassiar Mountains and to the east by an ever-reaching expanse of rising forest that seemed struggling to reach heights it would never know. But it tried. The tops of the trees disappeared into heavy gray clouds that capped the valley and spit rain, snow, and sleet down at us with the impunity of a Nature that cared nothing for tiny men on tiny machines.

The lanes were mud and gravel and standing water, and somewhere under all that muck the oil and grease drippings of hundreds of big rigs worked their way into the very substance of the road muck and then up onto our tires, our boots, our riding pants, and our souls, the entire road made dark and hungry by the thin light that somehow crept through the overcast.

On each side of the road wide ditches, running full of water, tracked the lanes. In some places the ditches looked five or six feet wide. I had no idea how deep they were, and I tried not to think of finding out the hard way.

We kept the bikes at speed, trying to ride the surface of whatever the hell we were riding on, but now and then the bikes slewed to the side, the tires losing their tenuous grip on a tenuous surface and on our tenuous lives. Water and oily mud flew into the air, and we rode a hundred yards apart just to stay out of each other's way.

Our bikes threw paintball globs of muck up and onto our face shields, but we didn't dare touch them, just tried to see through the tiny spaces that were still open. To touch the shields would be to smear the pasty muck across them, blinding us. We would have to stop and clean the shields, looking over our shoulders through the gloom for huge trucks that weren't looking for us, that never changed lanes, trucks that would feel nothing, hear nothing, even if they rolled entirely over us. I'd never thought of trucks in that way before—machines so big, so heavy, that we'd be no more than a twitch of the drivers' steering wheels as they thundered over us.

But there were no trucks. Yet.

Snow had fallen in the night. Now, we did not know what was falling, only that it was wet and soaked into every tiny opening in our riding gear.

The guy at the lodge last night said that the "highway" was mostly paved. He lied.

I led, keeping up as much speed as I could, trying to reach the pavement that was never there. But this was the Cassiar, a place we'd been heading for, wanting, dreaming about for days, months. And now we were here, and it was kicking our asses.

I heard the roar first and then I think I actually felt the damn thing, even through all the mud. A truck was coming up behind me, coming hard. I could feel him closing in, could hear the primeval thunder of the engine, could feel my fingers squeezing grooves in stainless-steel handlebars. Problem was, I didn't even know if the driver knew I was there.

Slade was back there, and I was pretty sure that he was not between the truck and me, although I was afraid to look back, afraid of losing control of the bike. Just afraid.

Like my old friend Chaser had once said, "There are few problems on a bike that can't be solved by more gas." I gave the bike more gas and managed to open up a wider lead on the truck, praying to Sweet Mother Earth for a piece of pavement, a wide space, a gap in the trees, a break in the ditch at the side of the road—anything! Any fucking thing!

The road rose in front of me, a new steepness added to everything else. I felt the bike try to slow, and I twisted the throttle just a bit more, trying to increase my rpms without the rear tire breaking out. If the truck driver saw me, he might be slowing—*if* he saw me.

The road climbed for two hundred yards and then broke across the top of a rise where the trees had been cut back and an expanse of dirt cleared on both sides. Off against the trees piles of brush and other debris formed low walls, and between the walls and me there was only open space. I stood on the pegs and leaned the bike under me, trying to make a gentle turn without actually following the lean of the bike. The KLR carved a deep groove in the mud, and then I was in the open, off the road, out of the way of the truck.

The truck, a semi, was only yards behind me. As he went by he pulled his horn and flashed his lights. I'm not sure what that meant, but I think he was glad that he didn't have to stop his rig and pick pieces of my ass out of his grill.

As soon as he was gone I held the front brake, opened the throttle gently and spun the bike around, facing back the way I'd come. Slade was back there. The mud I threw in the air was still in the air when I saw him coming up the hill. He was standing on his pegs, his tall frame sticking up into the wet and the wind like some sort of mad stork riding a skeletal horse.

He spun into the opening beside me, geared down, and brought the bike around, a perfect 180. Everything about Slade and the bike was the same color—mud. There was mud on, and in, everything that was Slade. It was impossible to tell where the man left off and the machine began. Slade killed the engine, kicked the side stand, and leaped off the bike. He stomped forward a few steps, heading out toward the road. I got off my bike and waited. Slade stood looking at the road, staring down the way the truck had departed. Then, ever so slowly, he took off his helmet. He was laughing.

I stepped up beside him and took off my helmet.

Slade grabbed me by the front of my coat and shook me. I thought he had lost his mind.

"This is the best fucking idea you ever had!" he said, still laughing. "This is better than, than, hell, I don't know! This is just *better!*"

I laughed. I was standing at the side of a nowhere road in the middle of nowhere British Columbia with wet shit falling all around me, but I was standing there with Slade. And we were both laughing.

It couldn't get any better than this.

Thank God for the KLRs. The bony bikes stood upright and flew through the mud. We locked our knees to the tanks, trying to feel any slight lateral movement, adjusting our weight, re-minding ourselves to *stay the hell off the front brakes.*

We rode for miles in the mud, sometimes slowly, sometimes fast.

A hundred miles of mud.

A hundred miles of mud, the road seeming to writhe under us, sliding, shrugging, determined to cut our arrogance down to size.

# 23

# DAY 14—THE SAME DAMN DAY

Sunday, September 8
the same damn road

WHEN YOU RIDE IN the cold and the mud and the rain and the snow—when you ride like that, every time you stop you have to piss. So Slade and I stood there in the cold and wet, trying to fumble our hands through countless layers of riding gear, trying to take a piss while also trying to keep the mud from seeping inside our clothing.

We stood there looking at each other: here we were again, two grown men, standing in the middle of absolutely goddamn nowhere, both of us covered with mud so ingrained in our beings that some of it would surely be with us the rest of our lives.

Amazingly, the sun came out.

We took out our water bottles and cleaned our face shields. There was no place and no way to get rid of the rest of the mud, so we rode away still covered with it, a sort of dirt-badge of honor.

The road was still unpaved, but better now, and we were making good time. I was leading, joying in being able to finally feel the surface, my speed climbing. I was riding alone, and I loved it. Somewhere back there, Slade was taking his time, just resting his ass from the strain of a hundred miles of mud.

And, now and then, there were trucks, huge semis, square cargo trucks, trucks pulling trailers on which there were other trucks. The big ones would roar by, rooster tails of mud spraying up behind them and flying out from their sides. There was no place for us to go—we had to ride through the spray. If there were any small part of us the road hadn't coated with mud, the trucks did. The mud covered everything, including our face shields. It was a constant process of riding, going blind, and then stopping to clean our helmets.

The trucks did not look out for us. We had to look out for ourselves.

There was a truck behind me, not too close, but coming on fast. I could tell by the grille it was not a semi. But I didn't like what I thought it was—a box truck. It stood high off the ground, huge mirrors jutting out from its sides like tiny wings trying desperately to pull the heavy machine off the ground and out of the mud. I could see the grille in my mirror, could see the dual rear wheels churning water, mud and gravel, see the coating of mud that obscured everything that said "*truck!*" I couldn't see the driver, but I thought, if he hits me, he might not even feel it.

I wallowed around a curve, dropped into a slight grade, and saw the bridge coming up a hundred yards ahead. It was another one of those skinny, one lane, steel-tracked bridges that scared hell out of me, open metal floor grids slick as owl shit, the bridge hardly wide enough for one big car. The gapped surface lasted for years, did not buckle in the cold, and let your tires push snow and ice down into the gaps and into the water below. The bridges were common in British Columbia and the Yukon Territory, and I hated every one of them. I began to back off on the speed.

There was a courtesy about these bridges—whoever reached the bridge first had the right-of-way, and no one was in a hurry. We'd crossed a dozen of them, almost always seeing cars and trucks, and never once was there any problem. Everyone waited his turn.

But the heavy grid screwed up a bike's steering, particularly bikes with relatively narrow tires, like the KLR's. Slade and I rode these bridges slowly and carefully, trying to make the bikes go where we wanted, not where the grids tried to take us.

But I could not ride this bridge slowly.

There was no traffic on the other end of the bridge. I dropped down one gear and rolled hard onto the bridge, the bike clamped between my knees, every nerve waiting to feel the sideways slip of the tires on the wet steel.

And then I heard—no, I *felt*—the truck enter the bridge behind me.

I checked the mirror. The truck was picking up speed, the engine whining higher as the rpms increased. Even in the brief flicker of time that my eyes held the mirror, I could tell he was closing the gap, and that he intended to close the gap.

I tapped my rear brake lightly, rhythmically, not to engage the damn thing, but to make the rear taillight catch his attention. Either he did not see me, or he did not give a damn. I thought I knew which, but at that point it made no difference.

I had no choice. I had to open the throttle more. I felt the KLR lurch forward, the rear wheel coming out of its gridlock and slewing to the left. I wrestled the machine back where I wanted it, could hear the truck gaining, could feel the wet air drilling down inside my jacket. Could feel the fear behind my heart.

And the anger. I wanted to kill the driver.

If I could make it to the end of the bridge before the truck caught me, I might have a chance.

I was so close to the superstructure on the left side of the bridge that I was afraid I was going to snag the handlebars. I stood up and leaned the bike slightly to the right but the wheels seemed stuck in the steel grid, and the bike made no real movement away from the girders. I leaned harder. Suddenly the wheels broke away from the grooves, the bike wheeled heavily to the right, and I shot off the end of the bridge. I was too far to the right—the bike was immediately into a narrow lane of small, loose, muddy gravel that ran beside a deep drainage ditch farther to the right, the wheels grinding down into the stones. I had to stay up on the gravel—the ditch was running hard with water and beyond was a steep, muddy wall cut into the side of a low hill.

If I could have stopped time and waited for Slade, I know what he would have said. He would have quoted Chaser: "more gas." Fucking Slade was cut from the same mold as Chaser—both always had some simple answer when it was my ass on the line.

I twisted the throttle, feeling the bike jump forward, and I didn't see the basketball-sized rock snuggled into the gravel until it was almost too late. I stood higher on the pegs and leaned the bike hard to the left, trying for left movement without making the wheels dig too hard into the loose gravel. The front tire clipped the left edge of the rock and jumped a foot farther out toward the road. I thought I had things under control, that I could twist the throttle and beat the truck to some wider spot that I could escape into. But while I had been trying to stay upright, stay on the bike, stay alive, the truck was boring straight ahead.

Well, not exactly straight ahead. The bastard was veering to the right. I had no place to go. It was either hit the truck, or hit the ditch.

I chose the ditch.

The front tire, and then the bike, flew off the road. I was in the ditch, the water much deeper than I thought, the bike slopping around, diving down into mud-laden water that covered heavy, slick gravel and rocks, so far down that the edge of the roadway was level with my ass. I felt my body shoving forward.

"More gas . . ."

I didn't exactly apply a whole lot more power, but I did stay on the throttle. Before the bike could do anything to compensate for my clumsy riding, the front wheel descended into hell.

The bike dropped straight down, the front wheel falling into a hole big enough to take half the bike, the bash plate slamming hard into the bottom of the ditch. My body was, ever so briefly, airborne. And then it was not.

The bike spun sideways, the wheels angling badly into the water. There was nothing I could do about it—I was a few feet in front of the bike and in over my head. In more ways than one.

I landed face-first, sliding through the ditch, a whale-like blob of humanity doing something humans were never meant to do. The gravel tore off my face shield, muddy water and jagged stone ramming into my face, the water driving down inside my jacket and then into everything I was wearing. Everything.

I knew that I had to keep my head above water, but I didn't know whether my body would work. I'd had that feeling before—knowing I had to do something to keep myself alive, but not knowing if I could actually do it. I twisted my head and managed to raise my nose and mouth above the flow. At least my neck worked.

I was almost totally submerged.

I lay quietly for a few seconds, trying to let my mind wander through my body, looking for busted places, gradually moving my body parts. All I could hear was the rush of ditch water around my body.

I managed to roll slowly over on my side, keeping my face out of the water. It took a moment, but gradually I could see. The truck was stopped right above me, right beside me, just sitting in the road. On the filthy-creamy passenger door was the wolf's head, barely visible through the coating of mud. I couldn't take my eyes off it. The wolf was snarling, and somewhere along the way a rock had hit the paint and knocked off part of a tooth.

A snaggle-toothed wolf—on a truck I'd never forget.

The dirty passenger window slowly rolled down. Through the opening I could see the shadowy shape of the driver. He leaned over to the passenger window, his fat face staring down at me, his bald head still shining, even in the dim light. He sat motionless, staring at me, the truck idling, the smell of diesel exhaust drifting down into the ditch. He grinned, his big mustache twitching, his fat lips parting to show me a gold tooth. He must have been really proud of that fucking tooth.

And then he pushed his hand out the open window and slowly raised his middle finger. He jabbed the finger slowly upward a couple of times. The window rolled up. I heard the crunch of gears changing and the truck drove slowly away. In no hurry, in no hurry at all.

It was difficult to move. Somehow, the wreck had interfered with whatever made motion in my body, and I couldn't locate the right button inside me to turn it back on. My right side was still under water and thin, frigid mud was washing into the open front of my helmet and across the lower part of my face. I closed my eyes and concentrated, but still I couldn't move. I could barely breathe. It didn't occur to me that the layers of heavy clothing I was wearing, soaking wet, were heavy enough to trap a pregnant elephant.

Slade was back there, somewhere. Violent water was hitting my bike like a rock in a rapid, the water shooting up like a signpost. I wondered whether Slade would see it. If he rode on by, it might be a long time before he realized I was not where I was supposed to be.

*C'mon, Slade, goddammit, I'm down here! Eating mud!*

I passed out. It seemed the right thing to do.

\* \* \* \* \*

Motorcycles.

Fucking motorcycles.

Why did everything have to start and end with a goddamn motorcycle?

There were six of them, maybe seven. Hard to tell. The men would park the motorcycles that still ran next to junkers that would not run, so all the metal things would be in one place, so they could take wheels, gas tanks, spark plugs, and anything else that could be cobbled off the junkers and bolt them on their own bikes. Keep them running. I couldn't tell the good bikes from the bad ones. They were all flung together in a muddy flat beside the big hut.

But I knew one thing for sure—there were never any keys in the bikes. When you were in a hurry, not like when you were in a hurry to get home for dinner—there was no home, and there was no dinner—but in a hurry like when some other guy was shooting at your ass, you did not want to be fumbling for keys. And you did not want the battery to be dead and the starter dead because of it. No keys. Ignition hard-wired. Kick-start, all the way.

The bikes were all small dirt bikes, small gas tanks, knobby tires, the sort of bikes you could clamp between your knees and feel the very dirt you were riding on, or stand on the pegs and know that you could lift the machine completely off the ground if you had a good bump to help you. The bikes were always ready, most of them. They were the horses of jungle warfare.

The bikes and the greasy piles of parts were scattered randomly. It was hard to see the whole spread of the place from my position under a hut about twenty yards away. I was under the only hut that could be crawled under. None of the other huts was built up off the ground. I wondered about that. Maybe this was the original hut, the others thrown together in a hurry to keep jungle rains from washing the fight out of tired men. Huts built on the ground, the sleeping pads inside built up on low platforms of old lumber and jungle sticks to keep the meager, gnarled mattresses off the muddy floor.

In the movies, huts in the jungle always had thatched roofs. But I had never seen a hut with a thatched roof, outside of deserted resort areas, where rich Anglos had once come to drink and screw in the tropical sun. All the jungle huts I had seen had roofs of corrugated tin that had been stolen from military installations, or, in broad daylight, ripped off the houses of civilians in small towns, knowing the civilians would say nothing, do nothing.

So, no thatched roofs. Nothing for me to set on fire easily, create a diversion. Fuck. It was always easy to do that in the movies.

There was only one option. I had to grab a bike, start it, and get out of the camp faster than the bullets that sure as hell would be tracking behind me.

I tried to pick a bike that looked ready. Some were on side stands, some lying on the ground, their knobby tires looking worn and cracked.

I picked one that was standing up. At least its rider had thought enough of it not to just drop it on the ground. Maybe that was a good sign.

A light rain was falling. I knew it would only fall harder, the longer I waited. I slid from underneath the hut, staggered to my feet, and ran across the muddy ground, my feet slapping. I had no gear to slow me down, no pack, no food, no gun, no machete, nothing. They'd taken everything, even my watch and belt, when they had found me running through the jungle. I was a pretty good runner. Bullets were faster. One of these days I was going to have to stop letting these fuckers catch me in the jungle. Or anywhere else.

I threw my leg across the bike, hit the switch, put my

foot on the kick starter, and came down hard. The bike fired instantly.

My mind wanders, sometimes, even in times like this. I wondered, if this were a movie, would the bike have started? No way. We would sit there, in our seats, eating popcorn, tense, watching the guy try to start the bike, knowing that it would take a while. But then, just as the bad guys came running, it would start, and the hero would ride away.

I was going to have to stop fantasizing about movies.

This was no movie. And I wasn't a hero. I was simply a guy trying to live another day. I dropped onto the seat, kicked the transmission, twisted the throttle, and felt the muscular little bike throw mud behind me like a fountain gone mad. I shot forward and hit the first guy out of the hut square in the nuts with the front wheel. He screamed and twisted off to the side, flinging his arms up and then down, grabbing his crotch as he hit the mud. I swung a foot at him as I went by, but I missed him completely.

The narrow trail was my only option, the thick growth on both sides too heavy to let a bike pass through. Less than two hundred yards out of the compound a rickety wooden bridge crossed a sharp ravine. The bridge was held in place by ropes, the knots tied badly. I knew, because they had made me help build the bridge, and I tried to fuck up as many knots as I could. If I could get across the bridge with a minute to spare, I might be able to loosen the knots, or maybe just ram the bike into them. The ravine was running hard with more water than a man could safely wade across, even if he could get down to the edge of it. If I could cripple the bridge, I might have a chance at a decent getaway. Maybe.

I wondered about Slade. We were together when I got nailed, but I never saw what happened to him. When they took me to the compound, he wasn't there.

I was pretty sure Slade was dead.

I could see the timbers of the bridge ahead of me, a bridge that looked like it had been built by Boy Scouts on a Sunday outing. I risked a look behind me and saw the first riders wrestling bikes upright, some of the men not bothering with the bikes, just running down the trail toward me. Why the hell were they doing that? Did they actually think they could outrun my bike?

I gunned it toward the bridge, hitting the end of it squarely, giving the bike more gas and struggling to keep the wheels from whipping out from beneath me.

The other end of the bridge had already collapsed. I'd done my job of sabotage well—the ropes had come undone, the end of the bridge dangling down into the ravine. The bike and I shot into space, nothing below us but the torrential flow of a very small and angry river.

Cartwheel. The bike hit the water, my head hit the bike. I stayed conscious only long enough to hear the sharp cracks of automatic weapons, only long enough to wonder why the hell they were shooting when they must have seen that I was already fucked up, only long enough to realize I was in the water, and it was running over my face. And then nothing mattered anymore.

Slade was feeling me up. He was gripping my leg with both hands, squeezing, moving his hands. Then he did the other leg. And then my arms and chest. My feet were still in the water, but my head was up on the bank, and I could breathe. My face felt warm. I put my hand up and tried to wipe away the mud. The mud was red—I was bleeding into the ground like a hog hanging from its hind feet at butchering time.

I got my eyes clear. Slade was squatting beside me, an AK-47 hanging from his shoulder. (Where the hell had he gotten that thing?)

"You through swimming for the day?" he said.

*　*　*　*　*

Slade was feeling me up. He was gripping my leg with both hands, squeezing, moving his hands, trying to feel me through layers of heavy, sodden material. Then he did the other leg. And then my arms and chest. My feet were still in the water, but my head was up on the bank, and I could breathe. My face felt warm. I put my hand up and tried to wipe away the mud. The mud was red—I was bleeding into the ground like a hog hanging from its hind feet at butchering time.

I got my eyes clear. Slade was squatting beside me.

"You through swimming for the day?"

It must have taken me five minutes to stand up, water draining from every opening in my gear. I stood there until all the draining stopped, but the gear didn't seem to get lighter.

Sometimes you can fix a KLR with your knees.

I held the front wheel between my knees, twisted the handlebars back into line, checked the lines, spokes, and anything else that I could think of. Other than a dent in the aluminum bash plate, the bike wasn't damaged.

I don't remember how the hell I got on the bike—Slade probably had something to do with it. We rode up a rise and into a thick stand of trees, found the least wet place we saw, and parked the bikes under a heavy overhang. I worked my way out of the gear and dumped it on the ground, took a light mountaineering tarp out of my gear, and wrapped myself in it. I stood there, naked under the tarp. But I was not cold. I was too fucking angry to be cold.

After a while I tried to clean myself as well as I could, dropping the tarp and stepping out into the rain, letting it wash the blood off my face. The blood must have come from my nose, which felt like it was still being held in some sort of medieval clamp. Slade checked my face for damage but only found some scratches.

"There's a lot of ugly here," Slade said, grinning. "Kind of hard to tell if it's damaged or not."

Bastard.

Slade took all my riding gear out into the rain, hung it on branches, and draped it over bushes. He got rid of most of the mud.

And then Slade made the sacrifice that only a true friend would make—he gave me his last set of dry long johns.

The rain stopped. Right there in the middle of nowhere we built a fire. Maybe we weren't supposed to, but we didn't give a damn. We hung all our wet gear from limbs within reach of the heat, sat down on our tarps, and soaked up the warmth.

We wanted to ride on. Our gear was still filthy, but at least it was partially dry.

I'd already found the .45 in all the mud that had washed down into my riding pants. It didn't seem to be bothered by the bath. Now, I dug through my gear looking for my spare face shield. Before I found it, I found Curry's sunglasses. Both lenses were broken. I held them up for Slade to see.

"They're just sunglasses," Slade said quietly.

"No, they're not," I said, between gritted teeth. I picked up the .45 and gripped it as hard as I could.

Slade said nothing more.

"How the hell did he get behind us?" I muttered.

"Had to have been intentional," Slade said. "No other businesses or houses between the lodge and where we are now. He pulled off and hid, waiting for us to go by. He passed me a couple of miles back, kept easing to the right, crowding me. Had to pull off the road to let him go by. Couldn't really tell if it was the wolf truck."

The wolf truck. I could feel the anger boiling up around a vision of a fat face and a sneering smile and a huge mustache and a gold tooth.

I wanted to see that face again.

Late in the day we finally left the Cassiar Highway and crossed into the Yukon Territory.

To this point, the Cassiar was the most challenging piece of riding we had done. The low overcast made us jumpy, the constantly changing character of the road made us wary, and the on-again, off-again rain kept us fighting for vision. For miles the road surface would be hard and slick, then suddenly, without warning, it would turn into a black dough, the mud seeming to leap up from beneath the bikes, coating our legs and pants, tiny particles blowing up onto our faces. Nearing the end of it, I started thinking of the Cassiar as an enemy. But it wasn't an enemy. It was just a road. I thought about the mountains I had climbed and the good times with a glass of bourbon looking back on it all. Now and then someone would ask, "How did it feel to conquer the mountain?" You conquer enemies, not mountains. Nobody "conquers" the mountain. You merely survive. And the mountain, as the man said, "is there," and will be there, long after you've gone. You survive, or you don't, and the mountain doesn't care, either way.

And that's the way I finally felt about the Cassiar in the early winter. We survived. Later, I would sort of miss it.

Like I said, you get used to things.

I tried not to think about it, but there it was again, another one of those places—crossing into the Yukon Territory—that made me feel as though, yes, once again, we were really riding north. We were really doing this.

We took a side trip to the east and rode the few miles into Watson Lake, brilliant sunshine leading us into town.

We were covered with mud—mud plastered our bikes, mud in our gear, mud in our ears, mud in the pockets of our jackets. But the answer to that was simple: another car wash.

We found one in Watson Lake. We lingered in the thing for an hour, stripping down, turning on the soap that was supposed to be used for washing cars, putting our gear on the concrete floor and walking back and forth on it, turning on the hard-spray rinse, again and again. Pretending that we knew what we were doing. It worked. Later, in a hotel that looked left over from the gold rush days, we hung the gear to dry all over our room.

And Slade wanted his underwear back.

Watson Lake. I know I should write more about the town, but, truthfully, other than the car wash, only one thing there caught our attention.

The Sign Post Forest.

What the hell was it doing there?

What the hell was it doing anywhere?

We started to ride past it, and then, as though on some unspoken command, we wheeled hard across the road and down onto the gravel. It was impossible to ride past the place.

I'd seen pictures of it, but never really expected to be there, ever. It was confusingly fascinating. Wooden posts of various heights were planted in the moist earth in some sort of pattern that must have been thought out but appeared totally random. The tops of the tallest posts were too high for even Slade to reach. Every post was covered with signs nailed to them in some mad display of intolerance for order, signs from cities, towns, streets, burgs, villages, some of the places so small they had only a name and nothing else.

We walked around for the better part of an hour, reading the signs and looking for something. For something. For anything, and knowing that we had no idea what we were looking for.

The others who had been there before us must also have been looking. But, in the looking, they left something—these signs, signs that they had been there, signs that they were alive and had come to this far place to certify their identity, their lives, their being. All by carrying a piece of rusting metal or chipped, painted wood and nailing it to a post that only a handful of people would ever see except in photographs.

But a handful of people was enough, maybe. Maybe one person was enough, if that person now knew you were alive.

Neither Slade nor I had a sign. And neither of us knew what we were looking for. Perhaps that's the wonder of the place, the total fascination. It's a distillation of life, of people passing through, wandering around, looking for something, leaving signs. And leaving some sort of residual energy, something that ebbed and flowed around the signposts like sea water around the pilings of an ancient wooden pier. The energy, the emotion, was so real that it seemed to make the light waver when I looked at the thicket of signposts.

Slade and I stood beside our bikes, knowing it was time to find a place to bed down for the night but finding it difficult to take our eyes off the signposts.

And I wondered if we would leave anything behind.

# 24

# DAY 15

Monday, September 9
from Watson Lake, Yukon Territory

THE BED SAGGED BADLY. I lay on it like I was lying in a hammock. There was an ancient light fixture centered in the ceiling, and I watched it change shape as the early light began to tumble through the old rippled glass of the window.

Slade's bed was empty; he must have wandered off somewhere, looking for coffee, or checking the bikes, or just staring at the sunrise.

There was no sound, not even from the little highway in front of the weather-battered old wooden hotel that we were in.

I had been dreaming—gigantic signposts clustered in front of me, spiking into the sky, the signs hanging haphazardly, none of them proper, each seeming to silently scream their home place into the crystal air, a mute cacophony of places and names and long-gone people trying to find a place in the world. They had brought their signs, and they had disappeared. The signs held me, telling me of places I had never been and would never be. People lived there, in those places. They had lives.

They had lives.

Two weeks ago I left Wild Horse Canyon and rode through Santa Fe and straight on to the Yukon. Well, there was one small side trip to pay a quick visit to the Snake—it was one of my fondest memories. Without looking in my journal I tried to reconstruct the days, one day at a time, from memory. I couldn't do it. I couldn't remember what café went with what day, what mountain went with what stretch of road. This ride was a slowly building wave of joy, exhilaration, and grit, something that grew out of time and distance. For hours, sometimes days, I forgot the rolling boil inside my skull. I knew it was there—I just forgot about it.

We were in no hurry. Maybe we didn't want this trip to end. I would have to think about that. How do you make a trip not end? And what would I do when it did?

I'm tired of writing this miserable shit about the bike—the machine was really pissing me off. Each morning—and each morning seemed colder than the last—it seemed to take a little longer to start the bike, manipulating the choke and the throttle, fiddling with the idle screw, doing everything I could think of to make the bike take off, warm up, run. And then it jerked and coughed for the first mile or two, until it decided that I wasn't going to quit, that it would have to keep running, and then it ran as though it were determined to make up for all the jerking around it caused me in the mornings. The bike was diabolical, some warped bike-mind (maybe like my own) that tortured me just enough to make me angry and then straightened out long enough to keep me from pushing it off the road and over the nearest embankment. So I just kept riding it.

Slade's bike always started with a single touch of the starter button. I hated that bastard bike.

We left town in bright sunshine, riding again past the Sign Post Forest. We did not stop.

In less than thirty minutes, we were again under clouds, the temperature dropping. We stopped, and I put on extra clothes, and then some more clothes, and then we kept riding.

Somewhere back there, when Slade and I had been sitting with a stack of maps and marker pens tracing our route and circling the things we wanted to see, somewhere back there we had found Jake's Corner and marked it on a map. A nothing place.

And now we were at Jake's Corner, where the road kept on heading north but a part of it branching off and looping down to the southwest and on to the Alaskan Coast and to Skagway. If we turned left at Jake's Corner, we would ride into Alaska somewhere down that narrow, winding little road.

We turned left.

We crossed the border into Alaska.

*Alaska.*

*We had ridden to Alaska.*

Yes, it was only to the southern reaches of the state, but we were in *Alaska*!

Just across the border there was a huge, round intricately carved wooden sign, must have been twelve feet tall. "Welcome to Alaska," it said, among other things. I couldn't help myself— I got off the bike and hugged the sign. I felt like a fool.

Slade just looked at me, slowly shaking his head.

Alaska greeted us accordingly.

We rode hard along the crest of a low range of stony outcroppings, the road captured on the right by the rocks and off to the left hugging the edge of a glaciated valley. Below us, the valley floor appeared to have been scooped up and then dropped, countless pieces of rounded rock covered with moss, lichen, and a few stunted trees. Water was everywhere, a large lake down and to our left, countless smaller pools scattered among the rocks. Mists hung thickly on the slopes, and tiny drops of water condensed on our face shields. And then the real water collected in the floor of the valley, leaving not a square foot of dry land anywhere, pools of frigid water standing in every hard cup of stone, haggardly thin vegetation clinging to cracks as though trying to stay dry.

The shallow valley thundered beside us, just below the road, stretching to a close horizon and then disappearing as though the valley dropped off the edge of the world. It was a country as sparse, as bare, as hard as we had ever seen.

But we were in *Alaska!* And so we poured it on, opening the throttles and hunkering low in the saddles. The cold cut our bodies and numbed the ends of our fingers, but we could not seem to slow down. We screamed—we *sailed*—along the high edge of the valley, two riders in a paradise of rock and water, hard cold and wind.

We seemed high in the mountains, but I knew Skagway, at sea level, should be only a few miles ahead. How could that be? How could we be in such barren country, in such cold, and then fall to sea level in so short a time?

In less than an hour my question was answered. The road dropped away beneath us so quickly that I thought I could feel the bike rise on its springs, standing higher, ready for a descent into a canyon that made our breath catch in our throats. The road curled in dramatic twists down a steep side wall. I was running my bike at idle, coasting through drops and turns, tweaking the rear brake now and then, amazed to be losing altitude so quickly. It was as though we were dropping through thin atmosphere toward the Earth—only, we were *on* the Earth.

And then, as we dropped, I began to smell the sea, smell the warmth in the air, the salt, and feel the softening of the wind against my chest.

Warmth. At last, warmth.

We shot off the final ridge and into the valley of Skagway. Before us, there was only a flat run to the sea.

In Skagway, people were walking around in shirtsleeves.


I expected to ride into a near-deserted Alaska town, like all the other towns back in Northern Canada we had ridden through, the tourists gone, the RVs back at home in the garage, their radiators drained, their batteries unhooked.

Skagway was not more than four blocks wide and a quarter-mile long, a town of some 850 full-time residents. It should have been nearly deserted. Instead, nearly *7,000 tourists*, fresh from the enormous tour boats tied up to the town's docks, flooded Broadway, the town's main commercial street. By Wednesday, we were told, another 8,000 tourists would get off another three or four tour boats and roll through the town like a tidal wave. A tidal wave with money.

Broadway was lined with false-fronted buildings, designed to look like structures from the gold rush days. Local women, shilling for tour companies, walked through the crowd. They wore low cut dresses with huge skirts, high heels, and bright garters on silk stockings that showed through hip-high slits in the skirts. Men wearing top hats drove vintage-looking carriages loaded with tourists, the drivers keeping up a running patter of singsong information about the town and its history.

Watching it all, I thought of Disneyland. I thought of a movie set. I thought the crew had set up the shot, hundreds of extras milling around, moving through the action. I kept waiting for some unseen director to step out into the street and shout, "Cut!"

We wanted out of there as fast as we could go.

We didn't make it.

We didn't know what our plans were for Skagway—other than riding, we had no concrete plans—but thought we would check out the town and then catch the ferry to Haines, about an hour away down the inlet. But we arrived in Skagway too late in the day, on a Monday, in mid-September. At this time of year, the ferry to Haines ran only every other day, and we had missed this day's run. If we wanted to see Haines, if we didn't want to backtrack all the way to Jake's Corner, we were stuck in Skagway until Wednesday.

We didn't want to backtrack. Slade and I both hated re-covering ground we had already seen. We wanted to see Haines. We lay over.

# 25

# DAY 16

Tuesday, September 10
in Skagway, Alaska

We walked the streets of Skagway, ate in the restaurants, talked with the people. After a while all I wanted was . . . out.

Slade was always on a quest for the ultimate berry pie. He's a seasoned pro where berry pie is concerned. He watches pie pass by on the trays carried by waitresses. (It's always a waitress—guys don't wait table in Alaska and the Yukon.) He peers at pie through the glass of those round cases with the slowly turning shelves. (I've never seen Slade order pie out of one of those things.) He questions waitresses about the berries, the filling, the crust. Seldom do the responses come up to his standards. So far, he had actually ordered berry pie only twice. The first time was in Cruel Jack's, back in Green River, Wyoming. Blackberry. Slade's face lit up when he ate that pie.

"Good pie."

Slade pulled out his pie chart (yeah, Slade actually carried a "pie chart"—go figure) and duly logged in the experience and the rating of the pie. He gave it an eight on a ten-scale.

The second time he ordered pie was here in Skagway at the tourist-packed Skagway Fish Company, customers waiting outside, leaning against walls, huddled in doorways. Again, he ordered blackberry. He ate the pie in total reverence, nearly overwhelmed by the experience. His eyes rolled up, and he sank back in his chair, his legs splayed out in front of him.

"A nine," he said, closing his eyes as he spoke.

"You ever found a ten?"

"Nah," Slade said. "Can't give a pie a ten. If I did, the search would be over. And the search is the thing."

Slade was on to something. The search—the *journey*—was the thing. It was like this ride we were on. I wondered what it would feel like if we actually made it to the Arctic Circle, when we actually reached the uttermost point of the journey. What would we feel then? What would we do then? The search, the journey toward a specific thing, even if the thing is in our minds . . . such searches almost always end in disillusionment. The real searches are inside us. We search for things, we search for our limits. With any luck, we find neither. That way, we can keep searching.

I tried to think of where I was, inside. So far, what I did to Snake hadn't caught up with me. I'd freaked out in a café in Southern Canada, been wrecked and dumped in a ditch full of water. Was I emptied out? Did I know what I would feel tomorrow? How much anger was left? Did I care?

I had no fucking idea.

It was one of the things that Modene had talked to me about, more than once—did I ever, *just one time,* look inside myself? Or did I just react to what I was feeling, not caring where the hell those feelings came from, not really caring what my reaction was?

I knew the answer. And I didn't like it.

And then Lancey's face popped into my mind. I couldn't remember the last time that had happened.

Not remembering. That was a very good thing.


Slade had talked a rental car agency into letting us park the bikes in the rental lot. The bikes didn't move from there until we left on Wednesday. In the meantime, we slept, we ate, and we drank.

Oh, yeah, there was one other thing.

# 26

# DAY 17

Wednesday, September 11

from Skagway, Alaska

9/11

WE WANDERED OUT ON Broadway, interested to see what would happen in Skagway on the anniversary of 9/11.

Nothing changed. Hundreds, maybe thousands, of tourists filled Broadway, buying t-shirts and stuffed animals, filling the restaurants, talking, laughing.

Shortly before noon we walked slowly toward the waterfront and noticed a man carrying an American flag. We followed him to a small pavilion at the end of Broadway where some other men in uniforms of various types were silently waiting. These were not young men. These were men whose faces showed the long times and the hard times. Slade and I stood quietly and watched. One of the men stepped forward and said a prayer, then another man said a few words to the other men in uniform, his voice and his words so low, so reverent, that we couldn't really hear them. When he fell silent, the men came to attention, their slow salutes trailing off into the Alaskan sky. There was no noise, no shots fired, no fireworks. Tourists glanced at the men, but few slowed in their march toward the glitter of the jewelry stores of Broadway. As the tiny ceremony came to a close, the men turned and marched slowly and quietly away, down a side street and into the shadows. Slade and I stood still, watching them pass. The man with the flag was crying softly.

Slade and I, both veterans, stood silently.

"Those guys are not expendable," I muttered.

It would be nice, I thought, if one day we could talk about being veterans.

Slade said nothing.


Tourists still milled about in clumps along the street, the small town heavy with humanity. But we knew it wouldn't stay that way. A local barmaid had told us that the tour boats stopped coming on the last day of September, and when the boats stopped coming the town became, as it did every winter, virtually a ghost town. With no tourists to buy the jewelry and t-shirts, no hungry Germans, Norwegians, and Japanese to pack the restaurants, no Californians to charter the tour planes and buy tickets on the scenic railroad . . . the locals boarded up the town. The barmaid said that three days after the last boat, the town looked as though it had been raided by Home Depot—plywood nailed up everywhere. All the summer help was gone, maybe a couple of hundred hardy souls staying behind, sticking it out through the Alaskan cold. Throughout the winter, she said, only three restaurants stayed open: one served breakfast, one served lunch, one served dinner—taking turns, so to speak.

Everybody waiting on the return of the sun. And the tour boats. And the money.

Slade and I sat on a bench at the lower end of Broadway, basking in the weak sun, watching the tourists come and go from the waterfront and the boats. We were wearing our "civilian" clothes, not really looking like bikers, our heavy riding gear back at the motel, spread out across the room, drying. It felt good to sit there, staring at the huge boats tied up at the docks, watching the long snaking lines of humans coming and going. Watching the couples holding hands. I wondered what their problems were, or if they had any. Sure, I knew they did. I knew that in every one of those humans, every one of those couples, there was a universe of their own construct and experience, a horizontal existence that had depth only within their own emotions. And when each of those humans died, their entire particular universe would disappear with them and could never be recovered.

I knew what that felt like. I had been there when the only universe that ever mattered to me had disappeared.

I could feel the stirrings inside me to ride, to be on the bike, to be alone on the machine, to be away from the constructs of others. Now, we'd do exactly that. It seemed as though we'd been in Skagway for a week, but this afternoon we'd put the bikes on the ferry and make the one-hour trip to Haines. And then we would do what we came here to do—ride north. I felt better, knowing that.

Slade was looking at the docks. The usual piles of stuff that accumulated on docks were not there—carefully cleared away in order not to offend the tourists, I guessed, and to make room for the cars. Dozens of vehicles were parked there, most of them awaiting the ferry.

Slade was looking at the docks. I was watching the women.

I felt his hand on my arm. I turned toward him. He was looking at me, and he had a weird expression on his face, as though he had bitten into something he did not like. He slowly turned his face back toward the docks.

And so did I.

It took me only a minute to find it, the truck, the wolf truck. I could only see the back of it but I knew it was the truck—a dirty white box van, dual rear wheels, covered with mud. I jumped up from the bench and headed for the truck, half walking, half running, threading my way through the throng of tourists and zigzagging between the parked cars that were waiting for the ferry.

I stood at the passenger side and looked at the door with my hand under the back of my jacket, gripping the .45. I looked at the snaggle-toothed wolf and I could feel the blinding light washing behind my eyes, could feel the pounding of blood through every inch of my body.

I knew it then. I was not empty. I was stoked to my scalp with anger, and I could taste the coming of revenge in the far back of my throat. Francis Bacon said, "Revenge is a kind of wild justice." And that's where I was—in the court of wild justice. In the court of rage.

No one was in the truck. I tried the door. Locked. I went around to the driver's side and tried the door. Locked. I fingered the butt of the pistol. I could just take out the gun, break the window . . .

And then what? The fucking driver wasn't inside. He was

probably somewhere on Broadway, in a saloon or restaurant. And we had hours to go before we had to catch the ferry to Haines . . .

I walked quickly back to the bench where Slade waited. I looked at him and nodded and kept on walking. Slade jumped up and fell in beside me, both of us heading back toward the mass of humanity crowding Broadway.

We were on the sidewalk, walking quickly. I had no particular destination in mind, but I knew I would stop in every place along the street where I thought the driver might be killing time. We came to a narrow opening between two buildings, a small walkway leading off the sidewalk toward the back. Slade suddenly shouldered me into the space, grabbed my shoulders, and slammed me back hard against the wall.

"Give me the gun," he said quietly.

I hesitated. Maybe I could argue him out of this. "He's younger, and bigger," I mumbled. "Might need to even things up a bit."

"Fuck that," Slade said. "You're smarter. And you're meaner. I make it about even, without the gun."

"You know you could just reach around and take it," I said.

"I don't want to take it, pardner, I want you to give it to me." He grinned, but he wasn't happy. "That was our deal—when I ask for it, you hand it over. Pronto."

We stood that way for a long moment, Slade pressing me back against the building.

"Look, Morgan," he said, "I don't know what went down in New Mexico. All I know, and all I want to know, is that it was probably something that you shouldn't have done and probably something that's going to get us in a world of shit, one of these days," He waited. I said nothing. "And it's probably something you would do again," he said, letting out his breath in one of those heavy bursts that said "and there's not a damn thing I can do about it."

"But if you get us nailed up here, we'll never get to where we want to go. So—what's more important to you? And besides, we have a deal."

He was right. We had a deal. And Slade and I had never, ever gone against any understanding that we'd ever had. I slowly reached behind me and worked my hand up under my light jacket. I wrapped my fingers around the butt of the Colt and eased it out of the holster. I held it out to my side, away from the busy sidewalk. Slade let go of my shoulders, took the gun, checked the safety, and slid it into the back pocket of his jeans, his jacket covering the weapon.

Slade stepped back. "Okay," he said, "Show Time. If we find him, I'll distract, you attack."

*Hallelujah!* We were back in business!

Slade worked one side of the street, I worked the other. We ambled along, peering through the windows of shops and restaurants, threading our way through the crowd of tourists, a jumble of human bodies dressed in outlandish tourist clothing—stuff they would never wear at home—their hands on their wallets and purses, their eyes glazed, the thick scent of perfume, aftershave, and deodorant clawing through the atmosphere. The guy we wanted was not a tourist—he would not be getting on a tour boat. His truck was still parked at the far edge of the dock but, even so, I began to be concerned that we would not find him, would not find one single guy in this huffing, sweating, bloated mass of bodies. And I became angrier.

Slade found him.

We were keeping an eye on each other, and I saw Slade standing in front of an old hotel, its wooden sides painted a cheerful yellow. There was a restaurant and bar on the main floor—Slade and I had eaten there when we first got into town. Slade raised his hand and pointed casually at the big picture window—inside, the guy was inside.

I moved away from the direct line of sight from the window and crossed the street, then edged up to Slade. I glanced inside. The place was packed; two, three, four people at every table. Except for one table in the back, near the bar. The wolf-truck man sat by himself, dishes and bowls and bottles in front of him. His head was down—bald head shining—never looking up; he may as well have been alone in the restaurant. He again attacked his food as though eating were some sort of job that he couldn't wait to finish, his heavy mustache moving rapidly. When he wasn't forking food into his mouth he rested both arms on the tabletop, encircling everything in front of him, a habit born of some sort of childhood that I didn't want to know about.

The entry was a heavy screen door. Some people came out and the hinges squealed lightly, as though complaining that they had to last through the dwindling tourist season.

I wondered whether the guy would look up and see us. He knew what we looked like, from back at Belle Lodge, but I doubted that he expected to see us, ever again. To him, we were nowhere and nobody. Just a bump in his own personal history.

I was going to change his fucking opinion about that.

I walked into the restaurant. Slade stayed outside, just to the side of the door. We had nothing planned, but Slade and I had stood together in front of the fan so many times—when the shit

hit—that we didn't need to speak. We were extensions of each other. We knew what our jobs were.

The noise in the place was a steady stream of crumbling roar over a sea of gaudy clothing that held the noise above their heads like a jungle full of fat, exotic birds. Very large birds. Arms waved, heads flung back, feet stomped to underline some seemingly hilarious story. I wondered how every person at every table could be talking at once; no one paid any attention to me. I strolled to the guy's table and, without hesitation, sat down. On the table were hot sauce bottles, empty saucers, a partially eaten basket of French fries, an untouched glass of water, and two empty beer bottles. And a pair of expensive sunglasses.

The guy was working on a third beer, his meaty left hand gripping it like an axe handle. He looked at me, his expression clearly saying, "What the fuck?"

I picked up an empty beer bottle and slammed it down on the sunglasses.

I thought he'd come storming up out of his seat but he just sat there, looking like a gigantic bug ready to eat a smaller bug. He knew exactly who I was, and he was absolutely unafraid.

He pulled his lips back in a snarl, his gold tooth glistening, and growled, "I thought I was done with you, you old fuck."

I could feel the boil starting up out of my guts. I struggled to keep my hands on the table, struggled to get the words out. I leaned slightly toward him, speaking calmly, directly into his face. "You left me lying in a fucking ditch with water sluicing through my helmet." He didn't move, but I saw a flicker behind his hard little eyes. "I want your gold tooth," I said, my voice rising a notch. I was shaking, gripping the edge of the table.

"You want what?" he growled. "My *tooth*?!" His fingers

tightened on the beer bottle. He glanced around the room, started to ease forward in his chair, his right arm sliding from the table and out of sight down to his side. He still gripped the beer bottle and I wondered if he would try to backhand it into my face. He lifted his bulk slightly from the chair.

"If you get up from the table, I'll kill you," I said quietly.

He froze.

Out of the corner of my eye I saw a brief motion at the front door and I caught a glimpse of Slade coming inside.

It was time to get it on. A flood of sheer energized joy came up through my chest as I waited the half-second that I knew it might take—and then Slade slammed the heavy screen door so hard that I thought the damn thing would fly off its hinges and come winging into the restaurant.

The room went from conversational havoc to dead silence in a split second.

I did not look around. I knew that anyone in the place would be staring at the front door, wondering what the hell was going on. I was looking at the wolf-guy. I grabbed one of the narrow bottles of hot sauce and back-handed it, bottom first, straight into his mouth. His lips split and I heard again that wonderful sound of cracking teeth. The narrow bottle forced his mouth open and I realized the thing was partially inside his mouth and I slammed the top of it with my other hand. The bastard's head snapped back on his thick neck and then all of him flew backward, his hand losing the beer bottle, the chair splintering, and his huge body crushing it to the floor, the hot sauce bottle still sticking out of his mouth, his right arm flying out to his side. There was a knife in his hand.

I was on top of him before he even hit the thick planking. He tried to scream but only made some sort of gargling sound, and I thought maybe he was choking on his own blood and spit. And maybe some hot sauce. Slade's diversion would wear off quickly, and people were probably looking back toward me, but the wolf-guy and I were both thrashing around below the table. Before he could bring the knife up I grabbed the mother-fucker by his jacket, pulled him toward me, and then slammed him backward, his head whipping into the heavy planks and the knife flying across the floor. The hot sauce bottle shot out of his mouth and over his head as though he had spit it out in some majestic display of lung power. He lay still.

I slid to a kneeling position beside him.

People were leaning over us. I grabbed the guy's face, holding it between my hands. "He's having a seizure," I yelled. "He needs a doctor!"

"I'm a nurse!" A woman dropped to the floor beside me. "Let me see if I can help!" She listened to his breathing . . .

Someone else knelt and loosened the bastard's clothing, literally ripping his shirt open. A small glint of something lay on the floor beside his head. The gold tooth. I slid my hand over it and slipped it into my palm. No one seemed to notice.

I eased backward from all the commotion over the wolf-guy's fat body, almost crawling along the floor, not too fast, not too slowly. I glanced toward the front of the room and saw Slade casually walking out through the door. There was another door at the back of the room, and I slowly got to my feet and walked out. Everybody's attention was still on the guy on the floor, being worked on by the nurse and some other people. No one said a word to me.

\* \* \* \* \*

I strolled a block off the main street, turned a few corners, looked in some shop windows, and generally made my way back to the motel. Slade was already there. My body was still jangling, and I didn't want to stay cooped up the motel room. I told Slade I was going for a walk, and I changed my pants, put on my heavy riding coat, and tied a faded red bandana around my head—anything to change the way I looked back at the restaurant. Slade fell backward on the bed and was asleep before I got out of the room.

I spent a couple of hours walking the streets of Skagway, knowing I probably would never be there again, trying to get my vision to penetrate the fog that seemed to hang in front of me. I thought taking the wolf-guy down would make everything better, would make *me* better.

It did not.

When I got back, the afternoon was fading rapidly. We collected our gear, brought the bikes to the back of the building, and strapped everything on. We rode slowly down Broadway to the docks, parked, and settled on a bench. If the wolf-guy was looking for us, we wanted to be easy to find.

We didn't have a plan. We simply waited for whatever would come. No one paid any attention to us.

We could see the bikes, and over the tops of the cars I could see the roof of the wolf-truck. I hated to leave it there, untouched, but there didn't seem to be much I could do about it.

Slade gently nudged me. He was looking at the bikes. A guy wearing some sort of uniform and carrying a pistol on his hip was stopped in front of the machines, standing there, staring at them. Then he moved in a circle, walking completely around the bikes, never once raising his head. He came around to the back and stared at the license plates.

Fuck. How the hell did the cops know I was in Skagway?

I guess they didn't. The cop, or whoever he was, turned and walked away along the side of the docks. I realized I'd been holding my breath. Slade just grinned.

And then we heard the incredibly loud horns from the cruise ships, calling the tourists back to the docks. Like lemmings, the crowd seemed to turn as one huge mass of living beings, cooking in the bright sunlight, oozing its way down the street toward the docks and the boats, hundreds of arms holding thousands of bags and boxes. As if by magic, the shops and restaurants emptied of tourist life, and Slade and I found ourselves on a nearly deserted dock. In what seemed like an incredibly short time the tour boats were gone.

And we wondered where the wolf-truck guy was.

Riding the bikes into the bowels of the ferry was different from any riding I'd done. We rode the machines, heavy and awkward with gear, down sloping, damp metal surfaces, across bumps and gaps, trying to avoid small patches of water, riding into the bowels of the largest ferry I'd ever seen. In another life, I'd ridden ferries on the East Coast, boats that would carry maybe a dozen cars and a few tourists. But this ferry was something entirely different. Down in the lower hold, where our bikes were, there were enough cars to start a used car lot—and have enough room left over to play full-court basketball. Above the cars, several decks reached into the sky. The ferry was almost as large as one of the cruise ships but without the touristy glitz and over-organized activity crap. In other words, the ferry, as with everything else in Alaska, was large beyond belief.

It would probably be a half-hour before the ferry left, and then it was only an hour's ride to Haines. We went up a couple of decks to one of the lounges where we could see far down the waterway. We dumped our light packs in a couple of seats and made ourselves comfortable. I reached into my shirt pocket and came out with the gold tooth. I gave it to Slade. Slade got up and went outside on the open deck. He looked back through the window at me, holding up the gold tooth in his hand, then simply dropped it into the pocket of his jacket—I thought he would have thrown it overboard. He turned and leaned casually against the railing. He was grinning.

I stood up and went in search of a cup of coffee. Instead I found beer, bought two bottles, and went back to our seats.

Slade was gone.

\* \* \* \* \*

We took turns sleeping, the mosquito netting drawn tightly around the hammocks. One of us lay in his hammock, the other usually sitting on the tiny stoop at the front of the hut, holding the tiny radio, leaning back against the wall, both of us listening to the sounds of the forest underscored by the soft rush of the ocean, thirty yards away, gently running up on the sand like soft sheets being pulled up on a bed sparkling in the moonlight.

We knew we would not have much time.

Less than fifteen minutes, it turned out.

It was my turn to sleep. But neither of us really slept. I lay in the hammock, napping, fully clothed, my pack leaning against the wall of the hut, the rifle hanging from a hook just above. Slade sat and leaned back against the doorpost, his rifle across his lap, the earplug from the radio in his ear. We had been doing this for six days, the earplug either in his ear or in mine.

I dozed, my mind wandering across the lakes of upstate New York, the soft vision of Kateri fluttering, not in my mind, but across the vacuum of my chest, like the wings of a butterfly suspended in time. And then I heard the firm thump of Slade's open hand, drum-like, on the soft planks of the floor.

I twisted out of the hammock, tangled in the netting like a snake trying to shed skin that wouldn't release its hold. I whipped the knife out of its sheath on my belt and slashed at the cords, at the fabric, at the netting, everything falling at my feet. I grabbed the pack and the gun, took a quick look around the one-room hut—there was other stuff that we did not want to leave behind, stuff that we did not want anybody else to get their hands on, but too much to carry if we wanted to move quickly. And we really wanted to move quickly.

Slade was already standing at the foot of the wooden steps that led down from the front of the hut. He was stuffing the radio into one of the pockets of his pack. Not another person was in sight.

"They came in by sea," he said. "Landed on the point just inside the reef south of here. Nobody knew they could do that, or where they got the equipment." He started walking away. "Puts 'em a helluva lot closer than anybody expected."

"How much time do we have?" I growled.

"Maybe twenty minutes, maybe less. Maybe a lot less."

I had not put on my pack. "Wait a minute," I said. "Take my pack and move up the beach. I'll turn on the alarm." I handed

my gear and gun to Slade, seeing him grinning in the moonlight. Slade had installed the alarm. I was glad he was grinning—at least he wasn't singing. He took my stuff and slid silently away, a tall ghost in an alien land.

I took a tiny flashlight out of my shirt pocket, dropped to my
belly, and low-crawled under the hut, the flashlight stuck in my
mouth, a myriad unknown crawling critters scattering in front
of me. In the center of the hut there was a plastic water canteen
Slade had fixed tightly underneath the floor. Taped next to it in
a plastic bag were a piece of rag, a book of matches, two cigarettes, and another short piece of tape. The canteen was hung at
an angle; the cap could be unscrewed without spilling what was
inside. And that's what I did—unscrewed the cap. I ripped open
the plastic bag and stuffed about half of the rag into the mouth of
the canteen, taped the book of matches to the dry end, tore a cigarette in half—I only needed a short fuse—lit the short end, took
a long drag, and folded the hot butt inside the matchbook cover.

And then I started scooting backward as fast as I could go.

I felt the tug on my neck but kept moving, and it was a moment before I realized what had happened. I'd had a small silver chain around my neck. From the chain hung a tiny tur-
quoise buffalo, given to me by Kateri. Somehow the chain had
caught on something. It had broken, the buffalo gone, dropped
into the darkness.

I could feel the panic. I could not lose the buffalo.

I played the tiny light out in front of me, reached out, ran
my hands through the thick layer of sand, leaves, and rat shit. I
could not find the buffalo.

I glanced back at the Molotov cocktail and its crude fuse. I
could see the glow of the cigarette.

A pain went through my chest and I had trouble breathing, my heart hammering. But I knew what I had to do—I had to get the hell out of there.

I shot backward from beneath the floor, jumped up, and started running. I hadn't covered ten yards when I heard the heavy whoosh of the gasoline in the canteen bursting into flame, spreading fire under the floor of a hut that was nothing more than a tinderbox hovering above the ground. In seconds, I could feel the heat.

I caught up with Slade about a hundred yards up the beach. He was standing against the wall of one of the decrepit storage huts.

"Nice job," he said, "but how come you took so long?"

I was watching the hut become a funeral pyre for the tiny buffalo. Without taking my eyes from the hut, I twisted my body toward Slade and pulled my shirt open.

"The buff," he said quietly. "You lost the buff."

We stood, watching the hut burst and crackle, sparks flying into the forest and starting small fires.

Slade took out his macho wire cutters, sliced open the door of the hut and disappeared inside. In less than a minute he was back outside, holding two bottles of beer.

"I saw them put this in there yesterday," he said. "I guess somebody was planning a party." He handed me one of the bottles. "I think we need 'em more than they do." He opened the bottles with his wire cutters.

We stood, looking back at the hut where we had spent the last four weeks. In my mind, I could see the cigarette burning down, see the entire matchbook burst into flames, see the flames igniting the rag, see the rag flaming like a torch as it ate its way to the plastic canteen. And I could see the fires of my life turning the buffalo to a cinder.

* * * * *

I finished my beer and was working on Slade's when I heard the horn that signaled that the ferry was about to leave. That's when Slade wandered back into the lounge. He didn't sit down.

"There's a great view of the docks and the lower end of Broadway from up there," he said. There seemed to be a slight tinge of excitement in his voice. "C'mon," he said, jerking his head toward the door.

I got up, carrying the beer, and we walked out to the railing, Slade leading the way around the side of the big boat. The docks were almost empty, only a few cars parked far out on the edge.

And one truck, sitting by itself in the middle of dozens of empty parking spaces, flaunting its muddy sides and the bad artwork on its door. The wolf-truck.

Slade leaned on the railing on his elbows, staring at the truck. And so did I. Looking at the truck, I could feel the grit of the bottle ramming into the wolf-guy's mouth, could hear the drum-like sound of his head hitting the heavy wooden floor.

We felt the deck move—we were once again on our way.

Slade kept staring at the truck. "Any time now," he said.

"Any time . . . ?" And then I knew. Because I knew Slade.

"I installed the alarm," he said, "while you were out walking." He paused. "I armed it while you were looking for coffee. Or beer." He straightened up and fished in his jacket pocket, coming out with the gold tooth. He took out his wire cutters and carefully cut the tooth in half, then flicked both halves out over the rail, as someone might flick a cigarette. I lost sight of the pieces before they hit the water.

Slade took the beer bottle out of my hand. "This is probably mine," he said, taking a long pull from the longneck.

And then huge gouts of fire flared from beneath the wolf-truck.

Slade and I sat in deck chairs, sipping beer, watching the other passengers crowd the rail, binoculars and cameras in play, everybody looking back at the plume of smoke rising from the dock at Skagway.

Slade and I did not look back.

It only took an hour to get to Haines, the ferry sliding between mountains on both sides that came down directly into the water. When the ferry rounded the point to the west of us, a tiny town appeared in the distance, a few white houses glittering in the shafts of light that pierced the cloud cover, like golden columns that seemed to be holding up the sky. The town beckoned like an old friend, even though neither of us had ever been there.

We were among the very few to get off at Haines. I wondered about that. The ferry was packed with people and cars, bodies huddled against the chill, leaning against the guardrails, cameras pointed—but not getting off. As we were to find out—to our delight—unless you lived there, there's not much reason to get off the ferry at Haines, Alaska, except, maybe, to continue on up the wide valley on the tiny highway and back into Canada at Haines Junction, a long trip into the high, cold distance. And tourists didn't do that.

But we were travelers, not tourists.

We rode the bikes onto the dock and turned toward the small town lying in the far mist a couple of miles away.

Whatever Skagway was, Haines wasn't. There was no Broadway to glitter in a late Alaskan sun, no shoulder-to-shoulder jewelry shops, no women in long slit skirts. There was just Haines. And we loved it.

We checked in to an old slab-sided hotel near the waterfront, one of those places that looked like the builder couldn't decide what he wanted to do. Or maybe he did, and then he walked away, and another builder took over. And then another. The rooms were small and the doors were hollow-core, the sort of things you could cut through with an old Swiss Army knife. But the place had three things that we wanted: We could see our bikes from the tiny window in our room, the hotel served food, and the place was near the waterfront.

We left most of our gear on the bikes and parked them heading out, away from the hotel. At dinner we sat at a table by the window where we could see the bikes and see up the waterway that led back to Skagway. After dinner we were still too jittery to sleep, so I got the Irish Mist and cigars from my bike, and Slade and I sat on a tiny porch that fronted the dining room. It was full dark, cold and getting colder, so we put on heavier clothes and crunched our bodies down into old, heavy, hand-built wooden chairs that faced the waterfront. We smoked the cigars and sipped the Mist, both of us staring up the inlet. We were looking for any fast-moving lights on the water, a sure sign that somebody was heading for Haines in a helluva hurry, probably guys with badges.

We had already decided that seeing the fast lights would be our signal to bug out—grab our gear, abandon the hotel, and ride like hell for Haines Junction, the next town north. We would decide what to do about not being seen in Haines Junction before we got there.

"Fast lights," Slade said. "Fast lights could mean people wanting to talk to us about the wolf-guy, or maybe guys looking for you for the New Mexico thing, trying to get to you while you're in the US."

Something else popped into my mind. "Well," I muttered, "there was also a very small problem in Ute Junction . . ."

Slade sat upright in this chair, quickly. "Ute Junction?! What the hell did you. . . ."

I sat quietly, waiting for Slade to pick up the heavy chair and hit me with it.

"Goddammit, Morgan, you don't have *very small problems!*" He paused. "Ah, what the hell," he said, resignation in his voice, "it can't matter all that much now. And I really, really, don't want to know what happened in Ute Junction."

We sat quietly, looking through the darkness, waiting for lights that never came.

"Anyway," I said, "you're in it now," I said quietly. "I didn't mean to drag you into it, but it seems like it always happens."

"I've always been in it, Morgan. That's the way it works with you and me."

And that's the way it was with Slade. Up until Skagway he'd managed to stay out of the way of the effects of my deranged anger. But when he torched the truck he was sending me a message. We'd been partners a long time, and we still were. It didn't matter that what we did was right or wrong by someone else's standards. It only mattered that it was right by us. Although only I knew what Slade had done, still, it would be difficult for him when all of this was over. I'd dragged him back into the life that, sometimes, we tried to forget, but never would. I should have felt bad about that. Maybe I did. But my mind would not wrap around any sort of guilt. I was beyond that, so far beyond that I couldn't see the beginning. Nor the end. I could only see what was in front of me.

Slade was in it, now.

And I loved him for that.

We sat on the porch until midnight, and only then did we feel safe enough to go to bed. We lay on the small beds fully clothed. I knew that neither of us would sleep well. Or at all.

27.

# DAY 18

Thursday, September 12
from Haines, Alaska

SOMEWHERE IN THE SMALL darkest hours of the night I fell
asleep, and I dreamed. Wolves' heads. Burning motorcycles.
Coffee cups flashing through the air. Jumbled images of a life
too scattered and too insignificantly violent to figure out. Maybe
that was what it was all about—watching the fragmented bits
of images fall like the pieces of a jigsaw puzzle accidentally
knocked from the table. Maybe all of life was accidental.

When I woke up it was still dark and I was covered with
sweat, lying in a room where the air was only slightly above
freezing.

Slade was not in the room.

I eased off the bed, still dressed and wearing my riding boots.
I pulled on a fleece hat and slipped out of the room.

Slade was bundled up in all his riding gear and was sitting in
the dark on the tiny front porch where we'd sat before. His feet
were up on the porch railing, and he was watching the waterway. He looked at me and slowly nodded.

Seems as though that's the way it had always been. I was the one who blasted through his energy, lost his view of the wider situation, focused in on one target, and tried to destroy everything in my path to get the target under my control. And then I was empty. But Slade always had something left, something in reserve, something he could use to get us farther, safer, saner. And that's what he was doing now, watching the waterway.

A light glowed in the back of the hotel where I thought the kitchen might be. I went inside and found the kitchen door. There was an old guy in there cleaning the floor. He had the coffee on. That's all that mattered.

I took two huge mugs of coffee and went back out to the porch and sat beside Slade. Without a word, he reached under his coat and came out with the .45. He handed it to me, butt first. I checked the magazine, the chamber, set the safety, and slid the big gun down inside the back of my pants.

There was no need to say anything.

We sat there, drinking coffee, until light was softly flaring in the east.

The bike was doing its usual thing. But I finally started it, and Slade and I rode to the center of town and found what seemed to be the only café that was open. Or, perhaps, just the only café.

Inside, the place was dimly lit, which, at this time of the morning, was a blessing; it was barely daylight.

It smelled like a real café. The warm air was loaded with the aroma of coffee and the dripping smell of sizzling bacon. Potatoes were frying on a grill behind the counter—not frozen crap, but real potatoes that had been chopped up and dropped onto a hot grill slick with bacon grease.

And then there was the music. It wasn't too loud or too soft.

It was just there. Alaskans hang onto things. It seems to help them ease the passage of time as they work their way through the long nights, saving themselves for the joy of days when the light seems endless. They hold onto music, for example. We never intentionally went looking for music, didn't turn on a radio, didn't carry music with us. But we heard music in the small cafés, from the radios hidden back in the kitchens or tucked underneath counters. Sixties music, maybe some from the seventies. No rap. No crap. We got the feeling that any hard-core Alaskan over thirty would fold up a rap CD and use it as a funnel to put oil in his pickup. I loved music, but it didn't dominate my life when I was on the road.

While we were eating, a guy at the next table told us that Haines served as the inspiration for the television series, *Northern Exposure*. I believed him.

After breakfast, we rode slowly through the little town, heading north, back toward Canada. A stop sign was coming up and I began gearing down. As I went through the gears, pulling in the clutch lever, the rpms didn't seem to back off between gear changes. I rolled to a stop at the sign and plunked the bike into neutral. The engine roared at a steady 4,000 rpm. I fiddled with the controls but could not get the rpms down. The bike sat there, stock-still, roaring like the largest power saw ever built.

I shut the damn thing off. I climbed off and checked everything I could think of—throttle, levers, cables . . . every fucking thing. When I cranked it up again, there it was, 4,000 rpm, right on the nose.

I could keep riding, of course. I could ride at 4,000 rpm, even make my way through the small towns and stop signs, messing with the clutch and brake, maybe turning the bike off now and then. But the bike wasn't right, had not really been "right" since I left the rancho, and it was just a matter of time until being "not right" turned into "won't run at all." I didn't want the bike to be the ultimate focus of this ride. I wanted it to be the means, not the end. But the damn bike had lost its mind.

It was time for me to lose the bike.

The next stop north of Haines, where there might be some sort of service for the bike—or another bike for sale—was Haines Junction, more than a hundred miles away. Too small a town; too big a gamble. I decided there was no reason to leave Haines with the bike acting like that. If I really was going to dump the cranky bastard, Haines was the place. In real life, relationships sometimes come to an end. I knew that better than anyone. Today was the day. It was time to end the relationship with the KLR.

It was still early and we doubted that any business would be open at that hour, so Slade and I were still messing with my bike when I looked up and saw a lady casually watching me fume and cuss at the KLR. She was middle-aged, wearing jeans and an insulated jacket, had a small dog on a leash. She didn't seem to be in a hurry to leave, and since I suspected that everybody in Haines knew everything about everybody else, I thought she might know where I could take the bike, once the town was fully awake.

And, of course, she knew. There was no motorcycle shop in town, she said. If I wanted to buy a bike, I was probably out of luck. But there was a guy down on the waterfront who worked on outboards and snowmobiles. A genius with small engines, she said.

Snowmobiles? I didn't want a fucking snowmobile! I wanted a motorcycle that would run when I turned the goddamn handle!

Slade saw the anger rising in me and stepped in front of the lady, thanked her, and then told me to get my ass on my bike.

I roared my way to the waterfront, the bike screaming in some sort of hysterical death rant. Slade hung back. I think he didn't want to be associated with an insane motorcycle roaring like something out of NASCAR ripping through a town that was just coming awake. With an insane rider.

We were wrong—a business *was* open at this hour.

Rick Conneaut (I had to ask him how to properly pronounce his last name, and I'm still not sure I got it right), the guy who worked on outboards and snowmobiles, was a forties-something guy who looked like he'd been born and raised in Haines. He was tall, had a short beard, and even at this hour in the morning had fresh grease on his hands. He squatted beside the bike and listened to the engine over-rev. I stood off to the side, my arms tightly wrapped across my chest, my face red, staring at a motorcycle that I wanted to kill. Slade had parked off to the side and was leaning against his bike. Rick started following cables from the controls to the carburetor and engine (I'd already done that). He fiddled with the choke cable (I'd already done that) and poked his fingers in among the cables and tiny metal pieces around the engine (I'd already done that). Finally, he took the choke cable loose from the carburetor and inspected the end of it (I'd not done that), did some things with a pair of long-nosed pliers, and reinstalled the cable. He made some other small, mysterious adjustments and then started the bike—4,000 rpm, right on the nose. Ah, I thought, another mechanic baffled by a schizophrenic machine that should be shipped off to the junkyard.

And throughout the process, Rick had not said more than a dozen words. And then he said, "This is a '91."

"Yeah."

"Not many miles on it, for a '91."

"Yeah."

"I think I know why. You get it used?"

"Yeah."

"Defective carburetor. Probably came that way from the factory. Whoever owned it tried to fix it. Messed with the carb so much that it's hopeless. Probably stuck some bad parts into a carb that was already bad. Has to be rebuilt."

"Screw that." I said.

Rick looked at me, like a parent looks at an unruly child. "Some things just can't be fixed with small fixes," he said, still looking me square in the face. "They have to be dealt with as they are."

He caught me off guard. I thought maybe he wasn't talking about the carburetor. But where does a small-town mechanic get off messing with my head?

I tried to switch mental gears. "Is there a bike in town I can buy? Something that will get me farther north?"

"Doubt it," he said. "I see most of the machines that might be for sale. You don't want any of 'em."

"Can you order a new carb?"

"Sure."

"How much time?"

Rick rolled the question around in his mind. "Could take a week. Ten days. Have to order it out of Anchorage . . ."

"Can you rebuild this carb?"

"Sure."

"Same amount of time?"

"Nope. Longer."

We could hear some sort of sea birds calling from behind his shop, a light breeze springing up with the coming of the sun. "Fuck it," I said, looking at Slade. "I can ride at 4,000 rpm, all the way to Fairbanks, if I have to."

"Why would you do that?" Rick asked softly.

"What fucking choice do I have?"

Rick ambled over to an old shed with a sliding door. He still had a screwdriver in his hand and he used it to pry open a rusted sliding bolt. He pulled the door back. Inside the shed was a KLR.

If there ever were a KLR that looked worse than mine, this was it. Both tires were flat; the front wheel was twisted hard to the left and had somehow been pounded into an oval shape; the forks were smashed back against the engine; the left handlebar was bent straight up, like some sort of oversized antennae; a hole in the gas tank big enough to put my fist through. The seat had been ripped apart, pieces of it lying on the floor of the shed. But there, snuggled inside all that damage, untouched, pristine, seeming almost to glow, was the carburetor.

We had a couple of hours to kill. Turns out, we were not too far from the old hotel we'd left earlier that morning. Slade left his bike at Rick's place, and we walked back there, sat on the porch, drank coffee—and kept an eye out for fast-moving boats.

When we went back to Rick's my bike was sitting out front. I stood beside the machine and started it up, my frustration already building, sure that the bike would do its usual thing. The engine started without minimum choke, and then settled in to an idle a little below 1,000 rpm, running as smoothly as I'd ever heard it. Rick stood in his doorway and didn't say a word, just stared at the motorcycle, listening.

I couldn't believe the sound of the engine. If a 650cc single-cylinder engine could be described as "purring," then the KLR was, indeed, purring.

Gently, I swung my leg over the bike—I was afraid it would die or over-rev if I jolted it, dropped it into gear, and rode slowly away from Rick and Slade, heading back down the narrow blacktop that led to the ferry docks. At first I rode slowly, gently, waiting for whatever the damn bike was going to do. And then I gently increased the throttle, again waiting for the unscheduled change in rpms.

Nothing. Just smooth acceleration.

I tightened my fingers on the throttle and twisted it violently. The KLR leaped like it had been kicked, the engine winding smoothly, no variations in rpms unless I made them. I backed off the throttle, then got on it again, then backed off. I couldn't make the bike backfire, couldn't make it jerk, couldn't make the engine forget where it was, and how much power it was supposed to put out. The fucking thing ran perfectly.

I rode back to Rick's place and shut the bike down, got off, and shook Rick's hand.

"My friend, you must have an engineering degree from MIT," I said, grinning.

"Nope. Psych degrees, two of 'em, Berkeley," he said with a straight face. "It's a fact. Had a therapy practice in Oakland."

In the background was his rambling shop, the waterfront. Behind us was the weather-beaten little town of Haines.

"Yeah, I know," he said, "you're wondering why I'm here. Got tired of dealing with crazy people. Came to Alaska, where everybody's sane, or everybody's crazy. Either way, it's the norm." He paused, looking at me. "'Course, now and then, somebody comes along who's still off the chart.'"

And then he laughed. A genuine, deep-chested laugh. And I laughed. And Slade.

Rick charged me fifty dollars. I would have paid him anything he asked.

Some things can't be fixed with small fixes, you have to deal with them as they are. I know, because that's what Rick told me.

I loved Haines.


We rose out of the river delta that shelters Haines and followed the shallow, wide water through an eagle preserve. There was a single, lonely eagle in the top of a dead tree across the river, and that was the only eagle we saw.

At a break in the trees beside the road, Slade pulled over. I knew he had to piss. Slade had to piss every twenty miles.

I got off the bike (I actually patted the gas tank, once again in love with the machine) then worked my way through the trees and brush to the edge of the river. For some reason, I wanted to feel the water.

I squatted down and put my hand into the flow, and in seconds I could not feel my fingers. I dug my fingers into the icy mud, but it wasn't mud—it was fine shale and even finer gravel, washed out of the wilderness and being wrangled to the sea by a never-ending flow of water, the water itself turned gray by the load it carried.

I let the gravelly earth dribble between my fingers.

And then Slade was there, towering over me. "Couldn't build a mud doll out of that," he mumbled.

I said nothing.

At the summit the road looped over the pass and then dropped slightly, running north toward Haines Junction. The temperature fell back to that familiar, frigid range that we'd become used to, the landscape looking truly Arctic, the most tundra-like of anything we'd seen yet. We stopped and looked at it, the treeless, rounded ridges; the stunted shrub growth, no higher than our knees. In its own way, as with everything else we'd seen that had been Arctic-like, it had its own terrible beauty, a bone-bare starkness that hid nothing and offered nothing but an ultimate landscape layered with hard days lived through by harder men. It seemed as though every astounding thing we saw on the ride was simply a preparation for seeing something else the next day that would exceed the day before. What we were looking at here was no exception.

The air was quiet, the sky overcast. I knew there was, more often than not, fierce weather that clapped down on the very ground we were standing on. I didn't want to wait to see it. In spite of the stark beauty of the place, I was glad when we got on the bikes and kept heading north.

Somewhere in there, we crossed out of Alaska and back into the Yukon Territory. We were in Canada for the last time.

We got to Haines Junction a little after 2 p.m. There was a bakery there. People I had talked to who had been in Haines Junction said we had to stop at this bakery, *the* bakery, the best bakery on the whole damn highway, with absolutely the best . . . pie.

Slade was ecstatic—maybe he would find the ultimate berry pie. Maybe even a ten?

The bakery was closed for the winter.

Haines Junction was closed for the winter.

We rode into the gravel parking area of three restaurants, all closed. The sky was closing down, too, the temperature still dropping, even more than it had on the ride into the Junction. We were tired, cold, and hungry. It would not be a problem; we had road-food in our saddlebags, but it would be nice to sit in a warm place and eat warm food. It would be damn nice.

We managed to find a gas station that was open, and we fueled the bikes. Looking out through the window of the station, I saw a rambling clapboard motel across the street that had an open sign dangling from what looked like a front porch. The sign hung from a single hook, swinging and twisting slightly in the cold air. Off to the side of the porch and around the right side, another sign said "restaurant." It didn't say "closed."

We rode the bikes across the street. The motel and the restaurant looked deserted, one large, wooden, slab-sided building standing by the side of the road in a town that was all but boarded up, the wind beginning to rush across the tops of sleeping trees, moisture trying desperately to turn to snow, the cold of it all seeping into our clothing and our bones.

Slade and I walked up on the porch. We were wearing full riding gear—helmets, heavy jackets, overpants, insulated gloves, boots. We looked like very large and very bad actors out of a cheap biker movie. Slade tried the door. It was unlocked. He opened it, and we stepped inside.

The place was big, empty, and silent. Dozens of naked tables, dozens of chairs, some of the chairs stacked onto the tables. It was the empty shell of what, during the season, must have been a huge restaurant. But the room was warm. We pulled off our helmets.

The place was not completely empty. At the far back of the cavernous dining room a large Asian family was seated at an enormous, round table. There must have ten of them. They were eating, talking, laughing, a family very much at ease with itself. When they saw us standing there, all conversation stopped. A short man, older, probably the head of the clan, jumped out of his seat and stomped quickly toward us, his feet thumping on the wooden floor, his steps amplified by the huge, empty room.

Slade glanced at me, then at the little man marching across the floor. I knew what Slade was thinking—everything else in town seemed to be closed, so maybe we didn't belong there, maybe we'd wandered into a restaurant that was closed, the owners having a late lunch before going home. Or to Hawaii.

The little man marched up and fronted Slade, puffing out his chest and trying to rise on his toes—Slade was at least a foot taller.

"How you get in here?" the man asked, his voice stern, challenging.

Slade didn't move. "Through the door," Slade said, his voice taking on that edge that meant he wasn't in the mood to take shit from anybody. Neither of them spoke for a moment, then Slade asked, "Are you open?"

"Was door locked?" the little guy wanted to know, his voice rising slightly.

"No," Slade said, his voice edging farther toward a growl.

"Then we *open!*" the little guy said, his face breaking into a broad grin. "If door locked, we *closed!*" And he walked away laughing.

We heard giggles from the women at the back of the room.

Slade and I peeled off some of our outer layers and sat down, still trying to shake the cold out of our clothing and our bodies. The little guy, Mr. Wong, appeared with menus. Slade ordered a hamburger. (We were the only people in a huge, empty Asian restaurant, and Slade ordered a fucking hamburger.) I ordered wonton soup. Some folks got up from the table and hurried into the kitchen. It was obvious that no one had planned on cooking anything, but they were going to cook something for us.

We sat there, glad to be inside in the warmth, watching the others at the large table in the back steal looks at us, grinning, nodding.

Mr. Wong brought our food. My enormous bowl of soup was rich, steaming, with stuffed wontons that sat on the tongue like soft, succulent pillows. It was the best wonton soup I'd ever had. It was the best meal on the entire trip.


When we left Haines Junction, I thought the cold would finally get to us, the wind picking up, maybe cause us to go back and lay over for the night. But it didn't. We kept riding.

Ten miles out of town the wind died, the clouds slid away, and bright sunshine poured down, all the way to Kluane Wilderness Village.

# 28

# DAY 19

Friday, September 13
from Kluane Wilderness Village, Yukon Territory

IT WAS NOT REALLY a village. It was an ancient motel at the edge
of a long, narrow lake, the buildings hunkered down for another winter in the Yukon Territory, a maintenance guy sealing
up doors and windows. Tacked onto the south side of the main
building were a few rooms that looked as though they had re-
cently been added, rooms from manufactured housing that had
been bolted together. A narrow porch ran along the front, opening out into a large gravel parking area.

We checked in and walked across the highway to the Village's restaurant. The only other patrons were some boisterous
fishermen, clustered around a table in another room, drinking,
telling fishing stories.

We sat in a booth. A waitress came out of the kitchen, walked
over and leaned her hip on our table. She was young—compared to us—but she was no kid. She was taller than most, attractive, and ample, her curves filling out a fifties-era waitress
uniform—complete with apron, her breasts barely contained
inside the buttons. I thought she looked tired, from working

long days in the restaurant, dealing with cranky tourists, waiting for the Village to close for the winter. Turned out, she was the only waitress in the place, but there was only Slade and me and the fishermen in the other room. We ordered, and she went back into the kitchen. I don't remember her saying a word.

But as we ate, she kept stopping by the table, more often than necessary. I thought she had eyes for Slade, but I couldn't be sure. Ever since Marie's Café in Wasa he'd been in some sort of musing space around women, as though he were comparing, or remembering, or maybe just thinking. Maybe all of that. I couldn't tell. And I wasn't going to ask.

Her name was Lorena. The waitress. And she finally started talking, her voice low-key, almost somber. She kept asking us about our trip, where were we going, when did we start, why were we doing this? We sat at the table for a long time after we finished eating, talking with her. She seemed almost depressed, but we couldn't figure out why. She'd been at the Village since it opened in the spring, and now, in a few days, would head south, back to Vancouver, she said. Or maybe someplace else. It didn't really matter. When she said that, she paused, giving us time to think about that. But Slade and I said nothing.

We heard a heavy voice from the other room, apparently one of the fishermen. Lorena made a face—what now?—and disappeared through a door. In a few moments she was back, carrying a platter with a single, large, whole, eel-like fish on it. The fish was black and wrinkled, dry, as though the cook had broiled the thing over a too-hot fire, skin and all, its eyes burned out, the empty sockets still staring as though blind but not dead. I wondered if he'd taken out the guts. If ever there were a competition for the ugliest fish in the Yukon, the thing on the platter would have won easily. Lorena said the fishermen had caught several, and the cook had broiled them for the fishermen's dinner. They were offering us the fish, she said, to go with our dinner.

We politely refused. Lorena carried the fish back into the other room.

In less than a minute a huge guy came through the door, carrying the platter in front of him. He had a slight wobble to his walk, as though he'd been drinking and the booze had started to work its magic. He wore expensive fishing clothing—some sort of heavy canvas pants and a vest with more pockets than I had on my entire body. Lorena was a few steps behind him.

He came straight to our booth and clunked the platter down between us. "I'm from America," he said. He paused, letting that sink in. "Where I'm from, when somebody offers to share their food, you don't turn it down. You Canucks need to learn some manners."

For a moment, no one said anything. The air was thick with tension and the smell of the burned fish came up through it like an oil slick. Lorena did not move.

And I knew I was going to have to pay the owners of the Village for the furniture I was going to bust up by trying to put this guy on the floor.

Slade beat me to it. And he didn't even move.

"Here's how this is going to go down, you *American* asshole," Slade said softly. "You are going to back your ugly *American* ass away from this table and go back to your *American* buddies," Slade paused, "or I'm going to ram this ugly fish up your ass and light the end of it like a fuse."

Slade kept looking directly into the guy's eyes. So did I. I could see the indecision there, and then the fear. The guy took a small step backward, blew air out through his nose, and made a small backward movement with his head, as though we weren't worth messing with. He turned and took a step toward the door to the other room.

"Hey, *American!*" Slade said sharply.

Oh, shit, I thought.

The guy stopped and turned.

"You forgot your fish," Slade said sharply. "I don't want it on my table."

Richard Ford once wrote that the extraordinary things in life can start from otherwise ordinary events—and start in the blink of an eye. I blinked my eyes and waited for this one to start.

The guy knew there were only two ways to end it. He had to take on Slade, or he had to take the fish. Even through the alcohol, he made the right decision. He took the fish.

As he picked it up, Slade said, "I don't want to see you again."

The guy didn't look at Slade, just took the fish and left. He had to slide by Lorena to get through the door.

Slade and I got out of the booth, separated a couple of feet, and waited for the sound of many feet pounding across the floor. Nothing happened. Not a single sound came from the other room.

Usually, it was me.

But Slade had his moments.

\* \* \* \* \*

Yeah, Slade had his moments. Sometimes, one hell of a lot more than "moments." Usually, those moments involved keeping me alive. Or out of jail.

*  *  *  *  *

The pickup truck looked like it belonged there. A thirty-year-old beater, the fenders hanging on by bolts probably stolen from an ancient tractor, the paint eaten to the metal by the scouring of desert sand blown at the speed of gunfire. No bumpers. The passenger's windshield was spider-webbed with cracks, as though a large rock had been dropped on it from above. There was no glass in the rear cab window. The door windows would not roll up, or were missing. We never bothered to find out.

But the engine ran, sort of. We'd driven the truck to El Paso from Antelope Wells, where we'd crossed the border into the United States and then turned east across dry, burning country. Now, the truck was parked in a trash-strewn alley off a narrow, trash-strewn street, the truck's one headlight staring blankly out into sunlit heat strong enough to bake brains. The truck had Mexican plates. But that didn't matter—half the trucks in El Paso had Mexican plates. Besides, we'd stolen the plates in Mexico, which is where we'd stolen the truck.

Yeah. It looked like it belonged there.

Slade and I stood in the mottled shade of a tattered canvas awning that hung in front of a tiendita that sold baskets from Mexico. A mixture of smells blanketed us: meat cooking somewhere, probably over an open fire; car exhaust; urine, from the alley where we parked the truck. Sweat poured from us. After the drive across the desert in a rhythmically clunking junker with no windows, the super-heated air trying to melt our shirts, I thought we didn't have enough body fluids left to make sweat. But I was wrong.

We stood silently, at one of those points in our lives where the past was dimming quickly, and the future did not exist, and all directions were open to us. But most of the directions would be bad, and we did not know which ones.

And so we stood there, in the oven that was El Paso, and tried to let the world identify itself.

Down the street, a dead neon sign hung partially out over the sidewalk. The sign said "air condition" in both English and Spanish. Not air "condition-ing," just "condition." Slade and I moved slowly down the sidewalk and stood under the sign. It was over the door to a store, which, from the stuff in the windows, seemed to sell hardware, work clothes, a few groceries. And guns. There were bars over the windows. A fat guy stood behind a counter. He didn't seem to be sweating. The "air condition" must work, I thought.

"Let's go inside and poke around," I said to Slade, "at least until we can stop sweating."

A door of heavy metal grillwork was pushed back and tied open with a tattered piece of heavy rope. The other door was thick, scarred glass. We pushed it open and went inside.

The "air condition" was working. We could hear its rattle from somewhere far back in the store, struggling to keep ahead of the heat. The store was jammed with hardware and rough workman's clothing, a few shelves in the far back loaded with bread, crackers, and small pop-top cans of food that laborers might buy for their lunch boxes. The place smelled of damp cloth and old leather.

A narrow, glass-topped display counter ran the full length of the left side. The case was full of pistols. Behind it, long guns stood in racks against the wall—shotguns, rifles of all calibers and ages and conditions. The fat guy was Anglo, big, looked young, a smirk on his face, a revolver on his belt. He was wearing some sort of tan, military-type shirt, every button buttoned as though he were waiting for an inspection. His huge belly bulged the shirt out over his belt. A large tattoo peeked out above his collar, but I couldn't tell what it was.

Slade and I went to the counter, nodding at the guy, looking at the pistols, basically just trying to cool off. The guy didn't say anything, just looked at us. We were wearing our "invisible" clothing—jeans, floppy shirts hanging outside our belts, ankle-high canvas shoes with lug soles. Slade wore a ball cap. I wore an old western hat, the brim slightly tattered. No loud colors, no patches, no logos. We might have been day workers. We might have been one step up the ladder from bums.

We stood in front of the case, looking down through the glass, Slade standing to my left. The guy moved over in front of us and rested his big hands on the counter. "Show you anything," he said. It might have been a question, but didn't sound like it.

"Yeah," I said, "I'd like to see that old 1911." I pointed down through the glass at a .45 that looked like WWII vintage, maybe even older.

"Sure," the guy said, the smirk still on his face. "Expensive. Collector's gun." He had already decided that Slade and I weren't really customers. We weren't, of course, but it still pissed me off a little.

The guy took some keys out of his pocket and opened a tiny padlock, took out the gun. And pointed it directly at my chest. His finger was on the trigger.

I could sense Slade tensing up beside me. Slade seemed to send out vibes when that sort of feeling came over him, vibes that, over time, I'd come to recognize. And appreciate.

The bore of the .45 looked like I could crawl up inside it and build a campfire. I didn't know what the guy had in mind. For once, I kept my mouth shut, waiting for the scene to play out.

"That piece loaded?" I heard Slade growl as he stepped up right against me.

The guy was enjoying this. We must have been his only entertainment for the day. "Don't know," he said, sounding as though he were talking to children. "Not supposed to be loaded, but you never know." He actually chuckled softly. "Either way, kinda gits your attention, don't it?"

I felt Slade's hand in the small of my back, felt my shirt move, felt my belt become suddenly lighter.

"Man should always assume a gun's loaded," Slade said. "This one is, for example." And he pulled my—our—.45 from behind me and stuck it in the guy's face. There was a tiny clicking sound as Slade thumbed off the safety. The guy's face turned instantly white, his eyes bulging and riveted to Slade's gun. He did not move.

"Do I have your attention?" Slade said. It was obvious that he didn't expect an answer. "That hammer on your piece is down," Slade said, the tension in his voice hard enough to use as a weapon. The guy was still pointing the gun at me. "If you touch the hammer, I'll open up your fat face like a stopped-up sewer." And then Slade leaned forward across the counter and jerked the guy's revolver from its holster and handed the gun to me. I stood stone-still. I hadn't said a word.

"Now listen carefully, fat boy," Slade said softly. "Put that .45 down gently on the counter and then put your hands flat on the glass and lean on them." The guy put the gun down. His hands went to the glass, his fingers spread. I could see the pressure of his weight on his wrists. Slade's gun hadn't left the guy's face, the fat guy staring so hard at it that I thought his eyes were crossed.

Slade nodded to me. I took the guy's .45 and moved slightly to my right, out of reach. I glanced at the door of the store. It hadn't opened since we'd come inside.

The revolver went into my pants pocket. I dropped the magazine from the .45—empty—and jacked back the slide—empty. I put the gun on the floor and kicked it toward the back of the store. It went out of sight under some shelving. I fished the revolver out of my pocket. It was chrome plated and had ivory handles. A show-off piece, loaded. I popped the cylinder and dumped the ammo on the counter, then slid the back of my hand hard across the glass, scattering the rounds. I threw the gun toward the back of the store. I heard it hit something back there, glass breaking, and then something spilling on the floor.

Slade hadn't moved. I eased behind him, sliding toward the door.

"One more thing," Slade said, "you're going to shoot left-handed for a while." And he brought the butt of his .45 down hard on the back of the guy's right hand, so hard that the glass in the counter broke. And so, I supposed, did the guy's hand.

The guy screamed and fell backward, hitting the long-gun racks, slamming into the floor, his bulk taking up all the space behind the counter.

Slade put the .45 in his belt under his shirt, and we walked slowly out of the store and up the street. We crossed the street to the alley where we'd parked the truck. The truck was gone.

We didn't stop, walked down the alley into the shadows, and kept on going. It felt familiar.

"Gracias," I mumbled.

"De nada," he said, lightly.

Like I said, Slade had his moments.

* * * * *

The next morning, we ate quickly in the same restaurant. The cook came out and brought our food. The fishermen were gone, and we didn't see Lorena anywhere. We went back to our room and saddled up the bikes. We started the engines, sitting on the bikes for a moment, waiting for them to warm up, me listening to the calm working of the engine of my KLR, me grinning.

I thought it was too cold to rain. Snow, maybe, but not rain. I was wrong. The frigid rain came again.

I glanced back toward our room. Lorena stood on the porch, looking through the water running from the roof, the open door of one of the motel rooms behind her, a vacuum cleaner off to the side. She was wearing her waitress uniform, although it was obvious she also cleaned the rooms. She was holding what looked like a battered suitcase pressed hard against her chest. I imagined I could see the whites of her knuckles as she squeezed the sides. She stared at us, not moving, not speaking. Off the porch, in front of her, an old Buick sedan was parked, the rain from the roof pounding on its hood. Lorena jumped from the porch, whipped open a door, and threw the suitcase inside the car. It was an exaggerated movement, done to show us the finality of where she was and what she was doing.

In a moment she was back on the porch, this time holding an armload of sheets, again pressing them against her, as though, somehow, they might escape into some other world before she did. She stepped into the parking lot and into the rain, staring after us, motionless, still holding the sheets, making no effort to protect herself from the blowing rain that lanced through the heavy mist that came down from the high ridge behind the Village.

We dropped the bikes into gear and rode slowly away. As we eased up the narrow highway I kept checking the rear view mirror. Until we were out of sight of the Village, I could see Lorena through the mist, standing like a wet statue, watching us ride away, the rain soaking her and the sheets that she still held.

We were again headed north, the sound of the rain dampening the rush of air around our helmets.

I was on a motorcycle, riding away from an ancient car and a woman I did not know . . .


After an hour the rain stopped. We pulled off the road and took off our helmets, letting suddenly hot sunshine bake our faces.

"If one of us had nodded his head, Lorena would've been on the back of his bike," Slade said. "I don't think she would have even changed clothes."

I said nothing. I looked back down the highway, knowing that Lorena was still cleaning rooms, and I knew she was desperate to be someplace, anyplace, other than where she was. I knew what she felt like. Jesus Christ, I knew what she felt like.

We felt good. We were closing in on it.

The border crossing was the largest operation we had yet seen. Crossing into Canada the first time, then into Alaska, back out of Alaska and into Canada again—all of that had been simple and easy.

This place looked like the parking lot of a Walmart.

But that isn't what bothered me. From the Canadian side I looked across into Alaska and saw the Alaska state trooper's car, parked facing back into Alaska, ready to give chase. I reached over and tapped Slade on the shoulder, nodded toward the car.

Slade raised his face shield. "Nothing we can do about it," he said. "It's not like we aren't going to cross the border because there's a cop car sitting there."

That did not make me feel any better.

We went through the border processing without even a sideways glance from the agent. If a bulletin had been issued for me, this border is where it would have come into play. It didn't. We rode past the cop car at *very* slow speed. The car did not move.

We'd crossed the border back into Alaska for the last time. We'd been in Alaska before, when we dropped down into Skagway. But now, when we crossed the border, it would be . . . the last border. The border we'd been looking for since we got on our bikes in Slade's driveway and rode out into the rain.

We didn't know what we were in for.

# 29

# DAY 19—THE SAME DAY

Friday, September 13
from the border crossing, Yukon Territory

THE DAY HAD STARTED with misty rain, then brief sunshine, but the sunshine didn't last.

I'd become fixated on the weather. Nineteen days of riding since I'd left the rancho, and in that time only three half-days of sunshine, three half-days of calm. The weather was beating me down. I wasn't cold, not really, even though I bitched about it. I wasn't wet—our riding gear really was waterproof . . . except when I was wearing mine while lying in a ditch. But the world was wet, and the harder I tried to ignore what was outside my face shield, the more energy it took. Sometimes it felt as though I were not going anywhere—just sitting on a bike, upright, stationary, while the rain beat the hell out of me. In between the rainstorms nothing changed. The world was black outside my helmet. The world was black inside my helmet.

Everything about this ride seemed to be about water. From the time I'd ridden into Ute Station is Southern Colorado, water had been with me—with us. Even ripping across Yukon wilderness, water was still filling our lives. Water ran inside our coats and down the middle of our backs; water was in our long johns (might have been piss; it was hard to tell at this point); water was inside our waterproof boots. The wind cut through our clothes as though we were riding nude. But sometimes I didn't know if the chill was coming from the outside or the inside.

I'd come out of the Southwest, an arid and bone-hard land where water was gold, and gold was good only for jewelry. You could not drink gold. Now, I had to wrap the .45 in a plastic bag before I stuck it inside my coat. Even so, I made sure I dried it every night, usually putting it inside my sleeping bag.

I was pretty sure my own personal drought was over.

To hell with it. It was just weather. I had been in weather before. I had been in weather all my life. I wanted to get to the Arctic Circle, so I was going to have to suck it up and ride like I knew how to. Screw the weather.

And besides, the bike was running like a dream.

When our wheels rolled across the line into Alaska there was the thrill of knowing this was the last border we would cross. But I knew, and Slade knew, that we were back in a state where cops from the lower forty-eight, and Skagway, would have buddies. But there was nothing we could do about that—we weren't going to quit, and we weren't going to cut and run. Fuck it. We rode on.

We were two hundred miles from Delta Junction, as good a target as any.

Slade and I looked at each other.

Let's do it.

*  *  *  *  *

Ten miles out of Delta Junction the wind seemed to slip into our world without our knowing it was coming. We'd been in a lot of wind before, but there was something different about the hard air blowing against us, as though it had come a long way and was used to sweeping everything from its path. It even smelled different. At first, it was only a slight push from the south and west. But the push became a shove, and the shove became a constant weight. Five miles from Delta Junction the wind was blowing at a constant forty miles per hour, directly onto our left shoulders. And it was constantly increasing its pressure. Maybe fifty, maybe more. Maybe I'm exaggerating.

I tried to keep a straight line, but it was useless. In a single gust, the KLR was moved from the centerline to the edge of the berm. The berm caught the front wheel and pulled it off onto the gravel. I let it go, waited for the rear wheel to slip in behind it, then gunned the KLR into a hard drive until I knew the wind wasn't going to take me off into the rocks. I tilted the bike to the left and let the wheels take me back onto the blacktop.

That happened twice more.

Finally, I slowed to about twenty miles per hour. If the wind were going to blow me down, at least I wouldn't slide very far.

It was, maybe, the worst wind I had ever been in on a motorcycle. There was no question about setting up camp in that wind.

We hid the bikes behind the wall of a tiny motel in Delta Junction, fixing them in place with prop sticks to keep them from being blown off their side stands. The motel had a café that was bigger than the motel. Maybe another restaurant was somewhere on the highway, but Slade and I damn sure weren't going to ride around looking for it. The place was almost deserted, empty booths along the left side and a thrown-together collection of tables and chairs that filled the dining area, only one table occupied. We sat and sipped coffee, watching through the window as pieces of tin roofing from some unknown building sailed, spinning, across the road. If we'd been on the bikes on that road, the sheets of tin could have decapitated us.

When Slade and I were on the road we stayed out of any restaurant with a name we recognized. We haunted the tiny cafés, the board-front places with names painted on planks nailed across the porch, names like Skinny Dick's, Sled Dog Annie's, and Bertha's Pie Shop—But We Ain't Got No Pie. (Slade wouldn't stop there.) Slade and I always sat in the no-smoking section, usually nothing more than a tiny table in the corner, less than three feet from the smoking tables where early morning chain-smokers sat sipping coffee and working a deck of cigarettes down to the last stick, a blue haze hanging in the air, ashtrays full, waitresses stealing a quick toke from a favored customer.

Those cafés were special. They had their own rules. When you went inside you knew, automatically, what you could do and not do. One of the things you did not do was order anything that wasn't on the menu; you didn't order anything "special." You didn't order anything, well . . . "froufrou."

Slade is the only guy I know with balls enough to walk into a classic, smoke-filled Alaskan roadside café and ask to taste the gravy before he ordered it. Once, he walked into one of those places and said to the waitress, loud enough for everyone to hear, "I'll have a bran muffin, yogurt, and a decaf coffee." All conversation in the place stopped instantly, the grizzled locals looking hard at the newcomer who wanted . . . yogurt? We sat at our usual table in the corner. It took Slade an hour to get the grin off his face.

In almost all those cafés there was a café community, two or three guys, sometimes more, who were gathered for the morning, perhaps even the day. They had "their" table, maybe even "their" coffee mugs. They joked with the other locals who came in, made lame comments to the women, and stared openly at customers they didn't know. They weren't hostile, only openly curious about others with the audacity to invade their territory.

We got to Delta Junction by mid-afternoon. In the café when we were drinking our coffee the regulars were already at their table. The "chairman" joked with us, ribbing us about riding bikes in that country, in that weather, at that time of year. After they tired of laughing at us, the chairman explained that there was a gap in the mountains to the south of Delta Junction. Cold air capped the mountains. The only way the warm air off the ocean could get through was to be forced through the gap, bearing down on anything in front of it like a freight train—and Delta Junction sat squarely on the tracks.

"Does it always blow like this?" Slade asked one of the guys, who had a full beard and was sipping beer through his missing front teeth.

"Hell, no, boy, sometimes it blows harder!" The standard comeback for tourists. They all laughed, and one of his buddies clapped him on the back.

We drank some more coffee and left.

When we came back for dinner, the café community was still

there, the chairman still holding court. A few other people were there, mostly keeping to themselves, trying to ignore the chairman and his buddies. Slade and I sat in a booth. All the other booths were empty. Maybe too windy for the locals to come out. They were smart.

A waitress of some undetermined age sauntered over to us. I could smell the cigarette smoke on her clothing, and I knew Slade could, too. I wondered if he would say anything. He didn't.

We both ordered beer. Slade ordered chicken-fried steak; I ordered meatloaf. We drank our beer silently, each of us lost in some other thought-world, exploring, our eyes wandering around the room. On the wall above the front door there was a framed photo of a wolf. The photo was old, fading, the frame cracked. But the picture held my eyes, and my mind flashed to a wolf's head badly painted on a truck door.

I sipped my beer. "Do you think we'll ever be rousted over the wolf-guy, and the truck?" I muttered.

Slade sat quietly for a while. Then, "Been thinking about that, wondering why there wasn't anybody at the border after we left Haines and nobody at the border when we came back into Alaska, east of Tok." He sat for a while, still thinking. "Only one reason," he said. "The wolf-guy is a bigger outlaw than you or me. Maybe he was carrying something in the truck that he shouldn't. Maybe when the truck burned he had a lot of explaining to do.

"Or," Slade said, "maybe we are just lucky. Like I said, never question good luck."

The waitress brought the food. I don't know how she carried it all. Each serving was big enough for two people. Slade and I could eat good-size piles of food, but this was ridiculous. One thing we were beginning to learn about Alaskans: they could eat, drink, tell stories, and chain-smoke cigarettes. And their cafés were a testament to all of that.

We were making a valiant effort to eat all the food, taking our time, half-listening to the chairman and his cronies. The door opened, and a hard burst of wind crashed into the dining area. It knocked over the first two chairs and swept the salt and pepper shakers off the table. No one paid any attention. Right behind the wind, as though being blown into the café, was a heavyset guy and his family—wife and two early-teen kids, a boy and a girl. They looked happy, content, ready for a good meal. A damn big meal, I thought.

They sat in the booth next to ours. Slade and I were paying attention to our own food, but we overheard their conversation with the waitress. Mom ordered a bowl of soup and some sort of sandwich. The kids ordered burgers and fries. And then it was Dad's turn. He ordered a steak, baked potato, beans, and all the other trimmings. A salad came with his order. The waitress told Dad that the steak would take a few minutes.

"How long?" Dad asked.

"Oh, maybe fifteen minutes."

"How long will a burger take?" Dad wanted to know.

"Burgers will be out in less than five minutes," the waitress said. I had the impression that she knew where Dad was headed.

"While I'm waiting for the steak," Dad said, "you can bring me a burger and fries.

"You got it," the waitress said.

And she brought the food—for Mom and the kids and Dad's

burger. And when he finished the burger and fries, she brought the steak. Mom and the kids sat easily, talking about everyday things, in no hurry, while Dad finished both his dinners. Nothing unusual.

Slade and I thought about ordering dessert. But then we figured that neither of us was man enough to eat it all. We sat sipping coffee, in no hurry to go back to a room that was too small and get into beds that were too short and listen to wind blow against walls that were too thin.

We watched food being brought to the chairman and his buddies, the plates large, the food piled high.

"If this is just an ordinary night," Slade said, "I wonder what the hell it's like in here at Thanksgiving." He sipped his coffee, then slid his eyes toward me. "Um, sorry, Morgan. Didn't mean to bring that up."

I looked at him, grinned a little and shrugged my shoulders. The memory hadn't completely faded, but it was getting thinner.

\* \* \* \* \*

Thanksgiving Day.

I was never one for holidays. They came and they went, like all other days. Maybe it was because I'd spent so many of them in places where it was the right holiday in the wrong place.

But I liked Thanksgiving. It was the most quiet of the holidays, a day when you could sit beside someone and say nothing. Maybe for hours. And I knew, sooner or later, it would be completely absorbed by the creeping length of the American Christmas season. Thanksgiving would grow old and disappear. I could relate to that.

Sylvia wanted to cook Thanksgiving dinner at the ranch, use the old wood burning stove that still kept the kitchen warm on sharp winter mornings. Roast a turkey. Bake something. Serve dinner in the early evening when we would have to light a kerosene lantern, eating by the sort of glow that kept families together for generations. Be together. Maybe like in the old days when the ranch had been nothing more than a frontier outpost.

The day before Thanksgiving she drove her little red sports car into town to get everything she needed.

She knew that I was going to help Arturo take a load of food to his relatives down in the southern mountains, something we did every Thanksgiving since I'd been at the ranch, since before I'd met Sylvia. I wouldn't be back until late afternoon, probably just in time for dinner, with enough time left over to step to the side of the creek and wash off the trail dust and then put on a clean shirt. But she didn't seem to mind, seemed glad, in fact. I would be out of the way while she cooked and did whatever women do in the kitchen when it's Thanksgiving.

There was a small room off the kitchen. It had a single window and room enough for one big chair and a footstool. I kept books in there; I enjoyed sitting and reading in a place where I could reach out and touch other books. But Sylvia had wanted to set it up like a formal dining room. So I took out the big chair. As a dining room, there was hardly space for a small dining table and the two of us. But we would have Thanksgiving dinner in there. A dining room. It was the way it was supposed to be; it was what normal people did.

It was turning cool and crisp when I turned the old pickup into the narrow lane that led to the house. I always liked turning onto the lane, seeing the house up there under the cottonwoods, the rocking chairs on the porch. I stopped the truck and sat there, looking at a place that was mine, a place with another human inside that I knew, a place I wanted to be, for the first time in my life.

The front door was closed against the chill of the late afternoon air, but a soft lantern light shone behind the windows as though in anticipation of my coming home.

I didn't see Syl's car, but I paid no attention.

I was home. I'd waited for years to have the feeling of being home.

I pulled up at the side of the house, walked around and did a quick washup in the creek, and stepped up on the front porch. Even standing there, outside, I could smell all those smells that came from Thanksgiving kitchens. Maybe Thanksgiving was more than just a holiday. Maybe, for me, it was a reminder of something that I'd once had and now maybe had again. I had my books, I had a home, and inside the home there was a woman I could pay attention to.

I opened the front door and stepped inside. The house was silent, but filled even more with the scents of the meal that had been in preparation all day.

I eased through the room and stood in the kitchen doorway. The kitchen was clean, the pots put away, the cupboard doors shut, the stove cooling.

No one was in the kitchen.

I looked into the dining room, our dining room. The table was set perfectly. I didn't own a tablecloth, so Sylvia had taken a sheet and folded it to fit the tiny table. In the center of the table was a small turkey, perfectly roasted, the skin glistening in the light from a kerosene lamp that sat on a windowsill. Beside the turkey there were some small bowls with lids, bowls that I seldom used and had not looked at in months. Mashed potatoes, and maybe green beans. A basket of bread, covered with a small towel, sat at one corner. Next to the turkey one tall candlestick, made from the thick, dried base of a cholla cactus, the candle unlit, stood sentry over the meal. A bottle of wine sat at the edge of the table, unopened. Waiting for me, I thought. All I had to do was light the candle and open the wine, and it would be Thanksgiving.

The table was set for one.

At the chair farthest from the kitchen door a single plate and wine glass sat, empty and pathetic. There was nothing in front of the other chair.

In the center of my chest a mass of stone formed and instantly grew into something that I knew I would have for the rest of my life. I stepped backward out of the room and leaned against the doorway into the living room, still looking at the table, everything on it untouched, unlit, unopened.

"Syl," I said. But I knew there would be no answer.

I stumbled to the doorways of the few other rooms, then went back through the kitchen and out the back door. Sometimes Sylvia parked her car back there. There was no car. I was the only human on my ranch.

I walked slowly back through the kitchen to the doorway of the dining room. I leaned against the doorframe and let my head ease back against the wood, listening to the silence, groping mentally for any sound that would tell me that Sylvia was there, somewhere, just out for a few minutes . . .

I knew better.

I took a step backward, away from the table. Inside me,

something was shoving the stone aside and struggling to get out, to come screaming into the world in a rage so pure and blue that I was almost euphoric. But I realized it was not euphoria. It was a rage beyond rage, a glittering, electric sheen that wrapped my mind and turned my vision into tiny spots of focus that could only see where I was now and saw nothing of any future that was known to man.

What I felt then is not worth writing. I had been intentionally damaged, in a way that would never allow full recovery.

Carefully, with controlled motion, I gathered up the corners of the tablecloth—the sheet—and gripped them together above the table, slowly taking out the slack until I could feel resistance from some of the platters and bowls that were now inside my large, improvised bag.

And then I whipped the entire thing off the table and smashed it into the wall.

Glass and crockery shattered, and stains formed almost instantly as gravy and cooking juices and wine began soaking through the sheet.

The bag was still intact and I didn't let go. I flung the bag over my shoulder, stomped through the living room, across the porch and out onto the high desert that spread away from me in the fading light.

And then I ran.

I ran with the bag banging into the backs of my legs, unknown wet things still soaking through the sheet and my shirt and pants. I ran south, stomping through brush and weeds until I could see the small road that ran off to the west. I angled off toward the corner of my property. Without stopping, I heaved the bag. It landed in a crash of gritty breaking sounds just short of the road, in the corner of the fence. It was still on my ranch.

I backed slowly away from the mess, knowing I would never touch it again. As I eased backward, back to the road, and then toward my house, I never took my eyes from the mess I'd created on land that I thought I loved. As I moved, I began stripping off my clothes, flinging them in front of me as I went. When I reached the stream I kicked my way into the icy stream and sat down, the liquid needles of the water growing dull as my skin grew numb from the cold.

On a flat rock by the side of the stream there was always a bottle of bourbon and a small Mason jar. I poured some whiskey into the jar and sat sipping it, feeling the burn on the inside and the freeze on the outside.

It was the first time I clearly realized there was something inside me that I would never be able to capture. And the color of it was black.

Tomorrow I would burn the clothes. But not now.

Now, it was Thanksgiving.

But how many more of these could I survive?

30.

# DAY 20

Saturday, September 14
from Delta Junction, Alaska

THE WIND BLEW ALL night, still blowing when we rose before daylight the next morning.

All we wanted to do was get the hell out of Delta Junction.

The café was open, and we ducked inside for a quick breakfast before heading out. The chairman and his buddies were already there.

We talked it over at breakfast, both of us a little tense. It wasn't the weather. It was where we were, and where we were going. Today we easily would be in Fairbanks, about a hundred miles away, and early the next day we'd ride due north, leave the paved road, jump onto the Dalton Highway, still north, and officially be on our way to the Arctic Circle. Maybe spend the night somewhere near the Yukon River. The morning after that . . .

*The Arctic Circle.*

Two days away. Neither of us could relax.

Looking back, I had no idea what this day would bring.

We rode out of Delta Junction with the wind at our backs, blowing so hard that I thought we could stay upright and moving, even if we turned off the engines. The wind caught our jackets and found every tiny wrinkle and pocket, filled them, and drove us forward. The wind speed matched the road speed of the bikes, and it was as though there were no wind at all. I could hear the engine clearly, every little tick and groan of it, hear the tires on the pavement, hear everything. We were riding at sixty miles per hour; I knew that if we stopped, the wind would blow us over.

Twenty miles out of Delta Junction the wind stopped.

When we got to Fairbanks it was still early in the day, and the weather had turned, spilling warm sunshine into a landscape that lay gentle and inviting, pastoral, reaching into the distance. We pulled into a supermarket parking lot, went inside, sat at a tiny counter, had some coffee, and checked the maps, taking our time. Knowing, just knowing that, hell, this is where we would turn north, *really* north, a road that had damn few side roads, a road that was a dead run to the Circle.

We sat there sipping coffee. We were edgy. It wasn't hard to make the decision—we weren't staying in Fairbanks. We'd top off our tanks, grab some food, ride a little farther north, put on a few miles before dark, whatever excuse we could think of for not sitting still, for getting on the road. Heading north.

Maybe just ride up to a little place we saw on the map called Livingood, maybe stay overnight there, make an easy run tomorrow, cut a day off our time to the Circle.

As we came out into the parking lot a petite woman dressed in expensive winter clothing was standing by our bikes, looking at them like people look at animals behind the bars at a zoo. Next to her was one of the biggest RVs I'd ever seen, one of those Greyhound-size things, this one pulling a cargo trailer the size of a small mobile home. The woman wanted to know about the bikes, where we were going, and why. We tried to explain. I told her that we were riding north, to the Arctic Circle. I don't think she believed me. We got on the bikes and rode out, the little woman standing there looking after us, her hand on the door of the RV. She knew that she'd never see us again. There was something a little emotional about that, but I didn't think about it for very long. I just rode on.

We headed north.

The weather was holding. The sun baked our backs, and the air was tender and sweet—the warmest day's riding we'd had. Odd that we had to get north of Fairbanks to find warm riding.

The highway north out of Fairbanks was briefly four lanes, then two lanes, then two lanes that became very narrow, and then two lanes that went off into the wilderness with no good reason, or so it seemed.

When we got to Livingood there was nothing there. No houses, no store, no fuel, nothing. It was only a name on a map, and on a wooden sign leaning beside the road.

We could have camped there, of course; we had everything we needed. But why camp there? There was lots of daylight left, and the Yukon River was only . . . somewhere to the north.

We kept riding.

From the beginning, the weather had tested us. But now, north of Fairbanks, with our ultimate goal a hundred miles farther north, the weather gave it up. It was almost as though we were being rewarded for having kept at it, for riding when riding was insane, for being wet and cold and muddy, for being driven by the wind. Now, there was no wind, the road was dry, and the sun bore down into the gentle valleys and the low ridges with a bright, cool light that painted everything we saw in colors that our eyes had trouble believing. We crossed low, rolling hills that gave a view north for miles on end, and we knew we could see to the edge of Earth.

The turnoff to the Dalton Highway was just there, suddenly. We'd passed Livingood, passed a few houses, passed landscapes too incredible to describe. But we could not pass the turnoff to the Dalton Highway. We'd come too far, and there was still light left in the heavens. The Dalton Highway, called the Haul Road by the locals because of the enormous trucks hauling supplies and equipment all the way to Prudhoe Bay on the north shore of Alaska, carried trucks in a hurry, trucks with drivers sitting ten feet above the road surface, and drivers who were not looking for motorcycles.

But that was the way of things on the Dalton. We swung the bikes into the turn, onto the loose surface of the road.

If the rest of the road was like the first quarter mile, I knew I was in trouble. There was a steep grade covered with some sort of crushed rock too big to be called gravel and too small to be called boulders. The stuff was the size of baseballs, a foot deep and shifting. The bike squirmed, the wheels digging down into the stones, flinging them aside in a spinning search for traction.

I managed to work the bike up to the top of the grade, and I stopped. To hell with it. If I were going to ride through this crap I'd have to sit here for a while and get my mind, and my gut, into it. I wanted desperately to go to the Circle, but I knew that riding this huge, loose rock would take everything I had, and I didn't know what I had to begin with. Or what I had left.

I raised my helmet and looked north. At least I could let my eyes rove over the north country while I got my courage up. And right in front of my wheel there was no more of the monster stone. Instead, there was the unpaved track of the Dalton Highway. The huge gravel was gone and the dirt track that passed for a road was smooth and even, drifting north in long straight stretches and leisurely curves. The road snaked over the far horizon, tracking the oil pipeline that would always be beside us, sometimes out of sight, but never far away.

Slade and I looked at each other.

Decision time.

There were hundreds, thousands, of places we could stop and camp, even right here, right where we were. We could pitch camp, watch the sun go down, make coffee, heat up some food, sip Irish Mist, smoke a cigar . . .

But Slade and I could make decisions by just looking at each other. We knew what we were going to do—we were going to keep riding.


Riding the Dalton was an experience like no other, but it was two entirely different rides. The narrow road swept up and away through country too beautiful to believe. There were no immediate high hills, only ridges that rose and fell in front of us like some sort of benign waves rolling across the top of the world. When we left Fairbanks, the trees and other vegetation along the road were still green, but as we rode north on the Dalton we could track the change of colors, actually see the deep greens turn to reds and ambers, golds, and hard glistening browns. The road was actually somewhat gentle, and as we rode we could pay attention not only to the road but to the wild and alien environment that moved past us.

But then there was the other ride. Yes, the road was somewhat gentle, but it changed personalities by the mile, and sometimes instantly. We rode on hard-packed earth, the KLRs eating the miles and sticking to the surface like glue. And then the road, without changing color, would change density. It would shift from hard to soft, the bike wheels slashing grooves in the soft loam, speed dropping, the bikes struggling to move through the gripping, mushy surface.

We hit mud. But there had been no rain and the mud was a mystery—right up until I slid the bike over a small rise and realized that I was only about ten yards from an enormous water truck, stopped in the center of the road, the driver standing beside his open door, pissing. He paid absolutely no attention to me as I squirreled the KLR to the right, the rear wheel sliding slightly. When I got even with the truck, there was no mud. I gave the bike more gas and roared on, knowing that Slade had seen the whole thing.

The Dalton Highway, north. We rose and dropped through almost-barren land so beautiful our eyes ached, then through groves of birch trees, their leaves long gone. The highway was being kind. It was a time to daydream and to float steadily north, taking the road as we found it.

We dropped down a grade and made a gentle turn to the left and found another water truck. We learned later that crews watered the road to soften the hard-packed surface, intentionally

making mud—easier for road graders to handle. I knew ther
was a grader somewhere up ahead—it had left a two-foot-high
ridge of dirt running down the center of the road. The left lane
was only about one-third of the road width, then the dirt ridge,
then another lane of soft surface, just scooped up and moved by
the grader. I was leading, Slade about a hundred yards behind.
There was no traffic, no grader, nothing, only us riding through
a soft dirt road in the wilderness. I opted to ride in the left lane,
the dirt wet and slick but still firm enough to grip the wheels.
As I swung around a gentle turn, there was the grader, coming at me, smack in the center of the road, moving the ridge
of dirt even farther into my path. Coming up hard behind the
grader was a heavily loaded flatbed truck. I was in their lane,
and neither of them cared—they probably didn't even notice
me. They were not going to slow down, not take any evasive
actions. Whatever happened was going to be up to me. And besides, they were right, and I was wrong. There was a steep bank
to my left, an almost vertical wall of dirt that flew up from the
edge of the road, much too steep even for the KLR. To the right,
the road simply dropped off into nothing, the drop too sheer for
me to see anything but the tops of scrubby trees barely reaching
up to the road level. I had no choice. I got up on the pegs and
cranked the throttle, the bike's rear wheel dancing a little on
the greasy mud as it picked up speed. I shot past the grader on
my right, directly at the oncoming truck. I could see the driver's
face, and now he saw me; he thought I'd lost my mind. At the
last moment, I tilted the bike to the right and the front wheel
dug into the ridge of dirt left by the grader. The bike blasted
through, off to the right of the truck. I could feel the wheels digging into the soft road surface, and I backed off, letting the bike

quickly drift down to walking speed. The truck was gone; the grader was gone. I looked in the mirror. Slade was right behind me, pumping his fist in the air. He'd made the same move as I.

And then, there was the Yukon River.

I'd thought about the Yukon, seen pictures. But the pictures were deceptive. I thought of the river as a picturesque, deep green stream running gently toward the sea, a stream where we could spend some time, just listening to the babbling of the water, resting, watching the sun sparkle from the water . . .

What the hell was I thinking? The Yukon was a frigid brown freshwater ocean, two hundred yards wide, moving at eight knots, a force so frightening that I couldn't take my eyes from it. Fall in that water, I thought, and you'd never be seen again.

A bridge soared—really *soared*—over the river. Riding across it was like being on a motorcycle on some ride in Disneyland, floating high into the air and then swooping back to Earth.

Just over the bridge on the north side of the river there was some sort of motel/café/truck stop, with some trucks parked in the lot. Slade and I hadn't eaten since we left Fairbanks, but it didn't seem to matter. We weren't interested in the café. We wanted to touch the river.

We wheeled into the big gravel parking area and rolled slowly to the side next to the river. We parked and walked down to the water, watching some men load a metal boat with enough gear and food for a couple of weeks. The boat had an enclosed metal cabin, and two giant outboards dominated the stern. A fifty-five-gallon drum of gasoline was attached to the cabin with metal straps. The men were going moose hunting and didn't really know when they would be back—or really care, for that matter. They could reach their favorite hunting area only by boat. On the Yukon.

Slade and I stuck our hands in the frigid water. About a foot from the shore, I picked up a smooth, half-rounded stone, polished by some unknown glacier far into the interior of Alaska, and washed down to my hand over countless years. The stone held my eyes. It lay in my palm, seeming to glow. Strangely, although I'd just taken it from near-freezing water, it was warm. Arturo talked about manitou. He said that some people believed that everything, *everything*, had manitou, a spirit that formed life as we know it. And so the stone had manitou. It held my eyes, seeming to grow warmer in my hand. I squatted by the edge of the water and carefully put the stone back exactly where I had found it. Perhaps its journey was not yet over.

Nor was ours. We rode on.

31.

# DAY 20—THE SAME DAY, PART 1

Saturday, September 14
at the Hot Spot, north of the Yukon River

SOMEWHERE FARTHER NORTH OF the Yukon, we knew, was a tiny rest stop called the Hot Spot. We had been told there was food there, and gas, and even a room for the night—a warm room. And five miles north of the river, we found it.

The Hot Spot was a collection of portable buildings and miscellaneous huts down a short dirt road off the west side of the highway, cobbled together at the edge of a parking area wide enough to turn a semi trailer rig. If you drove past the Hot Spot in any other place in America, you'd take one look at the joint, and you wouldn't stop there. No way. But this wasn't any other place; this was five miles north of the Yukon River and less than an hour's ride from the Arctic Circle.

All the buildings at the Hot Spot had been salvaged from the oil development site at Prudhoe Bay and hauled south on a flatbed truck. At Prudhoe, latrines for the oil workers could not be dug into the permafrost, so a large incinerator had been installed to burn the human waste. The complex that housed the incinerator was called "the hot spot." Now, those buildings were going to house us. I had only a slightly uncomfortable feeling.

We rode into the huge parking-turning lot and up to what looked like the office—and we realized we were the only customers anywhere. It was still full daylight, but the lack of anybody else around made us hesitate.

We stepped inside the tiny office. The Hot Spot was owned by a husband and wife, and the two of them did everything that had to be done—rented the rooms, took the money, did the maintenance, cooked the food. The wife rented us one of the three cubicles they used as motel rooms. We unsaddled the KLRs and dumped our gear inside the room, wondering only briefly what the room originally had been used for.

There was a small café at the Hot Spot—outside. We stood in the rapidly chilling early evening weather and ordered through a small window. The wife who checked us into our rooms also took our orders and cooked the food. We had two of the best hamburgers we'd ever eaten.

With little more than an hour or so of daylight left, Slade and I sat at an outdoor table and drank steaming coffee, content to wait for the southern sun to go down. We pulled fleece caps down tightly on our heads and jipped our riding jackets tighter against the coming chill of an Arctic night and dreamed, and talked, about tomorrow.

Tomorrow, we would ride to the Arctic Circle, no more than forty miles farther north.

This was the *best*—the best *day*, the best *weather*, the best *riding*, the best *evening*, the best *place*.

Until the trucker pulled in.

He sat at our table and made the usual polite conversation, three guys in a sort-of inn where no inn should ever have been. The trucker ordered coffee and asked us what we were doing there, and we told him.

"Going to ride up to the Arctic Circle tomorrow."

"Why?"

"No particular reason. Just to say we've done it, I suppose."

He looked at us, a sad little smile on his face.

"You ain't gonna get there," he said. "There's a bridge a few hundred yards south of the Circle. Construction people have it closed. Ain't gonna open it for days." The driver shook his head slowly. "Take my word for it. I just come from there. They got temporary barriers up now, but at dark tonight they're gonna put up them permanent concrete ones."

Slade and I couldn't believe what we were hearing. We'd ridden thousands of miles, and now we were going to be stopped, forty miles short of our target.

"How did you get across?" I asked.

"I was the last 'un they let cross goin' south. They stopped everything behind me a few miles farther north. Ain't no more traffic goin' over that span for a whole bunch of days."

We sat in silence. Forty miles short of the target.

Fuck that.

"How long's the bridge?" I asked.

"Not long. Probably throw a baseball 'crost it, if you had a good arm."

"Is it a steep canyon?"

"Nah, don't think so. Never really looked too close at it, but it don't look all that steep."

The driver finished his last gulp of coffee and stood up. "C
more thing," he said, "the crew boss up there is a son of a bitcl.
He gets off on holding truckers to a standstill, and everybody
else, too. Even if you do go up there, I doubt you'll talk him into
lettin' you across." He walked back to his truck, slowly shaking
his head. He stopped and looked back at us. "I'm sorry, boys,
but this shit happens on this road now and again. We just have
to live with it."

Fuck that. Again. I wasn't going to live with it. I could feel
something building inside me, something that I recognized.
There was a time when I knew what it was and didn't like it.
Now, it was different. What I felt was exactly what I wanted to
feel.

Slade and I looked at each over cups of coffee swiftly going
cold in the fading Arctic day. Each knew what the other was
thinking: we were in a situation we'd been in many times before—stopped, stymied, dead in the water, cut off at the knees
by forces beyond our control. But not once, in all those other
times, did we quit. And this time was no different—we'd come
all this way; we weren't going to turn around now, bridge or no
fucking bridge.

We had a mission.

The world would not come to an end if we did not make
it. Some country would not fall into anarchy. Some economy
in some shaky shit-covered nation would not collapse. None of
that had ever rested on what Slade and I did in another life—we
were never that high up the food chain. Or the gun chain, as the
case may have been.

But, now, we had a mission. It was *our* mission, and, goddammit, we were going to pursue it.

All of this, without either of us saying a word.

A smile slowly spread across Slade's face. It was one of those smiles that said, "Are you ready?"

The bridge, and the Circle, were forty miles away.

It was worth a try.

32.

# DAY 20—THE SAME DAY,
# PART II

Saturday, September 14
from the Hot Spot, north of the Yukon River
attempting to reach the Arctic Circle

WE LEFT OUR COFFEE cups sitting on the table, yelled at the woman behind the tiny window that we would be back, ran to our room, and grabbed our riding clothes, trying to haul the heavy gear onto our resisting bodies as we headed for the bikes. In less than five minutes Slade and I were again riding north over the Dalton Highway.

We had to reach the bridge before nightfall. The sun was still where we could see it, behind us, but hanging there in a soft red glow that made us think maybe we should be back at the Hot Spot, having another cup of coffee, maybe some Irish Mist, maybe even—for God's sake—trying to get some sleep in our tiny room.

All we did was go faster. We started away from the Hot Spot at forty miles per hour, gravel flying, thinking we were actually going fast. Gradually, the gravel became smaller, and patches of hard dirt showed through. Fifty miles per hour, the bikes doing little dances when the wheels left the dirt and crunched back into the gravel. We could never tell what sort of gravel would be there, but it made no difference—we kept grinding away on the uneven road.

Sixty miles per hour. And then seventy.

The country broke open. The trees fell away into low shrub and clumps of grasses, lit by a sun that was retreating south as fast as we were riding north. I topped a low ridge, and there was nothing in front of me but the Arctic, stretching away to the Brooks Range in the distance, the snow-covered peaks glowing in the falling sun. I tried to concentrate on the road, on the ruts and patches of gravel, but I couldn't help looking at the terrain, a country so beautiful that, for a brief moment, I thought about slowing down, forgetting about the damn bridge that would close before I got there, enjoying a piece of the earth that I'd never seen before and might never see again.

Thirty miles north of the Hot Spot we hit *pavement*.

Then we jumped the bikes up to eighty, maybe a little more, reveling in the hard gripping surface, the wind roaring past our helmets. The bikes were responding well—we'd left most of our heavy gear back at the Hot Spot—and so we just kept twisting the handles, feeling the rpms steadily increase.

Until the pavement ran out.

It ran out instantly, and suddenly we were doing eighty miles per hour on gravel that we could hardly see beneath the swift passage of the bikes. I thought I could feel the front tire bounce free, ever so slightly airborne. I was leading, and I got off the throttle as soon as I could, hoping Slade wouldn't run up on my back tire. I tried not to fight the bike, letting it ramp down by itself to a speed that I could handle. When I thought it was safe to take my eyes off the road, I checked the mirror. Slade was back there about fifty yards, seeming to cruise through the rocky shit with no particular problem.

I checked the odometer. We were almost there, but daylight was slipping away over the horizon.

The gravel got smaller and more packed, and we got faster. We screamed over a small rise and could see the bridge in front of us, down a long gentle grade, could see the shallow canyon, could see across the narrow gap to where we knew the Circle was . . . and we could see the dozen northbound trucks that were stopped on the road in front of some sort of wooden barrier.

Through the barrier, across the bridge, and up a short rise . . . and there was the Arctic Circle, even if we couldn't see it.

But the bridge was closed. No one was going anywhere. According to the trucker back at the Hot Spot, it might be days before we'd be able to cross, if at all.

We rode slowly to the end of the line of trucks, then eased around them to where we could again see the bridge. Wooden barricades, hastily erected, stretched across the road. A construction crew truck was parked at an angle behind them, a further message that the road was closed. We shut down the engines, got off the bikes, pulled off our helmets.

And heard the silence. The truckers had turned off their engines. Somebody told me that truckers only do that when they know they aren't going anywhere for a long, long time. Some of the drivers walked around in the fading light, smoking, swapping stories. They didn't seem upset by the blockade, perhaps used to the unknown and unexpected conditions that cropped up on the Dalton Highway.

Slade and I walked to the very front of the line of trucks. Everybody looked at us. You could see it in their faces: "What the hell are these bikers doing here?"

A little wiry guy wearing a hard hat stood in the middle of the barricade, leaning back against it, his legs crossed at the ankles as though he had nothing at all to do, nothing to think about, as though he were only trying to stay awake.

A trucker was standing next to us, a huge guy with a wild beard that came down to his jacket collar. He was half a head taller than Slade, his arms folded across his chest. I couldn't see his hands, but his arms were the size of small logs. He paid no attention to us. He stared steadily at the guy leaning against the barricade.

"Is that the road boss?" Slade asked, flicking his hand toward the guy.

The big trucker slowly turned his head toward Slade. "Yeah, that's him," he muttered. "Muthafucker thinks he's the boss of Alaska." His eyes took Slade in, took me in, took in what we were wearing. "Where the hell's yer bikes?"

"Back there a bit," Slade said, tilting his head back toward the trucks. "Wanted to see what was going on before we rode up here." Slade stared across the bridge. "I don't see any construction. How come this bridge is shut down?"

"Construction is more to the north," the trucker said. "Workin' on another bridge. Road boss blocked this bridge so truckers wouldn't be sitting up the road there where they can see what's goin' on. Must be we make construction crews nervous." The trucker turned slightly toward Slade, unfolded one of his tree-like arms, and reached his hand out. "Name's Harley," he said, "like the motorcycle." His voice was like gravel being poured out barrel.

Slade shook his hand. "Slade," he said. "That's Morgan," Slade said, nodding at me. "Morgan's a little weird," Slade said, grinning. "Doesn't talk much. And when he does, doesn't make much sense."

Harley leaned forward and looked at me, like he was looking at a bug. I kept my mouth shut.

Fucking Slade.

Slade stared across the bridge. I could tell he was looking at the barricade, looking for gaps, figuring out our chances of crashing the thing.

"Where you boys goin'?" Harley asked.

Slade looked at him. "Ain't it the shits?" he said. "We're just going another quarter-mile or so, right over there." He raised his arm and pointed across the bridge.

"The Circle?" Harley said. "You come all the way up here just to stand on a line on the ground you can't even see?"

Slade looked at me, and then at Harley. "Yeah, I guess that's about it. Sounds a little stupid, now that I think about it."

Harley surprised me. "Nah, it ain't stupid. First time I drove a truck up here, I stopped just so I could read that big wooden sign. Hell, you can see the top of it, stickin' up out of the bush over there. Must be ten foot tall." He pointed one of his log-arms across the bridge.

And there it was, the top of the sign. The Arctic Circle within sight, but not within reach.

"Well," Slade said, looking at me, "we're here. Might as well go talk to the road boss and see if we can cross the bridge, even for just a few minutes."

Lots'a luck," Harley said. "That little shit just loves to fuck
ith people. And he's usually got a buncha construction humps
to back him up." Harley kept looking at the road boss. "But if
you boys are goin' down there, mind if I tag along?"

Harley was grinning. Slade was grinning. I was the only one
with a straight face. I could feel a noise inside me getting louder
,and I didn't like the sound. But I felt comfortable with it.

We ambled down toward the road boss. He watched us
come, not moving from his place against the barricade. A couple of construction guys eased over in his direction, trying not
to be obvious.

I glanced behind me. Some of the truckers had gathered at
the front of the line of trucks, exactly where Slade, Harley, and I
had been standing. *Damn*, I thought, *this could get really fucking
interesting.*

Without turning his head, even the slightest, Slade said quietly to me, "Scout now, ride later. I'll be along."

I knew what Slade was doing; he was going to keep the road
boss talking until I could figure out the ride. If, in fact, we could
make the ride.

As Harley and Slade approached the road boss, I angled off
to the right and strolled slowly to the end of the bridge. Nobody
at the barricade paid any attention to me. The bridge spanned
a narrow, dry cut in the earth—an arroyo, we would have called
it in New Mexico. The sides were steep but not impassable, falling away to the bottom of the narrow cut. Some sort of trail
seemed to run at a shallow angle from the end of the bridge
down-canyon to the bottom. The trail was old, weeds and brush,
alive and dead, cluttering the pathway. Parts of it had washed
away, but it was still a trail. On the other side, the trail came up

again, as though, at some point, there had been a need to walk down one side and up the other. But the bottom of the canyon was very narrow, rocks scattered in it, exposed by periodic run-off of rain and melting snow.

Steep sides, narrow cut, rocks. But it was the only chance we had. I thought the KLRs could handle it, if Slade and I could handle the KLRs. Once we rode down there the bottom might be a problem—the width down there was narrower than the length of the bikes, but somehow we would have to turn the KLRs back up-canyon toward the bridge and the trail on the other side.

I'd done my scouting, such as it were. Slade was still talking to the road boss, some other truckers now standing idly by, chipping into the conversation now and then. Slade glanced at me. I gave a slight nod of my head: "*I think it might work.*" Slade flicked his head to the north: "*Go.*"

It looked as though I got to test the new route.

I started walking quickly back to where we'd left the bikes, intentionally bypassing the men talking at the barricade. The conversation was becoming heated. I sneaked another look at Slade and could tell that things were not going well. "Hell," Slade was saying, "I'm trying to be nice. But see that guy there?" Slade flicked his head at me. "He wants to rip off your jawbone and use it to open beer bottles."

I walked faster.

Another trucker was standing by the KLRs. As I threw my leg over and hit the starter button, he clapped me on the shoulder. "You got balls, old man," he said. And I rode away toward the bridge.

I made no pretense of riding to the barricade. I put the bike on the right side of the road at the end of the bridge and stopped, the front wheel dropping slightly onto the steep slope at the edge of the canyon.

Why was I doing this? I'd ridden bikes on some gnarly pieces of Earth, but this was definitely new territory. I could get off the bike and start walking. If the road boss would not let me walk across the bridge—and I knew he would not—I'd climb down into the canyon and up the other side. There was a rudimentary trail already there. The road boss may have owned the bridge, but he didn't own all the dirt in the state of Alaska. Fuck him, I could *walk* to the goddamn Arctic Circle from here. It would take a while, but I could do it. *We* could do it.

But that wasn't what we'd set out to do. We had set out to ride motorcycles to the Circle, and now that we could actually see where it was, some clown was telling us this was as far as we could ride. I couldn't get off the bike and walk. I just could not.

Sometimes my decisions suck.

The road boss knew what I was going to do. In the mirror I could see him running toward me, waving his arms, his mouth open, shouting. I could not hear him. It would have made no difference if I could. I dropped the KLR into low gear and drove the front wheel past the point of no return, and then the bike was off the road and onto the top of the old trail. The bike headed downhill immediately, the wheels dropping and digging to stay on the narrow trail, loose dirt squirting from underneath the tires. I stood on the pegs, letting the engine hold the bike back from free fall. It wasn't working. The rear wheel started to break away from the trail and slide downhill. If I touched the brakes it would all be over. The bike and I would slide down the side of the cut, gathering speed and rocks as we went. Whether either of us would be functioning when we hit the bottom was a matter of considerable debate. And I had no one with whom to debate.

I was more than halfway down the wall.

I let the bike do what it wanted—and what it wanted to do was break completely free of the wall. And it did. Both wheels shot out to the left, my right foot came off the peg, and the bike slid away from me. The bike was sliding down the wall; I was sliding only a few feet behind.

The bike came to a stop at the bottom. The engine had died. I came to a stop also, on top of the bike. I hit the seat, then bounced into the handlebars. The left mirror dug into my rib cage and spun me around, and I ended up in the dirt beside the bike.

I got up and pulled off my helmet. I had dirt down inside my jacket, but all my body parts seemed to be working.

And then I heard the yelling, and the applause, from up at the end of the bridge. A bunch of truckers were up there, clapping, yelling, pumping their fists in the air.

I could not see Slade.

The cut was so narrow that the bike wasn't really lying down. I got it upright easily and checked the controls and the running gear. Everything worked. Hey, it was a KLR—you probably couldn't kill it with a sledgehammer. The bike started immediately when I touched the button.

I sat on the bike, looking over my shoulder at the steep bank on the north side of the little canyon, and all I could think of was . . . what I'd just done was the easy part.

The trail up the other side started right there, right next to my rear wheel, but the cut was too narrow to turn the bike. I thought about getting off, grabbing the front wheel, and trying to muscle the thing around in the other direction. The KLR was not that heavy, something less than four hundred pounds, but still too heavy for what I had in mind. I'd probably drop the thing, screw up the machine in some way, and never get up the other side. I'd have to try to let the bike do the work.

I saddled up, put the bike in low gear, twisted the front wheel to the left, jamming it into the bank, then gave it a little gas, and let out the clutch. The front wheel lurched into the bank, climbing slightly, and then the rear wheel started to spin. I hit the rear brake, twisted the front wheel back to the right, and let off the brake. The bike rolled back slightly, but the front wheel was pointed slightly higher on the bank than when I started. And so I did it again, and again, and again.

I got the bike turned around. The sweat ran down from inside my helmet and my arms were shaking.

And the truckers were applauding again.

I sat on the bike, still slightly shaking, and looked at the steep trail up the north side of the cut.

And then something occurred to me that I hadn't really thought about before. I'd ridden the KLR down into a small, steep canyon. If I couldn't ride it up the other side, the KLR might end its life right where it sat. Maybe one of the truckers would help me haul it out. Maybe not. Fuck it. I'd deal with that problem when I came to it, which, of course, was my usual tactic.

I knew I wasn't going to make it.

I sat on the KLR and looked at the side of the cut. The longer I looked at it, the steeper it became. The trail was too narrow, too old, too washed out. The side of the cut was too soft. The wheels would dig in and then slide, and I'd end up right where I started—in the bottom of the canyon.

I thought about leaving the bike and climbing out, hiking up to the sign that marked the Circle.

That was stupid.

There was nothing wrong with the bike. The only thing wrong was my lack of skill as a rider. I thought maybe I was not good enough to make it, not good enough to take the bike to its limits.

I kept staring at the wall, but it never got any more gentle, the old trail running sharply up toward the road. I twisted around and looked behind me. There were some basketball-size rocks in the bottom of the cut, but I thought I could maneuver around them. About thirty yards down the canyon the north wall seemed to fall away into a shallower angle, and the bottom of the cut was a little wider.

I left the bike in neutral and turned off the engine, then got off and started to push it backward, guiding it around the rocks. If I could push it far enough down-canyon, I might be able to gain a shallower angle of attack on the north wall. The climb would be longer, but maybe easier. I wouldn't be able to use the trail, but that didn't matter. All I wanted was to reach the top. No matter how.

The starter button glared at me like some sort of little, dark, evil eye, daring me to touch it.

I touched it.

The KLR made soft rumbling sounds. If I hadn't known better, I'd have thought it was talking to me: "I can do it, you angry jerk! Can you?"

I dropped the transmission into low, gave the bike gas, and lurched forward, attacking the slope immediately. A KLR has amazing low-end torque and I'd have to use that as well as I knew how. I knew better than to open the throttle too far. If the rear wheel started spinning out of control, it would dig downhill, get far below the front of the bike, and I'd have to stop and try to back down.

Well, at least the truckers would have a good laugh.

The bike started up the slope. I clamped my knees to the gas tank and hung on, my ass rising off the seat, trying only to keep both wheels in the same groove. Frankly, I didn't know what else to do.

In less than a minute I was more than halfway up the slope. I felt the rear wheel slip downhill a little, and I thought the climb was over, but then it seemed to find a grip on something it liked, and it began to track properly again. Twenty feet from the top the engine began to lug, and I carefully opened the throttle the smallest amount. Immediately, the rear wheel spun and dropped downhill, turning the bike at an almost impossible upward angle. I was suddenly riding the KLR in a dead-on hill climb.

A microsecond of a vision of Chaser went through my mind, Chaser leaning on the handlebars of his own KLR and looking at me lying in a heap at the side of a dirt track, where I had not properly made a tight turn. I had tried to be too cautious, had not let the bike help me out.

"More gas," I could hear Chaser saying.

Okay, pal. I twisted the throttle.

The big single-cylinder engine roared as though I had stuck a blowtorch into the cylinder head. The rear wheel spun wildly, throwing dirt and gravel completely back down the slope and into the bottom of the cut. All I did was stand on the pegs and hang on.

The front wheel broke over the top of the bank. I was on the north side of the canyon.

I was so stunned by the fact that I was out of the cut that I hung onto the throttle a second or so too long, and the bike shot across the berm and onto road. I kept it upright, slammed on the rear brake, and skidded to a halt. Without looking back at the bridge I turned the bike quickly and pointed it up the road toward the turnoff to the sign that said Arctic Circle, sure the construction crew would be in their trucks and coming hard across the bridge to drag me back, bike and all.

I wheeled into the turnoff, eased to the left, pulled up in the middle of the parking area in front of the huge, beautiful sign, killed the engine, leaped off the bike, and stood there in the fading gold of an Arctic sunset.

Across the bottom of the sign were the words, *Latitude 66° 33'*.

I was standing on the Arctic Circle.

Slade was leaning against the sign, his arms folded across his chest.

33.

# DAY 20—THE SAME DAY, PART III

Saturday, September 14

at the Arctic Circle

SLADE HAD ONE OF those silly grins on his face that said, "Why do you always do things the hard way?"

I took off my helmet and hung it on a mirror. "*What the hell?*" I yelled, standing there with my hands on my hips, sweat pouring from every inch of my skin. "Did you *walk* over here?"

The grin never left his face. He nodded his head a little to the side. His bike was parked at the edge of some brush, his helmet sitting on the saddle.

"A 'committee' met to discuss the situation. Convinced the road boss to change his mind," he said. "'Course, you were already gone by that time. I rode across just after you started up the north side. Been waiting ever since. About time you got here. Not much daylight left. Got to go back across the bridge before dark."

Committee? I thought.

Christ, I guess I do always find the hard way to get things done.

"And the best part was," Slade said, laughing, "you didn't punch anybody!"

I loped across the gravel and wrapped my arms around Slade, hugging him as tightly as I could. Slade hugged back, both of us giggling and shaking ourselves.

*Latitude 66° 33'.* We had made it.

We were standing on the Arctic Circle, with only minutes of daylight left.

Once, climbing with a guy named Pownall, we reached the summit of the mountain and saw a storm coming hard on the other side. We spent less than a minute on the top. The time we spent there did not matter, it only mattered that we were there.

And now Slade and I stood on the Circle, almost in awe. It wasn't as though this ride had never been done before; lots of riders had done it. But it had never been done by us. Until now.

We spent a few minutes looking at the countryside, breathing the air, wondering, dreaming. There was nothing at the Arctic Circle, only the big wooden sign saying that we were, indeed, at the Circle. But we were there and, below us, to the south, lay almost the entire planet. We loved it. *We fucking loved it!*

We were out of time, and we were rapidly running out of daylight.

I looked at my odometer. I had ridden exactly 4,400 miles from the road in front of my house in New Mexico. That is, counting the short side trip to visit the Snake.

The Snake. I hadn't thought about him for a while. Maybe I was losing my edge. Or losing something.

We sat on the bikes, turned our backs to the Arctic Circle,

and stared into a distant sun that hung low, soft, and cool in that far and mystical place where we were going. I had never before been so aware of what "south" meant.

South. Away from the Artic Circle, away from the destination we'd had out there in front of us for all those cold, wet days, a misty image of some sort of icy grail that we might reach. Or might not.

We rode slowly back across the bridge.

And then I understood about the "committee." A dozen truckers stood in a group at the south end of the bridge. The few guys in the construction crew were on the inside of the wooden barricade, as though that would protect them. From the truckers? It took me a few seconds to find the road boss— he was almost invisible standing next to Harley. Harley had his arm around the road boss's shoulders, as though hugging his best friend. Only trouble was, the boss's feet were off the ground. He hung there like a sack of beans, Harley grinning from ear to ear. The road boss was not smiling.

As we rode by, now truly heading south, the truckers broke into cheers, waving their arms.

I've always loved truckers. If you can't be a cowboy, be a trucker. Might be the same thing.

34.

# DAY 20—THE SAME BEST DAY

Saturday, September 14
South, from the Arctic Circle

IT WAS OVER.

In the early morning light of this day, Saturday, September 14th, all we'd wanted to do was get the hell out of Delta Junction. Maybe lay over in Fairbanks. It didn't turn out that way. Instead, we'd ridden all the way to the Arctic Circle. Now we'd ride back south to within five miles of the Yukon River—on the same day.

Not bad. For old guys.

It got darker, colder, but both of us were so high from the experience of reaching the Circle that the darkness and the cold didn't bother us. We rode south on an empty dirt track that seemed to roll on forever. And we could have kept riding until the bikes gave it up. For days, for thousands of miles, we'd been pulled toward one point on Earth, an imaginary line that wasn't even very far north. And we had made it; we had been there.

Now, it was over.

And it was really no big deal. I mean, c'mon, the motorcycles did all the work. All we did was sit on the saddles and stay awake.

No big deal.

Was that what this was? No big deal? Was this just some tiny adventure that two old guys clamped onto as the most exciting thing they could think of?

Is this what it would have meant, to me, to have seen the buffalo?

Now, there was only the riding south.

The ride south was a mystery thing, a not-quite-real flow of images, scents, and the bass humming of the engines. Riding across low tundra-covered ridges in the pale red light of sunset and knowing the Brooks Range was rising on the horizon behind us, guarding the silent presence of the Arctic forever from guys like us. I could feel those mountains pressing against my back, pressing against my mind, producing a sensory overload, a high that cleansed me. It was as though we were riding on the roof of the world, and if we kept going we would simply ride off the edge of the planet and into some state of being where there was only more of everything in front of us, nothing behind us, and the low, sweet singing of the engines was the only music we would ever hear, or ever need to hear.

I hung back, letting Slade get farther ahead, and then farther, until he was out of sight. I was now riding on a road that had no beginning and no end, nothing in front of me, nothing behind. In all four directions there was nothing on the quickly darkening far horizons but unidentifiable undulations that edged up into the sky like gigantic, old sawteeth, cupping me, keeping me. The bike was moving, but the space I rode in seemed to make the movement immaterial. I was suspended, and I stayed that way until the bike eased into a gentle turn in the road, and my sense of movement came back in a rush.

There is something about making a turn in a road that has no known end. On the map, of course, the road ends. And that's where we'd been riding, on a map, to the end of the road. But not in our minds. In our minds, we rode on a single track of dirt that seemed to fade into the rain and mist and white light, as though we could ride into some other dimension where all the curves were sweeping and long, and the air was warm and honeyed with sunshine.

That's what we had set out to do.

That's what we had done.

We had screamed over roads never meant to be screamed over, ripped past scenery that, at any other time, would have stopped us cold. Everything in Western Canada and Alaska was beyond our imaginations. For every river and lake we had ever ridden by in past years, now there were dozens of rivers and lakes. For every mountain, there were a hundred mountains, sheer walls, the fingers of glaciers probing the lower reaches, phalanxes of trees coming to an abrupt halt at a line beyond which only the most determined could survive.

But this was not about survival. We could easily survive— and had done so.

This was not a test of endurance. We could easily endure— and had endured many things more stressful than this ride.

In fact, this was not a test at all.

This was about an experience, a thing to do, a long stream of perceptions that infused the mind.

This was about being at the end of the road. At the end of the world.

Was this nirvana? Or just the end of all of it?

I remembered, somewhere back there on some tiny road—they had *all* been tiny roads—we had pulled into a café hardly bigger than the inside of a bus. We sat and stared out the window, looking at the misting rain and sipping coffee.

"They have berry pie here," I said, nodding at a handwritten menu on a chalkboard behind the counter. "Might be a ten. Might be pie nirvana."

Slade was silent for a moment, seeming to be thinking. Then he said, "Nah, I think I'll pass this one." He paused. "After all," he mumbled, "reaching nirvana is not all it's cracked up to be. After you get there, then where the hell are you?"

That was Willi's question, an old mountaineering buddy, now long dead, killed in an avalanche. Willi's life goal had been to reach the summit of Everest by a new route. He'd done that. We'd sat on a ledge on another mountain, about halfway to the summit, staring into the distance. And Willi had said, "Ever since that summit, I've been trying to figure out what's left . . ."

I did not understand, at the time.

I did now.

I hung back, riding so slowly that I could feel no pressure from the still, cold air against my chest. I stopped, took off my helmet, and strapped it onto the luggage carrier behind my seat. I wanted to feel the air on my face. In front of me, on the right, a seldom-used track headed off the road and into the west. It looked like nothing more than faint parallel grooves made in the tough, short vegetation by some sort of ATV. Hunters, probably.

I thought about the world and the fact that I was not in it, at least not in the world known to everyday humans. Alberta,

British Columbia, the Yukon Territory, Alaska—epecially the Yukon. I could simply ride up a faint road like the one right there until it turned into a trail, then ride the trail until it became a track, then ride the track until it became a game path, then ride the path until I couldn't muscle the bike through the bush anymore. The KLR had a range of more than three hundred miles. No one would ever find me.

Nirvana. Maybe I could find it by just turning the KLR and pointing it west, down the faint track in front of me.

And if I found it, what would I do then?

The engine was idling. I dropped the bike into low and let the idle rpms move it gently forward, turning carefully, and finally pointing down the nearly invisible track. Just to see what it felt like, I told myself.

I went only a few yards, and then stopped. I turned off the engine. What was I doing? Was I really thinking about doing this?

I sat on the sleeping bike in a darkening Arctic silence, staring to the west, trying to gather the last of the northern light into my brain where I wanted to keep it, forever. I was immobile, absolutely still, unblinking. I'm not sure I was breathing.

The track disappeared into the low growth and the darkness. I searched along it with my eyes for as long as I could see the indentations in the spiny vegetation—and until I saw the soft, moving glow somewhere between me and the western horizon. The glow was far away, and yet not, one of those images that seemed within reach if only I rode on. But I knew clearly that I wouldn't reach it, that it wasn't meant to be reached, only yearned for, and seen. I had never before seen it, not really. But I saw it now, and I didn't have to reach it to know what it meant.

It stood there, an iridescent outline in a wilderness where few men had walked, its glow wavering and seeming to change, deep molten reds and dark golds. Colors ordinary living things would never have.

The buffalo.

I was seeing the buffalo. In the Arctic. Its head, huge even in the distance, turned slightly toward me, looking. And then, knowing that I had seen it, it simply turned and walked slowly away, its hooves seeming not to touch anything beneath it, the soft, shimmering glow growing dimmer until it disappeared into the far reaches of my mind and the distant places of Earth.

I had seen the buffalo.

It wasn't over.

I wasn't over.

This ride could not end.


By the time I got back to the Hot Spot it was pitch black, and the temperature was dropping like a stone through clear water. But I was wired, too hyper to even think about going to bed.

Slade was sitting at the outdoor table under a bare lightbulb that hung from a wire. He was still wrapped in every piece of riding gear he had. The tiny kitchen in the building beside us was dark, the cook nowhere to be seen. Without stopping, I went to our room and dug into the saddlebags that we'd left behind when we made the speed run to the Circle. I came out with the Mist and cigars.

Slade and I sat at the heavy wooden table, sipping Irish Mist and smoking cigars, the smoke drifting straight upward through air so it pressed against us like black crystal. Our bodies were still jittery with leftover adrenaline and our hands shook as we tried to keep the Mist from vibrating out of the tiny metal cups, feeling the Arctic air seep into our bones. We drank the Mist, and we smoked. We said very little. There was nothing, really, to be said. What we had experienced that day, the images that had blown through our minds, sometimes it's better not to try to put all that into words.

I did not tell Slade about the buffalo. He'd find out soon enough.

We finally forced ourselves into bed in our tiny room, but I knew that I would not sleep. Fifteen minutes later, the northern lights came out and played in the sky, a fitting finish for a day that would live in my mind forever.

But I did not know how long forever was.

# 35

# EPILOGUE

Early February
Wild Horse Canyon
Southern New Mexico

Modene

WHEN THE SNOW STARTED piling up in Colorado Springs in late December, Slade and I decided to come down here. The days were cool, but not really cold, and the little adobe house was tight and warm. We had been here many times, and I knew the house as well as my own. And so we lingered on in the Southern New Mexico winter.

The days were quiet. Now and then one of the Apache kids would come by and ask about Morgan, but no one ever stayed for long. Slade got the old pickup running and spent his time clumping around the old rancho, mending fences and picking up deadwood, piling it behind the house for firewood. He drove the truck to the far southern corner of the rancho and used a pitchfork to load up the remnants of an ancient Thanksgiving dinner. He never said what he did with the trash, and I never asked him.

I brought my computer—Juanito had told us about Morgan's computer and the steer. Juanito said the Apaches had laughed about it for days. Another crazy white man story, he said. I spent the weeks transcribing Morgan's journal, wrestling with the awkward notebooks and Morgan's atrocious handwriting. When I finished the transcription, Slade and I sat in the warm little living room, a fire in the fireplace, the aromas from dinner still lingering in the rooms, and we read to each other from the journal, carefully placing in our minds the words from each day. And sometimes crying.

To the side of the fireplace there was a nicho that once held a tiny wooden carving that one of the Apache kids had given Morgan. We put the carving on a bookshelf and brought in the bottle of bourbon from the porch, the bottle unopened. We put the bottle in the nicho. It would stay there, Slade said, until Morgan came back.

But I began to realize that there was something missing. Morgan's journal ended, but the trip had not. When the journal ended, Slade was still up there, at the Hot Spot, alone. There had to be an ending to the trip, as well as to the journal, an ending that Morgan would never write, because Morgan never intended the ride to end.

And neither would it be written by Slade. "Morgan's the writer, not me," Slade said. And so I sat with Slade while he told me the story of Day 21. And I wrote it, as faithfully as I could.

36.

# DAY 21

Sunday, September 15
South, from the Hot Spot

Slade

MORGAN AND I HAD gone off together, and I would come back alone. That had never happened before.

That night, after we came back from the Circle, I tried to sleep, thrashing around on the narrow bed at The Hot Spot. I'm not sure Morgan even tried. In fact, I'm sure he did not. Several times during the night I woke up and saw Morgan sitting up in his bed, writing in his journal, his little headlamp glowing like some misguided star, riding low on his forehead. He did not even look at me, his face frozen in concentration, his hand seeming to write words that he was not consciously creating. I had learned long ago that Morgan wrote when the energy hit him—any time, any place.

I tried to sleep.

When I awoke the next morning in the still blackness before the coming of the Arctic light, Morgan was not in his bed. There was not a thing of Morgan's in the room.

I wandered outside in a darkness being eroded by soft glowing on the far eastern horizon. It was easily the coldest morning yet. There was ice on my bike cover, and small pockets of water in the big gravel parking lot were frozen over.

There was only ice on one bike—mine. Morgan's bike was gone.

How could I stand there in the darkness of an Arctic morning, wearing nothing but my underwear, knowing that he'd been there only a short time ago? Knowing that I had no idea where he'd gone.

Somewhere up or down that goddamn road there would be, in the distance, a tiny red dot in the darkness—the light on the back of his bike. It would grow tinier in the rolling distance, disappearing and then reappearing as the road made gentle deviations, caressing the curvature of Earth. But I did not know which curvature.

How could I just stand there knowing the red dot would fly totally beyond my reach? How the hell could I do that? I should have jumped on my bike and ridden off into the dark . . . but where? North? Or south?

And then I knew I had seen the last of him.

There was something in my eyes. I wiped them with the back of my hand.

I mean, what could I have done about it anyway? He always did what he wanted to do, what felt right to him. Or what felt wrong to him. When nothing felt right, he would want to fix it, find some way to get us both in some part of the world where we did not belong, doing things that we could never even talk about except around campfires when there were only the two of us trying to stay warm, or huddled in a tent so small that our bodies made bulges in the walls, or taking a break on the edge of the road, our bikes leaning hard on the side stands, our dicks in our hands, pissing into the wind. Doing things that turned our blood hot and shot the very essence of our being out through the tops of our heads. Things that no one else would sign up for. Things that only we would believe.

Things we talked about only with you, Modene. And long ago with Kateri. Things he never mentioned to any of the other women, especially Lancey, because he knew they would not understand. Lancey: "Smart, but no wisdom," he'd said. "Don't think she's strong enough to run with the buffalo."

Those are the things I did with him. Those are the things I loved.

I could feel the cold begin to seep up through my bones, and I knew it wouldn't be long before it would grip my chest. I knew that he was already feeling it, the cold. He was riding somewhere in the far north in a darkness and a cold as solid as the wall of infinity, riding with his body curled hard forward into air thick with winter, his eyes following the beam of the KLR's one headlight, a beam so insignificant that he was not really paying attention to it, his eyes raised to a horizon he could not see, looking for a specter that was not there, except in his mind.

If he went north I knew he wouldn't stay on the Haul Road. Somewhere up there he would bust across the Brooks Range and then swing west, maybe having to go cross-country. No, he wouldn't stay on the Haul Road. He might meet someone on that road, and he was weary of meeting.

If he went south, he'd ride the Haul Road until he lost it, then probably work his way back to the Yukon. He'd come to love the Yukon. He could, over there, truly ride to the edge of the world.

I had found him in a cage in a river in the jungle. He was sitting there, watching a big ugly bird that was sitting on top of the cage and seemed to be talking to him. I never really believed that the fucking bird was talking to him, but he really liked birds, and when he really liked something he made it his, even if only in his mind, so I don't doubt that he, at least, thought that the bird was speaking to him.

I thought maybe he'd been trying to get out of that cage all his life.

But he changed quickly after Lancey. He grew more remote, quieter, lost some of his voice, didn't take the joy in his own bullshit that would always end up in near-hysterical laughter when he thought someone believed him. Now, instead of laughter, he had anger.

Maybe Lancey was one too many.

He began to walk that old rancho of his, naked in a desert wind blowing tumbleweeds like giant balled spider webs. Wearing that big .45 and his hat. The only other living animal on the place that he paid any attention to was a big fucking snake that lived under a shed. Hillbilly, he called it. I always thought it was a metaphor for something else, someone else. But I never knew. Sometimes he loved that snake, sometimes he hated it.

It hurt him when Lancey left, but that wasn't the real problem. He could fix that. She was just a Smoke Woman. And, down deep, he always knew that at the first breeze she would drift off in some other direction.

No, the real problem was that he began to believe there was nothing left to fix.

Nothing left that he could fix.

He began to believe what Arturo had said about the buffalo. Or maybe not.

He spent the visions of his life looking for something that even I didn't understand. He always tried to clearly see what was in front of him, but he always wanted it to be something other than what it was.

I wondered if he had ever seen the buffalo.

Maybe there never had been a buffalo.

Maybe I would never know.

When I finally realized there was no reason for me to stay where I was, I got dressed and hauled my gear to the bike and pulled off the icy bike cover. And that's when I saw the flat, worn leather case strapped to the seat. I knew it was from Morgan. I unstrapped it and started to open it, but then realized that whatever was in it would probably take some time to deal with. After all, Morgan had left it there, and he never left anything simple. I would wait for daylight. And I wanted to ride, to be somewhere else, not where I'd last seen him.

I put all my gear on, everything I owned that I thought would keep me warm, mounted up, started the KLR, turned it south. And then sat there. Surely, he would come to his senses. *Surely* he would wheel his bike in a hard, digging turn and scream back to the Hot Spot, laughing so fucking hard his helmet would shake. Surely he would see me waiting there.

No fucking way.

He had already come to his senses.

He was riding away, in the cold, because he wanted it that way. Because, for him, it wasn't over.

By the time I got back to the Yukon River it was full light. I rode past the café and up the long arc of the bridge and stopped in the center in the quiet, frozen air that drifted silently with the river. I probably wasn't supposed to stop there, but I didn't really give a damn.

I knew the river would have spoken to Morgan, and I wanted to see if it would speak to me. It did not.

I rode south, then pulled off the road at a high point where I could see far back into the north. I unstrapped Morgan's leather case and sat on a flat rock in the early sun, the light golden against the hard surface of the Arctic.

The old case was tied closed with a wide strip of doeskin. The stuff inside was wrapped in a piece of white cloth—Jade's apron. I spread out the apron on a flat rock and piled everything on top of it. In the bottom of the case, under a thick bundle of paper and a fistful of notebooks, were a flat silver flask and a narrow plastic bottle. I knew what they were: some Irish Mist and a few cigars.

What was not in the case was the .45. I was not surprised.

I put the flask and bottle aside and pulled out the bundle of papers, most of it the notebooks, the composition books, full of his awful handwriting. The books were numbered. I opened the first one. The title page said, "Magnetic North." I flipped through some of the pages, reading paragraphs here and there, words scratched out, pages torn, but always the words coming back to where he wanted them to be, the words either singing like poetry or dripping with darkness. Sometimes, it seemed to be the same thing.

Modene, I knew you were going to have a tough time making sense out of some of it.

There was another, smaller envelope in the bag, one of those ancient, brown almost-hard things that looked like it should be

DAY 21          351

on the shelf of an old bank, hidden away somewhere in the West. It wasn't sealed. I opened it and pulled out a long sheet of paper that had been folded several times. It was the deed to Wild Horse Canyon, and it had been signed over to me. And to you.

And a note. It said, "Both of you, or neither. You don't get to choose."

I cried.

And then something in my life changed. It was a good day for things in my life to change.

I knew I should have told you this a long time ago. Maybe I did. But if I did, I think I would remember.

I love you.

I rummaged through my pockets until I found my little black book. ("One of these days I'm going to steal that thing and burn it," Morgan had threatened.) I shook all the tiny pieces of paper from between the pages, all the names, addresses, and phone numbers of women that I had known, or thought I wanted to know. I dumped them in a small, neat pile on the ground. I added some twigs and bits of grass, and then balanced the black book carefully on the top.

I set fire to the pile.

It was not a big fire, but it warmed my hands. The little black book took longest to burn.

I took out a cigar, bit off the end, and lighted the thing in the flames of the black book. And then, of course, I opened the flask of Irish Mist.

A cigar and Mist, before breakfast. Morgan would be impressed.

Later, with my warm hands and my warm belly making me feel things I had thought were long past me, I cried again.

I stopped, rolling the bike into the edge of a small stand of stunted trees, and took out the cell phone. I was close enough to civilization that it worked.

You answered. "Modene."

"Are you at . . . our house?"

"How do you know it's 'our' house? You never paid any attention before."

I thought about it. Before anything other than Morgan banged into my mind, you said, "Yes, Slade, it's our house."

You waited for a while, and then you said, "Slade, are you okay?"

I didn't know then if I could keep talking. But I had to. "No."

"Slade, you have known, all along, that he would have to pay the price for the things he does."

"He's already paid. He paid when he rode away from the ranch. He paid. He can't go home again. And he knew that."

"He's gone?" Your voice was softer than I had ever heard it.

"He's gone."

There was silence on the phone. You didn't speak for a long time.

"I thought he might . . . go," you said softly. "Yesterday a package came for me. From the ranch. He had Juanito send it." I thought I heard your voice break slightly. "It's the wampum belt, Kateri's belt. The Seneca Alliance Belt; the Death Belt. It hung over the desk where he wrote. He would never have let it go, not even to me, unless . . ."

You didn't have to finish the thought. We both knew what the ending was.

"But Modene, he went off into the cold, he hated the *fucking cold*!"

"Well," you said, "it wasn't the only thing he hated. I could make a list."

"Modene, he loved you. Maybe more than anyone but Kateri."

I could hear the soft sounds of your crying. You hung up the phone.

I sat on the rock and tried to hear the sounds going on in my head. Always before, when I thought the world had changed, it never really had. But I knew, now, the world had truly changed. It would never be the same.

I called you back. You answered quickly, and I knew you had been waiting.

"Modene," I said, "I love you. Did I ever get around to telling you that?

"Not lately. I keep score."

I waited. I was having trouble with the words.

"Modene, will you . . . marry me?"

"Of course, Slade," you said, almost casually, as though you had thought about it for a long time, and it was no big deal.

And then you hung up again.


When I got back to Fairbanks, I knew the trip was really over. I'd lost all my energy, all my lust for riding. I went on to Anchorage, where I had the bike shipped back to Colorado Springs, and I caught the first plane home.

And the ride was over.

Wild Horse Canyon

Southern New Mexico

Modene

AND SO WE LINGERED on the ranch. Our ranch. But really Morgan's.

Back in early January a sheriff's deputy drove up to the house and asked about Morgan, a few questions about an altercation. The deputy said that he would very much like to talk to Morgan.

"So would we," Slade said.

# ABOUT THE AUTHOR

LEE MAYNARD was born and raised deep in the mountains of West Virginia, a location that drives the emotion and grit of most of his writing. He says he had never had a "career." Rather, he sought out "day jobs" while doing his real job—writing. Among several other things, he has been a criminal investigator, college president, and COO of a national experiential education organization. He now lives and writes at the edge of an Indian reservation in the high desert of New Mexico. He is the author of *The Pale Light of Sunset: Scattershots and Hallucinations in an Imagined Life* and the Crum trilogy: *Crum, Screaming with the Cannibals,* and *The Scummers.*